Braddock smiled to him
Dianne Ingleby who had c
the same emotion for h
ruined him and on reflection ne knew a bullet would
have been too good for him. Let him live and suffer.
Losing his wife hurt him, but coming so soon after last
night, news that Ray Braddock was sleeping with his
daughter would hurt him much, much more.

But there was something else he needed to do first
and that was to rid himself of Emma Crossley. She was
trouble, her and that brat of hers. She knew too much
and she was standing between him and Rebecca. The
sooner she was out of his hair, the sooner he could get
on with taking Maurice Ingleby for all he had.

Lesley Horton was a teacher in an inner-city Bradford school before writing her first novel, *Snares of Guilt*. She lives and writes in Yorkshire. *The Hollow Core* is the fourth book in the DI John Handford series.

By Lesley Horton

The Hollow Core
Devils in the Mirror
On Dangerous Ground
Snares of Guilt

The Hollow Core

Lesley Horton

An Orion paperback

First published in Great Britain in 2006
by Orion
This paperback edition published in 2009
by Orion Books Ltd,
Orion House, 5 Upper St Martin's Lane,
London WC2H 9EA

An Hachette UK company

Copyright © Lesley Horton 2006

1 3 5 7 9 10 8 6 4 2

The right of Lesley Horton to be identified as the author of
this work has been asserted by her in accordance with the
Copyright, Designs and Patents Act 1988.

A CIP catalogue record for this book is available
from the British Library.

ISBN 978-0-7528-8444-8

Printed and bound in Great Britain by
Clays Ltd, St Ives plc

The Orion Publishing Group's policy is to use papers that
are natural, renewable and recyclable products and made
from wood grown in sustainable forests. The logging and
manufacturing processes are expected to conform to the
environmental regulations of the country of origin.

www.orionbooks.co.uk

For my fellow Ladykillers, Priscilla Masters, Danuta Reah and Zoë Sharp, for their support and friendship.

acknowledgements

Many thanks go to all who supported and helped me throughout the writing of this novel. First to Detective Sergeant Colin Stansbie of the West Yorkshire Police, who has given of his time so generously to answer my many questions, and to Zoë Sharp, who explained the mysteries of the different firearms. I would also like to thank David Jackson, former Chief Executive of the Bradford NHS Trust, who organised a visit to Bradford Royal Infirmary for me; Oksana Wolstenholme who gave of her time to show me round and describe the many departments of the hospital, and all the members of staff who discussed their roles. My grateful thanks go also to Ismat and Razwana, who talked me through the problems of domestic violence perpetrated by some women on other women in the Asian community. Finally, my thanks go to the volunteers from Victim Support who give so generously of their time to support victims of crime and who gave it equally generously to me to discuss the code of confidentiality.

As always, I owe a debt of gratitude to my agent Teresa Chris, who is a constant source of encouragement; to my incredibly patient editors, Kate Mills and Genevieve Pegg, who are always on hand when I need them, and to Helen Windrath, who corrected my mistakes and inconsistencies.

Finally, I thank my husband, Brian, without whose help and encouragement the daily task of writing would be so much harder.

prologue

When he knocked, Kathie Lake was cleaning, one eye on *Coronation Street*, the other on the ornaments she was dusting. She ought to have looked through the window to identify her visitor, and if she'd been concentrating she would have, but she wasn't. She opened the door and there he was, huddled in a winter coat. As she stood in front of him she wondered why someone would dress like that in the middle of May. Then, as he lifted his head she saw his face and the loathing in his eyes and she knew. No one had ever looked at her like that except him.

Instinctively, she flung herself at him to push him away, but it was no contest and he flicked her aside like a spent match. He stepped inside and allowed the door to swing shut behind him. She backed along the hall and into the lounge. He stalked her, each step paced and deliberate. When they reached the room her way was blocked by the vacuum cleaner. As she manoeuvred round it her foot caught in the cable and she lost her balance to fall sideways over the arm of the easy chair.

The first blows came without warning – to her face and her head – not with an open hand but with his fist, closed and hard. She'd tried to protect herself. Her arms thrashed about as she attempted to parry each punch, but they were coming from all directions and as each caught her, she found herself slipping to the floor. Desperately she turned over to scrabble away from him, but he was there, hitting and kicking so that her only protection was to curl herself into a ball.

She'd felt her cheekbone go first and then her ribs – she wasn't sure about her skull. Blood poured from a wound on her head, the skin round her eye tightened and the lid swelled into a bulbous mass; hot flames seemed to be licking at her insides. She prayed for it to end. Yet ironically, before she floated into unconscious-ness, everything, his movements, her movements, had shifted into slow motion and she remembered having time to think that it if she lived at all she would need an operation to fix her face.

But he hadn't killed her; he'd stopped short of that. This had been no more than a warning, a warning to forget everything. It was over, he whispered in her ear, it didn't matter anymore; did she understand?

As best she could Kathie nodded; she understood.

She didn't know how long she'd been out of it, but as she came round she felt the pile of the carpet scuff against the bare skin of her arms and her legs and at the first cautious movement the room swirled and specks of light shimmered in front of her eyes. Initially the picture was blurred, but as her vision cleared she took in the damage he had done – ornaments broken, cupboards and drawers standing open, their contents strewn about the floor and James Bond, a drink in his hand, mocked her from the tele-vision.

The pain was excruciating as she dragged herself to the phone and dialled Emma Crossley's number. Her cheek stung as she mouthed the words in hoarse tones, her voice so indistinct that Emma had to ask her to repeat them. She'd been attacked, she croaked. Someone had broken in to the house and attacked her. She didn't say who.

'My God, Kathie, have you rung the police?'

'No police,' Kathie insisted. 'I don't want the police.'

chapter one

Karl Metcalfe lurked in the shadows of the multi-storey car park. It was late, going on eleven. The chimes from the city hall clock had struck the three quarters but not yet the hour. He'd do one more car and then he'd go. It wouldn't be long before those theatre-goers from the Alhambra who had left their vehicles here would be coming for them. There was no point asking for trouble, but he'd had his eye on the Hyundai that had come in while he'd been relieving the Fiesta of its stereo and he wanted to do that one.

He peered into the haze of the third level. A few of the ceiling lights were broken, the rest masked with grime and the illumination was poor, good enough to see by but not good enough for clarity. That's why he'd chosen this floor. If anyone noticed him he'd be no more than an indistinct outline, no possibility of a description or of the security cameras picking him up, even if there were films in them, which Karl doubted. Who cared anyway? It was nobody else's fault but the owners of the cars if their stuff got nicked. They should have been warned they were fair game by the notice which said the management took no responsibility for the vehicles or their contents.

He screwed up his eyes and focused on the middle distance. He couldn't distinguish much except the vague silhouettes of cars so he crept up to the passenger door of the Hyundai and shielding his eyes peered in. It was possible to make out a dark shape on the back seat. A briefcase he thought. Looking round, he prised his screwdriver beneath the handle. The sharp crack as the lock mechanism was released bounced between the concrete pillars. He pulled the door open and stretched over the back of the seat. Got it. But it wasn't a briefcase. This time

3

he'd struck lucky; it was a laptop. He'd get a better price for this.

Karl shoved it under his fleece and glanced round. The area was still deserted. He made a dash for the door to the stairs and pulled it open. From below he heard the sound of singing. Two voices, perhaps three, and the owners were coming towards him. Should the carry on and walk past them? He decided not, for in spite of the poor lighting they might remember him and if the driver of the Hyundai had come to pick them up after their night out it could be their car he'd nicked the laptop from. You had to consider every possibility in this job. He stepped back inside. There were two vehicles close enough to hide behind, a Citroën one bay from where he was standing and another, a Landrover, across the aisle a couple of bays further on. He scampered towards the Citroën and melted into the darkness of its shadow as he crouched down.

The door on to the floor opened and three people, two women and one man, boogied through and along the aisle. He held his breath hoping this wasn't their car. They passed it by.

'You're the one that I want,' the man sang and grabbed hold of the girl to swing her round.

Karl lowered his head. For fuck's sake, stop messing about and go. He stretched up to watch them as they danced past, towards the four-by-four. If it was theirs he might stand a chance of getting away without being seen. He edged forwards and as he did so his stomach lurched. There was a man in the driver's seat of the Citroën. He hadn't noticed him before and even now it was too dark to see who he was, but he was sitting forward, peering across the aisle. Karl ducked down. What the hell was he going to do now? He couldn't move out and he couldn't stay. The driver remained rigid, seemingly more interested in the man and the two women. Karl followed his gaze.

The older woman was giggling. 'Maurice, for goodness' sake, put Rebecca down and let's go home. I knew *Grease* was a bad idea; you've only got to hear the music and you get frisky.' Maurice released the young woman and slipped his arm round the waist of the one who had just spoken. He began to sing to her, 'Hopelessly devoted to you.' She gave him a playful push and he kissed her on the lips before stepping to one side. 'Fish and chips,' he said, as his bulky frame sashayed towards the driver's door. 'How about fish and chips to round off the evening?'

'Fine, but if we don't go now, the shop will be closed.'

Maurice felt in his pocket and pulled out his keys.

Rebecca made a grab for them, 'Oh no you don't, Dad. I'll drive; you'll be over the limit. Do you know you've drunk three double brandies tonight – one during the interval and two at the pub?'

Her father put his arm round her shoulder. 'So I drank three double brandies. It's a special occasion and I wanted to celebrate.' He turned unsteadily to the older woman. 'Help me out here, Dianne. Tell her it isn't every day she's twenty-five.'

She turned to him. 'True, and you don't want to round it off by being picked up because you're over the limit. Give Rebecca the keys.'

Karl was becoming stiff. He squirmed, trying to make himself more comfortable. The man in the car remained focused. *For God's sake Maurice, give her the bloody keys and go.*

With a sigh Maurice lobbed them over to his daughter. 'Go on then, they're all yours.'

The driver of the Citroën switched on his engine. It purred quietly and the car gently inched out from its parking space.

'Shit,' Karl muttered. Sweat prickled between his shoulder blades. He was more visible now, but if he side-stepped carefully to the left as it moved off, he might make the pillar. That should give him some shelter.

He waited until the car was a full length beyond him, then began to slide towards safety. And he would have made it too had the older woman not suddenly turned and peered in his direction. He froze. She must have heard him or seen him or something, and now she was watching him. Or perhaps not; perhaps it wasn't him she was looking at, perhaps it was the car, perhaps she'd recognised the man inside it. Karl didn't know, but what he did know was that he had to get out of here – and quickly. One, two, three and he would make a run for it. He had counted only two when the car came to a sudden halt and the driver dropped his window.

Fuck. *He* must have been watching him as well. Probably a copper, the creepy bastard. He'd been sitting there, pretending to be interested in the three across the aisle, when all along he'd been biding his time so that he could nick him when he knew he would have no chance of getting rid of the stuff.

Opposite, father and daughter were changing places. Maurice crossed in front of his wife, while the daughter slid round the back of her. As they did so, the man's arm appeared over the lowered window.

Karl saw the barrel of the gun a few seconds before it happened. It was so quick, over almost before he had time to work out what was occurring. The flashes, the explosions, the woman slumping to the ground, the screaming and the screech of tyres as the car sped away, took only seconds.

The laptop fell to the ground with a dull thud.

His hands over his ears, which were reverberating from the noise of the gunshot, Karl stood up. He stared at the four-by-four, trying desperately to make sense of what he'd just witnessed. The driver of the car he'd been hiding behind had shot her – three, possibly four times. Just put his arm out of the window and shot her! As easy as that. Images and sounds tumbled about in his head. The flash, the explosion, the outline of the man. The police would be here soon. He began to shake. He had to get away. Doesn't matter if anyone sees me, just get out. But he couldn't move. His head was telling him what to do but his body wasn't obeying. He watched, transfixed, as Maurice and Rebecca ran, crouched, to the woman, screaming 'Dianne' and 'Mum' in unison. They fell down beside her and her husband lifted her head on to his lap and rocked her.

Without warning, Karl's legs moved him forwards towards them. It was stupid. He should have gone, kept out of it; it was nothing to do with him. But he couldn't. He looked down at her. Blood was staining her blouse and she was moaning. Until now, Karl had thought himself hard. But he couldn't stand this. She was in pain, pain so intense that all she could do was moan. The sound, the smell. He'd never been so close to this kind of violence before. A few fights, the odd kicking, but nothing like this.

Still rocking her, Maurice searched in his shirt pocket. He pulled out a mobile phone and threw it to Karl. 'Ring for an ambulance,' he yelled. 'Tell them to hurry, tell them my wife's been shot.'

If there was one thing Detective Inspector John Handford hated

6

about his job it was disturbed sleep. It was said more people die at night than at any other time in the twenty-four hours but as far as he was concerned criminal acts came a close second. He left his car at Central Police Station and walked to the multi-storey. Police tape cordoned off the streets leading to the car park, and a couple of police cars and the scene-of-crime vans were placed across the entrance and along the roadside. He rubbed his eyes to banish the tiredness threatening to take over, then ran his hand over his chin and felt the roughness of the bristles. There hadn't been time for a shave before he'd left although he'd managed a quick shower in the hope it might bring him round, but it hadn't worked because his brain seemed to have coagulated into a mass of glutinous sludge. He wished he hadn't spent so long the previous night working with his daughter on her maths revision. Close to her GCSE examinations, Nicola was beginning to panic. He'd told her she had nothing to worry about, her understanding of mathematics was fine, but she'd insisted she wanted to make sure she completely understood calculus and if she couldn't ask her father, a maths graduate, who could she ask? He'd had no answer to that, and anyway she had always been able to twist him round her little finger, so they'd worked until late when he pushed her off to bed. If she wasn't tired, he'd said, he was.

He gave his name and rank to the officer stationed at the entrance to the stairwell, stifling a yawn as he entered, then cast his mind back to the phone call. He had been given very little except that a woman had been shot on the third floor of the multi-storey car park and there was a witness. At least that was a start. Handford hadn't had much experience of investigating gun crimes for they were usually handed to a more senior officer, but this victim wasn't dead – so for the moment no doubt, an inspector would be senior enough. What he did know was that it was likely the weapon would never be found. According to the duty inspector, Jane Charles, it hadn't been discovered at the scene and was probably, she commented acerbically, already on its way back to the dealer in Manchester or Liverpool from whom it had been rented. Five hundred to a thousand pounds, the gunman would have paid, depending on whether it had been fired or not when it was returned.

By the time Handford had climbed the urine-scented staircase and arrived on the third level, Inspector Charles had everything under control: the identified scene of the attack had been cordoned off with barrier tape, and a wider cordon isolated the whole of the third floor. Constables were positioned to log in essential personnel and to prevent any member of the public who had managed to get in from going further; lights illuminated the immediate area and the photographers and the scene-of-crime officers were well into their stride. In spite of the activity, there was an eerie silence about the place. The garish brightness of the lamps illuminated a patch roughly ten metres square, but waned in the gloom of the corners of the distant bays, adding to the unnatural atmosphere. It wouldn't be difficult to secrete yourself in the shadows while you waited for your victim, Handford thought.

He met Jane Charles, a small wiry woman with short curly dark hair, at the door to the stairs. She was arguing with an irate gentleman demanding access to his vehicle.

'I'm sorry, sir,' she said, 'but for the moment you cannot have your van. As I've already explained, this is a crime scene; it has to be preserved – that means it stays as it is – nothing comes in and nothing leaves. Wasn't this explained to you?'

He mumbled that he had a right to get to his own property and that he needed his van for work. But Jane was having none of it.

'I'm sorry, sir, your vehicle stays where it is until the area has been thoroughly searched. Give your name, address and telephone number to the officer over there and we'll let you know as soon as you can retrieve it.'

As the man walked away muttering something about bossy women and a police state, she turned to Handford. 'Bloody man,' she said. 'Pushes his way in here regardless and blames me when I won't let him drive his van over the scene. I ought to have arrested him for obstructing the police, but I'm too damned busy to do all the paperwork.'

Handford wasn't about to argue with her. 'What was he doing here at this time of night?'

'Been to the casino apparently.'

'Better than being woken up at two o'clock in the morning.'

'Believe you me, John, I'd rather this wasn't happening as well. I've got a scene on a main road that's hundreds of metres square, not to mention five floors tall, and I'm supposed to make it secure with three officers down, two more out on a rape allegation, and one on an aggravated burglary. And before you say anything, yes, it is the wrong time of the month.'

Handford held up his hands in mock surrender. 'The thought never entered my head, Inspector,' he said, then tentatively, 'The shooting?'

With a grin her annoyance abated and she led him to the four-by-four. The vehicle was parked, its engine close to the wall. 'We've recovered four cartridges, so for the moment we're assuming four shots. One bullet we know hit the victim, a Mrs Dianne Ingleby, one hit the back door of their vehicle … ' She pointed out the fissures webbing the paintwork from the puncture hole where the bullet penetrated the metal. 'Two more hit the wall of the car park, down there, see. Scene of crime have no idea of gun type, except they haven't recognised it as one we would expect to see on the streets at the moment.' That meant it was not a Browning, the weapon currently favoured by the Bradford gangs, and the shooting was unlikely to be part of any gang warfare. 'Mrs Ingleby was badly injured though alive, and has been taken to the Royal. The paramedics weren't hopeful,' she added, then turned towards Karl Metcalfe who was perched half out and half in the back of a police car, his head resting on his knees. A blanket was draped round his shoulders and in one hand he held a Styrofoam beaker, which was dripping liquid onto the concrete as it listed sideways.

'There's your witness,' the inspector said. 'As you can see he's very shaken. That's the third cup of tea we've brought him from the hotel next door, and he's spilt more than he's drunk. If it wasn't Karl Metcalfe you could almost feel sorry for him.' Before Handford could ask the obvious, she added, 'And yes, he was involved in theft from vehicles. Had quite a good night by all accounts. It seems a pity to have to arrest him for it, given what he's gone through. He ought to go down, the number of times we've had him in court, but perhaps this once we'll let him off with a caution. Poor lad; it's one thing for him to dodge security cameras, quite another to dodge bullets.'

A PC in uniform approached her. 'Ma'am …?'

'I'll leave you to it, John,' she said and turned to speak to the officer.

Handford nodded his thanks and walked towards the young boy, who lifted his head to look at him. Jane Charles had been right; Karl Metcalfe had lost his usual cockiness. His features were ashen and instead of arrogance there was a look of terror in his eyes. What he had witnessed was real crime – not the stuff he was used to.

Handford said, 'Hello Karl.'

'Mr Handford.' They were old adversaries.

'Come on, hitch up so that I can sit down.'

Karl pulled his feet inside the car and slid across the seat; Handford made himself comfortable beside him. 'You've had a nasty experience, how are you feeling?'

'All right, except me ears hurt.'

'When we've had a word I'll get someone to run you to the hospital. You ought to have them checked out.'

Karl nodded.

'Can you tell me what happened?'

Karl recounted the events. Some were hazy, others clearer. But he was sure about the car – cars were his speciality. It was a Citroën, a ZX, dark, green he thought, although he couldn't be absolutely sure. He'd been too scared to think about getting the registration, but he knew they only made them between 1991 and 1997.

Handford was impressed. 'You know a lot about cars.'

'It's me job to know.'

'Why were you hiding?'

Karl Metcalfe gave him a pitying look. 'I didn't want to be seen.'

'By whom?'

'By the people coming into the car park. I didn't know whether it was their car I'd done or not. So I hid.'

'What about the man in the Citroën? Can you describe him?'

Karl shrugged. 'It was dark.'

'Was he white?'

'I couldn't tell. He wasn't black, but he could have been Asian. I don't know.' Karl was becoming distressed. 'It was dark. I come up on to this floor because the light's bad, so that if anyone sees me breaking into a car, they can't describe me properly, so I can't describe him either. Honest to God, Mr Handford, I'd tell you if I could.' The boy screwed up his face. 'I think he was thin – at least he didn't look fat. And when he put his arm out of the car that was thin. I tell you something though; he was waiting for them three. He'd got the right car and he shot at them. It were no random shooting,' he ended proudly, obviously pleased with his choice of words.

Handford smiled at him and wondered if he'd learned the language from his frequent visits to the police station or from something he'd seen on television. But this wasn't a scene from an American cop show, this was real life and Karl knew it. He was frightened at what he had witnessed and probably about his position now it was all over. He frowned as his tongue slid over his lips.

'Are you going to do me for nicking from cars? I could have taken me stuff and gone you know,' he continued guardedly. 'It was nothing to do with me; I could 'ave just left, said nothing, then you'd know nothing,' He looked wistfully at the laptop on the floor, then up at the detective.

Handford considered. Like a lot of petty criminals, Karl was okay. Deep down he had a streak of morality that had forced him to stay on scene to help. He put him out of his misery, 'I can't make promises, but since you stayed to assist Mr Ingleby and then waited for us I think it's unlikely – a caution at the most, particularly if you return the stereo and the laptop, plus anything else you've picked up tonight.'

Karl licked his finger and rubbed at a mark on the back of the driver's seat in the police car. Handford watched him. He wondered how long it would take the boy to get over this. After a moment Karl stopped rubbing and returned his gaze.

'Why, Mr Handford?' he said softly. 'Why did he shoot that lady? They'd been out enjoying themselves and they were singing and having fun. The man didn't have much of a voice, but they weren't doing anyone any harm. Why would he shoot her?'

Why indeed? He placed his hand on the boy's shoulder. 'I don't know, Karl. But I'll do my best to find out.'

It was almost one o'clock when Handford entered the Royal's Accident and Emergency department. He grimaced as he always did when he walked in. Whoever had designed it had tried hard to make it feel both welcoming and efficient, but they hadn't been able to rid of the oppressive atmosphere which closed in on him.

Despite the early hour and the armed police on the door, the main waiting area was busy: medical and administrative personnel rushed from patient to patient, cubicle to cubicle, never seeming to push back the tide of men, women and children who topped up the red plastic seats and benches as they became vacant. A child was screaming in one of the cubicles. A harassed nurse opened the curtains and summoned a porter. 'He'll need to go up to the ward,' she said, 'although God knows how you'll get him on the trolley. He's got the strength of a dozen.' The staff coming to the end of their shift cast a weary eye over the people still waiting, some blood-soaked, others the worse for drink. The illuminated sign above reception read 'waiting time three hours'. Many of them would still be here when the night duty had left.

Mr Ingleby and his daughter were not in evidence, probably in the relatives' room and Handford was about to go to the receptionist to ask where they were when he spied the constable who had accompanied them in the ambulance.

'What's happening?' he asked.

'She's gone up to theatre, sir, been gone a while.'

Handford looked round. 'Has Sergeant Ali arrived yet?'

'Yes sir,' he nodded towards the cubicles. 'He's over there talking to the sister.'

He saw Khalid Ali, half hidden by a curtain. A young man in his mid-thirties he was slightly taller than Handford, considerably slimmer – and smarter. Typical of him that he had found time to dress in a suit, rather than the nearest casual trousers and shirt Handford had pulled on. He looked as tired as Handford felt. A deep frown creased his forehead and his demeanour suggested he was carrying all the cares of the universe on his shoulders. Perhaps he was. Ten days ago they had discovered a lump in his wife's breast and a couple of days ago she had had a biopsy. Now they were living in limbo as they waited for the result. Ali could have taken some leave to be with her, but Amina wouldn't hear of it and probably, at the moment, work was the best thing for him.

Ali spotted his boss, thanked the sister with a smile, closed his notebook and walked over to the inspector. 'Mrs Ingleby's still in theatre, sir. She's been there quite a while; it doesn't look good. She was hit the once. According to the sister there's an entry wound to the chest, but no exit wound, which means the bullet's still in there. That should give us something.'

'Where are her husband and daughter?'

'Upstairs in a room close to the operating theatre.'

'Have you spoken to them?'

'No, not yet. They're both in shock; I thought I'd leave them for a while.'

Handford sat on one of the chairs and indicated Ali should join him. 'Metcalfe was insistent the gunman was waiting for them to come back to their car,' he said, 'and when they got there, he pulled out from his parking space, stopped for a moment and shot four times. One bullet hit her, the other three missed. If the lad is to be believed, and for once I can't see any reason why he shouldn't be, it was quick and it was planned. Do we know anything about Dianne Ingleby?'

'Nothing much. Married, one daughter. Her husband's Maurice Ingleby. He owns a building firm.'

'Yes, I think I may have met him once or twice – at some meeting or other. Isn't he vocal in crime prevention – mainly us preventing his business premises being targeted by local burglars?' It was an attempt to lessen the tension in Ali, but the sergeant wasn't having it.

'Probably,' he said. 'But while he plays the big business man, Mrs Ingleby remains in the background. She helps him out in the office a couple of days a week, but most of her time is spent doing voluntary work – here at the hospital, takes library books to the wards and serves tea in the café, that sort of thing – and as a volunteer with Victim Support. Hardly a person I would expect to be the target of a planned shooting.'

'No,' Handford said pensively. 'Nor would I.'

'You don't think Metcalfe's exaggerating what he saw? Talking himself out of what he was doing up there?'

Handford shook his head. 'Not this time, Khalid. He was in quite a state when I questioned him and he didn't deny why he was there.' He thought for a moment and then said, 'Find out who Mrs Ingleby was working with for Victim Support. That might give us a lead.'

'Some kind of intimidation?'

'Why not, if she'd been supporting the victim of a serious crime?' Handford pushed himself off the seat. 'In shock or not, we need to have a word with the husband and daughter.'

They found Maurice and Rebecca Ingleby in a small office next to the theatre. It was not really a room, more a space where the staff wrote up their notes following each operation or drank coffee while resting. Everything about it was neutral: its decoration, its ambience. To the onlooker it lacked soul, for no matter what traumas were being played out close by, the relatives worried alone and without help. The door to the theatre where they were attempting to save Dianne Ingleby's life was guarded by two more armed officers.

At first sight, the Inglebys appeared as zombies. Pale and in shock, and staring at, but probably not seeing, the linoleum flooring. They looked up expectantly as Handford and Ali walked in.

Quietly, the DI introduced them both. 'I'm sorry, I don't want to intrude, but I wonder if you would mind answering some questions.'

'Didn't that young lad tell you what happened?' Maurice had aged more than his fifty-two years in the last few hours. He was haggard, his eyes sunken and red as though he'd been crying – but not now, not in front of the police. Rebecca, on the other hand made no attempt to stem the tears.

'He did, but we need you to tell us.'

Ingleby pulled himself from the settee and walked over to the inspector. He stood close. In build the two were similar – large framed and well made, but Handford felt himself overpowered by the man. His nearness was intimidating and Handford wasn't sure whether that was deliberate or not.

'Can't it wait until my wife is out of surgery?' Ingleby whispered. 'Look what it's doing to my daughter; she's in pieces.' Handford gave him the benefit of the doubt. He took a step backwards. 'I do understand, sir,' he said. 'But I need something to go on, so if you could bear with me for a while I'd be grateful, and then I'll leave you.' He paused as Ingleby returned to sit next to his daughter. He put his arm round her and pulled her towards him.

'Go on,' he said.

Handford perched on a chair opposite them and leaned forward. 'Perhaps you can tell me what you saw.'

'Nothing. We were coming back to the car, fooling around a bit. Rebecca wouldn't let me drive because she thought I was

14

over the limit. I gave her the keys and she went towards the driver's side, while I went to the passenger's.'

'Where was your wife at that moment?'

'I don't know.'

'Please, sir, try and remember.'

Ingleby frowned. 'She was at the back of the car. I crossed in front of her, and my daughter walked behind her.'

'Which way was she facing?'

'Us, I think.'

'Towards your vehicle, not away from it?'

Ingleby nodded. 'I think so.' He looked towards Rebecca.

'Yes, Inspector, she must have been because she'd follow us to get into the car herself.'

'And you didn't see her turn back towards the aisle?'

She shook her head. 'No.'

'What happened then?'

'I vaguely remember hearing the car opposite pull out, then the shots. It all happened so quickly. I couldn't see Dianne and think I screamed out to her and ran to where she'd been. She was lying on the ground and there was blood seeping through her blouse. Then the young lad appeared – I don't know where he came from. I threw him my mobile and shouted at him to ring for an ambulance.'

Ingleby was trembling. He bent his head forward and Rebecca grasped his hands to hold them in hers. For a moment the silence was interrupted only by their deep breathing as they attempted to calm themselves.

Eventually Handford said, 'As far as we can tell there were four shots, the one which hit your wife and three others; would you have any idea whether the gunman was still firing after your wife was hit?'

All energy spent reliving the event, Ingleby remained motionless. When he spoke his voice was drained of feeling. 'As I said it happened so quickly – he may have been.' He shook his head. 'I honestly can't say. Is it important?'

'I don't know; maybe.' Handford wasn't prepared to qualify his answer. 'Can you tell me who knew you were going to the theatre tonight?'

Ingleby took a deep breath. 'Lots of people; it wasn't a secret. It's my daughter's twenty-fifth birthday. We always celebrate her

15

birthday at the theatre.'

Handford sympathised. Whatever the outcome of the operation, Rebecca's birthday would never be the same. It would always be linked with terror.

'Perhaps as soon as you are able you can let me have a list.'

Too tired to argue, Ingleby nodded.

'I'm sorry to have to ask you this, but do you know of anyone with a grudge against your wife, anyone who would want to harm her in this way?'

'No, of course not.' Ingleby's tone was filled with revulsion. 'I don't know how you can suggest that.'

'I'm not trying to hurt you or your daughter, sir,' Handford said as compassionately as he could, 'but tonight someone waited for you to return to your car and shot her, and there has to be a reason for it.' It was harsh and cold and he knew it, but they needed something to go on.

Ingleby made no reply.

Handford nodded to Ali to take over. A new voice might help.

'I understand your wife's a volunteer for Victim Support, sir. Have you any idea who she's supporting at the moment?'

Mr Ingleby looked towards him. 'Her work there is confidential; she never speaks to me about it.'

Ali turned to Rebecca. 'Has she spoken to you, Miss Ingleby?'

Rebecca pulled at the tissue she was holding. 'No,' she said, 'Like my father said, her work is confidential; she will never break that kind of confidence.'

Ingleby drew in a deep breath. 'Haven't you got enough yet? Can't it wait? Please.'

Handford stood up. 'I think so, sir. We'll leave you in peace. We will need to speak to you again, but not now.'

He was about to move off, but as he did so the door opened. A man in blue theatre scrubs came in. His expression was serious. Maurice Ingleby and his daughter slowly pulled themselves from the chairs.

'I'm sorry, Mr Ingleby, Miss Ingleby. We did our best, but your wife was very badly injured and the trauma to the aorta caused an aneurism which ruptured. I'm afraid we couldn't save her. She died in theatre.'

chapter two

Detective Sergeant Khalid Ali left the hospital and returned home. In the kitchen Amina was preparing breakfast before waking Bushra and Hasan to get them ready for school. She was humming to herself.

Everything was so normal. How could she just carry on like this?

She turned at the sound of his footsteps. 'Khalid! What are you doing home? I didn't expect you until late tonight.'

The hospital had unnerved him and he put his arms round her. 'I needed to make sure you were all right,' he said. 'Are you?'

She pushed him away and picked up a box of cornflakes. 'Of course I'm all right,' she responded angrily. 'At least I would be if you stopped asking me that. Please don't fuss.'

He didn't want to keep his distance; he wanted to comfort her, support her, support himself. He moved back and stretched out his hands to her. 'Please Amina, don't reject me.'

Her arms flailed. The box of cereal fell to the floor spilling its contents. 'Now look what you've made me do!' she screamed at him and dropped to her knees frantically scraping the flakes towards her.

Ali crouched beside her and pulled her towards him. At first she tried to rebuff him, hitting out at him, refusing his advances, tears coursing down her cheeks. For a few moments he wrestled with her anger. Eventually it subsided and she stopped fighting and clung to him, sobbing into his shoulder. He held her until she was calmer, kissing her hair, stroking her as though she was a child, then gently raised her to her feet.

'Come and sit down,' he said as he manoeuvred her to the

nearest chair. He turned, rinsed out a glass and filled it with water. 'Here drink this.'

Amina looked up at him as she took it, her face stained, her eyelashes wet with her tears, and he watched as she sipped. He couldn't believe it was happening to her. She was so beautiful; someone so beautiful could not have something so ugly inside her. Her long black hair was tied back accentuating her slender face, but a tendril had escaped and she tucked it into the clip, her fingers trembling. Every movement was graceful, her trim figure flowed like that of a ballet dancer and she was so colourful, so vibrant and so happy – at least she had been until this. As he looked at her the sound of Maurice Ingleby's words surged into his memory. '*Why? What has my wife done to deserve this?*' Ali had asked himself the same thing over and over again. What had Amina done to deserve anything as cruel as this?

And it was his fault; he had felt it first when they had been making love. A small lump in her right breast. Fear had sparked through him like an electric current and he had snatched his hand away. She'd wanted to know what the matter was and to begin with he'd lied and said 'nothing', afraid of what the truth might mean, but she had insisted, entreating him to tell her if for some reason she repelled him. Repelled him? His beautiful wife whom his parents had chosen so carefully. That was the last thing she should be allowed to think. So he had told her.

She had more strength than him; he'd said to forget it, it was probably nothing, but she had made an appointment with the doctor the next morning. He had referred her immediately to the consultant at the hospital who had organised a biopsy. Now they were waiting for the result – it would be another four or five days before they knew anything for sure. How could anything as important as this take so long?

Amina handed him back the glass. She was calm now. 'Please go back to work, Khalid,' she said. 'It must have been serious for you to be called out in the middle of the night ...'

'A woman was shot. She died during the operation to remove the bullet.'

'Then I'm sure her family would want you trying to find out who did this to her rather than being here with me.'

Ali made to argue but she stopped him.

'I can deal with it much better on my own.' She stood up and

18

walked over to him. Stretching up her arm she stroked his cheek, 'Please, Khalid.' She took a step back from him, then turned and went over to the cupboard. She pulled out a small brush and pan and began sweeping up the cornflakes. 'I push it to the back of my mind and keep busy; it's your fussing I can't cope with.'

'I'm sorry, but I can't pretend it's not there; it's with me all the time. I couldn't bear it if anything happened to you.'

Amina threw the dirty cereal into the waste bin and replaced the brush and pan. 'We don't know if anything *is* going to happen. If the lump is benign, then the worst is that it will be removed; if it's malignant … then they'll do whatever they have to do.' She turned to face him. 'Now please Khalid, for my sake, go to work.'

He made one final attempt 'I don't have to; John would understand.'

'Then let him understand if and when there is something to understand.' She paused for a moment, her eyes fixing on his. He couldn't hold her gaze. 'You've told him, haven't you?' A hint of disappointment crept into her voice. 'You promised me you wouldn't.'

Ali embraced her. 'I had to Amina; he's my line manager. The test results will be through soon and I can't let you go to the hospital alone. I have to give him a reason why I'm going to want the time off. "Personal" won't be enough particularly now at the start of a homicide inquiry.' Gently, he stretched out, holding her at arm's length and looked into her eyes. 'I wish you would tell someone – my mother, your mother.'

Amina kissed him lightly on the lips. 'No. I understand why you've had to tell John, but you know well enough that both your mother and my mother would fuss even more than you do, and John or no John, murder enquiry or no murder enquiry, they will expect you to stay at home with me even though for the moment there's no reason to.' She paused and then said firmly, 'You can't give them the opportunity to criticise you for putting your job first and your family second.'

Ali fought against his feelings. This was nothing to do with job versus family; this was to do with him loving his wife and not wanting her to go through this alone. But what she said was true. His parents had never totally forgiven him for joining the police service; they would much rather he had become a lawyer or a barrister and because of that they forced him constantly to wrestle with the question of where his true loyalties lay. It was a problem many police officers had; the difference was that within his community commitment to the family overrode everything else.

He persisted. 'Now John knows, why not ring Gill Handford, she'll understand.'

'No Khalid, Gill is a busy woman with a career and a family. It's close to exam time and she must be up to her eyes in nervous students, not to mention her own nervous daughters who require her to be there to support them. With one coming up to school exams and the other to GCSEs, she has enough to cope with.' She took a step backwards. 'Please, Khalid, I don't want anyone else to know until we're sure there's something to worry about.'

His feet resting on the open drawer of his desk, Handford angled his body backwards in his chair, clasped his hands behind his head and stared up at the irregular-shaped water stain on the ceiling. It had been his focus since the heavy rains one winter when the water had found its way through the flat roof of the building into the top storey and eventually through the lower floors to his office leaving its profile behind. It cleared his mind and helped him think.

Dianne Ingleby's death was now a murder enquiry and when he had rung him, Detective Chief Inspector Stephen Russell had told him – much to his surprise – to stay with it. He'd managed to get home to shower, shave and change and Gill had insisted he have some breakfast. He'd complied with a piece of toast and a coffee – in matters like that he found it better not to argue with his wife.

He contemplated the watermark again. Dark around the edges, lighter in the middle. Maurice and Rebecca Ingleby must be feeling something like it at this very moment – a blackness surrounding a state of emptiness. Handford tried not to be affected by the distress displayed by relatives, even in a situation in which the husband and the daughter had seen their loved one gunned down. Ninety per cent of murders were carried out by or involved a close family member or friend and there was nothing to say Maurice Ingleby – or even his daughter – hadn't organised Dianne's demise; but equally there was nothing as yet to say they had. Certainly their pain and bewilderment had seemed real enough. After the surgeon had left, Maurice Ingleby had looked up at Handford. 'Why?' he'd pleaded. 'What has my wife done to deserve this?' It had been a question he couldn't answer, just as he hadn't been able to when Karl Metcalfe had asked. Perhaps eventually he would, but for the moment all he could give them was a promise to do his utmost to find both the reason and the person responsible. Small consolation, but it was the best he could offer.

A tap on the door broke into his thoughts and Detective Chief Inspector Stephen Russell popped his head into the room. 'You *are* here,' he said as he entered. 'I thought perhaps you might have gone back home, managed a bit more sleep.'

Handford grimaced. 'Not worth it,' he said.

Russell indicated the chair at the side of the desk. 'May I?'

Handford nodded his agreement then pulled his feet off the drawer and sat up. He watched as his boss settled himself. Russell was a good few inches smaller than him and eight years his junior, but he carried an air of self-assurance that spanned the inches and the age gap. Educated at public school and then Cambridge from where he'd graduated with a double first, Russell was on the fast track upwards. At least he had been until a year ago when a photograph of him as a student had been found in the purse of a dead girl. By default Handford had become embroiled in the case and much against his better judgement had been forced to investigate Russell's background. Eventually he had proven that his boss was not involved but in the process had learned that Russell senior had been both promiscuous and a bully and that Russell himself had fathered an illegitimate daughter. Apart from passing the information on to the senior members of the investigating team at the time, Handford had kept his boss's secret, telling no one – nor would he.

'It's been on the local news,' Russell said as he made himself comfortable. 'Just that there's been a shooting, nothing more, although the press have been clamouring; they're demanding a name.'

Handford shrugged. 'She's been formally identified – last night before her body was moved to Sheffield for the post mortem – so providing Mr Ingleby agrees there's no real reason why her name can't be released.'

'I spoke to him earlier. He said he's already notified those who need to be notified and as far as everyone else is concerned, he'll let the press do it for him. I suggested he might like more time, but he said no; it has to happen eventually. I promised we'd keep journalists away from him until he is ready to speak to them – if at all. He's no fool; he understands the way the media works as well as we do and I doubt we're going to be able to keep it under wraps for too long anyway; better coming from us than from the likes of Karl Metcalfe.'

'I'll have him done for theft from cars if he does,' Handford growled.

The DCI smiled. 'Well he won't get the opportunity; I've promised to hold a press conference at ten o'clock this morning. In the meantime the press officer is fielding all enquiries.'

'Right.'

'And to give you all the bad news at once, I've agreed to a trainee detective joining CID, although I'm not sure you're going to be happy with him, but I promise you I had little choice.' Handford studied his boss's profile as he tried to tune into what he was saying. 'What do you mean, you had little choice? Who is this new trainee, Stephen?'

'Parvez Miah.'

'Iqbal Ahmed's son?' Handford understood why choice hadn't entered into it. Iqbal Ahmed was an important member of the Muslim community who, when he wasn't criticising the police for their methods in handling the Asian youth, gave himself the right to interfere in other areas of police business. It came as no surprise he had been allowed to be involved in Russell's decision to accept Parvez into CID as a trainee, for even now, when relations between the communities were not as strained, keeping peace with Ahmed meant being his friend not his enemy. And it would suit the man to have his son out of uniform. What was more amazing was that he had allowed him to join the service in the first place.

'Wonderful,' Handford said with feeling.

Russell smiled. 'I thought that might be your reaction. Hand him over to Sergeant Ali; Ahmed can't complain at that.'

Handford wasn't sure he agreed; Ahmed had shown in the past that he could, and did, complain about anything and everything. He let his... on Russell. He hadn't noticed before, but although still only in his thirties there was a dusting of grey in his dark brown hair and the frown lines along his forehead were becoming more marked. The job was obviously getting to him; it must be hard having to be all things to all people.

'There are a couple more things I need to discuss with you before everyone arrives,' Russell said after a moment of hesitation. 'First of all you ought to be aware that I know the Inglebys – not well, more as acquaintances than friends. Natasha and I have been invited to one or two of their dinner parties and my wife's PR firm has acted for Maurice from time to time. He tends to mix a lot with people he thinks can be of use to him.'

'In what way?'

'In any way he sees fit. He expects me to use my influence in keeping his business premises safe; he seems to think I'm his own personal police service and security firm rolled into one. But I promise you, John, I'm not and never would be.' Russell paused. The frown creased his forehead even more and for a moment he was lost in thoughts he didn't seem to want to share.

Handford's interest stirred. It would be unprofessional to jump to conclusions, but the insistence that Russell would not pander to the business man's expectations coupled with the uneasy silence suggested he had more information on Ingleby than he was divulging. Hesitation usually meant something and with someone like the DCI it was probably something that could rebound on him in one way or another. As always there were two avenues open to Handford: he could force the issue now and get it over with or he could give Russell the chance to disclose the rest when he was ready. He decided on the latter, but with the option of using a modicum of persuasion should the opportunity arise.

Suddenly, Russell pulled himself back into chief inspector mode and asked, 'Where are we with it?'

Handford shook his head. 'Nowhere yet. There were four shots only one of which hit the victim, the others went wide. We haven't found the weapon, so we don't know the make of gun. The harvested bullets and the cartridges have gone to ballistics, so it shouldn't be long before we have some information. Apart from Maurice and Rebecca Ingleby our only witness is Karl Metcalfe, and if he is to be believed, and I think he is, it wasn't a random killing. The gunman was waiting for the family to return from the theatre.'

Again Russell was silent. Eventually he said, 'And you're sure she was the target?'

'At the moment I have no reason to believe otherwise.' Handford looked at him quizzically. 'You think she wasn't; that it might have been a case of mistaken identity?'

Russell sat back in the chair. He rested his elbow on the arm and placed two fingers across his lips. They were slim, the nails finely manicured. His gaze settled on the edge of the desk as though he was choosing his words carefully, then he took a deep breath. 'A mistake certainly,' he said, 'although not necessarily of identity, rather poor aim. Guns are not easy to control, especially in the hands of an amateur. No, I wonder if the bullet was meant for the husband.'

The early morning sun was still low enough in the sky to cast shafts of light into the room and Russell put his hand to his eyes as if to shield them from the glare. He leaned forward placing himself in shadow. 'Maurice Ingleby has made a good few enemies over the years. He doesn't suffer fools gladly and he hates shoddy workmanship. Dismisses anyone, his own staff or contractors, who doesn't work to his standards and doesn't easily forgive suppliers who try to fob him off with poor materials. Rumour has it that he's been instrumental in closing down at least one business, forced the owner into bankruptcy.'

'Who, do you know?'

'A builder's merchant called Ray Braddock.'

'And there was nothing else to it?'

'I have no idea, that's for you to find out. As I said, John, it's only rumour.' An answer, but not good enough. There was more to this, Handford was sure. It was time for persuasion. 'You don't like Maurice Ingleby do you Stephen?' he said.

At first Russell offered no comment, but allowed a smile to travel along his lips. 'Is it that obvious?'

Handford waited.

'All right, John; I don't like him. As well as everything else, he's a womaniser. He's had several affairs and made more than one pass at Natasha.'

It didn't surprise Handford; Natasha Russell was a beautiful woman. 'Don't get me wrong,' Russell continued. 'In his own way he was devoted to his wife. It's just that some women turn him on – particularly the beautiful or the successful ones, and if

24

they're vulnerable at all he has the charisma, the money and the power to snare them. He never stays with them long, drops them after a few weeks, months if they're lucky, and if there are signs of retribution from the women or the husbands he covers his own back by attempting to destroy them. Sometimes he succeeds, sometimes he doesn't.'

'Nasty,' Handford contemplated his fingers. 'Stephen ...' he began.

Russell pre-empted him. 'I know what you're thinking, John, in fact you've been leading up to it for the last few minutes. I'll save you the embarrassment of asking the question by giving you the answer. No, even though she has been vulnerable since she lost the baby, Natasha wasn't one of these women and I'm not one of the husbands.'

Sadness clouded his eyes. She wasn't the only one who was still vulnerable. A year ago, Natasha Russell had been rushed into hospital with an ectopic pregnancy. The fallopian tube affected had been removed and the other was found to be diseased. Handford knew how hard this still was for them. He nodded his thanks. 'Do you know who is?'

'Again no one I can be sure of. Maurice Ingleby's life is a constant source of rumour. All I can say is that like his business dealings, this aspect of his character is worth pursuing.' He paused seeming to weigh up his words. 'But there is something else much more worrying. If it's true and the papers get hold of it, it could rebound on a lot of people – particularly those from whom Ingleby has asked and been given favours.'

Including Russell. This was why he had been so insistent that he wasn't in any way involved with Ingleby – it was a covering your back exercise.

Handford waited.

Russell took a deep breath. 'Maurice Ingleby is widely suspected of being the money behind the local branch of the BNP ...'

Great, first Iqbal Ahmed's son on the team and now the husband of the murdered woman could be a member of the BNP and might have been the intended victim. The morning was just getting better and better.

'He's adamant he has no link at all with them,' Russell went on, 'but there are those who don't believe him and a while ago he received several death threats unless he pulled out.'

Handford frowned as he trawled his memory. 'I can't recall us being told about this; it's not something we have investigated.'

'No.' It was Russell's turn to contemplate his fingers.

'No we weren't told, or no we didn't investigate?'

'Maurice came to me with the letters and they were investigated, but not by us. They were passed on to Keighley division since he lives on their patch; they came up with several suspects, but little in the way of evidence. They must have warned off the people involved however, because the letters stopped.'

'They probably went underground and Dianne Ingleby's death is the result,' Handford said bitterly.

Russell shifted his position. 'You may well be right, John, but you must understand, there were political ramifications. At the time the BNP were gaining in popularity, but there was also considerable opposition. We didn't want it to get out of hand. It wouldn't have been a good idea for anyone to suspect that senior police officers in Bradford were involved. The BNP would have made political capital out of it and those who were opposed would have seen it as the police backing the party.'

'I don't suppose suggesting that the police are non-political or that making death threats is a serious crime would have done any good?'

'Not in this case, no.'

'Are you going to give me the names of the suspects?'

Russell took a folded paper out of the inside pocket of his jacket and slid it over the desk. 'I'm passing these names on because they may have a bearing on the murder. But, and I want this clearly understood, we don't want you to go back over old ground unless it becomes necessary. We're too near the local elections and there are a good few BNP candidates standing. Should the question of death threats to Maurice Ingleby hit the press then they will start to speculate and with journalists like Peter Redmayne around it won't take long for them to discover his alleged link with the party.'

Handford had to agree; he had clashed a few times with Peter Redmayne and knew that once on to a story he hung on like a ferret until he had all the answers.

'If that happens then I repeat,' Russell continued, 'it's likely both the BNP and their opponents will make political capital out of it and God only knows how that will end.'

Handford sighed; there was little more to be said. He knew the situation could be explosive, but sometimes it seemed that he had to investigate crimes – even murder – with his hands tied behind his back. He made a few notes then put down his pen. 'You said you had two things to discuss.'

Russell relaxed as a smile creased his face. 'It's not general knowledge yet and you're to keep it to yourself, but I'm taking over from Superintendent Slater when he retires next month. My promotion will be made official in a day or two.'

There had been talk around CID for some time as to who would replace Slater, but as far as Handford was concerned it had been a foregone conclusion. Russell was the right man for the job; he was much more a manager than a jobbing police officer. Paperwork suited him.

Handford stood up and walked round the desk, his hand outstretched. 'Congratulations, Stephen, I'm pleased for you.'

They unclasped hands and Russell looked up at him. 'I shall need a good DCI and you're good. You've just proven that. I know we haven't always seen eye to eye ...' *Now there was an understatement if ever there was one* ... 'But I think you're that man.'

Handford pulled a chair from the wall and placed it opposite Stephen Russell. 'I appreciate it, Stephen, don't think I don't, but if I'm honest as things are it would be second best. If I'm to be promoted I'd rather it was into HMET.'

HMET – the Homicide and Major Enquiry Team – was a new unit currently being set up in West Yorkshire. It was to consist of eight discrete teams working from different locations, dealing only with cases of homicide and serious crime, and Handford wanted to be part of it; he didn't want to end his career in a CID which dealt only with petty criminals and paperwork.

'And *I'd* rather you were with me,' Russell insisted. 'We know DC Clarke and DC Warrender are joining HMET and there's a strong likelihood that Sergeant Ali will be accepted on to the team. I can't afford to lose you too.'

Handford wasn't sure whether he should feel flattered or furious. 'Are you saying you won't back a transfer?'

Russell let out a long breath. 'No, John, I'm not saying that. I'm saying think about it. You'd be a DCI no matter what ...'.

'But working on petty cases – burglaries, muggings, criminal damage.'

'They're not petty to the victims.'

Handford felt his hackles rise. He stood up and walked to the window where he closed the blind, trapping the sunlight behind it. Then he spun round to face Russell. 'That was unfair, Stephen; you know what I mean. They are the kind of cases competent DCs can handle. I want more – something I can get my teeth into.' Russell raised an eyebrow and Handford realised he was letting his frustration show as the volume of his voice peaked. He returned to sit behind his desk. 'I'm sorry,' he said. 'I was just trying to make a point.'

Russell waved away the comment as though it wasn't important and got to his feet. 'Don't dismiss what I've said too readily, John; think about it. I want you as my DCI and I shall have no compunction in making my views clear to the senior officers in HMET. However if I can't persuade you to apply for the position and you're not accepted into the enquiry team, you'll probably remain an inspector for the rest of your career, still at Central, still working on petty crime. At least my way, you'll have your promotion.'

Trainee Detective Constable Parvez Miah stood in front of the mirror and considered his image. He turned to look at his wife who was sitting up in bed clutching her knees to her chest. 'Is this tie suitable? Would something a little more sombre be better?'

Aisha chuckled. 'It's fine,' she said. 'You might even be over-dressed. I think you'll find that most of the detectives don't bother with ties at all except when they're in court.' Aisha worked as a junior solicitor for the Crown Prosecution Service. 'If it's smart you want, you'll have to stay in uniform.'

He was about to respond when he saw the twinkle in her eyes. 'You're teasing me,' he said.

'You're right, Parvez, I'm teasing you. Stop worrying, you're absolutely fine. What I really want to know ...,' she pointed to the figures on the radio alarm, 'is why you're up and dressed at seven o'clock in the morning.'

'I want to be at Central early – give the right impression. And anyway, I've got a meeting with the DCI and then one with DI Handford.' He became serious. 'Do you think I'm right transferring to CID? You don't think I'm going to make a mess of it?'

28

Aisha knelt up on the bed and crawled towards the end. She held out her hands and he took them in his. 'How long have you been a policeman, Parvez?' she asked, 'How often have you made a mess of things?'

The problem with having a solicitor as a wife was they always went straight to the nub of the argument. 'Hardly ever,' he said, feeling he was on the stand.

'Then you're not going to make a mess of this. They wouldn't have accepted you for training if they thought you would.'

Parvez wasn't sure. He could never be sure, because he didn't know just how much influence his father exerted. 'Possibly, but I don't know if my father had any input into the decision.'

She pulled him closer to her. 'Even if he did, so what? You won't be the first and you certainly won't be the last to have been given a helping hand by his family. Come here and give me a kiss and forget your father for once.'

He bent towards her and kissed her gently. As he drew away, he said, 'You know you might be right about me being early. I could come back to bed.' Then he put his arms round her waist and lifted her towards him.

She flinched.

As he felt her discomfort he eased the pressure. 'I'm sorry, Aisha,' he said softly, 'does it still hurt?'

Her eyes flashed with a sudden burst of anger. 'What do you think, Parvez? Chanda pushed me to the floor and kicked me hard. Of course it still hurts.'

He took a step backwards. 'You talk as though she meant to harm you, when she has said over and over again that she didn't.' His voice had taken on a warning note.

If Aisha heard it, she wasn't about to acknowledge it. Instead she underscored each word. 'She meant it, Parvez, believe me she meant it.' She pulled aside her night-gown to reveal the yellowing bruises which spread over her right side and across the small of her back. 'Look, just look. How can she not have meant that?'

He attempted to explain. 'She was angry because she felt you were not pulling your weight in the house. Her temper got the better of her, and ...'

'Parvez, she's a bully, she's always been a bully, she was suspended from school for bullying. She's doing to me what she did to those girls – name-calling then kicking. She's been abusing me verbally for weeks and now it's become physical and the other women are egging her on. Last year she was the newest member of the household, the new bride; now I am and she's making the most of it.'

'I'm sure that's not it, Aisha. She's young; she's pregnant and she gets tired; all she wants is for you to do a bit more, perhaps help her look after my brothers' children or with the cleaning.'

'I don't care what she wants. I have a hard and responsible job, I bring work home with me, I haven't time for anything else. Your father agreed that if I continued working, I would contribute to the housekeeping, not that I would come home and do the cleaning. There are four women in this house who are here all day to do that. And as far as the children are concerned, I spend time with them when I can.'

He didn't want to argue, not today. 'Aisha …'

She met his gaze with a mixture of contempt and sadness in her eyes. 'No, Parvez. You can't see it, can you? Any more than your father could when he went into the school, taking me with him. "Chanda's a good Muslim girl; Muslim girls don't bully." Well this one does. How do you think I got these? Falling down stairs?' She pointed again to the bruises. She was crying now, tears of rage rolling down her cheeks. 'Chanda assaulted me and you all refuse to accept it. Well let me warn you; this time I've kept it within the family; but make no mistake, next time I *will* make a complaint against her.'

'No Aisha, that's the last thing you will do.' The words slashed the air. 'I forbid you to do any such thing.' He picked up his briefcase as if to indicate the conversation was over and walked to the door.

She climbed off the bed and closed in on him. 'Forbid me. Forbid me. This is the twenty-first century, Parvez; you don't forbid me to do anything, particularly when my safety's at stake.'

He stood, rigid, his back still to her. 'My father wouldn't allow it.' It was to be his final shot.

'Your father's not the one being abused,' she flung back at him.

He turned. 'He's a senior member of the community; what do you think bringing the police in would do to him? You can't shame him this way.' He was clutching at straws and he knew it.

30

She looked at him in disgust. 'I thought police officers were supposed to uphold the law. If you were any sort of a police officer, you would do just that. She assaulted me,' she said, emphasising each word. 'You should have had her arrested or got someone else to do it. You could still.'

Parvez loved his wife with an intensity he had never thought possible, but he couldn't do what she was demanding – not then, not now. His concern was that she might take it upon herself to take it further. In this frame of mind she could do anything. Her job meant she met plenty of police officers; she could complain to one of them; perhaps even to his new boss. And she would make her point. She was stronger and more articulate than he was; he didn't think he'd ever won an argument with her, but in this one he had to succeed. He had to make her see.

Aisha didn't give him time to formulate a reply. 'You won't though, will you?' Her voice was like steel. She took a deep breath and said slowly, 'Chanda assaulted me, Parvez, and I'm telling you she will do it again.'

'No she won't. I'll make sure she doesn't.' As he tried to reassure her, he felt the emptiness of his words. He dropped his case and folded his arms round her. This wasn't just between him and her; this was family business. He'd talk to his father tonight, ask him to stop what they were all aware was going on. But he knew already what the response would be. Iqbal Ahmed had had his reservations about them marrying at all. Aisha came from a good family, but she was too westernized, too ambitious. After a lot of soul-searching and praying, he'd given his consent he said, because his son was deeply in love and to refuse them could mean they would disobey him and marry anyway. That would bring shame on the family – shame he wasn't prepared to risk.

Parvez held on to his wife, trying to delete his father's words as they scrolled through his head. 'I've never prevented you from following your aspirations,' he'd said, 'or why else would I have agreed to you becoming a police officer, but this woman is clever and strong and will not be easily controlled. Even I have not been able to persuade her to act in the defence of members of our community, rather than prosecute them. You watch her, Parvez; you never take your eyes off her, because if she thinks she is right, she will disobey you.'

He'd thought this was over. He'd thought he'd managed the

31

situation. But how did you manage two explosive temperaments like Aisha and Chanda? The truth was he had absolutely no idea.

With a deep sigh, he kissed his wife lightly on her head, picked up his briefcase and left the room.

Emma Crossley held on to her young son's hand and knocked on the door of Ray Braddock's cottage. It was a few minutes before it was opened and when it was he stood in front of her dressed only in a pair of boxer shorts. His tousled hair and bleary expression suggested he was nursing a hangover.

He peered at her. 'What time do you call this?' he snarled, then pointed to the child. 'What 'ave you brought 'im for?'

She pushed past him, avoiding the staleness of his breath. 'Have you seen the local news this morning?'

'No, I've been in bed which is where I'm going back to.' He smirked. 'You can come and join me if you want.'

Emma ignored him. 'Dianne Ingleby died last night. Someone shot her.'

Cold water couldn't have brought him round more quickly. He blanched and for a moment it seemed as though his power of speech had become temporarily paralysed, then he said, 'Are you sure?' His voice was gravelly and he attempted to clear his throat.

'It's almost ten o'clock, put the television on; see for yourself if you don't believe me.' She propped Jack in the corner of the settee. It was cold in the room, but Braddock made no move to light the gas fire. Instead he pressed the TV switch, waited for the picture to appear, then stood close to the set as though he needed its nearness to take in what the newscaster was saying.

'A murder enquiry has been launched after a woman was shot last night in the multi-storey car park close to Central Police Station in Bradford. She has been named as forty-nine-year-old Dianne Ingleby, wife of business man, Maurice Ingleby.' Her picture filled the screen. She was smiling. 'She was taken to the Royal Infirmary where she died from her injuries in the early hours of this morning. Our crime reporter, Julian Green, has the story.'

The picture faded into a shot of the multi-storey car park. Police vans were still in evidence and uniformed officers stood at the entrance. The reporter described the scene but added little more to the information already given except to say that a press conference was to be held during the day.

Throughout, Braddock remained motionless and when the newscaster moved on to the next story, he continued to stare at the screen until eventually he picked up the control and lowered the sound. The silent picture switched from the anchorman to a woman holding a puppy in her arms. Jack squealed and pointed to it.

Emma grabbed Braddock's arm and swung him round to face her. 'Did you have anything to do with this?'

Angrily he pulled away. 'Don't be stupid, woman. Why would I want to kill Dianne Ingleby?'

'Kathie,' she suggested, a question mark in her tone.

There was a hint of fear in his eyes. 'What do you mean – Kathie?'

'You know bloody well what I mean. I warned you a couple of days ago she was close to telling Dianne who attacked her.'

He took a step towards her. 'And I told you it was nothing to do with me.'

'What are you saying Ray? That it's coincidence I let you know Kathie is on the verge of giving out the name of her attacker to Dianne Ingleby and forty-eight hours later the woman's shot? Shot, Ray – not beaten up or stabbed, but shot. Or is that a coincidence as well?'

He was now inches from her. 'The trouble with you is you're fucking obsessed,' he said through gritted teeth. 'I didn't beat up Kathie. The bitch would have deserved it if I had, threatening to shop me to the tax office and the receivers, but I didn't, and I didn't shoot Dianne Ingleby either.' He took a pace backwards. 'Ask Darren, I was out with him most of the night.'

'Out with Darren? You? He's twenty-one going on ten – why would you be out with him? You'll need a better alibi than him.'

Braddock blustered. 'And you'll keep your mouth shut or that kid of yours won't see his next birthday.'

She glared at him. 'That kid of ours.'

'Don't start that again. It could be anybody's.'

She scooped up the child. 'His name's Jack and he's yours. Whether you like it or not, Ray, he's yours.' She snatched at the door. A blast of cold air met her and swept into the room. She turned back to Ray Braddock who had folded his arms tight across his chest in an attempt to keep himself warm. 'The only reason I haven't been to the police earlier is that Kathie doesn't want me to and I don't want Jack growing up knowing his father beats up women. But ...' she lifted her eyebrows and left the rest unsaid.

As she walked to the bus stop, she heard his voice trail after her. 'If you think I'm paying for him, you've got another thing coming – you slag.'

chapter three

There was silence in the incident room as the detectives concentrated on the video taken in the multi-storey car park. It was not the most satisfactory method of viewing a crime scene, but it was the best on offer since trampling over possible evidence was not to be recommended. With the agreement of the senior SOCO and in full protective clothing Handford, as Senior Investigating Officer, had been the only one allowed beyond the cordon. But it had given him the opportunity to view at firsthand those elements which would give him some small picture of the attack: the four-by-four, the deep red stain, the bullet holes, and the witness for whom her final breath reverberated in his ears. Dianne Ingleby might have drawn her final breath in the operating theatre, but he was in no doubt that it was in the car park she had been murdered.

Handford set aside his memories and focused on the monitor. Mrs Ingleby had been taken off by ambulance and replaced by small numbered markers indicating the blood which had spilled from her chest as well as the locations of the three bullets that had missed their target. One had ruptured the metalwork to the left-hand side of the spare tyre on the back of Ingleby's Landrover and was, according to the scene-of-crime officer, probably embedded in the passenger seat's upholstery – they wouldn't know until they had removed the vehicle and checked it thoroughly. The other two had missed completely and penetrated the car park wall low down, powdering flakes of concrete on to the floor.

Apart from Ingleby's car, five vehicles remained stranded – the van belonging to the driver who had complained to Jane Charles, and four others. Only one was within range of the four-by-four – a Peugeot of a dark but indeterminate colour which so far no one had turned up to collect. Karl Metcalfe had been insistent the killer's car was a Citroën and had driven away at speed, but Handford couldn't risk that he'd been mistaken in the make, or indeed that the gunman hadn't arrived in the Peugeot and transferred to the Citroën for some reason. It was unlikely since Metcalfe had been there for some time and hadn't noticed anything. But it was never a good idea to throw out the unlikely, particularly at this early stage in an investigation and particularly if it had something to do with the more extreme opponents of the BNP – opponents who tended to be clever, meticulous in their planning and ruthless. Either way the owner would have to be traced and the Peugeot examined forensically, if only to eliminate it.

The Landrover was *in situ*; the front bumper hard against the concrete barrier at the edge of the building, the back end protruding into the aisle. The camera zoomed on to the bullet hole in the door; it was low down, lower than would be expected if the gunman had been aiming at Dianne Ingleby, suggesting it had probably been fired after she had gone down – possibly at her husband, who by this time would be low to the ground crawling towards his wife. On the other hand it could indicate that the first shot was on target and following the recoil the gunman hadn't been able to maintain his aim.

On the floor of the bay in which the Citroën had been parked was a patch of oil. According to the scene-of-crime officer it was fresh and may have leaked from the suspect vehicle. Towards the back wall of the same bay lay the laptop stolen and dropped by Metcalfe.

'What are we looking at here?' Handford asked as he turned off the television and ejected the tape. 'Is it someone who intended to kill Dianne Ingleby and succeeded, or was his victim meant to be Maurice Ingleby and the wife took the bullet by mistake?' He turned to the diagram of the scene and pointed to the bay where the four-by-four was parked. 'Ingleby is about to get into the car when his daughter tells him he is over the limit and insists she drives them home. They have to change places. They walk past Dianne – Rebecca behind her to the driver's door while Ingleby crosses in front of her. Dianne Ingleby was here, in the aisle, between the Landrover and the edge of the bay. Rebecca thought her mother had turned to follow them to get into the car herself, but according to Metcalfe she turned round, possibly because she had seen or heard him or perhaps because she'd recognised the car.' Handford moved his finger to where Karl Metcalfe had said the gunman's car was positioned. 'Either way she is facing the gunman when he pulls out of the bay. He stops here and fires. He hits Dianne in the chest, she goes down; he fires three more times – to the left where Maurice is, but misses him.'

Handford's eyes turned on the detectives who were listening intently. They were good at their job and enthusiastic, but for many of them this would probably be the last serious crime they would investigate – for him too if Russell had his way. 'As I see it we've two scenarios,' he said. 'The first is that Dianne Ingleby was the intended victim and the second that the killer got it wrong and it was her husband he wanted dead. We can't afford to ignore either.'

Detective Constable Chris Warrender spoke up. 'Does that mean, guv, that if Ingleby was the target he could be in danger? That whoever wanted him dead, still wants him dead?' An experienced officer in his early thirties, the ginger-haired man was resting back on his chair, his legs stretched out in front of him. He had little time for authority, was popular with his colleagues and took delight in annoying anyone he considered a fair target with remarks peppered with double meaning. Khalid Ali had suffered at his hands more than once. Nevertheless no complaints had ever been laid against him and he was astute and sharp-witted and knew the city and its under-class better than anyone – a detective worth having on any team.

Handford nodded his agreement. 'If he was then it's a strong possibility. It doesn't bear thinking about, but it's something else we can't ignore. The question is should we offer him protection?'

'Would we be justified in spending the money?' Ali asked. 'Particularly if we go with the view that we have an amateur on our hands and he killed Dianne by mistake, perhaps that will be enough for him. Either it will have frightened him and he'll keep his head down or he'll have made his point – whatever it is – and won't try again.'

Warrender wasn't convinced. 'And you're willing to risk another person's life on the possibility he's made his point?'

Ali frowned. 'I didn't say that, Warrender. I was simply

37

suggesting we could be wasting a lot of money on a maybe.'

Handford watched the two of them with interest. He had seen their relationship develop over the past couple of years from one ground firmly in mutual dislike to one that had changed subtly during the investigation into the death of a young black girl on which they had worked together. 'Sergeant Ali's right, Warrender, I doubt the DCI would sanction the cost at this stage,' he said. 'For the moment we'll treat them both as intended victims, maintain a police presence and warn Maurice of the risk.'

He turned to the photograph of Dianne Ingleby. A smart woman with a rounded face and fair hair, stylishly cut, she looked every inch the wife of a successful business man. 'Dianne Ingleby, forty-nine, married twenty-seven years, one daughter, Rebecca. Financially she didn't have to go out to work, though she helped her husband out in the office a couple of mornings a week. Most of her time was spent as a volunteer – mainly at the hospital and with Victim Support. On the surface it would seem she was someone to respect. From what her husband and daughter said, she was without enemies and went out of her way to help people.'

He stretched over and indicated Maurice Ingleby. 'At fifty-two he's an ambitious, hard-headed business man, who, rumour has it, will ride roughshod over rivals or those who try to fleece him by overcharging or passing on shoddy goods. More significantly, rumour also has it that he's had affairs with a number of women, mostly married and mostly with husbands known to him. Warrender and Clarke, I want you to take Maurice Ingleby. Check the bankruptcy list; see if there is anyone on it who has had any association with him that could have led to that person's financial ruin – specifically a Ray Braddock. Trainee Detective Miah can help with that. Also trace the women he is alleged to have had affairs with. According to Mr Russell they will be beautiful, successful and vulnerable – probably lonely if they spend a lot of their time alone at home. I want to know firstly how their husbands became aware of the affairs and secondly their movements last night.' Handford grinned. 'This should be right up your street Warrender, but I'm relying on Clarke to make sure you don't step off the path of discretion.'

Andy Clarke nodded. He was the oldest member of the team and had been a friend of John Handford from the time

38

they joined the police service together. He was experienced and thorough, and considered by all to be the person to whom they could turn for advice and encouragement. They had all done it – even Handford.

'Don't worry, guv, I won't take my eyes off him.'

Handford waited until the laughter had died down then said, 'Now, any ideas as to why Dianne should have turned to face the opposite direction? It could have been because she thought she saw Metcalfe ...'

'Or because she heard the car start up and wanted to check Rebecca had room enough to back out,' Ali said.

Warrender tossed the suggestion to one side. 'No, they were two bays away, and anyway she would back out to her right. I think there's more to it than that. Something happened to make her turn.'

'Such as?'

'I don't know, Ali.' There was a touch of impatience in the detective's voice. 'Perhaps it's like the boss said or because the engine misfired first time; it's possible, he was about to shoot someone; he can be forgiven for being a bit nervous. I think it's more likely to be that she'd recognised the car earlier but hadn't realised the driver was in it – Metcalfe didn't and he was closer. She might have turned to check or to wave or something.'

Warrender could be right; indeed Karl Metcalfe had commented that the killing wasn't random, that the gunman had been waiting for them. She might well have noticed him. 'I agree,' Handford said. 'The driver may have been known to her. In that case we need to track down all her contacts and the vehicles they drive.'

He turned to a team leader. 'Ken, I want you to get on to that; check on every friend, every acquaintance and everybody at the hospital and from her work with Victim Support ...'

'We may have a problem there, sir,' Ali interrupted. 'I rang Mrs Leighton, the coordinator, before the briefing this morning. She was horrified at the murder and said she will visit Maurice Ingleby, but she's not prepared to open her books to us. She cited the Data Protection Act and confidentiality as her reasons.' He let a smile run across his lips. 'She said she was surprised we'd even asked, and you ought to have known better.'

'What does she mean, the Data Protection Act?' Bloody woman. Who did she think she was? Handford tried to quell his irritation but failed as he had always did in situations like this. '*We give her* the information about the previous day's crimes and victims in the first place. If it wasn't for us, she wouldn't have anyone to support. Didn't you point that out?'

Ali smiled. 'Yes I did, although not quite in those words. She said once victims decide they need their support, then their code of confidentiality comes into play and that means she will not open her books to us. She said if you wanted to discuss it to drop in and see her sometime.'

'I might just do that,' Handford retorted. 'Or I might ask her to come in here – see how she likes that.'

'Do you want me to apply for a warrant?' Ali asked.

Handford took a deep breath to calm his annoyance. He as much as anyone knew it wasn't unusual for an inquiry to be frustrated by a refusal to cooperate. He didn't like it, although he could just about understand it when the rebuff came from villains or even from family members. What he found harder to take was when it came from someone like Eileen Leighton who was supposed to care. Just where did her compassion lie? Certainly not with Dianne Ingleby, her husband or her daughter – yet she had the cheek to say she would visit Maurice. To do what? To gain information that would help the police? He doubted it. Handford would have loved to walk into the Victim Support offices waving a court order in front of her but it was too early to apply to the magistrates; they needed to show opening the files was absolutely necessary and at the moment they couldn't do that.

'No, not yet,' he said. 'Let's wait until we know more about Dianne Ingleby. I'll pop in and see Mrs Leighton like she suggested, remind her of her loyalty to her volunteers as well as her clients. That might be enough. In the meantime find out which family liaison officer has been assigned to the Inglebys ...'

'It's Connie Burns,' Ali said.

Handford had worked with Connie Burns before. She was good and she used her common sense. 'Then make sure she knows that for the moment Eileen Leighton is not to be allowed to speak with the family alone.'

'Sir.'

'In the meantime I've asked for the CCTV tapes from the car park.' Handford went on. 'Paul, a couple of your team can trawl through them.' He didn't miss the groan that went up. 'A couple more can check the tickets from the machine. They won't give us much, but we shall know how many cars left the building immediately or soon after the shooting and how long they'd been there. We might even be able to match the car with CCTV. Also I want someone else on checking all Citroëns in the district as well as garages who've had drivers complaining their cars are leaking oil.'

A voice came from the back of the room. 'It could have been stolen, guv, used just for last night.'

Handford smiled. 'Then you know what your job is.'

'Check on all stolen cars, Citroëns or similar,'

'Got it in one. The rest of you, I want to know everything about Dianne Ingleby. Did she seem happy – in herself, in her marriage, what was her social life, did it include her husband or was she usually alone? Did she have any special friends, male and female? Was she a member of any clubs, golf club, Women's Institute, a church group? Also I want her movements over the past week or so. Go house to house, find out when she was on duty at the hospital, when she worked in the office, when she was at home, when she went out for coffee – everything. In the meantime Sergeant Ali and I will be with Mr Ingleby and can be reached on our mobiles. Any questions?'

Some detectives shook their heads; others muttered what Handford took to be a no. 'The murder of Maurice Ingleby's wife will be big news. It's already been on television and is bound to be in the first editions by midday, but don't talk to any reporter except to tell them there is to be a press conference later today. Understood?'

There was another murmur of agreement.

'Right let's get on with it and we'll meet back here at five to consolidate.'

By the time Emma Crossley arrived at work, the hospital was buzzing with the news of Dianne Ingleby's death. The nursery nurse in the crèche where she left Jack couldn't wait to discuss it, although her version probably had more than a sprinkling of imagination mixed in with the truth. Once Jack was settled Emma made her way to Kathie's ward. The nurse at the station was equally keen to talk, but her concern was for the patient rather than with the gory details. She said Kathie had been told as soon as it was practicable. 'Sister thought it better we let her know than she found out from the newspapers. The poor thing was very upset. We wanted to move her to a side ward but she wouldn't hear of it, she wouldn't even let us pull the curtains round her bed to give her some privacy. She's had a sedative so she's asleep now.' Then she smiled sympathetically. 'I'll ring down when she wakes up.'

The pathology lab where Emma worked was in the basement of the hospital with its cold tiled corridors lit by fluorescent tubes. It was usually referred to as the underbelly and not visited by other medical staff unless absolutely necessary. The pathology department for visiting patients was on the ground floor and was much more inviting. She stopped at the drinks machine for a tea which she'd decided some time ago was marginally more palatable than the coffee and grimaced as she picked the cup from the drip tray. The lights faded the liquid to a murky grey but it was hot and since she hadn't had time for anything that morning it was better than doing without. She carried it to the lab trying not to spill its contents. Everyone else was busy working and she slipped in quietly, placed the cup on the bench, took off her jacket and pulled on her white coat, then felt in her drawer for the KitKat she was fairly sure was there. She sat on her stool and picked up the drink and biscuit. She ought to be getting on with examining the blood tests, but she couldn't, not yet. She needed time to come to terms with everything – Dianne Ingleby's murder, Ray Braddock and Kathie, specifically Kathie.

Just how much more could her friend take? First the assault and now the murder of the one person she could trust not to broadcast her secrets – whatever they were. And whatever they were, they'd been pulling her apart since way before the attack. She was frightened too, had been for a while. Her house was secured with so many locks and bolts on the doors and the windows that if there was a fire it was unlikely she would ever be able to escape. She'd had spyholes fitted and rarely opened the door to anyone she didn't know. Even here in the hospital she hadn't wanted to be in a side ward or enclosed by curtains. She was only in control when she could see everyone.

At first Emma had thought Kathie might be being stalked by a former boyfriend, but after the assault she'd known that whoever was behind it, it wasn't as simple as a lovelorn admirer. Unless it

42

was a case of 'if I can't have her, no one else will', stalkers don't usually half-kill their victims – at least she didn't think they did. So if it hadn't been the work of a stalker had it been a burglary gone wrong? And if that was what it was why was Kathie refusing to say anything? In spite of the ferocity of the attack, she'd been and still was adamant she didn't want the police involved. At the best of times Kathie was secretive, but this made no sense.

Who even knew she was in hospital? Her, Dianne Ingleby, Ray Braddock, the Methodist minister who had visited a few times and the staff. Emma had offered to contact Kathie's brother, Jason, tell him what had happened, but had been told it wasn't necessary, the hospital staff had already done it. Yet as far as she knew he hadn't visited. Then there was the A4 envelope Kathie had asked her to keep for her. What was that all about and why had she insisted that she was to tell no one about it – not even Ray? She hadn't given so much as a clue as to what it contained and why it was so important yet it was sealed and marked 'Personal' and so well-hidden in the loft of her house that it had taken Emma ages to find it. Another secret.

Emma dropped the empty drinking cup and the biscuit wrapper into the waste-bin next to her. That was the problem with Kathie – she was one massive frightened secret.

That Ingleby's house belonged to a successful builder there was no doubt. It was well out of Bradford, on the outskirts of Baildon village with an incredible view of the valley below. It had once been a farm, which the owner had been forced to sell after the foot-and-mouth epidemic. Like many he hadn't been touched by the disease itself, rather by the fall-out from it. More farmers had gone bankrupt through not being able to move or sell their stock than had been ruined by their animals being culled.

The house was large and set back in a good acre of land tended by a gardener, who even today, the day after Dianne Ingleby's death, was busy working. But it was inside that the presence of the practical man was evident. Not that it would be noticeable to the casual visitor, but Handford was no casual visitor. As he'd wandered around, he'd observed the jobs that needed doing: the door handle drooping like a flaccid hand from its fixings; the old-fashioned stair-rod rattling as he climbed up to the bedrooms; the washer needing replacing on

43

the dripping tap – all easy to fix, but no time for a busy man in which to do it. He imagined Dianne complaining to her husband in much the same way Gill complained to him. 'It won't take two minutes.' An exaggeration, but he knew what she meant.

Handford returned to the lounge. Like the rest of the house the room was pretentious; everything in it was of generous size – the furniture, the television, the music system, even the grand piano, yet it had a homely quality about it. True at the moment it was tinged with sorrow, but so much of Dianne Ingleby was here. The ostentation was Maurice Ingleby's, the self-made man; the quiet calm of the decoration was hers; she had made this house into a home and currently the police were digging into its very soul. Upstairs Ali would be painstakingly leafing through letters and diaries, scrutinising and inspecting things which she would have considered private. Nothing would ever be the same again.

'I'm sorry we have to do this,' Handford said as he entered, 'but the more we learn about Dianne, the sooner we understand the motive behind her murder and the sooner we'll track down her killer.'

Maurice Ingleby shook his head. 'There *was* no reason for anyone to kill her. All she did was good. She kept house, she entertained and she helped me out at the yard, yet she found time to give of herself to other people.'

'How did you feel about that?' asked Handford as he sat on the chair opposite.

Ingleby lifted his head. 'I married Dianne because she was a kind and caring person. If you're trying to suggest I didn't like what my wife was doing you couldn't be further from the truth. Any attempt to change her would have made her into someone different and not the woman I fell in love with thirty years ago. So don't even go down that path, Inspector.'

Handford wondered how he equated that speech with his various affairs, but that was a question for later and he let it lie dormant. 'I'm sorry,' he said, 'I had to ask.'

Ingleby stood up and walked over to the piano. He picked up a piece of paper. 'I've made the list you wanted of people who knew we were going to the theatre.' He passed it to Handford. 'There may be others, but those are the only ones I can think of.'

Handford glanced at it; it was long, it would take forever to

44

go through it. 'Is there anyone on here who might have held a grudge against your wife?'

'No one; against me possibly, but not against her.'

'Why do you say that?'

'I'm a business man, Inspector, self-made and proud of it. But to get where I am, I've stood on some toes and people don't like that. I build high-quality houses, using high-quality materials and I use the best sub-contractors. No one puts anything over on me; if the materials or the work are substandard I complain and the suppliers and contractors don't get paid until I'm satisfied, and they don't do business with me or work for me again. Over the years some of them have tried to rip me off, to charge over the odds. But they soon learned it wasn't worth the risk. I know my trade, no one knows it better and as far as I'm concerned, if they're messing with me they're messing with my customers and with my reputation.'

As Handford listened, he knew why he'd felt overpowered and intimidated by the man at the hospital. His manner, his voice, his words overshadowed all in his path like an immense cloud.

Rebecca came in carrying a tray. She was pale, her skin as translucent as porcelain and her features strained. Her eyes were surrounded by dark circles as though she hadn't slept much.

'I've brought us some coffee,' she said as she put it on the low mahogany table. 'I've taken some to the officers upstairs; I hope you don't mind.'

'Of course not.' He thanked her for the cup she offered him.

'Oh, and Sergeant Ali asks if you can pop up and see him when you've a minute.' Tears welled in her eyes. 'He's in the bedroom checking through Mum's things.' She handed a coffee to her father, took one herself and sat down. 'Mrs Briggs has arrived, she's our daily,' she added by way of explanation. 'I don't know if you want to talk to her but she's in a quite a state; the family liaison officer is looking after her.'

'Perhaps later. I'll leave her with Connie for the moment.'

When Rebecca was settled, Handford said, 'How are you?' He'd always thought it a silly question, one that journalists ask when they've nothing better to say; even for him it was useful only to cut through the grief.

'Oh, you know. It doesn't seem real. I keep expecting her to walk in at any moment.' Her blue eyes, though filled with sadness were as hypnotic as her father's and held on to Handford's until finally she angled them away to gaze into their drink. 'I keep remembering, her lying on the floor of the car park, whimpering. Once or twice she pleaded for us to help her, but there was nothing we could do.' She stopped, guilt clouding her eyes. It was irrational, but at this moment she would believe that when her mother had needed her most she had failed her. There was nothing he could say to alleviate her self-reproach. Finally she took a deep sigh and said, 'She used to tell us that victims of crime go through a number of emotions – numbness, impotence, grief, anger, guilt. But all I feel is hollowness deep inside me and I can't imagine ever having the energy for any of the others to take over. I don't even have the energy to cry properly. Perhaps at the funeral.' For a moment she paused, then asked, 'When can we bury her?'

'It's up to the coroner,' he said, 'but it shouldn't be too long. I expect he'll open and adjourn the inquest in order that the funeral can go ahead.' He couldn't tell her that as murders go her mother's, although violent, was anatomically quite straightforward; the bullet had negotiated obstacles in her chest like the ball in a games machine until it caused damage to a major blood vessel so that in the end she'd bled to death. Nor did he want her to know that even now her mother's body would be undergoing a postmortem in the Sheffield mortuary and later today or tomorrow, the pathologist would report back in cold medical terminology exactly how that very small object had killed her. But hard as it was for her and her father they could no longer be treated as victims; they were witnesses to a murder and to the life of the dead woman and for Handford dispassion must now take over from compassion.

'I've asked you this before,' he said, 'but I want you to think about it again. Did your mother ever talk about any of the victims of crime she supported?'

'Not with us.'

'So you have no idea who she has been working with in the past few weeks?'

Rebecca shook her head. 'No. She took her work there very seriously; it was confidential; she wouldn't tell anyone.'

'Who did she talk to if the case was problematic, if it worried her?'

'The coordinator.'

'Never to you or your father?'

'No.'

'Did she work with victims of serious crime or just those involved in petty crimes – burglaries, robberies, that sort of thing?'

Rebecca put her cup on the tray and leaned forward. 'She supported both,' she said evenly. 'She cared about both. Victims are victims, Inspector, no matter how the police describe the crime.'

This was the second time today it had been suggested, however obliquely, that he didn't care about victims of petty crime, first by Russell and now by Rebecca Ingleby. He felt like telling her that he cared; but if they really wanted their mother's killer caught, then he couldn't let caring get in the way. 'I'm not suggesting for a minute,' he said quietly, 'that people aren't affected by any crime perpetrated against them, whether it be someone stealing their mobile phone, breaking into their house or assaulting them, but your mother has been shot. If she was helping a rape victim for instance, it may be that this was an act of intimidation by the rapist or his family that went tragically wrong. I don't know at the moment but I need your help to find out.'

Rebecca was weary but adamant. 'I can't help you, Inspector. I don't know.'

At the tone of her voice, the strain in Maurice Ingleby hissed from him like steam from a pressure cooker. 'Leave her alone, Handford,' he snapped, 'if she says she doesn't know, she doesn't know. Ask the coordinator.'

Handford was damned if he was going to apologise again or be treated like one of the man's sub-contractors. 'Mr Ingleby, like it or not I have to do this and the sooner it's over the better. I have to pull your wife's life apart – yours as well, and I have to ask questions which I'd rather not ask but the sooner I can put everything back together and find your wife's killer, the sooner you'll be able to move on.'

Ingleby opened his mouth to argue, but Handford stopped him. 'I know it's hard for you and it doesn't seem like it now, but believe me if a death is one of natural causes it's after the funeral that you stop living in limbo and slowly start to put your life together; with a murder it's after the trial. How far away that is, is up to me and up to you. I'm doing my job, and it's not always pleasant, so please don't use tactics on me that you use on

47

your suppliers and your contractors, because believe you me, if necessary, I have my own supply.' He paused to let his comments sink in.

Rebecca stood up and went to sit with her father. As she put her arms round him, her eyes found Handford's and she fixed him with a cool assessing stare. 'I really can't believe that was necessary,' she said.

Ingleby patted her hand as a sign of his assurance that he was fine. 'Ask your questions, Inspector, we'll answer them.'

'Thank you. Now, Rebecca said her mother had turned to get into the car, yet she was shot in the chest which means she must have been facing the other direction. As far as we can ascertain the car in which the gunman was waiting was a dark-coloured Citroën ZX, do you or did she know of anyone who drives such a model?'

Ingleby pondered for sometime and when he spoke his voice had flat-lined. 'I can't think of anyone,' he said.

'What about you, Rebecca?'

'No.' A monosyllabic answer – uncooperative, or was there nothing else to say?

'Did she give any indication at any time that she might have recognised the person in the car?'

Ingleby answered. 'No, none. At least if she did, I didn't hear her.'

'Rebecca?'

'I was at the driver's door; I heard nothing until the gun-fire.' Suddenly she turned on him, the anger she didn't think she had the energy for bursting out. 'Why did we have to identify her body? Wasn't it enough that we saw her shot, waited all that time while she was in theatre, put up with your questions and then stood by while the surgeon told us she was dead? Wasn't it enough we'd lost her; why did you have to put us and her through that indignity as well?'

Handford pushed her antagonism to one side. 'It's a matter of continuity,' he said. 'She needed to be formally identified to a police officer so that he could identify her to the pathologist at the post-mortem. It's procedure.'

Her face darkened, but she remained silent as did Handford. She needed someone to blame, he understood that; it was easier to hold the establishment and its rules and regulations responsible than the shadowy figure of the perpetrator. Or perhaps her attitude was common to the family. Maurice demanded special privileges because of his perceived status, Rebecca blamed the police and the coroner for what she saw as the pillaging of her mother's dignity, and Dianne insisted on complete confidentiality for victims no matter what the situation. He wasn't sure of the reason but he had the feeling the family was beginning to block his every move and since his brain was heavy from lack of sleep and the caffeine hadn't revived him, he decided to answer Ali's request before continuing. He pulled himself from the chair. 'I think we need a rest,' he said. 'I'll pop up and see Sergeant Ali; when I come back, Mr Ingleby, perhaps I could have a word with you on your own.'

Ali was sitting on the bed, staring into space when Handford joined him. 'Rebecca said you wanted me up here. Have you got something?'

Startled, Ali looked up. 'What?' For a moment he appeared confused. 'Sorry.' He turned and began to search through a pile of things on the bed. 'Sorry, John, I was miles away.'

'Thinking about what?'

'How much worse it must have been for Mr Ingleby and his daughter waiting for news, hoping Dianne would be all right, but knowing there was a possibility she wouldn't be.'

Handford sat down next to him. The words were about the Inglebys, but he knew Ali was voicing his own fears. They needed to be put into perspective. 'So much worse than what, Ali? Than us finding a body and turning up and telling the relatives a family member is dead?'

'It's the waiting that makes it worse.'

'Waiting always makes things worse.'

They didn't speak for a few minutes, then Handford said, 'How is Amina?'

Ali ran his fingers across his forehead as though to stem a headache. 'Worried, but trying hard not to show it.'

'And you?'

Ali shrugged as if there was no answer to the question. 'The same.'

'You *can* take some leave you know, if you think it would help.'

'I'd love to, but Amina won't hear of it. She says I make her worse when I'm there. On her own she copes by keeping busy.'

Handford wasn't sure how he would react in the same situation, but he felt for both of them. 'Then you've got to go along with her wishes, Khalid. It's the only thing you can do.'

'Probably, but it's hard.' Fleetingly his eyes closed. Finally he said, 'How are things going downstairs?'

'Slowly. They can't come up with a reason why anyone would want her dead. Ingleby has touched on the fact that he has enemies, but I don't think it has percolated through yet as to what that means. I'm going to talk to him again later; I'll broach the subject then.'

'This might give you something to go on.' Ali picked up an A5 hardbacked notebook from the things on the bed. 'I found it in her lingerie drawer – tucked away at the back. I think it concerns a current client.' He handed it to Handford who flicked through it while he listened to what his sergeant was saying. 'There are two names: Kathie and Emma – no surnames. I've only skimmed it, but it appears Kathie was the victim of a vicious assault and refused to involve the police.'

Nothing new there. Victims frequently keep quiet about an attack or their attackers, particularly if they're on the edges of crime or into prostitution or drugs. What interested Handford more was that Dianne Ingleby had made such copious notes. 'I wonder what it was about this case that made her decide to write everything down?' he mused. 'I didn't think the volunteers were allowed to keep diaries of their clients.'

'I'm sure they're not. Perhaps it was something Kathie said that persuaded her to keep a record. It might be worth trying to find out.'

'We'll have to locate Kathie first and that could be difficult. There's no indication she was on the game or into drugs?'

'Not as far as I can see. Do you want me get someone to check on it?'

'Yes,' Handford opened the book at the first page; it was dated the third of May. 'If they're working the streets, Kathie won't have been around for at least a couple of weeks and someone will have missed her.' He slipped the book into his pocket. 'I'll check with Maurice Ingleby, see if he knows anything about the two women.' He stood up. 'Have you finished here?'

'Just about.'

'Then let's go outside. I want us to talk without being disturbed.'

They walked into a spring day that was sliding into summer and settled themselves on chairs by the swimming pool.

Handford stretched out and watched the sunlight play on the water as he savoured the warmth. 'You know Khalid, I could just about manage this kind of lifestyle.'

Ali laughed. 'I'd give you twenty-four hours. After that you'd be champing at the bit to get back to work.'

Not for the first time this morning, tiredness engulfed Handford. He rubbed his hands over his eyes and yawned. 'You're probably right. Still it would be nice for Gill and the girls.'

'You said we had something to talk about.' Ali's tone was suddenly unremittingly matter-of-fact.

Handford cursed his carelessness – to build dreams for his family was not the most sympathetic of things to do in the circumstances. 'Yes, sorry,' He sat forward and adopted the same tenor as Ali. 'I know we're only a few hours into this investigation, but would you agree we're struggling for an obvious motive for Dianne's murder?'

Ali nodded. 'Yes I would.'

'And we already know there are a good few people out there who would be happy to see the end of Maurice? He has business enemies, has little compunction about ruining rivals and has affairs with other men's wives.'

'Yes, I'd go along with that as well.' Ali frowned. 'But we're already on to this, John, so I don't understand what you're getting at.'

'I'm getting at the fact that there's something we're not dealing with and I think we ought to be.' He exhaled slowly while he considered his words. 'According to Mr Russell, Maurice Ingleby is widely suspected of being the money behind the local branch of the BNP.'

Ali raised his eyebrows in astonishment. 'Are you sure?'

'No I'm not sure because he's adamant he has no link with them, directly or indirectly, and it's nothing to do with us if he has. It's not a crime to give money to political parties, however obnoxious. But it does seem there are those who don't believe him and think it is their business. A while ago he received several

51

death threat letters warning him to pull out or else. He handed them over to the DCI.'

'Were they investigated?'

'Yes, but not by us, by Keighley division – apparently it was thought to be too hot politically for Central to be involved and anyway it was off our patch.'

Ali pulled himself from the chair and walked over to the edge of the pool. He crouched down to dabble his fingers in the water. 'It's cold,' he said. Then he stood up and shook off the drops. 'Did they find out who was sending the letters?'

'They came up with several suspects, but little in the way of evidence.'

Ali regained his seat and dried his hand with his handkerchief.

'I want you to take over where they left off. Contact Keighley, find out what you can from whoever was the investigating officer.' Handford passed over the list Russell had given him. 'These are the suspects, check them again.'

Ali scrutinised the names, his expression suggesting incomprehension rather than surprise. 'Patrick Ambler, Matthew Hobson, Lee Sugden. I've never heard of them. Are they local?'

'Yes, they're would-be councillors; all standing in safe Labour wards; all up against BNP candidates and all have at some time had involvement with Maurice Ingleby in which they lost out.'

'So if they sent the letters the reason could be political or personal or both.'

'Exactly. It may be that these men are as much anti-Maurice Ingleby as they are anti-BNP and are using his rumoured link with the party as an excuse to frighten him – two birds with one stone, or in this case several letters.'

'Right, I'll get on with it. Am I working alone or can I borrow someone?'

Ali was astute. Under normal circumstances that wouldn't have been a question needing an answer. 'You're on your own, I'm afraid – at least for the moment. I'll be honest with you Khalid, Mr Russell would rather we didn't go over what he describes as old ground. He doesn't want it hitting the press and the BNP making capital out of it so near the local elections. But if we assume Dianne wasn't the intended victim and her husband was, then we can't pretend the letters didn't happen.

Whatever the motive behind them they need investigation – discreet investigation. The last thing we need is to spark off mob mayhem.'

When Handford walked back into the lounge, Rebecca was sitting with her father. She stood up as soon as she saw him. 'I'm going home, Dad,' she said, the strain of the past few hours showing in her voice. 'I need to pick up some clothes and I'll check my cats into the kennels for a few days. I'll go to the yard as well, let everyone know what's happening.' She bent to kiss him on the cheek. 'Don't worry, I won't be long.' She turned to Handford. 'I'm sorry about earlier, I'm not thinking straight at the moment.'

Handford smiled. 'Don't concern yourself Miss Ingleby, you've nothing to apologise for. Ask one of the officers to help you through the reporters.'

'I will,' she said and turned back to her father. 'Mrs Briggs is still in a bit of a state but she'll get you anything you want and if you need me call me on my mobile.'

When she had gone, Handford pointed to a vacant chair opposite Ingleby. 'May I?' he said.

Ingleby nodded.

'Your daughter doesn't live with you?'

'She's twenty-five, Inspector, she wants her independence. She has a cottage in Denholme.' Before Handford could probe further he said, 'I gave her the deposit for her twenty-first birthday; she pays the mortgage.'

'What does she do?'

'She works for me. She always wanted to be a builder, right from being about six. Her mother used to say she should have been a boy; she was never interested in dolls, but give her a carton of Lego and she'd have a house up in no time, windows, doors, chimneys, everything.' He smiled sadly as he relived the memory.

'She's been with me since she left school. I've taught her everything I know about the trade, but I insisted she went to college as well; get that piece of paper I said, and she did – passed with flying colours. I told her, you'll need those certificates when you take over the business; people are impressed with certificates.'

'And will she, take over the business, I mean?'

'Oh, yes, it's hers when I retire.'

Handford pondered his fingers. 'Look, Mr Ingleby, I'm going to be honest with you. We have no idea whether your wife was the intended victim or whether you or both of you were. There were four shots, one hit Dianne and it's possible from the trajectory the other three were meant for you. Maybe they were fired wide or by accident from the gun's recoil but until we know more we must assume he may have been trying to shoot you as well.' He refrained from saying instead of. 'If that's so, then you could still be in danger. He may try again.'

Ingleby stood up and walked over to the window. It overlooked a garden that stretched out to a tree-lined boundary. To the left was the swimming pool, the water shimmering in the sunlight. May had been an unusually warm month and Handford could imagine them celebrating Rebecca's birthday outdoors.

With his back still towards Handford he said, 'Could it be that he killed Dianne instead of me; that she got in the way?'

It was a question Handford would have preferred not to have to answer, but if nothing else Ingleby demanded and deserved honesty. 'It could be.'

For a few seconds there was silence. When Ingleby finally spoke his voice was terse. 'Then her death could have been the result of something I have done or someone I have upset?'

The answer was probably 'yes', but the man with his hunched shoulders and grief-stricken frame was suffering enough. Handford shied away from the direct reply. 'As yet we have no way of knowing, Mr Ingleby.'

Eventually Ingleby turned to face the detective. 'You see all this,' he said, indicating the view beyond the window. 'This was for Dianne. When we married we lived in a two-up two-down. Every bit of spare cash went into the business, but I always promised her a large house in its own grounds and I worked towards that. She saw one once when we were on holiday in Suffolk and she leaned over the gate and said, 'If I ever get that

55

house you promised me I want it to be like this'. I vowed she'd have it, Handford – even to the drive sweeping from the road to the front door. As soon as we got back from holiday, I taped its photograph to my filing cabinet, so that I wouldn't forget.' His eyes moistened and he coughed to prevent his voice from breaking. 'It took a good few years, a lot of building and a couple more house moves for us before I could afford it, but when the time came and I brought her to view this one she fell in love with it. And she was right to; she made it into a real home and we've been happy here – until today.' He paused and swallowed hard but didn't manage to regain his composure completely for he swayed and had to clutch at the back of the nearest chair.

Handford moved quickly to grasp him by the shoulders. 'Come and sit down,' he urged. 'Can I get you a glass of water?'

Ingleby collapsed on to the settee 'You can get me a whisky, over there on the sideboard.'

Handford poured a generous measure and handed him the glass which he took, drinking its contents in one gulp.

It seemed to do the trick for when he spoke again his voice had recovered its strength. 'If it was the gunman's intention to kill me he did his job the moment the surgeon told us Dianne was dead.' He lowered his head and rubbed his eyes with the heels of his hands. 'I just wish he'd got it right first time and spared her.'

Handford studied him wondering just how many Maurice Inglebys there were inside that well-built frame and how many of them were genuine and how many for the benefit of the outside world. He said, 'Perhaps we could assume for the moment the gunman had got it right first time and it was your wife he intended to kill and not you. You say she had no enemies?'

'No.'

'Has she seemed worried at all?'

'I've been busy, out a lot, but she hadn't given me any indication that she was concerned about anything.'

'Would she have told you if she was? Sometimes wives keep things to themselves, don't want to worry anyone, I know my wife does.'

'She would have told me; we didn't have secrets.'

'Except …'

'Except her work with Victim Support.' That wasn't Handford's 'except'; his had more to do with illicit affairs. He didn't pursue it.

'Have you seen anyone hanging around the house, perhaps a strange car sitting outside?'

'No.'

'Any unusual phone calls, the receiver replaced if you answered, has she received letters which have caused her concern?'

'Nothing like that, Inspector.'

Handford shifted his position; he was chasing shadows, not getting a grip on the woman. 'Tell me about her normal day. When did she come to help in the business?'

'She'd trained as a bookkeeper and did the books Wednesday and Thursday mornings. I have an accountant, but she kept everything up to date for me, sent out invoices, that sort of thing. Twice a week she went to the hospital to work in the café or on the wards. She was on a rota, so you'd have to ask the organisers about that or look in her diary. Visiting victims took up a lot of her time both during the day and in the evening.' His forehead furrowed and his eyes darkened, 'We didn't see as much of each other as we ought to have.'

Handford didn't want him entangled in his grief again. 'She'd been trained to work with those involved in serious crimes?'

'Yes, but she saw others.'

'Had she ever spoken about someone called Kathie or Emma?'

Ingleby thought for a moment. 'I can't say I've ever heard those names. But then I wouldn't if they were victims. I've already told you she never talked about them.'

'Your wife was a busy woman but did she have time for any other activities – clubs, the gym – anything?'

'She didn't go to the gym – wasn't into anything like that, exercise, that kind of thing, but she was a serious church-goer. She's been a Methodist all her life; she's always attended the chapel local to the area where we lived, now she goes – went – to the one in the village. The minister is Michael Iveson although I think he has other churches under his jurisdiction.' He sighed, 'I suppose I ought to tell him, but I don't want him up here. Can't stand the man myself.'

'Why?'

'He's a do-gooder and I can't stand do-gooders. Dianne said

he came to God late and they're always the worst. I don't want him up here spouting his platitudes or the woman from Victim Support for that matter telling me what a good person Dianne was. I know she was a good person.'

Handford leaned back in the chair and pondered on the dead woman. Was she really the saint everyone was making her out to be? He'd been in the job too long to know that no one was all good; except perhaps Mother Theresa and he was willing to bet she'd had her moments. Everything Maurice Ingleby had said about his wife suggested he adored her, would give her anything she wanted, yet if rumour was to be believed, he'd had more than one affair. That didn't suggest a perfect marriage.

'I'll have a word with Connie Burns; she'll make sure you're not disturbed until you're ready and I'll be seeing Eileen Leighton myself when I leave here. I'll ask her to give you some space.'

Ingleby nodded his thanks. 'And while you're about it, you can get rid of that pack of hyenas outside the gate.' For a brief moment the authoritarian was back in charge. He must be the very devil to work for. 'Dianne's parents are on their way home from Spain,' he went on. 'I don't want them mobbed when they get here.' He paused as he stared in front of him. 'I tell you, Handford, I've made some phone calls in my time, but this was just about the worst. I can still hear Marjorie screaming.'

Handford doubted the man could remember when he had last shared feelings of any consequence with anyone. 'We'll make sure the press are kept away from them,' he said. 'In the meantime perhaps we can look at last night's events from the point of view that you were the intended victim.'

Ingleby leaned his head back and closed his eyes. After what seemed like minutes, but could only have been seconds he opened them and said, 'Ask your questions.'

'You said earlier there are those who may well hold a grudge against you.'

'Yes.'

'Can you tell me who?'

Ingleby pulled a folded sheet of paper from his pocket and handed it to Handford. 'I made a list.' He shrugged. 'It was something to do.'

The detective studied it. 'There are quite a few names here, Mr

Ingleby. Are they all people who have worked for you or supplied you with goods?'

'Mostly, yes.'

'You must be a difficult man to please.'

'I am. When I set up my own business, I was determined right from the outset that whatever I built would be of the highest quality. My houses are expensive, but they're good and no one – no one Inspector – ever calls me back in to put things right. I check everything personally before I pay the sub-contractors and they don't get a penny until I'm satisfied, but when I am I pay on the dot. None of this thirty day nonsense. Same with suppliers.'

'And what about those on the list who are not in the trade? Why should they hold a grudge?'

'Various reasons, usually petty.'

'Like?'

'This one, James Mossman.' Handford pointed to a name halfway down the sheet.

'We were neighbours until we moved here in June of two thousand and two, got on fine until suddenly he decided he didn't like our boundary hedge, said it was cutting out his light. It was rubbish; it wasn't that high and I kept it well trimmed. Anyway it got nasty and when we were away on holiday he cut it down, right to the base. I called the police, but nothing happened because they said they didn't have enough evidence to say it was him.'

'And the hedge and a visit from the police was the reason for his grudge?'

'More or less.'

'What do you mean, more or less?'

'It wasn't so much the hedge that annoyed him it was what happened afterwards.'

'Which was?'

'That we were moving.' Handford waited. Ingleby took a deep breath. 'I was waiting for contracts to be exchanged on the house I'm living in now and I wanted a quick sale of my own, didn't want the rigmarole of house purchase – chains, that sort of thing.'

Handford could smell a scam. 'So what did you do?'

'I'm not without friends in high places, Inspector – your DCI for one.'

'Yes, he told me.'

'I'm also well in with some of the more influential councillors and I knew they were looking to buy houses for the asylum seekers assigned to the district. So I sold them mine. James Mossman wasn't best pleased when he found out, called me all the names he could think of and a lot more besides. Threatened me too, said it had taken thousands off the price of his house and put him into negative equity. He couldn't afford to sell and didn't want to stay. It's three years ago now and he's still there with asylum seekers living next door. They don't cause him any trouble, but he doesn't consider that the point.'

'What does he consider the point?'

'That I'd shafted him; did it on purpose.'

'And did you?'

'Does it matter?'

'Yes, Mr Ingleby, it matters. It matters that someone may have tried to kill you and that Mr Mossman would have had a motive.'

'It's three years ago, Handford. Why would he do it now, why not then?'

'He's angry; he's been angry for three years. He's seen you move into this house and thanks to *you* he can't move anywhere. Anger's a killer Mr Ingleby. I've experienced it more than once on my job. It destroys without compunction, particularly the person it's feeding on. Eventually the feeding becomes an obsession and is replaced by action. Do you know if he has access to a gun?'

Ingleby pulled himself from the chair and walked over to the sideboard where he poured himself another whisky. He turned, sipped at the drink and then said, 'I have no idea.'

Handford drew an asterisk against Mossman's name. 'Anyone else?'

'No.'

It was obvious Ingleby wasn't about to mention those with whose wives he'd had affairs. Perhaps he considered them too weak to do anything about it. Or perhaps the reason was just too petty. It was a pity also he couldn't ask him about the death threat letters, but it would be wise to see what Ali came up with first. With a transfer to HMET very much in the balance he didn't want to give the DCI anything he could pass on which would suggest his DI was a loose cannon.

Ingleby walked back to the window. 'I'll probably sell this place now; I don't think I can live here without her.'

There was a silence which for a while no one was prepared to break. Finally he faced Handford, his expression suggesting he would prefer the detective left him to grieve alone. But they both knew that wasn't an option.

'Let's have a look at the others on the list,' Handford said. 'The first name is a Ray Braddock. Who is he?'

Ingleby regained his seat. 'He is – or was – a builders' supply merchant.'

'Was?'

'He went bankrupt; blamed me for the collapse of his business.'

'And were you to blame?'

'I might have been the person who finally forced the bank to foreclose and him to pull the plug, but he'd been going downhill for a long time.'

'In what way?'

'He did quite well at first, had most of the business in the district, including mine until one of the larger conglomerates opened up and undercut his prices. Instead of riding it out, he tried to do the same thing, but provided substandard stock to make ends meet. Real rubbish it was. Most of us might have stayed with him and been prepared to accept price rises if he'd stuck with decent materials. Anyway I refused to pay him for the last order, he couldn't meet his costs, the bank foreclosed and he was forced into bankruptcy. It wasn't my doing; I was just the end of a long chain. He had an idiot of a nephew working with him, Darren Armitage, who probably had more to do with him going under than anyone else. But he wasn't going to blame him; no, I was a much better target. He threatened me with everything he could throw at me including bragging that he'd bedded my daughter, told everyone she wanted him and that one day he would marry her and have my business.'

'What did Rebecca say?'

'That he was lying, that he'd flirted with her but she'd told him to get lost.'

'And you believed her?'

'Of course I bloody believed her; she's my daughter. She'd not go with a loser like Braddock. I told him if he laid one finger on

61

her I'd make sure he never worked again.' A vein of anger ran through his words as his voice tightened. 'I'll tell you one thing though, if anyone can get hold of a gun, it's Braddock. He used to own them; had to give them up after the Dunblane killings. He does a lot of clay pigeon shooting now and he's a member of the Crosby Gun Club, shoots in competitions, that kind of thing. Yes, he's quite a winner with a gun is Ray Braddock.'

Rebecca Ingleby sobbed uncontrollably as she clung on to Ray Braddock. When she was calmer he sat her down and poured her a brandy. 'Here drink this.'

He waited until she swallowed the contents of the glass and handed it back to him. 'Another?'

She shook her head. 'I'm driving,' she said. Suddenly she banged her fist on the arm of the chair. 'How can I say that?' she yelled at him. 'As if it matters.'

He moved over to sit down beside her then pulled her towards him again. His arms were strong and she felt the warmth of his body against hers. She had clung to her father last night and he had clung to her, but neither had been able to give the other the support they needed, for both were immersed in their own grief. If she'd ever needed Ray, it was now.

'The police have been at the house most of the morning, going through Mum's things and questioning Dad.'

'What are they saying? Do they know who killed her?'

'They think whoever it was may have intended to shoot Dad not her, that he got it wrong.' Her eyes filled with tears and she wiped them away with her hand. 'They want to know of anyone who has a grudge against him. He made a list ...'

He took his arms from around her and she saw his face darken. 'I'll bet he did – and enjoyed doing it.' He stood up and took a few steps backwards. 'And I bet I'm at the top of it,' he flung. 'Well you tell him from me that if I'd gone out to kill him I wouldn't have missed. He would have been the one in the mortuary now, not your mother.'

He was visibly angry and for a moment her own flared to match his. 'Don't say that,' she screamed at him. 'Don't ever say that. Isn't it enough that my mother's dead?'

Swiftly his arms stretched out to her and he drew her towards him. 'I'm sorry,' he whispered. I was angry; it came out wrong.

All I meant was that whatever your father thinks, I wouldn't kill anyone, not your mother, not him, not anyone. I shoot clay pigeons and targets, not people – whatever they've done to me.'

But the tension between them remained and as she looked towards him the realisation of where she was, who she was with and what she was doing flooded over her. Ray Braddock had been her lover for over a year now. Knowing what had happened between him and her father, she'd come into the affair with caution, but convinced she could handle it; and she could, but not today. Everyone was hurting and whatever she did she would pile more hurt on to one of them. But at this moment Ray could cope with it more easily than her father could. She leaned down and picked up her bag. 'I can't stay here, Ray; it's not fair on Dad.'

As she made to stand up, Braddock grabbed her by the shoulders, his eyes meeting hers. 'It's always about your father, isn't it, Becky? Just for once forget about him; think about you, about us.' He wrapped his arms round her again.

A wave of tiredness engulfed her, and beyond argument, she allowed herself to be swaddled in his strength. She closed her eyes; so sad, but at the same time so secure. He kissed her, first on top of her head as you would a child, then on her cheeks and finally on her lips. She responded. She couldn't pretend; she needed him.

'Come on,' he whispered. 'You're exhausted.' And he guided her up the stairs and into the bedroom. She knew what was about to happen; he was leading her towards the inevitable and she couldn't pretend she didn't want it.

Handford stopped his car in a lay-by about a quarter of a mile away from Ingleby's house. Before he saw Eileen Leighton he wanted to check the contents of Dianne's diary. The coordinator of the local Victim Support was a good woman but she had strong beliefs and if she was to give him Kathie's full name, he would need to persuade her he already had much of the information and it would only be a matter of time before he found her. It was a pity he had so little to go on. On the surface there seemed no reason why anyone should wait in a car park the night the family was at the theatre and as they were about to leave shoot the wife. The only lead he had at present was that she was supporting a young girl who had been viciously assaulted. And the only thing

63

he knew about the victim was that she didn't want the police involved.

He picked up the diary from the passenger seat and began to read.

Part of this record has been written in retrospect and thus from memory; I can't say exactly when I decided to do it, probably when I began to feel uneasy about what had happened. I'm not sure I should be doing it; indeed I'm certain I shouldn't and Eileen would be furious if she knew. I'll destroy everything I write if I'm wrong, but the fact is I'm afraid for Kathie. I can't even say why; I've seen worse. It's no more than a gut feeling but I can't rid myself of it. Perhaps it's because her friend, Emma, reported it to us. She must have been concerned to do that. Perhaps she wanted someone else apart from the hospital staff to know about the assault. I've haven't met Emma, so I don't have any details but I hope by doing this I might be able to piece together what happened and why and break down Kathie's fear so that she can be persuaded to tell the police, because until she does she will never live without it.

May 4th
Kathie has been badly injured: broken ribs, fractured skull and cheekbone, and a ruptured spleen, not to mention the cuts and bruises. The doctor told me that whoever had attacked her hadn't spared her; indeed he'd come close – very close – to killing her. They've taken out her spleen and wired her cheekbone and although stable, she remains very poorly. What frightens me and probably Emma – I wish I could meet her – is that Kathie refuses to report the attack to the police. Some people do, but this was no burglary gone wrong; this was carried out with real venom. Someone really hates her. I sat with Kathie today, but she was too ill to speak. I told her who I was and if she wanted me to come back to squeeze my hand. It was a few minutes coming, but in the end she did.

May 5th
Kathie's a little better today although she still can't speak very well. What she did manage to make me understand was that I should not tell anyone she was in hospital or what had happened

to her – particularly the police. Of course I agreed. Our work is confidential whatever the situation, but for the first time I'm uneasy about it. There are times when complete confidentiality has to be wrong and I'm sure this is one of them. She hasn't said as much, but I'm positive she knows who assaulted her. I think be deliberately stopped short of killing her. It wouldn't have taken much more to do so – one kick to the head. I have a gut feeling the attack was a warning, although of what I can't begin to think.

I accept she is frightened, but it would be better if she told the police or let us do so. This man is brutal and sadistic and needs to be caught and if she does know him and he's allowed to go free, then she will spend the rest of her life afraid. I spoke to Eileen about it, but her response was what I expected. No matter what, you keep her confidence.

May 6th
Michael Iveson was with Kathie when I arrived today. Part of his duties is to visit the hospital. I was glad to see him, but I wasn't aware he knew her. He said he thought she went to one of his churches, although he couldn't be sure; the ward sister had told him about her. Apparently Emma had put Methodist under religion on the admission form so he'd called to see if he could be of any help. He hadn't realised she'd contacted Victim Support. I told him he hadn't, in fact she hadn't told anyone anything; it had been her friend who'd rung us. Michael said he would leave it to me and would perhaps pop in and see her again when she was feeling better.

Although he couldn't have explained why, as Handford read through the first couple of pages of the diary he felt as uneasy as Dianne Ingleby had done. There was no indication as to who Kathie was and no way of finding out except through the hospital, the Reverend Michael Iveson or Victim Support, yet by writing down every meeting she'd had with the young woman she had broken the rule of confidentiality, which according to Maurice and Rebecca she respected absolutely. Why? What was there about Kathie and this attack that concerned Dianne so much she would do this? So far he had read nothing to suggest the need. It couldn't be its severity that had upset Dianne; she was an experienced volunteer and had dealt with rape victims and the families of murder victims – work which was without a doubt as traumatic as this. Was there something about the girl herself? Kathie had refused to call the police, yet she must have come across that before as well and victims who refused to name their assailant. It was par for the course.

No, something had worried her right from the beginning and it wasn't simply a question of compassion for the young girl. He hadn't the time to read more now so he closed the book and replaced it in his pocket. One thing for sure though, the only way he would understand Dianne Ingleby's reason behind what she had done was to talk to Kathie. At least then he would know whether to take her out of the equation or place her firmly in it. He hoped Eileen Leighton would see it that way.

Ray Braddock descended the stairs of his cottage. He hated the place. It was minuscule and it was dark and it wasn't his – his home had had to be sold to meet his debts. Thanks to Maurice Ingleby he was renting this hovel where there was no room to own a cat, let alone swing it. The house was one of a row, probably built in the nineteenth century for the workers in the nearby mill. The front door opened on to the road, at the back was a square of paving bordered by a high wall with a gate which accessed an unmade alleyway. The small shack in the corner had at one time apparently been a toilet, but was now described as a storage area. A piece of rope was threaded through a hook and strung across the yard to a rusty metal pole. He could dry his clothes out there in the summer – if the sun ever penetrated as far as that or if he could afford a washing machine. Instead he took his washing to the launderette. He felt foolish, ashamed even, when he carried it in the supermarket bags and sat with all the young mums and their kids while it washed and dried.

He walked into the sitting room, picked up the brandy glass and took it into a kitchen that housed only a sink, a cooker and a set of cupboards. A galley kitchen, the woman renting it to him had called it. If that were so, remind him never to join the navy. Not that they'd have him; he was a bankrupt and likely to stay like that for some time. He rinsed the glass under the tap and placed it on the draining board then leaned against the cupboards. He glanced round.

Maurice Ingleby had done this to him. He hated the man with a loathing that consumed him; it should have been him who had taken the bullet not his wife. Although now, in retrospect, he wasn't so sure. Braddock had done something which would destroy the man completely; he had screwed his beloved daughter – and now his wife had died Braddock had taken the one person left to him in a way Ingleby would never forgive. And she hadn't resisted, quite the opposite – she'd wanted it. Her father ought to know that; in fact he would make sure he knew it.

Braddock smiled to himself. He was sorry it was Dianne Ingleby who had died, but he couldn't drag up the same emotion for her husband. Maurice had ruined him and on reflection he knew a bullet would have been too good for him. Let him live and suffer. Losing his wife hurt him, but coming so soon after last night, news that Ray Braddock was sleeping with his daughter would hurt him much, much more.

But there was something else he needed to do first and that was to rid himself of Emma Crossley. She was trouble, her and that brat of hers. She knew too much and she was standing between him and Rebecca. The sooner she was out of his hair, the sooner he could get on with taking Maurice Ingleby for all he had.

67

Eileen Leighton never failed to surprise John Handford. He didn't always see eye to eye with her, and sometimes she made him angry, but love her or hate her, he couldn't help but admire her. Close to sixty, her enthusiasm for her job and its clients had never diminished, constantly fuelled as it was by the anger for what she saw as the law's indifference to the victims she supported. Her constant complaint was that they went practically unnoticed while perpetrators of crime were well served by society even when they put two fingers up at a world they thought owed them a living. Until the judiciary and the police treated victims as the injured party, things would never change.

He wished he could ride her criticisms, but without fail he let them get to him. Why, he asked himself, did she make the police into the villains? And why moan at him? As she well knew, there were rules and regulations in place on the way in which victims had to be handled and for the most part they were followed but what was difficult to get over to a diehard like Eileen Leighton, was that sometimes it was necessary to be tough to get at the truth. Victims were not always victims and the alleged perpetrators not always perpetrators. But as she well knew, his defence usually fell on deaf ears; as coordinator and counsellor she had seen too much of the suffering caused to accept it, so generally they agreed to differ.

Handford doubted they would this time. She'd already made it clear to Sergeant Ali that she was not prepared to break the confidentiality of the clients and that was what he would be asking for. He only hoped that given the circumstances he could persuade her to tell him what he needed to know.

Perhaps he might, for from the anguish etched on her face it was obvious the death of Dianne Ingleby had affected her badly. 'Why?' she asked when he settled himself in her office. Always the confusion, the bewilderment and the same question. Not much use if she wasn't prepared to help throw some light on the answer.

'I don't know,' he said. 'Perhaps you can help me here.'

'I'll do what I can.'

He began with an easy question, one she could answer. 'Tell me about her as a volunteer.'

'She was good – more than good. She'd been with us a long time and was very experienced. Had she not been both I wouldn't have agreed to her training for supporting victims of serious crimes.'

'Would you say she was able to work on gut instinct? Pick up on things other people would miss?'

Eileen Leighton thought for a moment. 'Yes, I would say that. She came to me from time to time with concerns about clients that no one else would have considered.'

'And would you say her instincts were sound?'

'Usually. I would trust them.' She paused as she eyed him with suspicion. 'What are you getting at, John?'

'I've learned a lot about her as a person, now I want to know about her as a volunteer.'

'Rubbish. And don't give me that look of innocence. I know you, John Handford; you don't waste questions. What are you getting at?'

Love her or hate her, you had to admire her. He let his gaze rest on her. She was quite a handsome woman for her age. Good figure, clear skin, unlined features. It was the crêpe-paper neck and liver-spotted hands that were the give-away. 'I'm getting at the possibility that her death is linked to a client she was working with.'

Her response came at him like the bullet from a gun. 'Don't go there, John. I told Sergeant Ali I wasn't prepared to divulge the names of her clients and I meant it.'

This was a game, both of them deadly serious as the ball lobbed between them. But if the coordinator thought it was advantage Eileen Leighton she was sadly mistaken. 'I'm not talking about clients, Eileen, just the one she supported from the fourth of May. And I don't need her name, I have it.'

Her expression was one of incredulity; she hadn't seen that coming. Deuce. 'That was unworthy of you, Inspector. No one here would pass on that kind of information and Dianne would never have divulged her clients' names, particularly this one, and certainly not to the police.'

'I promise you it's true. I'm not trying to trick you, Eileen and you have my assurance no one has leaked the information, so you've no worry on that score.'

'So how . . .?'

He pulled the A5 book out of his pocket. 'We found this among Dianne's things; it's a diary of her encounters with the girl; in it are her name and the name of the friend who made the first contact with you.'

'She wouldn't.'

'She did, but only her Christian name.'

Relief flooded the coordinator's features. 'Only her Christian name?'

'Yes.'

She held out her hand. 'Can I see?'

He shook his head. 'No.'

'Then let me remind you that *if* it was written by Dianne about one of her clients, it's the property of Victim Support.'

Nine out of ten for effort. 'A good try, Eileen, but it's evidence. Now, are you going to tell me about Kathie, or am I going to have to get a warrant to open up your files?'

'Do what you think is necessary, but until I'm forced into divulging anything, Kathie will get the level of confidentiality she has asked for. I'll tell you nothing without her permission.'

Handford leaned forward, got in close. 'Even though Dianne Ingleby might well have been killed because of the attack on her client?'

Mrs Leighton wasn't to be intimidated. 'Even then.'

He opened the diary. 'Listen to this,' he said. '"She hasn't said as much," he read, "but I'm positive she knows who assaulted her. I think he deliberately stopped short of killing her. It wouldn't have taken much more to do so – one kick to the head. I have a gut feeling the attack was a warning, although of what I can't begin to imagine".' Handford looked up from the diary. 'Now wouldn't you say this man, whoever he is, is dangerous?'

'Probably, but not necessarily to Dianne.'

'She's the one who's dead, Eileen,' Handford said quietly. Her voice softened. 'I'm aware of that.'

'And you won't help me in spite of the fact that her death might be linked to the contents of this diary?'

'It's not a question of won't, John, I can't and certainly not on something as vague as a might be. Confidentiality and trust are the basis of our work. Give one up and we lose the other.'

As predicted, this was a waste of his time. Eileen Leighton was not going to tell him anything. One more attempt. 'If you're not prepared to tell me who Kathie is or where she is, then tell me who Emma is.'

She shook her head.

'Surely *she* can't have asked for confidentiality.'

'No, but Kathie has and the two go together.'

For a moment Handford remained silent while he managed his frustration; she was in control on the baseline and he was the one running round the court. If only he could give her something more positive. But he couldn't, he didn't know whether Dianne had been the intended victim or not; and if she was then his only lead was Kathie and for him to move forward on this he needed her identity. Bluntness was called for, even if it hurt.

'One of your volunteers has been murdered; I can't find any reason why she should have been; the only lead I have is Kathie, the victim of a brutal attack, an attack which worried Dianne so much that she wrote everything down. All right I accept Kathie is a victim and has the right of confidentiality, but so is Dianne and they seem to me to be linked. And what about Maurice and Rebecca Ingleby; aren't they entitled to answers? He let his comments lie in the hope of some response, but when none was forthcoming, he smashed it back to her, 'There are strands here linking one to the other, Eileen, and if I can't separate them how on earth can you?'

She returned it well. 'It's not a problem. I see Kathie as one victim and Dianne's family as another. They're quite separate.'

'And if the Inglebys have become victims because of Kathie – what then?'

Again she made no attempt to answer his question.

'For God's sake, Eileen, I'm trying to bring some meaning to what at the moment seems a senseless killing. We have very little else to go on but Kathie. I may be wrong, but I can only find out if I talk to her. Tell me who she is and where she is and give me the opportunity to take her out of the equation.'

Eileen Leighton pushed back her chair and stood up as if to make it clear the meeting was at an end. 'The best I can offer is to visit Kathie myself, build some kind of relationship with her, get her to trust me and ask her if she's prepared to talk to you ...'

'And how long is that going to take?'

'As long as it takes, John. I'm not prepared to rush it. And make no mistake, if she's still insistent that she doesn't want the police involved then there is nothing I can or will do. She's entitled to confidentiality just as you and I would be.'

Handford wished he could thank her, but he didn't know for what. Even if she got on to it straight away and by some miracle Kathie agreed, time would have passed and the initial impetus of his investigation gone. But if Eileen Leighton thought this was the end of the matter she was sadly mistaken. With or without her help he would find Kathie and rule her in or out of the inquiry.

In the meantime. 'Sergeant Ali told me of your intention to visit Maurice Ingleby. I don't know when you were anticipating going but he'd rather you didn't – at least not today. Dianne's parents have cut their holiday short and are flying home; they need to be alone to come to terms with what has happened. Until then he would be grateful if you would leave him and his family to grieve.'

Eileen Leighton nodded her agreement.

But Handford hadn't finished. 'We have a family liaison officer at the house; she'll let you know when he's ready to see you.'

She walked to the door with him. 'Is this your attempt to keep me out of harm's way?'

He placed a sympathetic hand on her shoulder. 'Just passing on a message,' he said.

Aisha Miah stared at the case notes in front of her, one half of her mind on them, the other on the argument with her husband that morning. It wasn't that Parvez didn't care; he did, but he also had the family's honour to consider. She understood that, and so did Chanda – in fact she probably relied on it. Talking to his sister-in-law wouldn't stop her from taunting his wife. She would flaunt her youth, take advantage of her pregnancy, squeeze out a few tears and promise she wouldn't do anything like it again, it was

72

just that she was so tired, and they would believe her, because it was easier than doubting her. Aisha had seen it all before – different reasons, the same outcome. The more Chanda got away with her bullying, the more she would do it. She had done so at school and she would do so at home; she was a past master at it. Just like this young man in the case Aisha was studying was going to get away with his crime – again.

Gary Marshall, a 22-year-old serial street robber with a good defence solicitor. This time he'd mugged – allegedly – an old lady. Mrs Shaw had been leaving the post office with her pension when he had snatched it, throwing her to the ground. She'd struggled with him, even tried to fight him and he had kicked and punched her – the police photographs were testimony to that. Then, his hood over his head, Marshall had – allegedly – run off, discarding the bag, but keeping the money. People had stopped to help her, rung for an ambulance, but that was as far as it went. Plenty of them had recognised him, given the police his name, but not one was prepared to come to court to corroborate Mrs Shaw's description. She was on her own.

Aisha could hear his solicitor in court: *'How can you be sure it was Gary Marshall who attacked you? I'm not doubting your word that you were robbed, Mrs Shaw; we have clear evidence of your injuries from the doctor's statement and the photographs. But what I'm saying is that perhaps you were mistaken in your identification of the defendant.'* The old lady would become flustered. Perhaps she might have been mistaken. It all happened so quickly you see, and she'd been trying to protect her face and her glasses, but she was fairly sure it was him. And there it would be – the word 'fairly', which would turn certainty into reasonable doubt. It wasn't worth the time of the court, the magistrates or the arresting officer to go on with the case. She'd take advice obviously, but it was unlikely her bosses would think it winnable. Someone might suggest Mrs Shaw go to the Criminal Injuries Board for compensation, they might even help her with the paperwork, but the physical and mental injuries she would have to cope with alone.

Just as Aisha would have to cope alone with hers. It was one thing saying she would make a complaint against Chanda if she ever assaulted her again, quite another making it stick. Not one member of the family would back her in bringing the girl to book, not even Parvez. They would close ranks and Iqbal Ahmed would use his influence to get the police to drop the investigation. *'We don't doubt Aisha's word that she was assaulted, Chief Inspector, and we want you to find out who did it to her. As you can see all the bruising is to her back; she cannot possibly have seen the perpetrator. Chanda came to her aid and she mistakenly assumed it was her who had attacked her. No member of the family would do this, particularly not one who is seventeen and pregnant.'* As with Mrs Shaw reasonable doubt would creep in, the chief inspector would designate it to a DC to investigate and when he or she came up with nothing because it would be her word against the family's, it would be pushed to the bottom of an ever-growing pile of cases. After which *she* would become the pariah of the family and Chanda would continue her bullying unhindered.

She was sorry she had argued with Parvez the day he was joining CID; she should have kept quiet, not sent him off with a worry he could do without. She wondered how he was getting on. He was a good police officer, everyone said so, and she shouldn't have suggested otherwise.

There was a tap on her door and Colin Jenkins, her senior came in. 'Any decision on the Shaw case, Aisha?'

She closed the file. 'I don't think it's winnable,' she said. 'There are no witnesses and Mrs Shaw is seventy, hard of hearing and her eyesight is failing. There's no clear forensic evidence either – it's a pity, but we'll have to drop it.'

'Not to worry, we'll get him one day.'

'Not with his solicitor. Mrs Shaw deserves better. I'd like to see him go down for this.'

He took the file from her. 'So would I; and you're right she does deserve better, but don't beat yourself up about it. It's not your fault.' He waved the brown folder at her. 'I'll let the arresting officer know we're not taking it further; tell him another vulnerable citizen bites the dust.'

After he had gone, Aisha pushed back her chair. It was hot in the office and she felt stifled; she needed to get out, take a walk, get some fresh air, rid herself of the images of the injuries Mrs Shaw sustained in the attack which, except for the bruises on her face, were very similar to her own. She didn't envy the police officer who had to tell her they were dropping her case.

74

She probably put a lot of faith in the law, people of her age often did. It would never occur to her that law and justice were so far apart they would never run parallel let alone meet in infinity. Too many factors opposed them for them ever to bond: a police service too busy with paperwork to investigate properly; a prosecution service more concerned with the evidential test for a realistic prospect of conviction, and people who looked the other way. People like Parvez and Iqbal Ahmed who should know better.

Suddenly she felt as vulnerable as Mrs Shaw.

Gary Marshall and Darren Armitage sat on the wall near the fish and chip shop eating pickled onions.

Armitage sucked on the vinegary juice before crushing the yellowing onion between his teeth. 'You 'eard from the fuzz yet?'

'Nah and i won't either. They can't prove it was me as did the old woman, blind old bat she was. If it goes to court my brief'll 'ave 'er banged to rights.' He laughed. 'You should have seen 'er counting 'er money when she came out of the post office, so close to it she could 'ardly see it.' He peered into his carton, mimicking the pensioner, then pulled out another onion, threw it in the air and caught it his mouth as it descended.

Armitage laughed and copied him. For a while they challenged each other as to who could catch the most. Finally, out of breath, they sat in silence until Marshall let out a long sigh. 'This is boring. There's nowt to do.'

'We could go down town.'

'No money.'

There was no talking to Marshall when he was in this mood. As far as Armitage was concerned he believed the possibility of being done for the mugging was worrying his friend, but he would never have said so. Marshall had a wicked temper. He tried tempting him. 'Awh, come on, it's Friday; there's bound to be some people getting money out of the walls. We could do a snatch.'

Marshall ran his fingers through his greasy blond hair. 'Don't feel like it.'

Armitage took the last onion from the Styrofoam box which he dropped on the grass behind him. 'They're good these onions. Want some more?'

'Nah.' Marshall half-turned towards his friend. 'Is Chand coming?'

Armitage aped him. 'Is Chand coming? Is Chand coming? She's all you ever think about nowadays.' When Marshall didn't respond he said, 'Don't know whether she's coming or not. She's got to get past all those women first.' He shook his head. 'It doesn't seem right does it? 'Er married and expecting when she should be out enjoying herself.'

Marshall grinned. 'She's fit is Chanda. I wouldn't mind 'er 'aving my baby anytime.'

'Yeah, right. As if they'd let her within miles of you. She'd be shipped back to Pakistan before she could get her knickers off.'

'As if.' The voice came from behind them.

The young men turned. A young Asian girl dressed in a pair of jeans and a baggy jumper which almost hid the eight months of her pregnancy, grinned at them.

'God, Chand, you made me jump. I didn't think you were coming.'

'You think I'm going to let a load of women stop me?' She climbed over the wall. Marshall stretched up to help her. 'Shove up,' she said and pushed herself between them. 'What we going to do then?'

Marshall sighed. 'Dunno.'

'We could do over the old man in the flats again. You two keep 'im talking, I'll ask to go to the toilet and do 'is bedroom while I'm there.'

'No we can't,' said Marshall. 'It's too soon since the last time. And anyway, he's got nowt much. Old folks, they're good for a few wraps or a night out, but they've got no real money.'

'All old folk have money stashed away if you know where to look. You should see what my father-in-law has. And it's not all in a bank either. What you need is something to show 'em you mean business.'

'Like what?'

'I don't know. Baseball bats.'

'Like we're going to walk into a house with baseball bats tucked up our shirts,' Armitage scoffed.

'Knives, then. We could do over a shop with knives. We'd get more money there.'

Perspiration prickled between Darren Armitage's shoulder

76

blades. He wasn't sure he was happy about the direction of the conversation. Jumping old folk was one thing, but going into a shop tooled up was something else. 'I've not done a shop before.'

Chanda rubbed her swollen belly. 'The trouble with you, Armitage, is you've got no balls.' She turned to Marshall, let her tongue slide over her top lip then, with her eyes wide and her voice stripped of the earlier challenge, she simpered, 'Not like Gary. You'd be up for it, wouldn't you?'

And Gary, who couldn't resist either a simper or Chanda, *was* up for it.

As he walked from the offices of Victim Support, Handford rang Ali from his mobile. 'Khalid, I've got the names of people Ingleby considers his enemies.' He began to read from the list. 'James Mossman ...'

Ali interrupted, his tone quizzical, 'James Mossman?'

'Yes, why? Do you know him?'

'I'm not sure. The name rings a bell. Just a minute.'

Handford heard the rustle of papers.

'Yes, I thought so. He's the owner of the Peugeot. He came to pick it up this morning; said he'd left it overnight because he'd been out drinking and thought he might be over the limit. When he demanded why we'd taken it for forensic examination, the PC told him to see me. I told him there'd been an incident last night and we were checking all vehicles in the vicinity. He became quite agitated, said he needed his car for work.'

'What is his work?'

'He's a salesman. According to him, no vehicle, no money. Anyway I told him someone would be in touch to let him know when he could pick his car up, took his statement and left it at that.'

'I don't suppose he mentioned he knew the Inglebys, that he lived next door to them until June 2000?'

'No, he didn't – not that he had reason to; he wasn't given information into what had happened, only that there'd been an incident. Although I suppose he could have heard about the shooting from the radio or TV news.'

'It doesn't much matter, does it? He was in the vicinity – at least his car was – and according to Maurice Ingleby, Mossman has a reason to hate him.' Briefly Handford explained about the house sale. 'Let's talk to him again and find out just how bitter he still is. Send Warrender and Clarke; they're experienced enough to sort the wheat from the chaff.'

'I'll get them on to it.'

'While they're there, ask them to find out what, if anything, he knows about the Ingleby's marriage. You'd think by the way Maurice is talking it was good, yet according to the DCI he's had more than his fair share of affairs, so there must have been something, and Mossman might be able to tell us what.'

'What about Miah, do you want him to go with them?'

'No, he can check the bankruptcy list against Ingleby's enemies.' He read out the rest of the names. 'Tell him to go back five years or so. There'll be a Ray Braddock's name there. Ask him to talk to the official receivers' office, see if they came across any firearms when they were assessing his possessions – either at his home or at the Crosby Gun Club where Braddock is, or was, a member. Pay a visit to the secretary; find out just how good a marksman Braddock is and I need a list of the weapons they hold up there. Tell him we'll need to check each and every one, and that until they're collected no one is to use them. I want the names and addresses of the keyholders, a list of current and past members and the names of anyone who has been there for whatever reason in the past week. And ask someone to check on Darren Armitage, he's Braddock's nephew, worked with him in the business before it collapsed. In the meantime I'll talk to Braddock.'

Trainee Detective Parvez Miah was equally as distracted as his wife and for the same reason. Their argument was buzzing round his brain like a swarm of bees. But deep down he knew Aisha was right – Chanda was a bully. Pecking at the edge of his reason, however, was the knowledge that she was his brother's wife, carefully chosen to link two influential Pakistani business families in the district. Whatever happened, this link had to be maintained and even a hint from them of wrongdoing by Chanda would sever it. If Aisha was to suggest for one moment that the girl was involved in assault, if she was to go to the police then he couldn't begin to conceive of the outcome. At best Aisha would be ostracised, him too if he supported her; at worst … He shuddered. Family shame was a powerful emotion.

He turned back to the bankruptcy list and forced himself to concentrate. There was only one person recorded who fitted the bill of bankrupt and adversary, and that was Ray Braddock. It was surprising he was still on it since the order had been made just over two years ago and normally the maximum time for one to run was a year. He should have been released from it by now. Parvez wondered why he hadn't been. Would it be worth finding out? Was the reason anything to do with Dianne Ingleby's death or would he be wasting his time? He was aware that in any investigation they took everything into account and didn't abandon it until they knew for certain it wasn't relevant. Better to have the information and not need it than to not have it and need it. He looked round. Warrender and Clarke had been sent out to question a James Mossman and Sergeant Ali was visiting the secretary of the Crosby Gun Club. There was no one of rank or experience to give him advice. It was his call.

He picked up the phone and dialled the Official Receiver's Office. He had a friend working there; if he could speak to him he would probably get the information he was after. The switchboard put him through.

'Asif, it's Parvez. How are you?'

'I'm fine, Parvez; it's been a long time.'

They made small talk for a few moments until Asif said, 'What can I do for you? Don't tell me you're thinking of applying for bankruptcy?'

Parvez laughed. 'No, nothing like that.' And without going into detail he told him they were interested in Ray Braddock and asked if firearms had been found when they were calculating his assets.

'I haven't got the information to hand, but I can check and get back to you.'

While Miah waited he worked his way through the credit ratings of others on the list. Quite a few had County Court Judgements against them – not that this was unusual in the current climate of easy borrowing and difficulty in paying back. What was more interesting was that three of the judgements were the result of cases brought by Maurice Ingleby. The DI had been right when he had said the builder was a hard-headed businessman who didn't suffer fools gladly. He made notes and began to word-process his report, the argument with Aisha almost forgotten.

It was half-an-hour later when Asif returned his call to say there was no mention of firearms in the report on Braddock.

Parvez thanked him then said, 'I'm not sure about the appropriateness of asking this, but can you tell me more about his situation?'

Asif laughed. 'Since it's you, I can't see why not, most of it is in the public domain anyway.' He paused for a moment. 'According to his file Ray Braddock owed a considerable amount of money when he was made bankrupt in January 2003 – almost a quarter of a million.' Parvez whistled. 'His firm wasn't a limited company so the debt was personal to him and since his assets didn't nearly cover what he owed a lot of people missed out.'

'Who were his biggest creditors?'

'The bank, the mortgage company and a builder, Maurice Ingleby.'

'He owed Maurice Ingleby money?'

'Yes, going on twenty thousand. Isn't he the man whose wife was killed?'

'Yes, last night.'

'And you're part of the investigation. I'm impressed Parvez – important or what?'

It was Miah's turn to laugh. 'Hardly. I've spent most of the morning trawling through lists.' They were getting off the subject. 'Do you know why Braddock owed Ingleby money? According to the DI, Braddock blames him for the bankruptcy because he refused to pay him for what he considered were shoddy goods.'

'That may be, but Mr Ingleby lent him quite a large sum when he set up the business in 2001 and as yet it hasn't been repaid. Nor will it be now.'

'I wonder why Ingleby didn't say anything.'

Asif laughed. 'I have no idea, Parvez, you find out, you're the detective.'

'You say the bankruptcy order was made in January 2003; shouldn't he have been discharged from it by now?'

'Yes. He missed out on the twelve-month ruling which only became law in April last year, but even so normally he would have automatically been discharged on the first of April this year.'

'So why wasn't he?'

'Two reasons. It's not his first bankruptcy – that was in 1996 – and because of that, discharge for this one can be delayed until

2009, but he knows that, we told him at the time. But we also think he's making money which he's not declaring to us. We're not sure what he's doing or where he's doing it, or even where he's salting his money away, and he's denying everything of course, so we asked the court to delay discharge until we're absolutely sure.'

'Does he know that?'

'I doubt it. He thinks the reason for delaying discharge is because of the first bankruptcy. And we'd rather he didn't know. Proving anything at the moment is hard enough; if he gets an inkling of what we're doing he'll go underground and we'll never find out.'

'So what made you suspicious?'

'Pure luck really. One of our bailiffs lives near him and happened to comment on Braddock's lifestyle. He may live in rented accommodation and be on benefit but it appears that doesn't stop him spending most nights in the pub not to mention nipping off to Europe for the odd week every month or so. He has a classy girlfriend so I suppose she could be subbing him.'

'Do you know who she is?'

'Sorry, no.'

Parvez scribbled notes. 'I'm really grateful for this Asif, I owe you one.'

'Perhaps if you find out who the girlfriend is, you can pass it on; it would be useful to know.'

Parvez wasn't sure whether this would be information that shouldn't be revealed. There was always the possibility it might affect the progress of the investigation, particularly if Braddock was a suspect in Dianne Ingleby's murder. He crossed his fingers and prayed this wouldn't be his first mistake. 'You can rely on me, Asif,' he said.

chapter six

Handford pulled himself out of his car and shivered. Unlike the mild weather he had left behind, here it was cold and windy. Eleven hundred feet above sea level, Queensbury was about as exposed as it could be and today, lost in swirling clouds, it seemed completely cut off from the city below. But in spite of the weather, the village held a special place in Handford's heart as the home of the Black Dyke Mills Brass Band, probably the most famous of its kind in the country. He had played the cornet in a brass band himself when he'd had the time to practise, nowhere near the level of Black Dyke but enjoyable all the same. Since he'd joined CID, however, he'd never been reliable enough to get to the practise sessions let alone the concerts. Now his enjoyment came from listening to CDs and cassettes at home and in the car.

His eyes took in the immediate area. It wasn't particularly busy, a few individuals were braving the gusty wind to struggle along the main street and one or two were standing at the bus stop. They're going to regret their scarves and heavy coats in the city, Handford thought. A blue Fiesta was parked outside Ray Braddock's cottage, a vehicle which Handford was fairly sure he recognised. It had been one of the four private cars on the drive at Ingleby's house when he'd arrived that morning but was not there when he'd left. He spoke to the communications room. 'Give me a check on vehicle registration YKo4LBY.' If he was right, he wondered what she was doing up here. Given she was meant to be going to her own home in Denholme to pick up some clothes and take the cats to the kennels, she had come a good few miles out of her way. He walked over to the car and peered in; the seats were empty, except for a road map and an umbrella, and since it was unlikely she'd had the time to deliver the animals, he had to assume she hadn't yet collected them.

His radio crackled. 'The car is a blue Fiesta, registered to Rebecca Ingleby ...' He was given her address and told that it had not been reported lost or stolen. Interesting. She was obviously visiting. Not the act of a daughter who would, to put it in Ingleby's own words 'never go with a loser like Braddock'.

Handford turned towards the house and knocked on the door. It was opened within seconds by a tall, broad-shouldered man dressed in jeans and sweater which, judging by the cut and the material, had at sometime cost him quite a lot of money. His dark hair was cropped short and even to the detective, he was good-looking in a rugged kind of way. He held up his warrant card and introduced himself.

Ray Braddock's expression gave nothing away and at first he tried staring at the detective. 'Surprise, surprise,' he said as he scrutinised the card. His voice was deep and gravelly, and he spoke in a Bradford rather than a Yorkshire accent. When Handford didn't move, except to put his warrant card back in his pocket, Braddock's eyes swerved away to look past him as though he was checking the weather. 'I suppose you'd better come in,' he said finally and stood to one side. 'Mind your head,' he warned. 'People were smaller when these houses were built.'

John Handford dipped down before walking directly into the sitting room. There was no sign of anyone else; if Rebecca Ingleby had been visiting she had either slipped out of the back door or was hiding in the kitchen or the bedroom. The stairs to the upper floor were to his left and opposite, at the far end of the room, was a wooden door that probably opened on to steps leading down to a cellar. To the right of that hung a colourful plastic strip curtain which hid the kitchen from view.

Braddock followed Handford. There was little natural light breaching the paned window and the room, which doubled as a lounge and a dining area, was illuminated by a single centre bulb hooded by a plastic shade. The walls were painted white to reflect what little brightness there might be but it was not enough to dispel the gloom. Even the furniture which was old and shabby and probably came as part of the rental mirrored the dreariness.

'I'll put the fire on,' Braddock said as he bent down to light the gas. 'I don't use it often – it's expensive. I'm not allowed to spend too much money – that's what it's like when you're a bankrupt.'

He made no attempt to hide the bitterness in his voice.

Handford frowned. Too much information, too soon. He wondered why. 'You were obviously expecting me, Mr Braddock; can I ask how you knew I would be coming?'

Braddock shrugged. 'It was on the television that Dianne Ingleby had been shot. I know the Inglebys.'

'A lot of people know the Inglebys but I'm not talking to all of them, so why did you think I would come to you?'

'It's common knowledge I hated Ingleby.'

'It was his wife who was shot not him. Did you hate her?'

'I'd nothing against her.'

'Then why were you expecting me, Mr Braddock?'

His hostility towards Handford simmered until he could no longer contain it. 'Because I know you don't think the bullet was meant for her and I have a dozen reasons to want Maurice off the planet. Is that enough for you?'

First over-confidence, now aggression that bordered on unease. Braddock was in danger of condemning himself if he continued in this vein. Handford made no attempt to answer the question but instead he played on the man's edginess as he waited for him to break the silence. He didn't have to wait long.

'If the bullet wasn't meant for Dianne Ingleby it had to be for Rebecca or for Maurice and there must be people lining up to see him off with me heading the queue. So unless it was some kid playing cops and robbers, I'll be top suspect. And that's as much as I'm saying without a solicitor.'

If the threat of a solicitor was meant to frighten, it didn't work. 'I can't imagine why you think you need a solicitor, Mr Braddock,' Handford said quietly, 'but we can wait for one if you like. In the meantime I still need to know *where* you got the information from that Mrs Ingleby may not have been the intended victim.'

'No you don't, you know already, her car's right outside the door, but if you want me to spell it out I will. Rebecca told me.'

Without waiting to be asked, Handford sat down. The chair was unexpectedly comfortable, which was more than could be said of the detective. He was angry with Rebecca Ingleby. She wasn't stupid, yet she had passed on information to someone who she must have known could be considered a suspect. For the first time, Braddock appeared more sure of himself. He leaned against the wall next to the fireplace and looked directly at Handford who returned the eye contact without flinching. 'Where is Miss Ingleby, Mr Braddock?'

Braddock's smile mocked him. 'Upstairs – in bed. She was exhausted. I told her to get some sleep.' He waited, but Handford wasn't prepared to ask the question Braddock obviously wanted him to ask, knowing the man would supply him with the answer anyway. He was right.

'We're together, a couple as they say. We sleep together and one day we'll live together. And our relationship is made all the sweeter for me because when Ingleby finds out, the bastard'll go ape-shit.' He pulled a cigarette out of a packet on the mantelpiece and lit up. He drew hard on it, seemingly savouring the taste before he blew the smoke into the room. They were cheap French cigarettes and smelt like cow-dung.

Handford stifled the need to cough. 'Why are you telling me about your association with Miss Ingleby? Is it because you're hoping I'll pass the information on to her father? Well let me tell you, Mr Braddock, not only is that childish but it's unnecessary because unless it impinges on the investigation into her mother's murder, then it has nothing to do with me. If you want to get revenge on Rebecca's father, you'll have to do it yourself and not use me as an ally. Now shall we get on with what I came to do? In fact let's start with your movements last night between eight and midnight.'

His smugness dented, the smile faded and Braddock sat down in the chair opposite. 'I was out,' he said. 'It was Rebecca's birthday and she spent it with her parents – it's a family tradition seemingly. They went to the theatre. I didn't want to stay in on my own so I went into the city with Darren.'

'Darren?'

'Darren Armitage, my nephew. We had a few drinks then went on to a club. We left about half-one, got back about two.'

'Which pub did you drink in?'

'Pubs. We started at The Speckled Hen but we weren't that keen, so we went on to the Shoulder of Mutton and then on to another one; I don't know its name, though Darren might. We left there about half ten and then to the Copper Coin night-club up near the college.'

'Were you together the whole evening?'

85

He smiled, 'Except when I went for a piss.'

Handford ignored him. 'Did you meet or talk to anyone else? Is there anyone who can verify your movements, apart from your nephew, that is?'

'I doubt it. We chatted to some punters in The Shoulder of Mutton, but I haven't a clue who they are. We didn't ask their names, I didn't think we needed to.'

'No women?'

'One or two. But you don't need to know them for a one-night stand.'

'And did you have a one-night stand?'

'Would it matter if I did? I've already said I didn't know who they were.'

So much for Rebecca. She was obviously no more than a way of getting back at Maurice Ingleby. Handford was surprised she couldn't see it.

'How did you travel to the city?'

'By bus.'

'And back?'

'By taxi.'

'Which firm?'

'I don't know. Darren booked it from a card at the night-club.'

Handford changed the subject. 'How long have you been bankrupt?'

Braddock's face darkened. 'I don't know what that's got to do with Dianne Ingleby's murder,' he said.

'Perhaps nothing, *if* she was the intended victim. But as you said yourself, she might not have been, and you were eager enough to tell me when I arrived that you were a bankrupt and that it was Maurice Ingleby's fault; indeed you almost revelled in it. You also knew that he, not his wife could have been the intended victim and for the moment, I only have your word for it that it was Miss Ingleby who told you. Now how long have you been bankrupt?'

Braddock shrugged. 'Two years. I've applied to be released, but they haven't agreed yet. Stupid bastards. They know I can't pay out any more; I haven't got anything.'

'Do you have a job?'

'Now where am I going to get a job? I've only ever worked in the building trade and Maurice Ingleby has made sure no one will hire me now. I've gone for everything – I spend more time at the Job Centre than I do here – but once the bosses know you're a bankrupt, they think you'll cook the books or pinch the petty cash.'

'And you blame Maurice Ingleby for this?'

'Of course I blame him; all he had to do was pay me for the stuff I'd sold him; if he had the bank would have kept going. But he couldn't do that could he? Everything had to be a hundred per cent perfect for him. And nothing's perfect in this life.' Ferociously he stubbed out the cigarette in the ashtray.

'So you're going out with his daughter to get back at him?'

'The man deserves everything he gets.'

'And Rebecca, does she deserve everything she gets?'

'She's enjoying herself.'

Handford looked at him with distaste. 'What about a dead wife, Mr Braddock, does he deserve that?'

Braddock leaned forward in his chair. 'No, copper,' he said, a note of self-satisfied malice in his voice. 'That's what Dianne doesn't deserve, not him.'

Aisha Miah had made a decision. After leaving the office she had bought herself a take-away coffee and sat in Centenary Square trying to make sense of what she was feeling. From the bench she could see the magistrates' court and the Central Police Station and she looked up at the windows of the CID offices. Was Parvez there now? What was he doing? She'd heard about the murder and wondered if he was part of the investigation. His father would expect him to be, but even he couldn't control everything and as a trainee Parvez would surely be involved in something more minor. Something like a street robbery.

It was interesting how the law categorised crime as major or minor or even petty. Certainly some were more serious than others, but however inconsequential they were perceived to be they affected the victims one hundred per cent. Burglary, mugging or common assault – it made little difference to the person involved. She had known one woman who, for weeks after her house had been broken into and her possessions stolen, never left one room to go into another without checking the windows were closed and locked – even in the height of summer and even though she was in the house. For a while it had become almost an obsession. It was the effect crime had on the victims that decided her to become a prosecuting rather than a defence lawyer.

She wondered how Mrs Shaw was coping. Was she picking up her own pension any more or was someone else doing it for her? From what PC Foxton, the investigating officer, had told her, the old lady insisted she wouldn't be cowed; no thug was going to spoil her life. She might have been bruised and he might have made it financially difficult for a week or so, but she wouldn't have the rest of her days ruined by him. 'She was such a brave old lady we had a whip-round in the canteen for her,' Foxton had said. 'She was grateful, but she told us to stop worrying about her and to go out and catch him so that he wouldn't do the same thing to someone else.' And now instead of giving her good news, he would have to tell her they were dropping the case and that is was very likely Gary Marshall *would* do the same to someone else. More than likely to some vulnerable old person who couldn't fight back.

As Aisha crumpled her empty coffee cup she made up her mind. If Colin Jenkins hadn't passed the information on to Foxton that they were dropping the case, she would ask him if she could have another look at the statements and photographs, see if she could find anything, however small, that could be used in court.

Her fingers tightly crossed that she wasn't too late, she lobbed the beaker into the waste-bin and ran back to the office. A fight was the only thing the likes of Gary Marshall and Chanda understood. She wasn't sure why her sister-in-law had come to mind, why she'd linked her with Marshall, but in that moment she'd made another decision: while she was dealing with Marshall she would deal with Chanda too; *she* wasn't going to be cowed by her or the family any more than Mrs Shaw had been by her attacker. If she was prepared to defend the old lady's apparent vulnerability, then why not defend her own? The girl was seventeen for goodness' sake; *she* was twenty-nine and a solicitor with the power of language. She'd been known to reduce people to tears in the witness box – so why not Chanda?

James Mossman's antagonism was evident as soon as Warrender and Clarke introduced themselves. He faced up to the older detective, leaning so close that Clarke felt and smelt his breath. He took a step backwards. When the man said he'd drunk so

88

much the night before that he was over the limit he hadn't been too far wrong.

'When can I have my bloody car back? No sales, no money, or don't you lot understand that?'

'I'm sorry, Mr Mossman, but we're investigating a murder and your car was in the vicinity.'

'You're talking about Dianne Ingleby's killing?' Clarke nodded.

'Then let me make it absolutely clear – my car might have been in the vicinity, but I wasn't. I told your sergeant this morning why I'd left it overnight in the multi-storey. But that's not enough for you is it? You've got to drag it away for forensic examination. How long are you going to keep it?'

'I don't know yet, if we find nothing, then it shouldn't be too long.'

'What do you mean, if you find nothing? There's nothing to find.' Mossman's anger was getting the better of him and for a moment he didn't grasp the significance of Clarke's answer. When he did, the blood feeding on his fury drained from his face and he took a step forward. 'Hang on a minute. You think I killed her? Don't be ridiculous. Why would I?'

'I don't think this is something we want to discuss on the doorstep, do you Mr Mossman?' Warrender said. 'Let's go inside.'

They followed him through the hall and into the kitchen. Considering he was a man living alone – or perhaps it was because he *was* living alone and out all day – everything was spotless. The walls in the hallway were decorated in a light cream and a dark blue carpet led along the passageway and up the stairs. On the telephone table was a framed photograph of a woman and two small boys who were so alike they had to be twins. 'Your wife and children?' Clarke asked.

As if he hadn't heard, Mossman made no reply.

The furniture in the kitchen was in light oak and the appliances up-to-date. A large picture window overlooked the garden. Spread out on the table were papers and a laptop sat open at one of the chairs which had been pushed back when he got up to answer the door.

'I'm going to have a drink, do you want one?' Mossman's antagonism gone, his voice was as pale as his face. He filled the kettle and switched it on. 'Coffee or tea?'

They elected for coffee. Warrender said, 'This is a fine kitchen Mr Mossman, your wife must love it.'

'She would if she was here.' He busied himself collecting up the sheets of paper and closed down the computer. 'I'm divorced.'

'What about your children, do you see them?'

'Whenever I want, except that she's getting married again and going to live in Dorset. I'll hardly ever see them then. Not that that will stop her taking my money every month.' He sighed. 'It's not that I begrudge paying towards their upkeep, of course I don't, it's just that it's hard making ends meet sometimes. That's why I want my car back. I can't work without it.'

'You're a salesman, I understand; selling what exactly?'

'Toys. It's at this time of year I make most of my commission.'

'It's May,' Warrender said.

'It might be May to you, but to me it's Christmas. I'm pulling in orders for Christmas stock as fast as I can write them. I need to get out there, beat the opposition, and I can't do that without a car.'

Clarke nodded towards the papers now piled on the work surface. 'Well at least it's given you the opportunity to catch up with some of that. If your work is anything like ours, there'll be plenty.'

The kettle clicked off and Mossman poured the water into the mugs. He handed one each to Warrender and Clarke, 'Help yourselves to milk and sugar.'

Warrender walked over to the window and stood with his back to them.

Mossman watched the detective for a moment and then turned to Clarke and sat down at the table. 'I told your sergeant where I was last night and why I didn't pick up my car. All you have to do is check it out.'

'We are doing, sir, but in the meantime we have a few questions.' He paused, took a sip of his coffee. It was strong and he added more milk and sugar to reduce the bitterness. 'I appreciate why you said nothing this morning, because you wouldn't know the identity of the victim, but now that you do can you tell me about your relationship with her?'

'We were neighbours for a few years, until they moved.'

'Good neighbours?' Warrender queried and continued to stare out of the window.

Mossman twisted round to face the detective's back. 'Most of the time.'

'But not all the time?'

'We had our differences. Don't most neighbours?'

'Mr Ingleby told us you cut down his hedge while he was away on holiday.'

Mossman flushed. 'No,' he said, 'Ingleby *thinks* I did. The police could find no evidence that it was me.'

'But it was, wasn't it?' Warrender turned and smiled conspiratorially and before the man could answer, he continued, 'You and the Inglebys parted on bad terms I understand.'

'No, *Maurice Ingleby* and I parted on bad terms; I had no problem with her; she was friendly, she was charming and she cared about people. She was far too good for him.'

'Why?'

'He was a swine to her. It was well-known round here that he had affairs.'

'Do you know who with?'

'Any woman who was attractive, rich and successful. Try Councillor Barker's wife for one.'

'Did he bring Mrs Barker here?'

'I doubt it. When you're playing about with the rich and successful, you don't bring them to a semi in Bierley.'

Warrender chuckled. 'No I don't suppose you do.' The smile faded. 'Did your divorce have anything to do with Maurice Ingleby? Your wife is an attractive woman and your job as a salesman must have kept you away a lot.'

Clarke frowned as he watched the fury rise in Mossman. There were times when the direct approach was needed, but not when all it did was upset and antagonise.

'No,' Mossman shouted, banging his mug on the table. 'My wife wasn't like that.' He pushed back his chair and strode to the sink where he picked up a dishcloth. 'The divorce was my fault, not hers and it's nothing to do with you.' Back at the table he scrubbed at the spilt drink and then walked over to Warrender. 'Don't you ever again suggest my wife was unfaithful with anyone, let alone with a shit like Maurice Ingleby.'

Warrender stared at him, seemingly unmoved by his outburst.

'So was that all you had against him, his affairs with other women? Because if it was, it seems very odd to me.'

Clarke interrupted. 'That's enough, Warrender,' he said quietly. He turned to Mossman. 'I'm sorry, sir, but all we're trying to do is to establish what, if anything, you may have against Mr Ingleby.'

Mossman backed away and returned to the sink where he slowly and deliberately rinsed out the cloth before folding and replacing it on the edge. By the time he had completed the task his composure had returned. He turned to look at Clarke. 'You think that whoever shot her got the wrong person, don't you? You think they were after Maurice or else why would you be so interested in him?'

'In what way?'

When he got no response, Mossman continued, 'If that's what you think, then you're more than likely on the right track. He had plenty of enemies. He always got what he wanted and he didn't care how, or what damage it caused.' He was into his flow now. 'He shafted me, like he shafted every one else. He *thought* I'd cut down his hedge, so he got his own back.'

'He was buying the mansion he's living in now and needed a quick sale for next door, but instead of putting it on the market like everyone else, he offered it to the council at below-market price for accommodation for some asylum seekers. He never said a word; in fact I didn't find out until an official came to check out what needed to be done before they could move a family in and he told me. If I'd known earlier I'd at least have had a chance of selling mine for a decent price. Now I can't sell it at all – not for what it's worth anyway. It's been three years and I'm still struggling to get out of negative equity – which is another reason why I need my car.' He emphasised the final sentence.

He sipped the last of his coffee and rinsed the mug under the tap then placed it on the draining board. He turned to lean against the drainer and for a moment contemplated his feet. 'Look,' he said eventually, 'I admit I don't like Ingleby; he's done me a lot of damage, but I wouldn't kill him and I certainly wouldn't kill his wife.'

Warrender and Clarke glanced at each other as a silence developed. Clarke asked, 'You say you were out with friends last night?'

92

'Yes.'

'Tell me about it. What time did you leave home?'

'I didn't leave from home. Tuesdays and Thursdays I work with the Air Training Corps cadets – I'm a Warrant Officer – so I go straight to the hut when I finish my visits. There's always quite a bit to do getting ready for them.'

'This wasn't in the statement you gave to Sergeant Ali.'

'No, it wouldn't be. He wanted to know my movements between nine and midnight. I was at the pub by then and later at the night-club. It's the CO's fortieth birthday tomorrow. We thought we ought to buy him a few drinks to help him on his way.'

'What exactly do you do when you're at the Air Training Corps?'

'I have various duties. I take the cadets flying, gliding, that kind of thing but specifically I train the drill team, and once a month I go with them to the range at the Crosby Gun Club.' He let his breath out with a deep sigh. 'I teach them to shoot, DC Clarke. But that doesn't mean I shot Dianne Ingleby. I had no need to; it was her husband I hated not her and anyway, I have too much respect for guns to point them at people – whoever they are.'

Handford was back at his desk. The file he was meant to be working on lay unopened. The interview with Braddock had left a nasty taste, the more so because Rebecca Ingleby appeared to be involved with him or why else had she gone straight from her father's house up to his? At one point he'd been inclined to ask Braddock to bring her downstairs, but had decided against it. It would have given the man too much satisfaction to produce her, and that would only have embarrassed Rebecca. One thing he *was* sure of was that Maurice Ingleby knew nothing of their relationship, although he did wonder if Dianne had – daughters often confide in their mothers. It was much more likely though that at twenty-five Rebecca considered her men friends none of her parents' business. She was an adult, entitled to her own life. Nevertheless, according to Ingleby she would inherit the business one day. Marriage to her would give Braddock a share in it; perhaps he had attempted to make it sooner rather than later, except – and he kept coming back to this – he was too good a shot to kill the wrong person – unless of course it had been his

93

intention to kill them both. It seemed a bit drastic to resort to a double murder to get hold of the business, when he could do it legitimately by marrying Rebecca. It would never have got to that; Maurice wouldn't have allowed it. He would either have changed his mind about handing it over to his daughter, or built a clause into any legal document which would preclude Braddock's involvement. Braddock would have known that the only way the man would have a clear path would be to dispose of Maurice and Dianne. Perhaps the mistake was not that the gunman had killed the wrong person, but that Maurice was not dead as well. Unfortunately this was no more than conjecture on Handford's part, because there was no hard evidence to back up the theory. Or if it came to that to suggest Kathie and Emma could be a link to the murder.

Who were these two women and why were they so important to Dianne Ingleby? If Eileen Leighton wasn't so pig-headed, he could probably have ruled them out by now. He needed the case to move forward, not just because there was a killer out there, but because he had to prove he would be an asset to HMET. He wasn't a fool – he knew he was under scrutiny from those setting up the team as well as from the DCI. He couldn't afford to stand still or to slip up.

He opened up the file and began to check on actions still to be completed when there was a knock on the door. Without looking up he called 'Come in'.

Parvez Miah appeared. Handford would have preferred not to have him involved in a murder investigation. It was his first stint in CID and he should have been investigating minor crime, instead of being shepherded through one as serious as this; but Russell had insisted. Why they always had to placate Iqbal Ahmed, Handford would never understand. The man was a menace, but as Russell intimated, better a friendly menace than a hostile menace.

As he stood at the door Miah appeared nervous, unsure whether to remain where he was or take a few steps forward.

Remembering how he felt on his first day as a trainee, Handford gave him a smile. 'Come in Parvez, what can I do for you?'

'I've got the information you asked for, sir.' He edged up to the desk. 'Ray Braddock is the only person on the bankruptcy list who is on Mr Ingleby's list, but there are others who have

94

County Court Judgements against them, three as a result of cases brought by Mr Ingleby. I've put asterisks against their names.' He passed over the paper.

Handford scanned it. 'This seems fine. Finish it off by taking statements from the three. You may well be able to do it over the phone, but if not make a visit. Just be sure to let someone know where you are. We're a bit pushed for detectives at the moment so take a uniformed officer with you.'

'Yes sir,' Miah hesitated. 'There's something else sir. You asked me to ring the Official Receiver's Office to find out whether they came across any weapons when they were assessing Mr Braddock's possessions ...'

'Go on.'

'They didn't, but I spoke to a friend of mine who works there. Mr Braddock owes about a quarter of a million pounds, at least twenty thousand of it to Maurice Ingleby.'

'Now that is interesting. I wonder why neither of them has mentioned it. Anything else?'

Again the trainee hesitated. 'I couldn't understand why Mr Braddock hadn't been discharged, with the new rules he should have been by now.' Miah went on to explain what he had learned.

Handford listened in silence. When the young man had finished he said. 'Well done, Miah; I'm impressed.' He indicated the chair at the other side of the desk. 'Sit down for a moment and let's look at this logically. Do we know why Ingleby loaned Braddock the money?'

Miah perched on the edge, his back straight. He looked uncomfortable. 'No, sir, unless it was to set up in business again.'

Handford tried to put him at his ease. 'I thought bankrupts weren't supposed to do that.'

'They weren't then; it's easier now with the new rules. But according to Asif, there have always been ways round it. It's someone else's business in name and the bankrupt becomes an employee.'

'But it doesn't make sense that it was Ingleby who lent him the money. I would have thought he was far too shrewd. Do we know anything about the first bankruptcy in 1996?'

'Asif said it happened after his father died. Apparently most of the old man's legacy was swallowed up by death duties and other debts, but his son had borrowed on the strength of a large sum coming through. When it didn't he was left owing thousands.'

'Not the luckiest of men, is he?' Handford commented. 'Have you done your report yet?'

'Not yet, sir.'

'Then get statements from the three with CCJs against them and then do your report and let me have it by the end of the day.'

'Yes sir.' He pushed back the chair and took a pace to the left.

'And Miah – well done.'

As Miah closed the door, Handford dialled the incident room. 'Is Warrender back yet? ... Good, ask him to come to my office would you, preferably with a cup of coffee in his hand. What about Sergeant Ali? ... Not yet, never mind, I'll see him later.' He replaced the receiver.

After a few moments Warrender entered pushing the door open with his back. He was carrying a mug of coffee in each hand. He turned and placed them on the desk, then without waiting to be invited sat down on the chair Miah had vacated.

'Did you get anything interesting from Mossman?' Handford asked as he picked up one of the mugs.

'We did, yes,' Warrender said and gave a brief resumé of the interview.

'Do you believe him?'

'I do actually. I doubt he's in the centre of the frame, but he might just be in a bottom corner. A lot depends on what the examination of his car reveals – if anything. He did mention a Councillor Barker though. Apparently his wife was one of the women Maurice Ingleby had a brief affair with. He lives near Mossman so we decided to have a word.'

'And?'

'We tried to be as discreet as we could, but he wasn't best pleased to see us. In fact,' Warrender looked sheepish, 'I'm sorry guy, but he threatened to complain to the DCI.'

Great. 'Probably inevitable.'

'Anyway, as far as the murder is concerned we can cross him off our list. He and his wife have been visiting relatives in Glasgow for a week. They landed at Leeds Bradford Airport at eight o'clock this morning. Mrs Baker gave us the names of four other wives who she knows were involved with Ingleby. She's not exactly thrilled with the man, or the women who followed her into his bed. Happy to drop them in it, so to speak.'

Handford stood up. He was becoming restless; he needed to pace. He wandered to the window then to the filing cabinet where he opened a drawer, fiddled with some papers and shut it again. He could do with a quick result, but the investigation was becoming clogged with dross, very little of which he understood and most of which, like Councillor Barker's wife's affair, was probably not relevant.

'Question them as soon as you can.' He returned to his desk. 'Ray Braddock might be in the frame.' He related the information Miah had given him as well as his own visit to Queensbury.

'Do you think Dianne Ingleby knew what was going on?' Warrender reflected. 'And that was why she was killed.'

'I've no idea, Warrender,' he said, 'but we need to find out. If the Official Receiver's right then Braddock may well be into something which is at least shady, if not downright criminal. I'll tackle Rebecca, see what she knows. I know you've a lot to do, but I want you to find out as much as you can about Braddock, his lifestyle, his finances, his friends and most of all his movements. According to Miah's information, he goes to Europe a lot. We need to know why. He's bankrupt so I doubt it's for pleasure. My feeling is that the OR's hunch is spot on and he's into something dirty – drugs perhaps ...' Handford cocked an eyebrow. 'Or guns?'

Warrender smiled. 'I'm on to it, boss.'

Handford shot him a look. 'I know you love a challenge, Warrender, but you can take that smile off your face. I want this done by the book. You understand.'

'Yes, boss, by the book.'

'I mean it Warrender. I want HMET as much as you did. You're there; I'm not and I'm never going to be if I'm seen to have a detective on my team that I can't control.'

chapter seven

Although it was looking more and more likely that the death of his wife had more to do with Maurice Ingleby than with Dianne, left alone to his thoughts Handford couldn't rid his mind of the gut instinct that Kathie overshadowed it. Superimposed on the image of the dead woman was that of a young girl, badly beaten, too frightened to go to the police, but eventually learning to trust the woman from Victim Support who had sat at her bedside and listened. He opened the book again. The next three entries told him nothing new. Kathie was still in intensive care and apart from confirming that Dianne had not informed the police she'd said very little. By May 10th, however, she was giving out information. Handford had to admire Dianne Ingleby's perseverance and patience.

May 10th
Kathie has been moved from intensive care to the high depend-
ency ward. Her face is still a mess, but it's less swollen. When
I arrived Michael Iveson met me at the door to the ward and
said Kathie was still upset but showing signs of coming to terms
with what had happened. I asked him if she was any nearer to
informing the police of the attack, but he said she was adamant
that she wouldn't and he felt we had to honour her wishes and
not worry her with it any more. Like me, he couldn't agree with
her decision, but he would respect it. He had other patients to
visit, but we arranged to meet for a coffee after my visit when we
could compare notes and work out the best way to help her.

Michael was right. Kathie was upset. When she saw me, she
clung on and cried. I comforted her as best I could and when she
was calm I asked her if there was anything she wanted me to do.

She said 'no'. I asked if her family had been to see her, but she told me her parents were dead and her only brother was working abroad. I offered to contact him for her, but she said Emma had already done so. I wonder why he wasn't on the first plane home. His sister has been badly injured and her life is at risk, surely a caring brother would have dropped everything to be with her?

The sister didn't want Kathie to get too tired and would only let me stay for half an hour. When I left I asked if her brother had been in touch at all. She said not to her knowledge. He hadn't been mentioned when Kathie was transferred, but she would check.

I met up with Michael in the canteen. He was as puzzled as me when I told him about the brother. Why would he stay away? Perhaps for the same reason she didn't want the police involved; perhaps he doesn't know what has happened. Michael advised that we should leave it alone. He said obviously Kathie has her own reasons for keeping the attack to herself and it's not up to us to make judgements. I didn't argue, but I'm not so sure. You can't go through what she has been through and want it to be kept secret. There are times when secrets can do more harm than good. I should know.

What exactly did she mean by secrets can do more harm than good? And why did she know it? Through her work with the charity or through personal experience? He read on hoping some light would be shed.

May 11th
Kathie was much brighter today. The doctor has said that if she continues to make such good progress she can be moved to a normal ward. I asked how long they expected she would have to remain in hospital and was told it would be at least another week to and who could look after her. With her parents dead and her brother seemingly not interested, that could be a real problem. I know we shouldn't get too emotionally involved, but I feel like suggesting she stay with us for a little while. It's not as though we don't have the room. I can't see Eileen liking it though. Perhaps Michael has a more suitable suggestion. However I did ask Kathie about the mess in the house after the attacker ransacked

it. Apparently Emma's been up and removed things that had belonged to her parents as well as some papers she wanted to keep safe and has made an attempt to tidy up. Perhaps Emma will stay with her for a while when she goes home. But when I suggested it, Kathie said no. Emma has a young son, Jack, who is into everything. And what if the comes back? She couldn't put a child's life at risk. At this point she became distressed and I changed the subject. As I was leaving she asked if Michael was coming today. I said I didn't know, but if she wanted to see him I would contact him for her. She seemed relieved and said it wasn't important. I can understand how she feels though; Michael can be a real old woman sometimes.

The more Handford read the more certain he was that he couldn't yet take Kathie out of the investigation. He made a note to have a word with the Reverend Iveson. Perhaps he would be able to throw some light on what was happening, he might be aware of something Dianne had not been told. The brother perhaps. It seemed odd he hadn't been to see his sister. For a couple of days it had been touch-and-go as to whether she would survive. Living abroad was no excuse.

May 12th
Kathie and I talked about her father today. Emma had brought in the box of photographs she had asked for and she showed me pictures of her parents and her brother, Jason. (So now we have a name). Most of them were taken when she was young – in fact I doubt she was more than fourteen in the latest ones – and were snaps rather than studio photos. They seemed a happy family, smiling, having fun and while she talked lovingly about her mother, she obviously had a particularly close relationship with her father. That's not surprising; Rebecca is much closer to Maurice than she is to me. I don't mind; it's natural; fathers and daughters, mothers and sons. Because of Kathie's father's job – he was an assistant bank manager – they had moved around the country to different branches, mostly in one city or another. They hated it. City life was too frantic for them. Her father in particular loved the sea she said; it was his ambition to buy a small yacht when he retired; in fact it was her parents' intention to sell up and move to the coast. They died before they could do

so – she didn't say how, except that their deaths happened within days of each other. Kathie had been in her final year at university at the time and her brother in his first year. Both had struggled through and gained their degrees. My parents would have been so proud of us she said.

The more I do this job, the more I feel that my family doesn't know how lucky it is.

Handford closed the book. Eileen Leighton had been right when she'd praised Dianne as a Victim Support volunteer. Not only was she supporting her client, she was teasing information out of her without demanding too much at once and without her need for confidentiality being compromised. Handford hoped when he found Kathie – and he would, on that he was determined – he could be just as discreet.

Aisha Miah set about checking the reports and photographs of Mrs Shaw's case with a grim determination. Colin Jenkins hadn't contacted PC Foxton when she got back to the office and although he'd been doubtful as to what Aisha would find that would make a difference, he said she could have until after the weekend. 'If you've nothing by then let it go.' She rang Foxton and suggested they meet; he agreed to come over in his lunch hour. Then she read and reread the statements. All of the witnesses knew Mrs Shaw and all had recognised Gary Marshall as the attacker. One remembered a young Asian girl standing on the sidelines and going off in the same direction as Marshall immediately after the attack, but he hadn't known whether or not she was involved. What was clear was that she hadn't made any attempt to help the old lady. Aisha made a note to ask Foxton if this girl had been traced and if she hadn't to talk to the witness again, get a better description if that was possible. The bag had been recovered near a builder's skip. It had been checked for fingerprints but the only ones found had been Mrs Shaw's. As for DNA, too many people, from passers-by to medical staff, had been involved with the victim after the robbery for it to be worthwhile checking and carrying out the expensive tests. The clear fact was that unless Aisha could come up with something, they were reliant on the witnesses, none of whom at the moment were prepared to stand up in court. Not that she could blame them, it was a traumatic experience. Nevertheless it might be worth talking to them again, there might just be one who had had a fit of conscience and could be persuaded to testify. It would only take one.

John Handford's next stop was to talk to the Reverend Michael Iveson. Not only did he know Dianne Ingleby well, but he also had had dealings with Kathie. From what he had read in the diary, Iveson was just as unlikely to divulge the young woman's identity or whereabouts as Eileen Leighton had been. He had taken the risk and rung all the hospitals in the district to ask if an attack victim with forename of Kathie had been admitted, but it had been a waste of time. One had said they had no patient with the name Kathie, Kathleen or Kathryn; another that he would need a surname if he was to check and two refused to divulge confidential information to someone who may or may not be a police officer.

As he was silently berating the Victim Support coordinator for her stubbornness, she rang him. 'I've seen Kathie this morning,' she said.

'How was she?'

'As you'd expect – grief-stricken.'

Grief-stricken – surely that was a bit strong. She'd only known Dianne for sixteen days so she could be expected to be upset, distressed even, but grief-stricken! He said as much.

'You have to understand Kathie is in an emotional state at the moment. She's been attacked, had her spleen removed and her face wired; she's still not well, John. Her reactions are heightened, more extreme than you would expect. You can't read anything into her response.'

'Could she be frightened?'

'She could be, but that wouldn't be surprising given what she's gone through.'

Or given that the woman she was opening up to had been murdered. Handford kept the thought to himself. 'Did you ask her if she would consider seeing me?'

'I didn't bring you into it. That would have been unfair to her and to Dianne. She didn't need to know the one person she trusted had in fact betrayed that trust by writing it all down. I asked if she still felt unable to inform the police. She was adamant she wants nothing to do with the authorities, nor does she want to see me again.'

'Did she tell you why?'

'Not in so many words, but not only is she emotional, she's also confused. I got the impression she wasn't prepared to trust anyone else now that Dianne was gone. Sorry John, I did try, but now there's nothing more I can do.'

'Will you attempt to see her again?'

'Not unless she contacts me.'

'Do you think she will?'

'It's possible, when she's got over the shock.'

Handford replaced the receiver. If Michael Iveson would tell him nothing, he was going to have to ask for a warrant to open up the Victim Support files or he was going to have to think of another way to identify Kathie, and the only route open to him, as far as he could see, was the press. Perhaps he ought to have a word with Peter Redmayne, ask him to plead with Kathie and Emma to come forward.

The secretary of the Crosby Gun club was as helpful as Eileen Leighton had been unhelpful. He gave Sergeant Ali everything he requested: a list of current and past members, names and addresses of keyholders and a full inventory of the weapons held. He had no objections to them being taken for testing, but did warn him that they had held a friendly pistol shooting competition the night before and all had been used. Every single one had been signed out and in – with times – and locked away in the presence of himself and the treasurer.

He enthused about Braddock and Mossman's ability as marksmen. They were skilled shots and both he insisted had a healthy respect for guns. He wasn't aware of any relationship with Mrs Ingleby – he'd never heard either of them mention her. Perhaps her husband from time to time, but never in a way that suggested they would cause him any harm.

Ali thanked him and agreed to let him know when the weapons would be picked up, then left to drive the ten miles to Keighley. Parking in the town was difficult at the best of times, today – Friday – it was impossible so he left his car in a pay-and-display and walked the rest of the way. The police station was split on to two sites, an old building on the main road with reception, offices, cells and custody suite, and behind it on the hillside a more modern building, part of which had been leased to the West Yorkshire Police by the owners. It was here he was to meet Detective Sergeant Aaron Tooley.

The sergeant was waiting on the steps for him. When he saw Ali he pulled on his cigarette, threw what remained on the floor and crushed it beneath the toe of his shoe. 'Sergeant Ali?' he said as he shook hands and simultaneously blew smoke above Ali's head. 'Sorry. Filthy bloody habit. I make a resolution to stop every New Year and the longest I've managed is two weeks. Let's go inside.'

Small and stocky with closely cropped dark hair, Tooley's accent suggested he hailed from the south of England – one of many who had made their way north for the cheaper housing and lower cost of living. He swiped his card and pulled open the heavy glass door. 'The boss explained what you wanted and why,' he said as they climbed the steps, 'so I think to be more private we'll go into one of the interview rooms.'

Ali followed him into the cramped windowless room boasting the customary table and four chairs. Tooley turned on the strip light which burred with an almost subliminal hum. 'We can go up to CID if you'd rather,' he said.

'No it's fine here.'

The sergeant passed over the file he'd been carrying. 'I'll get us a coffee while you read through it.'

Ali opened it. It was thin: four death-threat letters and their envelopes with Ingleby's home address printed on computer labels, statements from Maurice Ingleby and the three suspects, and a forensic report. There was also a short note to say that apart from a motoring offence by Matthew Hobson, the suspects were not known to the police. The threatening letters were computerised in bold, New Times Roman, font size eighteen he guessed, designed no doubt to make them appear more menacing. The wording in the first two was identical, short and to the point. It warned Ingleby that if he wanted to see his next birthday he should stop funding the BNP. The third was more explicit. It seemed he had ignored the first two warnings; if he refused to stop paying the BNP he would be killed. It ended melodramatically: 'Ignore us at your peril'. The fourth simply read: 'You're dead, Ingleby'. The envelopes were addressed to his home, two posted in Bradford, one in Keighley and one in Leeds.

Ali replaced them and picked up the statements. There was a short one from Maurice Ingleby describing when he received the letters and denying paying out money to any political party, least of all the BNP; the longer ones were given by the suspects who strenuously denied any involvement in death threats. The forensic report on the letters and the envelopes were interesting but did not constitute useful evidence. There were no fingerprints on the letters except Maurice Ingleby's and his wife's and various on the envelopes, but none matching the suspects. The stamps were self-adhesive and there was no DNA on the seal of the envelopes.

'Their English might not be of a literary standard, but whoever sent them had covered all forensic angles,' Tooley said as he came back into the room with two mugs of coffee. He handed one to Ali and sat opposite him.

'What made you suspect Ambler, Hobson and Sugden?'

'They have personal or business as well as political reasons for smearing him. Hobson and Sugden both had business dealings which fell through thanks to him. Sugden almost went bankrupt because of it. Ambler on the other hand came home unexpectedly from a business trip and found Ingleby in bed with his wife. Ambler's not a very forgiving man; threw his wife out and swore he would ruin him.'

'And the political reasons?'

Tooley leaned back until his chair was resting on two legs. 'Have you heard of the multi-faith group Concord not Conflict?'

'Yes, I think so. Aren't they trying to bring all faiths together peacefully?'

'Basically yes. Although at the moment so near the elections, the main aim of their work involves persuading people not to vote for the BNP.'

'And that's causing a problem?'

Tooley banged his chair back on to all four legs. 'No, not in itself, but like all groups there are mavericks who think writing articles and holding meetings will not do the trick.'

'Ambler, Hobson and Sugden?'

Tooley nodded. 'They have a lot to lose. All are standing for council this time and all in what they thought were safe Labour seats until the BNP put up their own candidates.'

'And why would they think the seats were still not as safe?'

'There's been a lot of ill-feeling on the estates that the residents are not being treated as well as the Asian community. They believe that a lot of money is being poured into their housing but none into their own. The BNP have latched on to it and they've managed to stir up strong emotions. There's a powerful mixture of anger, fear and uncertainty out there and as things are there's a real possibility they'll be elected.'

'So how are the three hoping to achieve their objective?'

'By breaking up meetings by whatever means possible; causing as much trouble as they can by instigating unrest among the Asian community, particularly the younger element. Get them to do their dirty work for them.'

'Couldn't that be construed as initiating hatred?'

'Not when it's against a political party – that's par for the course.' Tooley turned sideways hooking one arm over the back of his chair. 'Make no mistake Khalid, these men are not stupid.'

'What about their computers, have they been checked?'

'No. I wanted to but all three of them refused and I didn't have the evidence for a warrant. Also Ambler runs a small IT business from a shop in town. He builds and fixes computers, gives advice, sells toner, paper, that sort of thing, and visits customers' homes if they have a problem. He could have used any one of those he was fixing to write the letters. Given the need for secrecy and confidentiality so as not to upset the political situation, not to mention covering the bosses' backs, I was on a hiding to nothing with a request to check the computers of members of the public.'

The air conditioning didn't seem to be working in the interview room and Ali was beginning to sweat. He pulled off his jacket and hung it over the back of his chair. 'How did they come to the conclusion that Maurice Ingleby was the money behind the local branch?'

Tooley pulled a series of photographs from the back of the file and handed them to Ali. 'These. We found them in Ambler's house. He didn't deny having taken them. He said they were building up evidence.'

Ali sifted through them. Two were of Maurice Ingleby and several others at a black-tie event. He was laughing, seemingly sharing a joke with the man next to him. The rest of the photos were of the two men, some taken at Ingleby's business premises, others at a building site and three with a telephoto lens at Ingleby's house.

The Keighley sergeant pointed to the second man. 'That's Lawrence Burdon, a master builder from Huddersfield and chairman of the local BNP.'

'Do the suspects have any involvement with guns, do you know?'

'Not that has come to our notice and if you're going to ask me whether any of them would kill to get what they want, I'd have to say I saw nothing that would lead me to that conclusion.'

'So you don't think they could have been involved in Dianne Ingleby's death?'

Tooley smiled. 'I didn't say that. We have some hotheads in the town and all three of them have been winding them up. The leaders of the group have done their best to calm things down – specifically the chairman, the Reverend Michael Iveson, and committee members Canon George Stockdale, Sandeep Singh and Iqbal Ahmed. But as I said earlier: Ambler, Hobson and Sugden are quite happy to get someone else to do their dirty work for them – so yes, with the proviso that it's unlikely they were the ones to actually pull the trigger, they could have been involved in Dianne Ingleby's murder.'

Michael Iveson was working on a flower bed in his garden when Handford arrived at the Manse. 'Weeding,' he said. 'On a warm day like this I swear the little beggars grow a couple of inches.' He pushed himself off his knees and brushed his trouser legs with his hands.

Handford wasn't sure what he expected, but gardening seemed an odd occupation for a minister of religion on the day one of his parishioners had been shot dead. Shouldn't he have been praying in the chapel? The detective didn't know. Perhaps Iveson hadn't yet heard about the murder. Perhaps he was about to be the bearer of bad news.

As the minister approached him, he remembered how Dianne had described him in her diary as 'a real old woman at times' and looking at him he could understand why. He was a difficult man to age, probably between mid-to-late fifties but he could have been a little younger – or even older. Small and slightly built he was what Handford could only describe as grey. Everything about him was nondescript: the clothes he wore, the pallor of his skin, his bushy hair, his beard, even the colour of his eyes. Yet behind them Handford detected a shrewdness that belied the external persona. Perhaps it was the work he did, having to bring so many aspects of his character into play in different situations, yet having to remain sane in spite of it all. Rather like a police officer. As Iveson shook hands when Handford introduced himself, his voice was warm and welcoming.

'I expect you've come about Dianne. I heard of her death on the news this morning.' He shook his head sadly. 'I find it impossible to comprehend why anyone would want to kill her.' Then almost in a whisper, 'Yet someone obviously did.' He shook his head again. 'She'll be a great loss.' He paused for a few seconds – the exact amount of time to let his words settle before saying, 'I rang Mr Ingleby but was told he wasn't ready to see anyone yet. I didn't push. To be honest it was something of a relief. No I'm sorry, Inspector, that sounds callous, but I was sitting with Mrs Baker at the nursing home last night until she passed away. They're so short-staffed, so when there are no relatives the night sister calls me. It eases the pressure and ensures the poor thing doesn't die alone.' He paused for a moment to stare in front of him and turned to Handford. 'Anyway, the lady who answered the phone for Mr Ingleby was very kind and said she would contact me when he felt he could accept visitors. I will have to talk with him of course about the funeral. But in these circumstances I expect that can wait, it takes time to release the body doesn't it?'

Handford nodded. The Reverend Iveson wasn't exactly a caricature of a minister of religion and he preferred not to make snap judgements, but he wasn't entirely convinced by him.

'Come inside, Inspector; I'll ask my sister to bring us some tea.'

Handford smiled. 'Not for me thank you. I think I'd had my quota of drinks for the day by ten o'clock this morning.'

Iveson led him into the back garden, through the french windows and directly into his study. The house was old, built Handford guessed in the 1800s when Methodism was at its height, but the large study into which they walked was unexpectedly modern. Cupboards, drawers and bookcases were finished in a medium oak and fitted along two walls, and at the other end of the room facing the French windows was a large desk to the side of which was a workstation for the computer, screen and printer. Wooden crucifixes hung on each wall. At least one could be seen whichever way you faced – a sign perhaps that since he'd found God late, he was making up for lost time.

The minister seated himself on the tall leather chair behind the desk. He offered Handford a smaller, but equally comfortable one opposite.

'An impressive study, Mr Iveson and an equally impressive computer system,' Handford remarked as he sat down.

'I like them, although you wouldn't believe the fight I had to get them approved. Some of the Methodists in the city are very much the traditionalist; they didn't feel my ideas were in keeping with the rest of the house and if they had their way I'd still be using pen and paper to compose my sermons. They gave in eventually.' The old woman in him receded. 'I can be very persuasive if I have to be.' Then he smiled and the old woman was back. 'But I don't suppose you're here to discuss my taste in décor. Although I'm not sure how I can be of help.'

'I'm trying to fill in Mrs Ingleby as a person, because to be honest, sir, I'm having as much difficulty as you in understanding why anyone would want to kill her. As far as I can see no one has a bad word to say about her, yet whoever pulled the trigger had his reasons. I need something, however small, to help me find those reasons. Tell me, how long have you known her?'

'Three years, give or take. I became minister here shortly after she and her husband moved to their present house.'

'Describe her to me.'

'What can I say? She was a good wife and mother and a deeply committed Christian who lived, as well as practised her faith. I relied on her a lot. I'm not married and my sister helps when she can; but when she was off on one of her many jaunts, I called on Dianne. She didn't mind – in fact I think she quite enjoyed it. She had a caring nature – probably cared more about other people than she did about herself, particularly the victims of crime she supported. She was passionate in her belief that they were low down in the hierarchy of the law and even lower when it came to justice. In her own way she wanted to redress the balance – show them there was someone out there who cared. She worried about them. Sometimes I felt she tended to become too emotionally involved. Not always a good idea if you're dealing with the vulnerable. I used to tell her not to take them home – metaphorically speaking of course.' He seemed to have slipped easily into the past tense. Perhaps that was something to do with the mindset of a minister of religion. Death as a natural consequence of life.

'Did she talk about her family at all?'

Iveson contemplated before answering. 'Her husband and daughter didn't share her faith and I think that saddened her. I never once saw them in chapel, not even at Christmas.' His grey eyes made a quick circuit of the room and came to rest on his desk. 'There were rumours . . .' He stopped.

Handford urged him to continue.

'I wouldn't like you to think I was adding to them, because that's all they were – rumours – but in the circumstances . . .' He took a deep breath. 'The gossip was that Maurice Ingleby had a string of affairs.'

'Do you think she knew?'

'I'm sure she did, but she was far too loyal to say anything openly – not even to me.' He steepled his hands, resting his fore-fingers on the tip of his nose. Eventually he said, 'She'd seemed particularly worried over the past week.'

'Why?'

'I thought he must be indulging in another liaison.'

'Or there was a problem with a victim she was supporting.' It was a statement rather than a question.

Iveson slipped his hands down to clasp them on the desk in front of him. 'I wouldn't know about that, Inspector.'

'Oh, I think you would, sir.'

The minister gripped his hands tighter and his voice hardened. 'I can't imagine why you would say that. Her work was confidential. She never discussed clients with me.'

'Not even Kathie?'

For the first time the greyness disappeared as blood flushed upwards from Iveson's neck into his cheeks. At first Handford thought he was going to deny any knowledge of the girl, but then he said, 'How do you know about Kathie? What has Dianne told you?'

'You seem concerned, Mr Iveson.'

'Only because her conversations with her clients were supposed to be in confidence and because I know for a fact that Kathie had insisted to Dianne that she didn't want any police involvement.'

The atmosphere had thickened. Handford attempted to lighten it. 'Don't worry, Mr Iveson, Kathie has only come to my notice today.'

'How?'

Handford remained silent.

'Not from Dianne obviously, but someone must have told you.' When the detective still made no reply Iveson asked, 'Have you talked to Kathie?'

'Not yet.'

Iveson settled back in his chair, his mild nature reappearing. The act was so well-rehearsed he could switch it on and off as required.

But it was an act Handford wasn't prepared to rise to. He leaned forward. 'I'm concerned that Mrs Ingleby's death might have something to do with Kathie, that the attack on her is somehow linked to what happened in the multi-storey car park last night. If I'm wrong, then I need to know so that I can take her out of the investigation. If I'm right, I need evidence. Either way I have to talk to her, but at the moment I have no idea who she is or where she is, and no one will tell me.'

As Michael Iveson smiled at him, Handford knew his words had been wasted; the metaphorical knife was about to stab him in the back. 'We're all shocked by Dianne's murder, Inspector. But you have to accept that while we're coming to terms with it we can't forget the wishes of the living.' The sycophantic tone became more forceful. 'Kathie doesn't want police involvement; she has said that over and over again. So if you've come here to persuade me to tell you who she is and where she is, then I'm afraid you've come to the wrong person.'

The evening briefing was short and equally as unproductive, it seemed to Handford, as his day had been. No Citroëns had been reported lost or stolen, and officers were still trawling garages for any brought in with an oil leak. Uniformed officers had been seconded to check out the owners of all ZX cars registered in the area. So far nothing, and if it continued to prove fruitless, it would mean moving on to similar models and that would take for ever. The number in the city alone ran into the hundreds, and into the thousands in the whole of the Metropolitan District.

'We're putting out a request at the press conference for anyone who may have seen the car. It might bring something in,' Handford said. He turned to Andy Clarke. 'I want you to coordinate the information.'

Clarke nodded.

The results from the multi-storey CCTV and ticket machine were mixed. The suspect vehicle had driven in an hour before the shooting and left a minute or so after, but the pictures from the cameras were so poor that it was impossible to read the number plate or identify the car's make, its colour or the blurred shape of the driver. They had been sent for enhancement, but Handford held out little hope of getting much from them.

The news from ballistics was marginally better, but did not take them far. From the cartridges and the bullet harvested from Dianne Ingleby, the gun was probably a Luger semi-automatic.

'It's unusual,' the man at the other end of the phone said. 'We don't see many Lugers in Bradford, mainly Brownings. It's possible it was rented or bought from a dealer, but I'd bet my pension on it having been smuggled in from Eastern Europe: the Czech Republic, Slovakia, somewhere like that. Those countries are awash with them. You can buy any gun of any calibre in most street markets, no questions asked. It's easy; make your purchase, drive to Calais and through the tunnel, or come back via Eurostar. No baggage searches on the borders and little chance of checks on the train. Honestly, it's a trafficker's paradise.'

Is this what Braddock was doing in Europe? Buying a gun? Or guns? Is that how he was making the money the OR's suspected him of salting away – trafficking illegal firearms? There were plenty in the city, someone had to be dealing them, and the one thing Braddock knew something about was guns.

But gun-running or not – and Handford wasn't prepared to go with it without more evidence – Braddock was fast becoming a major suspect in Dianne Ingleby's murder. What didn't yet put him in prime position was that as far as they could tell his quarrel was with Maurice not his wife. Unless the link was Rebecca, although how she fitted into the wider picture, Handford didn't know. He doubted she had participated in her mother's death but she *was* involved with her father's enemy, either as a bona fide lover or as a pawn in his plan for revenge on Maurice. It was time to talk to her – and seriously.

There were more questions for Ingleby as well. Why, for example, had he given Braddock twenty thousand pounds and then forced him into bankruptcy? If ever a man had a motive to kill it was Braddock, and given his visits to Europe he could well have had the means and possibly even the opportunity if Darren Armitage was the best alibi he could come up with.

'Anything on those men whose wives Ingleby slept with?'

'Four so far, boss,' Warrender said, 'and every one with an alibi. I doubt any one of them would have known where to get a gun, let alone have the guts to use it. I'm not surprised their wives played away. No we're on the wrong track here; Dianne's death has nothing to do with Maurice's affairs, not unless there are more we don't know about.'

Handford turned to Clarke. 'What about Mossman?'

'His Peugeot's clean and his story more or less stands up – he was in a pub celebrating the CO's fortieth with the rest of the Air Training Corps staff. I've interviewed all but two of them. They're agreed he'd ordered a taxi to take him home, but none of them could say for sure that they'd had sight of him the whole evening. I'm seeing the others tonight and then I'll the coordinate

113

statements. To be honest, guv, unless something else crops up, I'll be surprised if he has anything to do with the shooting. He has too much respect for guns and anyway his quarrel, such as it is, is with Maurice not Dianne.'

'Isn't everybody's?'

Handford walked over to the board where the picture of Dianne Ingleby was pinned. He studied her; she was smiling, her eyes shining; even in a photograph he could see she was the kind of person who gave much of herself to others. So why her? And why weren't they moving forward? It wasn't as though there weren't clear lines of enquiry; the problem was none of them led to the victim – except perhaps Kathie, and until he knew who she was and where she was, she could hardly be considered a workable line of enquiry.

'Let's look at those we know whom Dianne was involved,' he said. 'Except for Kathie we do not have the identities of other victims she is or was working with, and Eileen Leighton won't tell us. So who else is there?'

'The minister, Michael Iveson.'

'He was sitting with an old lady at the nursing home who was dying. I checked with the night sister and she corroborated his story. His name was entered in to the visitors' book at eleven o'clock and it was two in the morning when he went downstairs to tell her Mrs Baker had died.'

'And he was there the whole time?'

'It would seem so. Staff popped in from time to time to check on the old lady and one of the care assistants took him some tea round about midnight. There were papers on the bedside table and she asked him if he was working on his sermon. He said it was a good time for him to do it, because in these circumstances he felt very close to God. When the night sister went in to check on the old lady, he was sitting close to the bed reading the Bible. He didn't have the opportunity and he has no more a motive to kill Dianne than Eileen Leighton or anyone else she worked with.'

Handford moved away from the board to perch on the edge of the table. 'We come back to the same question don't we?' he said. 'Why Dianne? In spite of all the interviews we've carried out with her friends and colleagues, we haven't been able to find one motive for her murder, plenty for an attempt on Maurice, but he's not the one in the mortuary. Did he mean to kill her or Maurice? Like it or not, we have to come to some conclusion as to who the intended victim was, and soon, if we're not to waste time and resources going in the wrong direction.' He paused while he made up his mind as to what to do. Finally he said, 'I'll give us the weekend before we decide where our priorities have to lie.' Forty-eight hours would be time enough for Ali to speak to the three suspected of sending out the death-threat letters, give Warrender time to check out Ray Braddock in more depth, and allow him to get a warrant to force Eileen Leighton to open up her books on Dianne, Kathie and Emma.

'Right, you all know what you have to do, so let's come up with something by Monday. Anything else?'

'Yes, boss,' Warrender said, 'I checked on Ray Braddock's nephew, Darren Armitage. He is known to us. He associates with Gary Marshall – a real toe-rag if ever there was one; mugged a seventy-year-old lady for her pension a couple of weeks ago. According to my informant, an Asian girl has been seen with the two of them recently. Apparently Marshall is smitten with her. I've only got a first name, and I can't say it's one I've come across before. I don't know if anyone else has.' He looked round. 'Chanda?'

A 'no,' rippled round the room.

Handford turned to Ali: 'Does it mean anything to you?'

'Sorry, guv, never heard of her.'

'Parvez?'

For a moment Miah said nothing. Then he shook his head, 'No sir.'

Handford sighed. He didn't like unnecessary false trails, but since Darren Armitage led back to Ray Braddock, he couldn't afford not to question them.

'You say Marshall has been involved in a mugging; has he been charged do you know?'

'It's with the CPS, boss.'

'Have a word with them; find out who's working on the case. As for the girl, I shouldn't imagine for one minute she's involved,' he said, 'but we'd better check her out. You can do that Miah. Have a scout around; see if you can find out who she is.'

Following the press conference Khalid Ali drove up to the

community centre on the Keighley council estate. He was early and Patrick Ambler's election meeting was still in progress so he sat in his car and chewed on a chocolate bar as he waited for it to end. Chocolate was meant to be a comfort food but it did nothing for him except quell his hunger pangs. A cigarette would have been better. He wasn't a habitual smoker, but when he felt the need of an emotional crutch out they came. And there was no doubt that that was what he needed now. He wished he could be as positive as Amina, but he couldn't. His fears were turning into nightmares – literally. 'The same every night – cancer spreading through her body like a supernatural entity; like an amoebic cell, it wormed its way into her organs, taking over every part of her. He would have preferred to take some leave, see her through this, but as she was having none of it, he had to make do with the occasional phone call. He'd rung her before he left the office on the pretext of saying he would be late home but hadn't been able to stop himself from asking how she was.

She'd ignored the question and instead said, 'I'm glad you called, Khalid; I spoke to Gill Handford earlier and she suggested that since we're hardly likely to see either you or John for the next few days and the weather is so good we should take the children to the sea tomorrow. She said it wouldn't do Nicola and Clare any harm to forget exam revision for a day, and Hasan and Bushra would love it. What do you think?'

He agreed. At least Amina would be with someone she could relate to. Perhaps she might open up to Gill Handford. 'I think it's a great idea; you go and if I don't get the chance to see them myself, tell the children to have fun.'

Immersed in his thoughts, he stirred as he heard a tapping noise in his ear. Momentarily disorientated, he looked up. Peter Redmayne mimed to him to let the window down so they could talk. Reluctantly he did as requested. 'Mr Redmayne,' he said, deciding formality was the best form of attack. 'What are you doing so far from home? You don't normally follow election meetings.'

The crime reporter for the local paper smiled. 'I could ask you the same thing, Sergeant Ali. As far as I understand it you're part of the team investigating Dianne Ingleby's murder so what, I ask myself, has a local election meeting twelve miles from the crime scene have to do with that? And to be honest I can't come up with a credible answer.'

'In that case Mr Redmayne I suggest you leave it at that and go home.'

The journalist ignored him. 'Unless of course you consider Patrick Ambler a possible suspect.'

Perhaps John Handford had been right to suggest the candidates' homes would be better places to question them than the hustings. But they hadn't been that easy to track down, for when they weren't at work they were busy electioneering. He'd accepted there might well be reporters covering the meetings, but even Handford couldn't have expected that one of them would be an investigative journalist who was more interested in the car park than the politics.

Redmayne was still talking. 'And if you do consider him a suspect, I have to wonder why.' He searched the detective's eyes. 'What do you know Sergeant Ali that I don't?'

Ali made no reply.

'Come on Khalid,' he coaxed. 'I'll refer to you as a police source; I won't name you.'

'Go home, Mr Redmayne.' The detective pressed the electric button to close the window, but the journalist put his hand over the top. Ali stopped. 'What now?'

Redmayne indicated the passenger seat. 'Can I join you?'

With a sigh Ali stretched over to open the door to allow him to slip in, then waited while he made himself comfortable.

'Tell me – is there a link between Patrick Ambler and Mrs Ingleby's death?'

Ali maintained his silence but Redmayne persisted. 'Or does the link concern the BNP?'

'Why should you think that?'

'I've been checking out Dianne Ingleby and I can't find a single motive for her murder. Now, Maurice Ingleby is a different matter altogether. Enemies in just about every camp I'd say. And among other things I've heard rumours that he has links with the BNP and that Ambler and the other Labour candidates have been more than vocal in their condemnation of him.'

Ali wondered what else he knew. 'So that's why you're here, because of a rumour?'

'No, I came because the BNP are contesting the seat and I thought they might cause trouble.'

'And have they?'

Redmayne pushed his glasses up his nose. 'No, not yet. Pity really; a political meeting makes boring copy, which is why I'm out here instead of in there. However,' he said, stretching the word as though he wanted it to last, 'a political meeting that turns violent is much more interesting. And a political meeting that involves a detective investigating a murder case makes for even more interesting reading.' He waited for a moment and then repeated his question, 'Does the reason why you're here have anything to do with Ingleby's links with the BNP?'

Again Ali made no reply.

'That's a police no comment is it?'

'That's a police "it's nothing to do with you" comment.'

Redmayne smiled and opened the car door. 'Have it your own way, Sergeant, but I think I'll hang around a little while longer anyway, see if we can't turn boring into something more worthy of note.' He sauntered back to his own vehicle, giving Ali a wave. When he reached it, he didn't climb in, but leaned against it, his head turned firmly in Ali's direction.

Ali banged his fists on the steering wheel. Damn the man. The self-satisfied, self-righteous ... He ought to get uniform up here to move him on, and would if he could think of a good enough reason. More to the point was what he should do now. Wait or leave? Ali didn't want to drive away; it would mean he had allowed a journalist to make the decision for him, but not only that, it might give credence to Redmayne's suspicion that Ambler was a suspect and that he wasn't prepared to question him while the reporter was loitering. Ali's anger began to bubble; no way was that going to happen. Peter Redmayne or no Peter Redmayne he would do what he came to do. He broke another piece of chocolate off the bar and pushed it in his mouth.

A few moments later the doors of the hall opened and a crowd of people flooded into the evening sunlight. He was impressed – it was quite a turnout for local elections when fewer than thirty per cent of the country hardly ever bothered to vote. Whether it had to do with the emergence of the BNP in the area or whether Ambler had employed a rent-a-crowd was impossible to say. He glanced towards Redmayne's red Fiesta. He was still leaning against it, obviously not going anywhere.

Ali pulled himself out of his car. He wiped his mouth with his handkerchief as he made for the door. Inside the hall three men were stacking chairs and setting them against the walls. 'Can I help you?' a well-built balding man asked.

Ali showed his warrant card. 'I would appreciate a word with Mr Ambler,' he said.

Ambler was small, round and sweating. He wore the smile most politicians wear when he thinks he is about to discuss issues with a would-be voter. 'I'm Patrick Ambler,' he said. 'What can I do for you?'

Ali introduced himself. 'Is there somewhere more private where we could talk, sir?'

The smile faded. 'It depends on what you want to talk about.'

'It would be better if we could find somewhere less public,' he said quietly.

Ambler stood his ground. 'I'm going nowhere until you tell me what this is about.'

Ali sighed. The man was quite within his rights, but it would be less embarrassing for both of them if he just took him into another room.

'I'm investigating the murder of Dianne Ingleby and would appreciate it if I could ask you a few questions.'

Ambler shrugged but acquiesced. 'I can't think why, but we'll go in here.'

As they moved towards a door leading to a kitchen, the man who'd greeted Ali came up to them. He inclined towards Ambler's ear. 'Call me if you need me,' he said in a stage whisper while maintaining his gaze on the detective.

'I will, George,' Ambler said. Then, 'my agent,' he added by way of explanation as they walked.

The kitchen smelt of stale food which didn't mingle well with the lingering taste of the chocolate Ali had eaten. He closed the door behind them. Ambler leaned against the cupboards. 'I don't know what I can tell you; I hardly knew her.'

'But you do know her husband?'

Patrick Ambler pulled out a chair from the table and sat down. 'Yes.'

'Can you describe your relationship?'

Ambler frowned. 'What has my relationship with Maurice Ingleby to do with his wife's death, Sergeant?'

Ali made no reply, but his silence demanded an answer. Ambler capitulated. 'I can't see the point,' he said, 'but if you insist. I didn't have a relationship with him, which is more than can be said of my wife – or more correctly my soon to be ex-wife. She had quite a relationship with him. It involved beds and sex.'

'When was this?'

'I don't know when it began exactly, but it ended as far as I was concerned a year ago this January. I can give you the precise date if you want – Thursday, January 22nd 2004 at three o'clock in the afternoon when I came home and found them in bed together. I threw him out, followed by her and her clothes. Then I filed for divorce.'

'You're still angry?'

'Of course I'm angry. He stole my wife, broke up my marriage and I lost my kids, not to mention her grabbing about a quarter of my salary. She's too busy being a mother to go out to work she says, so I have to support her and the kids. It'll come as no surprise that he doesn't put his hand in his pocket. Of course I'm angry, bloody angry.'

'Angry enough to threaten him?'

'Ah,' Ambler said as comprehension dawned. 'I know where this is going – we're back to the letters.' He leaned forward. 'I didn't send Maurice Ingleby those threatening letters and you know I didn't.' He emphasised the final four words. 'That case is closed.'

'No case is closed until it's solved, Mr Ambler.'

'And you're going to solve it by linking me to the letters and the letters to the murder of his wife. You really are clutching at straws aren't you? He pushed back his chair and snatched at the door. 'George,' he called. Then he turned back to Ali. 'This is harassment Sergeant Ali and I'm not prepared to stand for it.'

The man who had greeted him appeared, sweating from the exertion of tidying up the hall. 'You've already met George,' Ambler said. 'From now on anything you have to say you say in front of him. Either that or you arrest me and say it in front of my solicitor.'

George Midgley took the chair Ambler had vacated. He crossed his arms and stretched out his legs; he obviously had no intention of moving.

What had the DI said – be discreet? Discretion was rapidly

120

disintegrating and Ali attempted to limit the damage. 'I have no intention of arresting you, Mr Ambler, but we can continue this conversation down at the station if you wish.'

Ambler ignored Ali and gave his agent a summary of the conversation to date.

Midgley listened without interruption and when Ambler had finished he said, 'You know your trouble Detective Sergeant Ali, you're too transparent. You're not looking for the person who killed Dianne Ingleby, you're looking for the person who missed Maurice. Whoever pulled the trigger got the wrong person, didn't he? That's why you suspect Patrick.'

The man was astute and there was little point in refuting his hypothesis. Instead he met George Midgley's stare but waited a moment or two before he answered him. 'We're not sure who the bullet was meant for, Mr Midgley, but you are right Maurice Ingleby could have been the intended victim.'

'So you come here and rake up an old investigation in which Patrick was a suspect, even though there was absolutely no evidence against him. Now you're accusing him of attempting to kill Maurice Ingleby.' This sounded like political spin and Ali felt he was the one being spun.

'I haven't accused Mr Ambler of anything, sir.'

'As good as.'

'No, not as good as, in fact not at all.' He turned to face Patrick Ambler. 'However, since your agent seems to think you might be a suspect, perhaps you could describe your movements for me between nine o'clock and midnight so that we can begin to eliminate you.'

Before Ambler could answer, Midgley said, 'He was with me. It may have escaped your notice but we have an election to win. Thanks to Maurice Ingleby and his tainted money it's harder than it should be. We were out canvassing and then went to my place to discuss strategy for tonight.'

'Can anyone verify this?'

'We talked to plenty of people on the streets and doorsteps, and I'm his alibi from half past nine to midnight. You'll have to take my word for that, Sergeant.' He emphasised Ali's rank.

Enough was enough. He glared at the man and when he finally spoke his words were as cold as he could make them. 'Mr Ambler, I was hoping to go through a few points and leave. Mr Midgley,

121

however, seems intent on hijacking the interview, so, I'm sorry, but I'll have to ask you to come to the station where we can talk more privately. Tomorrow at eleven would suit me.'

'Do I have to?'

'I can't force you; but since you're hoping to represent the people of this ward and you consider yourself a law-abiding citizen, I hope you will not refuse. It wouldn't add to your credibility.'

'It won't add to his credibility either if he's thought to be involved in Dianne Ingleby's murder. Our opponents will have a field day and you'll give the BNP a wide open door.' Midgley stood up. 'I would have thought you of all people would not have wanted them in power.'

Ali stiffened. 'This isn't about politics, Mr Midgley, it's about the death of a woman.'

'Is it? Maurice Ingleby is pouring money into the BNP's coffers and I'm fairly sure some senior police officers are in his pocket as well.' Angrily, he pulled open the door and walked out into the hall. He pointed to the entrance. 'There's a reporter out there, Sergeant Ali; has been all evening. Shall I call him, tell him how you're interfering in the democratic process and at the same time implying that somehow Mr Ambler is implicated in the death of Dianne Ingleby? It should make a good story.' And with the look of a man who had just won the battle and was well on his way to winning the war, he marched over to Peter Redmayne who was still leaning against his car.

Parvez Miah was worried; more worried than he'd been for some time. He'd just blown his chances of staying in CID and by doing that he'd let his father down, himself down and DI Handford down. Whatever had induced him to deny knowing a woman called Chanda? And what did he do now that he was the one given the task of finding her? It wasn't as though she would be difficult to find – Warrender had been right; there weren't that many girls around of that name; his sister-in-law had to be one of only a few. Perhaps he could keep it from the family by having a quiet word with her – but then what? Would she admit to knowing Darren Armitage and Gary Marshall? He doubted it. And if she did should he tell the DI? To do that would put him in a lot of trouble. Mr Handford would want to know why when she was a family member, he'd denied any knowledge of her, and even if his boss accepted that he didn't want the whole team knowing, he had no explanation as to why he hadn't asked to speak to him privately. It was a mess.

What had concerned him from the moment the name had been mooted was that given Chanda's track record, it could well be her. She was never where she should be; she'd had questionable friends when she was at school and was very likely still in touch with them, although he thought – he hoped, he prayed – she wasn't involved in street robbery.

At first he considered discussing the problem with Aisha, asking her advice, but deep down he knew she wouldn't be in any doubt as to what he should do. She would tell him to go back to work and confess to DI Handford that he did know a Chanda and let him visit her, see if she was the person they were looking for. A fright wouldn't do her any harm; indeed it might even do her some good. And anyway it was his duty as a police officer. He remembered his wife's words this morning, so bitterly spoken: *I thought police officers were supposed to uphold the law. If you were any sort of a police officer, you would do just that.* A woman was dead and he was more concerned about his family's honour. What sort of a police officer was that?

He needed advice and there was only one person to give it to him – his father. It wouldn't be easy for he would be angry his son had lied, but at least he would understand why and know what to do.

He'd wanted to get it over with, but his father insisted whatever it was would have to wait until they'd returned from the mosque and dinner was over. Finally, more than a nervous hour and a half later, Iqbal led him into his study and closed the door. As father and son, they were physically very different from each other. Iqbal was small, slim to the point of thinness. Although only in his late fifties, his hair was grey and his face webbed with wrinkles, yet he had an air of strength – almost arrogance – about him. Parvez, on the other hand was taller, rounder and altogether softer. His black hair though neatly shaped had a tendency to curl and even now, as short as it was, it sat on his head in deep waves.

When they were settled, Parvez described exactly what had happened. Iqbal's reaction was mixed. At first he was angry.

'How could you even think that Chanda would be involved

with two white men, particularly those who might be implicated in a murder?'

'I don't,' Parvez assured him. 'Neither does Mr Handford, but the name has come up as being associated with these men, one of whom is the nephew of a serious suspect. If she isn't the Chanda we're looking for then there's no harm done, but if she is he has to talk to her if only to learn what she knows. He gave me the task of tracking her down, father, and I lied to him; I denied any knowledge of her.'

His father's voice softened. 'You safeguarded the family, Parvez. That was your duty.'

'I'm not sure Mr Handford will feel the same.'

'It's not up to Mr Handford to condone or condemn our family loyalties.'

'But he can condemn how I act as a police officer.'

Iqbal flicked the comment aside. 'That's of no importance Parvez.' He pulled himself from his chair and stood by the fireplace, staring into the blackened grate. Eventually he faced Parvez. 'Do *you* think Chanda is the girl he is looking for?'

Parvez wanted to say no, but that wouldn't be true. She'd been a bully at school and now – even though no one in the family would admit it openly – she was bullying Aisha. 'I think she very well might be. You know as well as I do that she's difficult. Marriage and pregnancy have made little difference to her. I don't doubt she's involved with Darren Armitage and Gary Marshall – she may even have known them at school.'

'They're criminals, Parvez. Why would she want to associate with criminals?'

'Because to her they're exciting and she craves excitement. She's hardly ever in the house. She goes out when she's expressly been forbidden to do so. Chanda does as she wants and she gets away with it.' He refrained from adding, 'like she did when she beat up Aisha.' Instead he said, 'The women don't seem able to control her at all.'

'I agree she's picked up the worst features of this country's values.' Iqbal turned towards the fireplace again. When he looked back at Parvez, he seemed to have come to a decision. 'Tell me more about the two young men.'

'They're into petty crime; involved in street robbery and burglary. Gary Marshall mugged a seventy-year-old lady only a week

124

or two ago and stole her pension. He's also ...' he paused as he attempted to find the right words. 'According to DC Warrender Gary Marshall is besotted with Chanda. I worry as to what she will do with him; what they will do together if she continues to spend time with him after the baby is born.'

'Then she cannot be given the opportunity. If she were not so heavily pregnant I would send her to Pakistan tomorrow, but no airline would take her at the moment. Once she's had the baby I will give it to the other women to care for and she will go to our family at home. She *will* learn the ways of Islam; of that I am determined.'

'In the meantime, what do I do?'

'Either you tell Mr Handford that you cannot find any girl of that name or you say there are some, but not of the right age; apart from that you do nothing. You do not mention your brother's wife. Do you understand? I am not prepared to bring shame on our family or hers and I am not prepared for her father to think we cannot look after her. Our honour and our livelihood depend on this.' Iqbal Ahmed shot his son a look that told him he would brook no dissent. 'Do not let me down.'

Parvez closed his eyes. He was caught between two cultures and two authorities: that of his father and that of his senior officer. Neither would understand the dilemma; from their conversation tonight his father wasn't even prepared to. To both him and the police service there was no problem. Obey me. Yet obeying one meant he disobeyed the other. And as far as he could see there was no way out of that.

Leaning forward, his head sinking on to his chest, his elbows resting on his knees, Parvez took a moment to consider his next question. 'Can I tell Aisha?'

His father came to stand behind him and placed his hands on his shoulders. 'This is to remain between you and me alone. You tell no one, not even your wife. Indeed I would say particularly not your wife.'

Parvez digested the silence; he felt sick. His father was asking too much of him. Iqbal returned to his chair. 'You can talk to Chanda if you feel you must, but whatever the outcome, the conversation remains in this house. I will also have a word with her; inform her of my decision. The family will be told that after the baby is born her wish is to return to the roots of Islam. I promise you, Parvez, she *will* adhere to my request even if I have to force her on to the plane myself. And she *will* return here a better person, or she will not return at all.'

chapter nine

At the time Sergeant Ali was remonstrating with Peter Redmayne, Chris Warrender was huddled in his car opposite Ray Braddock's cottage, watching and waiting. Between the briefing and the drive up to Queensbury he had checked into the man's background. It hadn't been a complete waste of time although apart from the bankruptcies and the failure of his business there wasn't much of interest to learn. There was little anyone could tell for few people knew much about him, except what was visible on the surface of his life. He'd been born in the district and had lived in or near the city. When he'd left school he'd joined his father in the building supply business. His mother walked out when Ray was a teenager. She died a couple of years later when she went to the rescue of her dog who had got himself into difficulties in a particularly fast-flowing section of the River Aire. Both her and the dog had drowned. His father coped with losing his wife and bringing up a young boy by drinking heavily, so that when Ray was in his early twenties, Braddock senior died from sclerosis of the liver, leaving his son to cope with heavy debts and a business going under. At first he tried to build it up, but eventually had to admit defeat and declare himself bankrupt. Warrender wasn't sure how he managed to start up again, although it probably had something to do with the twenty thousand Maurice Ingleby had loaned him.

Ray Braddock hadn't married, but he was linked with various women over time most of whom had either money or connections. Currently it was Rebecca Ingleby – and she had both. According to the secretary of the gun club, he had never shown any sign of committing to any one of them, although rumour had it that one young girl had had a baby by him. 'Must be about two now,' he said.

'How often does he come up to the gun club?'

'Not as often as he did unless we have a competition, he doesn't have the money now. Pity because he's just about our best shot.'

'I understand he goes abroad from time to time.'

'Wouldn't know about that, although I can't see it myself – I doubt he could afford to, not even with cheap fares. I've heard he drinks and that must make a hole in his benefit. You can't blame him but if he's not careful he's going to go the same way as his father.'

Perhaps tonight he *was* following in his father's footsteps, for as far as Warrender could tell there was no one at home at Braddock's house – no lights, no movement, nothing. Another half hour, that's all he was prepared to give it and then he was going. Friday night was his night out – the one night he paid the day nurse overtime to stay with his sister who had been left paraplegic after a car crash, while he went for a curry and a few beers with his mates. He'd stay another half an hour – not a minute more.

Bored with the wait, he was about to settle back in the seat when a dark-haired young woman, leading a little boy by his hand stopped outside the house. The girl who'd had his child? Perhaps so. Warrender let his window down.

She banged on the door and shouted at the top of her voice.

'Come on Ray, I know you're in there.'

There must have been a reply for she stood tapping her foot on the ground until the door opened and Braddock appeared, a towel wrapped round his waist, his expression hostile. Either he'd been having a bath or he'd got a woman in there. He stood back to let them both in but it couldn't have been more than ten minutes later when the door opened again and mother and child were pushed roughly on to the pavement. They'd obviously been having some kind of an argument and the young woman had come off worst. The little boy was crying loudly. She picked him up, turned, yelled something which Warrender couldn't quite catch and left. Braddock slammed the door. The detective smiled to himself. He was willing to bet that the argument, whatever it was about, would trigger the need for a drink. Perhaps the evening wouldn't be wasted after all.

On cue a quarter of an hour later, Braddock marched out of the cottage and down the street. He would give him a few minutes

128

then follow him to the pub. Unexpectedly Braddock by-passed the Stag's Head and instead a hundred yards further on turned right into a rough lane between two sets of houses. Warrender climbed out of his car and shivered as the cold air curled round his body. That was the trouble with Queensbury – it had weather all of its very own. In the city, they were on the cusp of summer; up here it felt more like January. Pulling his coat closer to him, he followed, hoping his prey had not disappeared into one of the houses through the back door. The track led on to a patch of ground behind the second group of dwellings. Braddock pulled a key out of his pocket, unlocked the door to one of them and disappeared inside. A few moments later the detective heard the sound of an engine starting up and then saw the car slowly reverse out. Its wheels on the turn, it stopped; Braddock pulled himself out, walked over to the door, dragged it closed, locked it and pocketed the key. Interesting. As far as Warrender knew Braddock didn't possess a vehicle. His back-yard had been taken as part of his debt.

By the time the car emerged from the lane, Warrender was back in his, had switched on the ignition and was waiting for a return call on the registration. It wasn't long coming and when it did it made the waiting and the lost curry worthwhile. The car was a 2003 silver Volvo estate, registered to Rebecca Ingleby. There was always a way round bankruptcy orders, particularly when you had a rich girlfriend.

So close to Bradford and on direct routes to Halifax and Keighley, the evening traffic was still fairly heavy. Warrender kept a couple of cars behind the Volvo and hoped he wouldn't be stopped at the lights and so lose Braddock. Luck was with him and eventually the man turned down Station Road. Warrender followed him. This was a road that led to nowhere. Queensbury had had its own railway station until the late 1960s when the lines were closed. Now all that was left were various landfill sites and a badly potholed road that did little for a car's suspension.

He followed Braddock as far as he dared. To go much further would have meant being seen. Instead he parked up and walked, keeping himself hidden as much as was possible in the bushes growing along the roadside. Close to the end in a fenced-off piece of land was a detached house. Braddock had parked under the trees and was letting himself in through the front door. First a car no one knew about, now a house. Warrender would have liked to get inside, have a look round, but that would mean knocking on the door and for the time being he had to avoid recognition. The other option would be to wait until Braddock left and force his way in. That was not on the cards either since the DI had insisted this had to done by the book. It was a pity because as far as Warrender was concerned the book did nothing but slow down – if not completely eradicate – the detection of crime.

Although detached, the house was small and appeared uninhabited. Scruffy curtains hung at the windows, the paintwork was peeling and the area around it was unkempt. Warrender wondered who it belonged to. Certainly not Braddock – the ORs would have found it and sold it – probably for a pittance. Rebecca Ingleby? Possibly, he was after all using a car registered to her, why not a house owned by her? Come tomorrow Warrender would make the necessary inquiries. What intrigued him for the moment was what he was doing in a house that appeared unlived in, at the end of a road that was hardly ever used and close to a railway station that had long ago been torn up and landfilled.

Emma flopped on to the settee and picked up her glass of red wine. As she drank, it laced her palate with the bitterness of a cheap plonk, but at least it rid her of the taste of Ray Braddock. The slime-ball. How dare he threaten her with what Kathie had been subjected to? She'd told him, if he thought she was frightened of him he could think again. 'Do to me what you did to Kathie and I *will* go to the police.' As usual he'd denied it, shouted and yelled that he'd had nothing to do with the attack. She didn't believe him – no, that wasn't strictly true; she half-believed him. For whereas he blustered when he denied Jack, he was more definite, more convincing, more sure of himself, when he denied assaulting Kathie. But there was history between him and Kathie, just as there was history between him and her. The difference was that because Kathie hadn't as much to lose, she was less forgiving towards him. More than once she'd threatened revenge by shopping him to the Official Receiver's and more than once he'd threatened to stop her. Perhaps this time he had.

It didn't alter the fact that he'd used both of them – others too probably – but it was Emma who had learned early on that he never took responsibility for his actions. No responsibilities, no ties was his maxim. There was no way he was going to be bound by a child for the rest of his life; he'd rather accuse her of sleeping around and insinuate Jack could be anyone's kid.

'*If you think I'm paying for him, you've got another think coming – you slag.*' The words had accompanied her to work. She knew, and he knew, even if he wouldn't admit it, whose son Jack was and as far as she was concerned there was one sure-fire way of proving it. A DNA test. After this morning she'd determined there would be no more messing around, no more prevaricating, and on her way home, she'd jumped off the bus, knocked on his door and with her heart beating hard in her chest, had demanded one. He'd been livid, called her every name he could think of and a few more besides. She'd countered with the threat of taking him to the CSA. They would get a court order to force him. It was at that point he'd grabbed her by her hair and thrown her and her son out. She'd yelled back at him that she would get his DNA one way or another, whether he liked it or not. And she would too – even if it meant sleeping with him again.

She leaned her head against the back of the settee and closed her eyes. Between him and Kathie, she'd just about had enough for one day. A quiet night in front of the television with the bottle of wine, however cheap, was what she needed.

She got up, switched on the TV and flicked through the channels. Nothing – at least nothing she wanted to watch. She could pop out and get a video or a DVD but she reckoned she'd fall asleep halfway through it. Perhaps a bath and an early night would be better. Jack was staying with her mother, the choice was hers. Except she was too tired to make it.

Earlier she'd visited Kathie. She had looked dreadful; it wasn't just the injuries, for they were beginning to fade, it was the look in her eyes. The fear that Dianne Ingleby had slowly managed to dispel was back. Except for the Victim Support coordinator, she'd refused to see anyone apart from Emma. In fact she'd told Mrs Leighton she didn't want any more help now that Dianne was gone. Even when the Reverend Iveson had come to the ward he'd been asked to leave.

Initially, they'd made small talk, hardly mentioned the events of the previous night until Kathie asked if Emma thought Dianne's murder was her fault.

Emma was aghast. 'Don't be ridiculous, Kathie. How can it possibly be your fault?'

'Because she was helping me.'

'You and several others, I would think. Why would anyone want to kill her because she was supporting you?' Emma had wanted to say Kathie was becoming paranoid, but that would have been cruel, so instead she'd held her hands and made light of the suggestion, giving her as many reasons as she could think of why she must put the thought right out of her head.

But now, as unthinkable as it was, she wasn't sure – not that Kathie was the direct cause, but that she might, conceivably, be the indirect cause, although she had no idea how. Kathie had not been herself for two or three years now. At first she had been edgy, jumping every time someone knocked on the door, then the edginess had turned to anxiety and eventually to fear. Each time Emma had asked her what was wrong she'd laughed it off, said she was imagining it, but she wasn't imagining the heightened security, the spyholes and the insistence on keeping the door permanently locked. Nor had she imagined the result of the assault on her friend and the mess the attacker had made of the house. Even though they were best friends and had been since they were at university, there was so much in Kathie's life that was hidden. Why had Kathie asked her to go back to the house, take the envelope marked 'Personal' from the chest in the loft and keep it safe? Why had she been so relieved when Emma told her she had it in her possession? Whatever was behind it, Emma was absolutely sure it contained more than birth certificates and insurance policies, and that whatever was in it underscored her friend's fears.

Emma swallowed the last of the wine in the glass and poured herself another. One thing she was sure of above everything else was that there was a lot she didn't know about Kathie. In fact all she did know when she thought about it was that her parents were dead and Jason was her brother – a brother she was fairly sure she hadn't contacted. According to Kathie the hospital had rung him, according to the hospital Dianne Ingleby had done so, and according to Dianne Ingleby, who had spoken to the ward sister, Emma had been the one to ring him. For whatever reason Kathie wanted him kept out of it, but what that reason was she had no idea. He was her brother; she had no one else; they had been very close before he went to work abroad – surely she would want him with her and for his part he would want to be with her?

Emma pushed herself off the settee and walked over to the cupboard built into the alcove next to the fireplace. When she had been asked by Kathie to bring the envelope and a few other things from the house, Emma had included an address book. The envelope she had hidden, but the book she had put in the cupboard. She flicked through it. As far as she knew Jason was in Brussels working for the European Commission. There must be a telephone number for him. She flicked through to 'J' and there it was – a landline and a mobile number. Should she? Dare she? What would be Kathie's reaction if she did?

She had to.

She picked up the phone and dialled. Now that Dianne Ingleby was dead and Kathie had refused to confide in anyone else, Emma didn't feel she had a choice. Someone had to save Kathie from herself.

Handford arrived home late to find Gill in the kitchen preparing a pile of sandwiches.

'You've got enough there for an army,' he said. 'Are you planning a trip?'

'Didn't Khalid tell you? I rang Amina today and we're going to have a day out. I thought perhaps Scarborough. Bushra and Hasan will love the beach and the sea, and our two will be all the fresher for a day off from revision.'

'Sounds good.' He felt almost jealous. 'You could do with a rest; you're working too hard at the moment.'

Gill smiled at him. 'That coming from a man who left home at two in the morning and has arrived back at – what time is it? Nine thirty.' She gave him a friendly push. 'Go into the lounge, pour yourself a whisky and I'll bring you in a plate of sandwiches.'

He slipped his arms round her waist and kissed her through her hair. 'What would I do without you?' he said.

'I can't begin to imagine. Now do as you're told. And don't fall asleep until you've eaten something.'

Handford wandered into the lounge. He loved this room. In

winter the heavy velour curtains and the warmth from the fire shut out the cold, and in summer the sun streamed through the windows casting a welcoming glow. It was this room that had sold them the house when they first looked round. It wouldn't have mattered whether it had been summer or winter, they would have fallen in love with it.' He poured a whisky and settled himself on the settee. Brighouse, one of their two cats, was sitting on the windowsill looking out into the garden. He turned his head slowly, then without warning, leaped across the divide to land next to Handford who held his drink up high to avoid spilling it. Assuming this was an offer of a comfortable seat the cat curled up on his knee and purred loudly.

As he stroked him, Handford wished he could do the same as Gill and the others and take a day off for no other reason than the weather was good and the felt like it. That kind of spur-of-the-moment trip out was a thing of the past as far as he was concerned. He couldn't remember the last time he'd said to hell with it and gone off for the day. Perhaps if he wasn't accepted by HMET and he missed out on Russell's offer, he might be able to; he could become a nine-to-five DI. The trouble was that as good as it sounded, he didn't want to be.

He lifted the cat from his knee and stood up to pour himself another drink as he considered the implications of whatever decision he made. If, as Russell intimated, the post of DCI at Central was his, at least he would get the promotion he wanted – and God knows he could do with the extra money with two daughters looking towards university in the not-too-distant future. It was tempting to play safe, but he couldn't help feeling that if he showed interest the senior officers would think he wasn't as committed to HMET as he ought to be. But if he didn't, then Russell was right, he could lose both and remain a DI for the rest of his career.

He sat down and picked up the cat again. 'What would you do in my place, Brighouse?' he asked. Brighouse refrained from comment, but rested his head on his paws and closed his eyes. He opened one a few moments later when Gill came in to the room with a plate of sandwiches. She urged the cat off Handford's knee and pulled the coffee table closer to him, then made herself comfortable in the corner of the settee, curling her feet under her.

'You look worried, John. Is the case not going well?'

134

Handford met his wife's gaze. 'Not very, no. We have a victim who to all intents and purposes shouldn't have been the victim with a husband who should. So we don't know whether the gunman meant to shoot at her and found his target or at her husband and missed.' He picked up a sandwich. 'Then we have two suspects, both of whom have a motive to kill Maurice Ingleby, but are expert shots and would be unlikely to have hit the wrong person. Then,' he pulled Dianne Ingleby's notebook from his pocket. 'We have this. It's a diary Dianne kept about a young girl she was supporting following a vicious attack. I have a gut feeling it has something to do with the murder, but no one else does, including the DCI, and this case is complicated enough without wasting time on a wild goose chase. Mrs Ingleby was worried about Kathie – that's the only name I have – or why else would she have written her fears down. In spite of that and in spite of the fact that what happened to her may be connected with the murder, Eileen Leighton the Victim Support coordinator won't tell me who Kathie is or open her books to me. He mimicked her. 'It's confidential, John, you ought to know that.'

Gill smiled. 'It gets in the way a bit doesn't it – confidentiality?'

'You might well mock,' he grinned, 'but that's exactly what it's doing in this case – at least it is as far as I'm concerned.' He became serious. 'One way or another I'm going to have to find her if I'm to count her out of the enquiry. I wish I could do what everyone else thinks I ought to and drop it, but I can't because I have a feeling that the diary and Mrs Ingleby's murder could be linked.'

Gill moved to sit beside him. She picked up a sandwich. 'You've always respected your instincts before and you're hardly ever wrong.'

'I know, but it's the "hardly ever" that worries me.' He drained his glass. 'Russell is refusing to back my application for HMET.'

Gill was aghast. 'Why?'

'No, that's not fair. It's not that he won't back me, rather he's not prepared to actively support me. He's being made up to superintendent when Slater goes next month and wants me as his DCI. What he said was he would have no compunction in making his views clear to the senior officers in HMET and that if he couldn't persuade me to apply for the position he's offering and I'm not accepted into the enquiry team, I'll probably remain an inspector at Central working on petty crime for the rest of my career. At least his way, I'll have my promotion.'

Gill stroked his arm. 'Oh, John, I'm so sorry. What are you going to do?'

'I don't know and at the moment I'm too tired to get it clear in my brain. What I do know is that he'll keep an eye on me in this enquiry and if I put one step wrong he'll make mincemeat of me and in the process get his own way.'

They sat in silence until Gill said, 'Has his appointment been made official?'

'No, it'll be a day or two yet.'

'Then you don't have to do anything for the moment do you? Come on John, think about it. They still have to advertise the DCI post and at best it will be a couple of days before they can do that. Then they'll have to wait a fortnight for applications, so if you're going to apply you don't have to do so until the last minute and by that time you'll more than likely know one way or another about HMET.'

Handford closed his eyes. There were times when he was so stupid. Why hadn't he seen this morning's meeting for what it was: Russell's attempt to provoke him into agreeing? 'Of course you're right. What's the matter with me?'

Gill sighed. 'Nothing's the matter except that you were called out at two o'clock this morning and you've been working without a break all day. And like it or not you can't do what you could do when you were in your twenties.'

He leaned over and grabbed her. 'Are you sure about that,' he said.

She gave him a push. 'Just finish your sandwiches and go to bed.'

He smiled. 'It's under protest,' he said. 'But I'm going.'

He pulled himself off the settee. As he was nearing the door, Gill said, 'John, you're a good detective. If he believes in you otherwise Russell wouldn't be so keen to keep you. If he believes in you, the least you can do is believe in yourself. If you think Kathie is somehow involved in Dianne Ingleby's murder, then stick with it whatever the DCI says.'

*

The dialling tone on Jason Lake's landline was different from what she expected and at first she wasn't sure whether the phone was engaged or ringing. She was just about to replace the receiver and try his mobile when it was picked up and a voice said, 'Jason Lake'. She had only met him once or twice, but it was as she remembered it, deep and cultured.

'Jason, it's Emma; Emma Crossley.'

For a second or two there was a silence as though he was working out exactly who Emma Crossley was, then as recognition dawned, he said, 'Emma, how nice to hear from you. How are you?'

She wasn't sure what to say next; it was difficult. 'I'm fine,' she said, answering his question. 'But it's not me I'm ringing about; it's Kathie.' Like all bad news there was no easy way to break it to him, so she outlined as briefly as she could what had happened. She ended with, 'She's not out of hospital yet, but she is improving.'

'What do you mean she's not out of hospital yet? When was she attacked?'

This was not her fault and she tried to keep the guilt from her voice 'At the end of April?'

Again there was a short silence, then, 'Emma, it's nearly the end of May now; why didn't someone tell me? Were you going to wait until she died?' His voice was controlled but Emma could feel the anger underlining his words.

'I'm sorry, Jason; we all thought someone else had been in touch with you. At first she was too ill and then when she was able to talk she told everyone who asked that someone else had rung you. I only found out today that it wasn't true.'

He changed the subject. 'What are the police doing?'

'That's another thing; she was adamant she didn't want them involved.'

'Why on earth not?'

'She wouldn't say.'

The anger which finally escaped him, exploded into Emma's ear and for a long moment there was silence. Eventually he said, 'I'm coming home. Someone has to talk some sense into her. It appears you lot can't do it.' He paused. Then, 'Did she give you any indication as to why she's being so pig-headed?'

'No, she won't talk about it. The only person she's opened up

137

to is Dianne Ingleby, the worker from Victim Support.'

'Then I'll talk to her.'

This was getting worse by the minute. It would be funny if it wasn't so tragic. 'You can't Jason.' She ran her fingers through her hair. 'Oh God, this is awful. Dianne Ingleby's dead. She was shot last night.'

'What?'

'She was coming home from a night out and someone shot her. I don't know any more, except ...'

Jason interrupted her. 'You think this has something to do with Kathie?'

He was perceptive. 'No ... yes ... I don't know. All I can tell you is that Kathie is frightened but won't open up to anyone. I'm fairly sure though she knows exactly who it was who attacked her and I think she was close to giving Dianne Ingleby his name, but I can't believe that Mrs Ingleby was murdered because of that. Her work was confidential and she wouldn't have passed on anything Kathie didn't want her to pass on, so how would he know? And anyway, things like that don't happen ...' Her voice trailed off.

'Don't be so naïve, Emma, of course they do. It's a way of silencing people, just like attacking them is.'

Emma frowned. 'You think she might have been attacked to keep her quiet and Dianne Ingleby shot to stop her passing on whatever it was Kathie knew?'

He brushed it off. 'I don't know; probably not. Like you said, things like that don't happen. You say you think she might know who attacked her; you're her friend, do you have any idea who it was?'

Emma closed her eyes. She ought to say, 'Yes it could be Ray Braddock,' but the words wouldn't come. Instead she said, 'No.'

His voice softened. 'Look, I'm sorry if I seemed to blame you earlier for not telling me; I know it's not your fault. I've one or two things to sort out here; I need to let my boss know what's happened and he'll get me on a flight out tomorrow. It might not be commercial but there's not much point in working for the European Commission if you can't get back home in an emergency. Give me your landline and mobile numbers and I'll ring you as soon as I arrive. I'll see you as soon as I can after that. Oh,

138

and it's better you don't tell Kathie I'm coming; the mood she's in she'll probably do something stupid like discharging herself and disappearing.'

Refreshed after an uninterrupted night's sleep, John Handford was at his desk early. A major enquiry generated an excessive amount of paperwork and he wanted to make inroads into it without interruption. But more importantly he needed to read the rest of Dianne Ingleby's record of her meetings with Kathie. If he was to ask for a warrant to open up the Victim Support books, he needed all the ammunition he could get and the only ammunition he had was in this A5 hard-backed notebook. He took it from his briefcase and opened it at the last page he had read.

May 13th

When I arrived at the High Dependency Unit I found Kathie had been moved to Ward Eleven. This is one of the old Nightingale-type wards, with beds along each wall and no bays. It could make things difficult to talk since there won't be much in the way of privacy. Kathie was sitting in the chair beside her bed looking at the photographs of her family; It's good to see her up and about. She's still pale, but closer to recovery – physically at least. I'm not so sure about emotionally and mentally; I wish she'd tell me exactly what is wrong; I might be able to help her then.

We talked about Emma today. She has been her friend since university and Kathie doesn't know how she would have managed without her over the past couple of weeks. At one point she asked me if I knew Ray Braddock. I said I did but not very well. According to Emma her little boy is Braddock's son, although he denies it. From what I know about him that seems to be the kind of thing he would do – never take responsibility for anything; certainly he never felt responsible for his own bankruptcy. He tried to have a relationship with Rebecca a few years ago, but

Maurice soon put a stop to it and he was right to do so. I asked Kathie how well she knew Braddock; she said well enough, then after a pause, 'better than he would like me to'. I asked her what she meant, but she shook her head and was quiet for a moment, then picked up one of the photographs of her parents. I couldn't help noticing she was trembling and I wonder if whatever it was she knew about Ray was important enough for him to attack her.

I took the picture from her and commented on how happy her parents seemed. At first she said nothing, then without warning she told me how they had died. Apparently her father committed suicide. Kathie didn't say how and I didn't ask. The one thing I've learned in this job is that people will tell you when they are ready. Her mother suffered from asthma and had a serious attack when the police informed her of her husband's death. Both Kathie and her brother rushed home to be with her, but by the time they got to the hospital she had died. Both parents dead in so few days and in such tragic circumstances.

Poor girl, life hasn't been good to her of late.

Handford sat back. So Kathie, Jason and two dead parents, one of whom took his own life. Why? She was also linked with Ray Braddock and not just through Emma otherwise she would have explained. And Ray Braddock was linked to the Ingleby's. Could it be that Maurice had paid him the twenty thousand pounds to keep him away from Rebecca? If he had, it clearly hadn't worked. But that still didn't explain why he might have killed Dianne. Unless … unless, she'd been aware of the relationship her daughter still had with him and had threatened to tell her husband. Losing the chance of owning the Ingleby firm would be a powerful motive for killing the two of them. It would make sense of both her death and of the stray bullets, probably meant for Maurice. He read on.

May 14th
We talked about Kathie's parents again today. She asked me as she always does when she is about to tell me something important to her if our conversations really are confidential and I assured her they are. Nevertheless she made me promise I would not pass on what she was going to tell me to anyone. I promised. I got the

impression that whatever it was it would be a relief for her to talk about it. It took her a while to find the words, but once she did I felt for her. Her father was in prison when he killed himself. He had been accused of fraudulently setting up a bank account into which he transferred funds electronically from clients' accounts.

Only small amounts and from those who probably would never notice it had gone until it was too late. By then the money had been transferred to a holding account and withdrawn. It was the manager, James Gould (she spat his name at me), who first suspected him. He was the only member of staff who understood the system well enough to do it, he said. He passed his suspicions on to the bank's investigative branch but by that time the money her father was alleged to have stolen had disappeared and the account closed. This kind of investigation by the banks was in its infancy and a lot of evidence had been lost by the time they passed it on to the police. It didn't make any difference because they charged her father anyway. In court the prosecution maintained the money was for the vessel her father was keen to buy when he retired. The jury were blinded with computer science then shown leaflets of yachts for sale found in his possession, yachts, it was claimed, he would never have been able to afford out of his savings, his lump sum and the sale of his house. The defence argued they were no more than a dream and that what he intended to buy he could have afforded. The jury believed the prosecution.

By the time Kathie finished her story tears were rolling down her cheeks and although I suggested she took a break, she refused. She had to make me understand her father was innocent; he would never do anything like that; he had been set up, but set up so well that he was found guilty and given a five-year prison sentence. He tried but he wasn't tough enough to take prison life and one night was found hanging in his cell. There was a note saying how sorry he was and the authorities took that to mean sorry for his crime. But he didn't mean that, Kathie said. He was sorry for not being able to cope in prison and for leaving them behind.

By now Kathie was distressed and exhausted and it was time to stop. As I was leaving the sister called me into her office. Michael Iveson was with her and when she said she wondered if my visits were doing Kathie more harm than good, he agreed *with her. He said he knew how caring I was and how committed to my work with Victim Support, but perhaps in this case I ought not to visit him for a while. I told him, Kathie was distressed because she had been talking about the deaths of her parents and not because of anything I had said. In fact I had listened rather than talked. Then before he could ask questions, I explained that I couldn't discuss it with him because she'd insisted on complete confidentiality. He understood, bless him, and didn't press me. That's one of the things I like about Michael; he might be an old woman at times, but he understands. He accepts that, a bit like my clients, you tell him things when you are ready and not before. Perhaps one day Kathie might confide in him, he said. I think it's unlikely but said nothing. Instead, I asked him if he knew anything about Ray Braddock. He didn't, except that he had attempted to visit Kathie once while she was in the High Dependency Unit but that she'd said she didn't want to see him and he had been asked not to come again.*

As Handford read he made notes. The obvious person to ask about both Emma's and Kathie's identities was Ray Braddock. He doubted anyway that what he had so far would be enough to persuade a magistrate to allow him a warrant. His information was still, as Eileen Leighton had put it, made up of several vague might-be's. What he needed was someone else to read the diary so that he could judge their reaction. Andy Clarke was the obvious choice if only because he hadn't argued that the murder was more likely the work of someone who wanted Maurice Ingleby dead. That was one thing he admired about Andy; he kept an open mind until it was necessary to close it and, just as important, he accepted the need for discretion. Handford gave a deep sigh; he didn't like it, but for the moment that was how it had to be. Working like this was alien to him. Even when he was the only person to believe in something, he had never before had to work underground; he'd always been able to argue his corner openly. Thanks to Russell and his desire to have him as his DCI, the man was watching every move he made; if he could trip him up with some misdemeanour that could be used to hurt his chances of being accepted into HMET, he would.

He flicked through the rest of the book. Three more entries, ending the day before Dianne's murder. He glanced at his watch.

Eight o'clock. Except for the DCI, it was unlikely anyone else would be in the office before nine – particularly as this was the weekend. Weekend working, although it had its advantages in the form of overtime, was not popular with detectives or their families. He stood up and stretched. The sun was already streaming through the window, casting rays of light over the desk and on to the floor. He thought of Gill and Amina preparing for their day out and wished he could be with them – weekend working was not that popular with him either, even more so since, as an inspector, he didn't have the bonus of overtime pay.

He wandered into the incident room. It was deserted except for Parvez Miah.

'You're early Parvez,' he said smiling at him. Trainees were always keen.

'I thought I'd get on with my reports, sir.'

Handford lifted the kettle and shook it, then switched it on. Had he wanted to see him, he would have knocked on the DCI's door; he was always good for a coffee – well almost always. Ever since his arrival at Central, Russell had prepared coffee in his office from beans freshly ground and percolated each morning. It was one of his idiosyncrasies and it was a good way of finding out if you were in favour. An offer of coffee meant yes, no offer meant trouble.

'Do you want one?'

'No thank you, sir.'

Handford spooned the instant into a mug, and poured the boiling water over it. He took a half-empty carton of milk from the fridge, sniffed it, decided it was fresh enough and poured some into his drink. He was about to leave when he remembered. 'Anything on Chanda?'

'No sir, not yet.' Miah appeared embarrassed.

Handford was sympathetic. 'Don't worry about it, she's probably not important. Let me know when you have.'

In his office, Handford rested back in his chair with his feet on the bottom drawer of his desk and picked up the diary.

May 17th
I didn't visit Kathie over the weekend and was relieved to find that today, far from being upset, she was in a more positive frame of mind. For the first time since I had met her, she smiled

144

when I walked in. We chatted generally for a while and then she said, 'I tracked him down.' I asked who, although I had a terrible feeling I knew exactly who she meant. 'The man who set up my father.' She didn't name him. I asked if she was sure. She said she was sure but when I asked her to name him she shook her head. She said, ' My father wasn't allowed an appeal unless we could get new evidence, but now we have a witness, someone who was a junior teller at the time of the investigation and wasn't questioned, presumably because the police assumed he would know nothing. After he learned of my father's death be found me. He has written it all down – everything he knows. I intend to get the case re-opened and there's a reporter who never believed my father was guilty and who is prepared to help. All the information is in the envelope Emma has.' I asked if the man she was talking about was the person who had attacked her, but she didn't answer me, except to insist I keep the information confidential. Again I promised her.

The conversation was surreal; it was the kind crime novels are made of, except that I imagine most publishers would think it too incredible to print. I'm not even sure I believe it. Is she fantasising because she can't accept anything bad of her father as true? I'm not sure. I get the impression that the bank manager, whoever he is, is in Bradford, but I'm not even sure about this. What I am sure of is that someone beat her up because of something she knows. The obscure bank manager or Ray Braddock? My money's on Braddock.

If only she'd tell the police; but she won't and I can't.

Handford sat back. Dianne Ingleby was right; this was what fiction was made of, except he'd been a police officer too long to believe that. Things happened to people that none of them could ever have envisaged. They experienced events or were given information that were way outside their remit as human beings. If Kathie was right, then the chances were that the man, whoever he was, was saving his own skin by threatening her and possibly by killing Dianne Ingleby, the only other person who knew something. He wasn't to know she didn't know everything. Then there was the reporter. Handford knew of only one in the district who would take on something like this and stick with it. Peter Redmayne. He'd get in touch and hope the journalist

145

wasn't bound by Kathie's code of secrecy and refuse to divulge the information. He returned to the diary.

May 18th

We had an emergency at the yard today and I couldn't make it to the hospital. I rang to tell Kathie then once the problem was sorted out I went into the Victim Support offices to talk everything over with Eileen. (So Eileen Leighton did know more than she was telling. They were back to shifting the rock of confidentiality).

Her feeling was that she was paranoid about her father. It wasn't unusual for families not to believe the worst of one of their members, particularly a family as close as Kathie's. The police must have been satisfied that he had defrauded the bank and some of its clients otherwise her father wouldn't have been charged, much less found guilty. I mentioned the new witness. She insisted that what Kathie did with that information was up to her. If and when she decided to pass it on to the police we would support her, but we couldn't force her to do anything she didn't want to do. And if the man who set up her father was the one who attacked her? As far as Eileen was concerned it made no difference and her advice was to continue to do what we were meant to do, to listen and if necessary to advise on personal safety. It is not up to us to decide what is best for any of our clients or to notify the authorities behind their backs. I came away feeling that not only had I spent an hour with a headmistress but also that we are letting Kathie down. I won't – can't – do anything without Kathie's permission, but I will do everything in my power to persuade her to tell me who this man is and then to go to the police.

May 19th

As I arrived at the hospital, Michael Iveson was just leaving. I mentioned that I thought Kathie was almost ready to tell me the name of the man who attacked her. He was delighted and congratulated me on a job well done. He asked if she had made any moves towards informing the police and I had to admit she hadn't, although I would try to persuade her to do so. He said he would keep his fingers crossed for me. We talked for a little while longer about the theatre visit for Rebecca's birthday and as he left he said to enjoy the show.

The doctor was with Kathie when I walked into the ward. He

was pleased with her progress and said he would probably be able to discharge her next week. He asked again if I could find out if there was anyone to look after her when she left hospital; he would prefer she wasn't on her own. I agreed to do my best, although I doubt my best will stretch very far.

After the doctor had gone, Kathie asked if I would draw the curtains round the bed. We had hardly begun talking when there was a commotion on the other side. A man's voice demanded to be allowed to see her. The colour draining from her cheeks suggested she knew exactly who it was. I heard the sister shouting to someone to call security when the man burst through. It was Ray Braddock. Kathie who was sitting on the bed, drew herself into a ball hard against its head. I pushed him backwards and told him she didn't want to see him. He was too strong for me and forced his way through demanding to know what she was telling me. Kathie was crying and at the same time shielding her head with her arms. He yelled at her, 'What are you telling her? You say one word . . .' He lifted his fist, but by now the security men had arrived. They grabbed him and dragged him backwards. The sister came up to the bed and muttered something about it not being fair to the other patients and that whether she liked it or not she was going to move Kathie into a side ward. I managed to dissuade her, insisting Kathie needed people around her.

It was an hour before I could leave her, an hour in which we had taken several paces backwards. Whatever it was Ray Braddock didn't want her to say – and I think it was to tell me the name of her attacker – he had made his point. She hardly uttered a word.

Handford closed the book. Perhaps Eileen Leighton was right, Kathie was paranoid. Reading Dianne Ingleby's record of her support of Kathie you could put that connotation on it. But Dianne clearly didn't think so; she'd heard the words, seen the reactions and then, against all the rules, had written everything down. Kathie knew something about Ray Braddock that he didn't want anyone else to know and she had also tracked down the man she considered to be responsible for her father's suicide – who was probably in the city or why else would she have remained? Finally she had a witness statement of sorts and a local reporter who believed her. Handford was with Dianne Ingleby – Kathie

147

might be vulnerable, she might be frightened, but she was no fool. Whatever it was the girl feared was mixed up with what she knew, and what she knew was the reason for the attack. By supporting her, Dianne Ingleby had become unwittingly involved of that Handford was sure, but proving it wasn't going to be easy.

Mentally he went over what they had already. First they had a dead woman who may or may not have been the intended victim, and her husband who may well have been, either because he had made a number of business and personal enemies, or because he was considered to be the money behind the local branch of the BNP, or both. Secondly they had a series of suspects: James Mossman, Ray Braddock and three would-be councillors who were suspected of but never charged with sending death-threat letters to Maurice Ingleby. Handford knew little about the councillors and was waiting for Ali to complete his inquiries and get back to him. What he did know was that the case against the three men wasn't closed and if opened further, it could well cause a political outcry which would be felt across the city. Finally they had the hazy individual of the diary who may or may not have wanted Dianne dead, and who may or may not have assaulted Kathie.

James Mossman seemed the least likely suspect because, although he blamed Maurice for putting his house into negative equity, he had nothing against Dianne, in fact he felt sorry for her. He was also too good a shot to have killed the wrong person. Even so, they couldn't clear him completely until they had spoken to the rest of the people he had been out with that night. Ray Braddock on the other hand was a firm favourite with everyone on the team, albeit for different reasons. He was a sworn enemy of Maurice Ingleby, blaming him for his bankruptcy. The Official Receiver's were suspicious that he was making money which he wasn't declaring to them, and coupled with that he spent time each month in Europe. Suggesting what? That he was being paid cash, no questions asked, for work he was doing, or that someone was keeping him more than solvent, or he was involved in something illegal. Handford didn't know which and wasn't prepared to speculate until Warrender came back with more information. If there was anything, the detective would find it. Ray Braddock was also sleeping with Rebecca Ingleby, which could be a way of getting his own back on her father or could mean something more sinister. Again Handford wasn't prepared to assume anything until he had spoken with Rebecca. Then there was Kathie. Whatever the relationship between her and Braddock, it was causing him no end of problems. *'What are you telling her? You say one word ...'* One word about what? Was he the person who had attacked Kathie and then thinking she had told Dianne about him had killed her? He could have done it. One bullet for her, another for her husband? Why not? Kill both of them and the way would have been clear for him to marry Rebecca and take over the business. Handford had to admit that Ray Braddock was prime suspect for the murder.

The only other person it could be was the man Kathie had tracked down; the man who she alleged had set up her father and as a result driven him to his death. The man who was very likely in the city, safe in the knowledge that no one knew his identity.

Handford sat back and clasped hands behind his head. He couldn't let it go without finding this man and to do that he had to locate Kathie whether she liked it or not. It shouldn't be that difficult – Dianne Ingleby had left him enough clues as to where she was. She had described Ward Eleven as a Nightingale ward, and Handford was fairly sure that had to mean the Royal Infirmary. Dianne wouldn't be supporting anyone as far away as Leeds, Wharfedale or Halifax, and the Keighley hospital was comparatively new. Ray Braddock knew both Emma and Kathie; he had been to visit Kathie in hospital so he knew not only where she was but who she was. If Handford couldn't track her down, then he was not much of a detective.

He was just about to turn his attention to the paperwork when his phone rang. 'Detective Inspector Handford.' He picked it up.

It was Russell. 'My office, now,' was all he said.

Parvez Miah's eyes followed John Handford as he walked out of the incident room. He was still lying to him and in spite of all the reasons given him last night he couldn't rid himself of the guilt he felt. This was a murder case and he ought not to be hiding information. It was unlikely Chanda was involved directly – or even indirectly – with the murder, but she might know something

149

about Ray Braddock's lifestyle through his nephew – she may even know him personally.

His father had left it to him to talk to her and he would – tonight. If she denied knowing Armitage and Marshall then that would be an end to it and there would be no need to say anything to the DI – not even that she was his sister-in-law.

Unless she was lying of course and that didn't bear thinking about.

The fact was he didn't trust her and he didn't want to be forced into believing her lies by the family. He sat back and stared at the computer screen. The words of the report he was writing suddenly transformed into a myriad silent stars sweeping towards him, but at the same time drawing him into the blackness of the screen. He shifted his mouse and the words returned and with them the decision to tackle Chanda, and if she was involved with Darren Armitage and Gary Marshall he would leave it up to his father to deal with her. But this was the last time he would allow family matters to clash with his work.

John Handford made his way to Stephen Russell's office knowing that whatever the reason for the abrasive instruction it did not include a cup of coffee. He was right.

The DCI was behind his desk, and watched as Handford approached it. He didn't waste time with niceties. 'Can you tell me why I should have Peter Redmayne on the phone asking me if I would care to comment on why Patrick Ambler has been questioned regarding Dianne Ingleby's murder and what ...' he emphasised the word, 'I can tell him about Maurice Ingleby's involvement with the BNP and the death-threat letters sent to him?'

The question was almost rhetorical, but not quite, and Handford felt the need to answer it. 'I have no idea sir. I haven't spoken to Redmayne.' He waited a moment before asking, 'What did you say?'

'What you would expect – that I would not discuss an ongoing investigation. He told me that Ambler and his agent were prepared to go public, if only, he said, to clear the man's name. I've had a word with the editor and he has agreed to sit on the story for a while, but I can't prevent Ambler from making use of it politically.' He waited for a moment and then said, 'This

150

should never have been allowed to happen, John.'

Handford would like to have sat down rather than almost standing to attention and feeling he was the one in the dock. 'I asked Sergeant Ali to go back over the file with Keighley police and to take over where they left off. I can't understand how Redmayne has become involved. He's a crime reporter, not a junior who attends political meetings.'

'He was there because he thought the BNP might get involved. He was looking for a story and by God, thanks to you, Ali gave him one. He waited in the car park outside the hall until Ambler ended his meeting then walked in and began to question him about the murder. He was aware Redmayne was around and looking for a story, even spoke to him for goodness' sake. Is the man stupid?'

'I warned him not to confront any of the three at their meetings for the very reason that the press might be there. He ought to have spoken to each man privately.'

'Then obviously your authority is not enough for him.' Russell came round the desk to move in closer to Handford. 'I thought I made it clear that I didn't want you to go back over the letters unless there was a very good reason, and then discreetly. Discreetly does not mean involving the press, John.'

'No, I'm sorry, Stephen. I did make it clear to him that he had to tread carefully.'

'Not clearly enough it seems.' Russell paused to let his words settle then said, 'Perhaps you chose the wrong person for the job.'

The meaning was implicit, but Handford was not about to spell it out. 'No, I don't think so.' He could feel his anger mounting. 'Ali is a good detective; he wouldn't let anything affect his judgement. If Peter Redmayne somehow became involved then it wasn't his fault.'

'You can be sure about that, can you?'

'Yes, I can be sure.'

Russell returned to his desk. He sat down and indicated to Handford to do the same. The aroma of the coffee was becoming overpowering, but there was obviously not to be an offer of a cup. Handford wasn't off the hook yet. 'I did after all spell out the political ramifications if it was realised how and why Maurice Ingleby had been threatened before. It wouldn't take people like

Redmayne long to work out that Dianne was killed by mistake and once it became public the BNP wouldn't be able to prevent themselves from making capital out of it. A wife killed, probably by someone in the Asian community, because of the assumption that her husband was involved with them. They would even suggest we had not investigated it properly in the first place. The fact that we did and that at no time were we looking at anyone in the Asian community would mean nothing to them. It would be a chance to stir up trouble. I would have thought you of all people would understand what that could lead to.'

Handford held on to his temper. Of course he understood. He was the one who had been blamed by his bosses for the night of mayhem a couple of years ago after he had arrested a young Asian boy for the murder of his sister. But this was different; then he was censured for doing his job, this time he could be censured for not doing it. Russell was doing what he was good at – covering his back in case trouble broke out – and at the same time implying that Handford was not a suitable candidate for the depth, judgement and caution needed by officers seconded to HMET. Well for once he was not prepared to play the DCI's game. 'I'm not sure I could avoid the letters, Stephen. If we assume Dianne wasn't the intended victim and her husband was, then we can't pretend they didn't happen. Whatever the motive behind them they need investigating; they did involve threats to kill after all. And to be fair, it was you who first suggested we had the wrong person in the mortuary and then brought the letters to my attention.'

Russell's face clouded over, 'And it was me, Inspector, who told you not to bring up the past until it became absolutely necessary. As far as I can see, unless you were sure that Dianne Ingleby was killed by mistake you had no reason to go there. Are you sure?'

'No, not yet.'

'Then when you are, and only when you are, will the letters have any relevance. Is that clear?'

'Perfectly, although I want it noted that I don't agree with you.'

Russell didn't answer, but instead opened the file in front of him and picked up his fountain pen. The interview was clearly over. As Handford made to leave, Russell fired his last shot. 'I am aware you have a …' he paused, visibly trying to decide on the

152

appropriate words, 'working relationship with Peter Redmayne, Inspector, but don't attempt to get in touch with him or to speak to him if he contacts you. Do you understand?'

He did. Russell was telling him his future depended on it.

He said, 'Yes, sir,' and closed the door as carefully as his temper allowed.

chapter eleven

'I'm sorry, John. He crept up on me. One minute I was waiting in my car, the next he was tapping on the window. I hadn't expected him to be there.'

Handford fixed Ali with a hard stare. This morning the DCI had put his DI firmly in the wrong over this. His future was on the line here and he was damned if he would allow a sergeant who hadn't followed his orders to damage it. 'I told you not to go to the hustings for the very reason that the press would be hanging around.'

Ali attempted to make his excuses. 'The suspects were proving impossible to get hold of, they're too involved in electioneering at the moment, I could have been running around after them for days; the hustings were the best place. The last person I expected to be there was Peter Redmayne. He wasn't covering the meeting. He'd only gone up in case the BNP made trouble; he was looking for a decent story.'

'Well, you certainly gave him one didn't you, Sergeant?' Handford held Ali's gaze for a few seconds.

Ali made no reply. There was nothing much he could say.

Handford slipped off the corner of the desk and returned to his chair. 'I know you're worried about Amina, but that's no excuse for sloppiness.'

Ali stared at him as though he couldn't believe what he was hearing. 'You don't understand ...,' he began.

'Of course I understand, but this is a murder enquiry and I can't carry you. So either take some leave or deal with it. It's up to you. I mean it.'

'I'm not taking leave; not until I know something for sure.' He looked at Handford, his eyes cold. 'I'll deal with it.'

'Make sure you do. I backed you to the hilt with the DCI this morning Ali, so don't you dare let me down again. You do as I say and if for any reason you can't, you let me know.' He emphasised his words with a curt nod. 'Is that firmly understood?'

Ali let his eyes slip from the DI's. 'Yes it is,' he said tightly.

Handford allowed the atmosphere to cool for a few seconds. He didn't like himself very much at this moment, but it couldn't be helped; he couldn't risk Ali messing up again. He turned the conversation back to the investigation. 'Give me the gist of your talk with DS Tooley and with Ambler.'

When Ali had finished, Handford said, 'Where do you suggest we go from here?'

'There are two areas we need to cover: Ambler's statement and the fact that the computers weren't checked.' Ali hesitated, as though he wasn't sure how what he was about to say next would be received. 'When George Midgley became involved he did all the talking, mainly giving Ambler an alibi it will be difficult to disprove. I wasn't getting anywhere, so I invited Mr Ambler down to the station today; he's due in at eleven.'

Handford showed his surprise. 'And he agreed?'

Ali allowed himself a brief smile. 'He didn't disagree.' After a moment he said, 'Do you want me to cancel the interview?'

Handford was cautious. He ought to say yes but would prefer not to. It was a question of the best way to limit the damage as far as the DCI was concerned and at the same time either clear Ambler or put him on the starting grid. Russell had given a direct order that he was to leave the letters alone, but the DCI needing to avoid political fallout was not a good enough reason to do so. They were an issue here that had to be resolved, if only to take them out of the equation. There were too many equations in this case and he had to lose some, but not by hiding them away. Unless he did something about it, secrecy and confidentiality would remain the slogan of the investigation. Somehow he had to turn it round.

'No. Leave it as it is, but first I think we should make inroads into checking the computers. We're not going to be given permission by Ambler and company, particularly with George Midgley involved so let's get a warrant. We'll need Ambler's records as well in case we have to visit his customers.'

'You think we'll get one? Tooley couldn't.'

155

'He was investigating death threats, we're investigating a murder. With the evidence we have, we're unlikely to be refused. If you're not back, I'll make a start on the interview. I was going to sit in anyway ...' As the question 'why?' formed on Ali's lips, he said, 'Leave it, Khalid. I could sideline you altogether – in fact I ought to – but I won't, partly because I don't like the idea of people like Ambler and Midgley winning, and partly because Russell can't hand us the kind of information he has and expect us not to follow it up. But thanks to you we're in a position of damage limitation and if it becomes necessary I want to be there to do it.' He watched the play of emotions in Ali's eyes: disappointment, frustration, anger even, but he had neither the time nor the inclination to psychologically stroke his sergeant. They were all feeling the heat, they had to get on with it. 'Now, is there anything else I ought to know about progress made overnight?'

Ali turned to his notes. 'Not much. We haven't found the Citroën. The whereabouts of all but one in the city has been accounted for, and none of them has or has had an oil leak, nor has any garage been asked to fix one. The last one is the right age and colour and is registered to a Mrs Elizabeth Dutton, a widow in her mid-to-late fifties. She wasn't in when Elliot called on her; apparently she hardly ever is. She moved to the area a few months ago and the neighbours don't seem to know much about her, except that she almost always uses a bicycle to get around and the car stays in the garage. He enquired if anyone had heard it or seen it on Thursday night, but no one seems to have done. It doesn't sound likely that it's the one we're looking for, does it?'

'No it doesn't, but we'd better eliminate it properly. Tell Elliot to keep checking until he has spoken to her. We're probably going to have to go out of the city on this one. Anything else?'

'Yes, we haven't managed to back up James Mossman's alibi. There's definitely a half to a three-quarters of an hour we can't be certain of. He'll have to be questioned again. The time is tight, but he could just about have made it. He would had to have picked up the Citroën, waited, shot her and disappeared, and taken the car back to where it came from, or left it for someone else to pick up and get it out of the area, then returned to the night-club to be ready for his taxi. So unless he and the fifty-something widow are in league with each other ...'

Handford laughed. 'Don't even think it. Can you imagine an

aged Bonny and Clyde? Ask Clarke to go back to him. I doubt he had anything to do with Dianne Ingleby's death but we can't take any chances.' Under normal circumstances he would probably have put him at the bottom of the list and concentrated on the others, but circumstances weren't normal. Even the connection between Braddock, Armitage, Marshall and Chanda had to be checked out. Probably a complete waste of time, but he had to be seen to be covering all angles.

'How's Miah doing?' he asked as Ali made to leave.

'Fine. He's a good worker; gets on with the job, eager to learn.'

'He was in very early this morning – seemed a bit uneasy when I spoke to him.'

Ali allowed himself a smile. 'That's probably because you terrify him.'

'I'm glad I terrify someone,' Handford said with mock severity. 'And for that you can take the briefing, make sure everyone knows what they're doing. Keep them busy, Khalid, I don't want their weekend to be wasted. In the meantime I'm going to pay another visit to Rebecca Ingleby.'

He began to shuffle his papers into a neat pile, but as Ali closed the door, Warrender opened it and popped his head round. 'Have you got a minute, boss?' he said.

With a sigh Handford waved him in. 'How did it go last night?'

'Interestingly.'

'Go on.' Handford indicated for him to sit down.

'To begin with Braddock has use of a car. It's a silver Volvo estate and is stabled in a garage on some land behind a row of houses in the village. I checked it out and it's registered to Rebecca Ingleby.'

Handford tried to keep his expression as neutral as his voice. 'Is it? Now that is interesting. It must be love; an affair with Braddock behind her father's back and now a second car registered to her for his use. Well done.'

Warrender leaned forward. 'It gets better, boss.'

As he caught the twinkle in the detective's eyes, Handford found his excitement building. If secrets were to be unearthed – and there were several lurking beneath the surface of this family – then Chris Warrender was the man to do it.

'I followed Braddock, but he didn't leave the village. Instead he drove down Station Road. It used to lead to the old railway station which was demolished in the late 1960s when the lines were closed; the whole area is a landfill site now. The road leads nowhere, just to a bank of tyres that fence off a field someone uses to practise their horse jumping. He parked towards the bottom end outside the old stationmaster's house. He doesn't appear to be occupied, but Braddock had a key. He let himself in *and* turned on the lights, so someone is paying the electricity bill. It can't be his house because if it was he would surely be living in it; and he's not, he's in a pokey little rented cottage paid for by the DSS. Equally the Official Receiver's can't know about it or they would have seized it.'

'How long was he there?'

'An hour give or take, then he took the car back to its garage and went to the pub where he stayed for a couple of hours. He had a few beers, a game or two of pool, shared some jokes with a couple of regulars, then hung round a young kid who couldn't have been more than fifteen, but looked like twenty-five. Eventually they left together and the last I saw of them they were disappearing into his cottage. I doubt she'd gone there for a cup of cocoa.'

'Did he have any other visitors – Rebecca Ingleby for instance?'

'Yes, there was one, but not her. She was a dark-haired woman in her late twenties with a little boy about two years old. She didn't stay long and it was obvious when she left – or rather was thrown out, quite roughly actually – they'd been having an argument.'

Handford was willing to bet it was Emma. 'You didn't talk to her?'

'No, she caught a city bus and it was shortly after that Braddock picked up the car and drove down Station Road.'

'We need to know who owns that house, Warrender. If it isn't Braddock, then who is it?'

Warrender's eyes twinkled even more. 'Oh, I can tell you that, boss. I had a word with the owner of the corner shop. He knows everything that's going on in the village. I'll check it with the council tax list and land registry in Nottingham just to be sure, but …' He paused for effect.

'Warrender,' Handford warned. 'There were times when he could fill in for a diva.'

'The old stationmaster's house in Queensbury is owned by Rebecca Ingleby. Now that bit of information was worth missing my weekly curry for, don't you think?'

As Handford drove up towards the Ingleby's house and took in its façade he could understand why Dianne Ingleby had fallen in love with it. Constructed in Yorkshire stone and bathed in sunlight, it was tucked away among farmland, fields and woodland where trees were covered in the fresh green leaves of spring. It was open yet private. A place where family secrets remained secret – and this was a family with secrets: Maurice's affairs, his business dealings, his alleged involvement with the BNP; Rebecca's affair with Ray Braddock. And Dianne who kept other people's secrets, hiding them under the guise of confidentiality. Somehow he needed to get beneath them for no matter who the intended victim was, no matter what the reason for the killing, it stemmed from the inhabitants of this house. The sad fact was that, wittingly or unwittingly, victims often contributed to their own deaths.

In their private world the Inglebys had been happy. Maurice and Dianne had been married twenty-seven years – a lifetime for most people; they had a daughter to whom they were close and on whom they doted. Would Maurice continue to dote on her if and when he knew the truth about her and Braddock? Probably – you don't necessarily stop loving your children when they hurt you – particularly your only child. *Rebecca is much closer to Maurice than she is to me. I don't mind; it's natural; fathers and daughters, mothers and sons.* Suddenly Handford wanted to go home – spend time with Nicola and Clare – except of course they had gone off to the sea with Gill and Amina. They were probably having a great time – hardly missing him. They'd had to grow used to him not being around and they had learned how to cope – or at least he hoped they had.

He slowed the car as he approached the journalists and photographers clustered outside the wrought-iron gates chattering and smoking. As soon as they realised who it was, they surrounded him, throwing questions at him all at the same time so that he didn't catch any of them. Peter Redmayne was at the front, bending down to make his voice heard. He gave Handford an inscrutable smile. Of the others, some he recognised some he didn't, which probably meant the nationals were interested. The photographers' cameras flashed, reflecting their light off the windscreen. It seemed such a waste; they must have hundreds of pictures of him in his car. But not at the house of the wealthy business man whose wife had been murdered. He wondered if Redmayne had told them about Ambler. He doubted it – he would want to keep that snippet to himself until the time was right to publish it, and that would depend on the lawyers who would be sifting through his copy with a fine toothcomb.

As the crowd parted, the officer on the gate let him through and he drove up the curved driveway so beloved of Dianne Ingleby. He parked alongside the stretch of lawn. If he was honest he wasn't looking forward to this. It was always at this point, twenty-four to thirty-six hours in, that he began to peel the layers from lives already torn apart. After which he shredded each one into its component parts, unearthing the secrets they had worked so hard to maintain, knowing that in the process he could wreak more havoc than the perpetrator had done.

The family liaison officer, Connie Burns, met him at the door.

'I've warned them you're coming, sir.'

'Good. How are they?' He turned to look out over the fields. It was so quiet and secluded that he couldn't see or hear the journalists and photographers bent on getting their story and their pictures. It was odd how the house and its grounds had taken on the grief of the family. He'd seen it before. Even the grass seemed careworn, its freshness somehow stolen.

'As you would expect,' she said. 'They're still in shock; they don't really believe it. They need some news, something they can cling on to, something that will give them a reason to understand her death.'

'How about she was in the wrong place at the wrong time and the bullet was really meant for her husband?'

Connie Burns's eyes widened. 'Was it?'

Handford sighed. 'I don't know yet, but it's looking likely. I'll have a quick word with Maurice, but it's actually Rebecca I want to talk to. How is she now? She was very angry yesterday.'

'She still is; but it's difficult to know who with – her father for insisting on carrying on with the ritual of the birthday party treat; her mother for agreeing with him, or us for not leaving them alone to grieve. She needs someone to blame but can't settle on who that should be. The actual perpetrator is too hazy for her to fix on. Whatever, it was a rotten day for it to happen; her birthday will never mean the same to either of them again.'

Handford scanned the young woman who was squinting into the sunlight. 'Have you ever thought of becoming a family liaison officer, Connie – you'd make a good one.'

She grinned at him and they turned to climb the steps into the house. 'You know, sir, I might be wrong, but I can't help feeling Rebecca has more than her mother's death on her mind. She was alarmed when she heard you were coming again – panicky even. She covered it by saying you ought to be out catching the murderer instead of pestering the family – but that wasn't it, that was an excuse. She demanded I tell you they didn't want you up here. I think if she could have left the house again, she would have done.'

'She has reason, Connie. I'll fill you in later when I've spoken to her.'

Connie Burns held open the door of the lounge. A heavy silence met him as he entered. An elderly couple were sitting on the settee, Maurice and Rebecca on chairs opposite them. There was a tray on a small table on which were a cafetière and several cups, none used. The family looked up expectantly. Maurice Ingleby pulled himself from his chair and walked towards him. 'How's it going?'

'It's early days sir, but we're following some leads.'

'What leads?'

Handford shook his head. 'I'm sorry, I can't be more specific at this stage. As soon as I can I will, I promise you.'

Ingleby's shoulders dropped. It wasn't the answer he wanted. Like his daughter he needed someone to blame. He turned to the man and the woman on the settee. 'Let me introduce Dianne's parents, Marjorie and Eddie Kilvington.'

Mr Kilvington stood up and shook his hand, but his wife remained where she was. Except for the white hair, Handford was looking at a mirror image of Dianne Ingleby. He stooped to touch her lightly on her arm. 'I'm sorry we have to meet like this,' he said.

Under the tan of a holiday in Spain, her face was pale but she gave him a weak smile. Her eyes had the redness of old age, but also the redness of weeping. 'You don't expect your child to die before you,' she said. 'Will you catch him?'

'I promise you I'll do my very best, Mrs Kilvington.'

'Would you like a coffee, Handford?' Ingleby asked.

He stood upright. 'No thank you, sir. I would like a word with Rebecca though, if you don't mind.'

Maurice Ingleby raised his eyebrows interrogatively and colour flooded into his daughter's cheeks. She pulled nervously at her handkerchief.

'I didn't get the opportunity yesterday, sir. You remember she went home to pick up some clothes and to take her cats into kennels.' Then to allay any further question, he added, 'It's important I talk to you all. Is there anywhere we can go that is more private?'

'You can use my study, although I don't know what she can tell you that I can't.'

Rebecca led him to a door to the immediate right of the lounge. The room they entered was large and as ostentatiously furnished as the rest of the house. It was typical Maurice Ingleby – a large mahogany leather-topped desk, a couple of veneered filing cabinets, a modern computer with a flat screen, two leather three-seater settees, and in one corner a well-stocked bar. He might work in here, but this was his den, his escape route. Handford wondered if his wife had had somewhere she too could escape to. God knows, she needed it. He walked over to the windows that looked out on to the patio and swimming pool – the same vista as the lounge.

As soon as she closed the door, he turned. Rebecca came towards him, a frown bringing a vertical crease to the centre of her forehead. She was as Connie had suggested, nervous, but she came straight to the point. 'Are you going to tell my father about Ray and me?'

He was equally as straight. 'Mr Braddock would like me to.'

'I doubt it,' she said defensively.

'I can assure you, Miss Ingleby he was quite specific about it when I met him. But I'll tell you what I told him – that if your relationship does not impinge on the investigation into your mother's murder, then it has nothing to do with me and there will be no reason for me to say anything. If he wants revenge on your father; he'll have to get it himself and not use me as an ally. So in answer to your question I will not be telling your father – yet. It might be an idea for you to come clean though in case it becomes necessary for me to do so.'

She relaxed visibly and her body language suggested a newly found confidence. 'Are you always so forthright, Inspector?' she asked as she sat down.

He smiled. There was no doubt she was her father's daughter. 'I'm a police officer; it comes with the territory.' He sat opposite her. 'Tell me, how long have you and he been involved?'

She shrugged. 'We've been involved, as you put it, on and off since I was seventeen, but lovers for just over a year, since just after he went into bankruptcy – thanks to my father.'

'You blame your father for that?'

'Of course. All he had to do was to pay him. It would have given him breathing space to find a buyer for the business.' Her voice was cold. 'I love my father, Inspector; but there are times when I don't like what he does.'

'You mean refusing to pay Ray Braddock for what he considered shoddy goods? That seems reasonable to me. And it wasn't only your father, you know, other builders were having the same problem with him.'

'No, but it was my father who finally forced the issue.'

There was little point in pursuing it. She saw more wrong in her father than she did in her lover. 'You told Mr Braddock that we were unsure as to whether your mother was the intended victim.'

'Yes.'

'You shouldn't have done that. You gave him time to consider his answers to any questions I might ask. He has good reason to want him out of the way – not least so that he can marry you and take over the business.'

'He's also a perfect shot; if it had been his intention to kill my father he wouldn't have missed. And he has no reason to want my mother dead.'

'Are you sure?'

'Yes of course I'm sure. I love him, Mr Handford and he loves me. Why would he want to hurt me by killing my parents? Why would he want to hurt me at all?'

Why indeed? Perhaps he ought to tell her about the young kid her boyfriend had picked up in the pub. Not that it was any of his business and not that she'd believe him anyway. He changed the subject. 'Do you know a woman called Kathie?'

'No, I don't.'

'Emma?'

'If you're talking about Emma Crossley, I've never met her, but I know *of* her. She insists Ray is the father of her child.'

'Do you believe her?'

'No I don't. I think she's lying. I think she hasn't the vaguest idea who the boy's father is, but she's blaming Ray because it suits her. He offered her a DNA test, you know and she refused. Now why would she do that?' When Handford made no reply, she sighed as though she couldn't understand why more explanation was necessary. 'He met her once at a night-club. She kept coming on to him, wouldn't leave him alone. You can't blame her; he's a good-looking guy. She says she went home with him and they ended up in bed. The next thing he knew she was insisting he'd made her pregnant. It's rubbish; he was with his nephew ...'

'That would be Darren Armitage?'

'Yes. *He* went home with Ray, not Emma Crossley.'

This was the second time Ray Braddock had used his nephew as his alibi – the second time he'd been on a night out with him when he was in need of an excuse. He would have thought Darren Armitage who hung around with the likes of Gary Marshall would not have been the best companion for a mature man in his thirties. Good for an alibi though it seemed. 'Do you know where Emma Crossley lives?'

'No idea, but it can't be far away because she has been known to drop in on him on her way to and from the Royal where she works, usually to demand that Ray pays towards the upkeep of the boy.' Rebecca stood up and walked over to the window. The sun streamed through, casting a halo round her. She turned to him. 'I'm sorry, but I can't see what Emma Crossley has to do with the death of my mother. I doubt she even knew her.'

Handford wasn't about to enlighten her; instead he said, 'Your father gave you the deposit on your cottage in Denholme and you pay the mortgage?'

'Yes.'

'And you work for your father?'

'Yes.'

'You're an employee, not a partner?'

'No, not yet.'

'How do you feel about that, after all you are a qualified builder?'

She returned to the settee and sat next to him. 'My father controls people; even you must have realised that – he's already attempted to control you.'

Handford smiled.

'While he is the owner and I am a member of the workforce he can control me; once I become a partner he can't. He's not ready for that yet.'

'How much do you earn?'

'He pays me well.'

'Well enough to buy a car for Ray Braddock? Well enough to purchase a house in Queensbury?'

Rebecca looked at him for a long moment her expression a mixture of anger and puzzlement. 'You're checking up on me?' she said.

'This is a murder enquiry, I'm checking up on everyone. Perhaps you could answer my question.'

'No, he doesn't pay me well enough to do either of those things. My aunt died last year and left me some money. I used part of it to buy Ray a car; he needed one and the Official Receiver's had taken his.'

'And the house?'

'It was going cheap; I bought it to rent out as a holiday cottage; this summer if possible. Ray is doing it up for me.'

'You pay him?'

'No I don't, except for the materials; he doesn't want money, just something to do.'

'Miss Ingleby, were you aware that your boyfriend makes frequent trips to Europe?'

The tension in the room thickened. This was news to Rebecca. 'I don't know where you've got that from but there is no way Ray could afford a day in Blackpool, let alone Europe. And even if he could, I can't see what it has to do with my mother's murder or what business it is of yours.' She stood up. 'So if you want to question me about my relationship with my father or about my relationship with my mother, or even about the events on the night she was killed which you already know anyway, that's fine,

165

but I will not answer any more about my relationship with Ray. He did not murder my mother; he wouldn't hurt me like that.' Tears were streaming down her face, but she managed to retain her dignity. 'And now, if you don't mind I'd like to rejoin my family.'

As far as Rebecca Ingleby was concerned the interview was over.

Aisha Parvez would have much preferred to go into the office to work, but she had been tasked with looking after Chanda. The women were out shopping, and Iqbal and his sons were at the mosque. Parvez was at the station; the murder of Dianne Ingleby was taking up everyone's time. At first he'd been excited at the thought of being on a major enquiry, but since last night he'd seemed to have lost his enthusiasm. He'd spent a long time closeted with Iqbal in his study and then had refused to discuss the reason. Whatever it was, it was worrying him. He'd gone off to work early almost before she was awake. She vaguely remembered him kissing her and telling her to go back to sleep.

In the meantime she was trying to work with Chanda's music at full volume. She could tell her to turn it down, but it wasn't worth the argument. She went out in the garden and thumbed in PC Foxton's mobile number. 'Anything on the Asian girl?' she asked when he answered.

'Nothing. If they know they're not telling.'

'Keep at it; we need something or Marshall will walk.' She closed her mobile.

'That Gary Marshall you're talking about?'

Aisha started; she hadn't heard Chanda come up behind her. It was quiet; she'd turned her music off. They walked back into the house together. 'Yes. Do you know him?'

Chanda shrugged. 'What if I do? It's not against the law to know someone.'

'Do you know him well?'

'No, I just know him.' She eased herself into the chair and scraped at the nail varnish on one of her fingers. 'Why?'

Aisha wasn't sure she believed her. She hoped to God, the girl wasn't Chanda, but she answered her question anyway, 'He mugged an old lady.'

Chanda smirked. 'Allegedly.'

Aisha glanced at her. 'Yes, allegedly,' she agreed. This was the problem with Chanda; she wasn't stupid; in fact she was quick-witted and intelligent or perhaps she was just streetwise. 'I'm trying to find witnesses – well one in particular, an Asian girl who was there when the mugging took place.'

'You got a picture of her?'

'No, there was no CCTV by the post office, a witness told us about her.'

Chanda grinned. 'Then you've got nothing, have you?' She struggled out of the chair and made for the door.

'Where are you going?'

'Out. It's doing my 'ead in being here with you.'

Aisha took a step towards her. 'I don't think so, Chanda. Iqbal said you were to remain indoors. He expects you to obey him; I expect you to obey him.'

The girl snatched at the door. 'I expect you to obey him,' she mimicked. 'Who do you think you are, you stuck-up cow?'

Aisha took a step towards her and made to grab her arm. This wasn't how it was meant to be.

Chanda pulled it away. 'Don't you touch me.'

'Chanda you are very near to term; it's not a good idea to go out on your own. What if you go into labour? Think about your baby.'

'I don't care about the bloody baby. I never did. If I could have, I'd have had an abortion. You can have it when it's born, because I won't be around.' She was shaking and crying at the same time, tears running down her cheeks, snot sliding from her nose.

'Chanda …' The girl kicked out at her, catching her on her shin. Aisha stumbled backwards. She tried to regain her balance but Chanda came at her again, this time forcing her to the ground. The punches came hard and fast, worse than the last time she had attacked her. Aisha attempted to cover her head, but as soon as she did Chanda kicked her in the stomach. She stretched her arms out in front of her in an attempt to parry each blow, but Chanda towered above her and there was nothing she could do to stem them. Each one was contributed to someone. 'That's for Gary; that's for Darren; that's for the stupid old cow who wouldn't let go of her bag.' And the last one, straight to the head was for her and no one else. Aisha lay on the floor, the room spinning, every part of her on fire. She tried to turn, to look at the girl who had done this. She'd taken out her mobile phone, was taking pictures, and the tears had turned to laughter. Aisha reached out her arm towards her, pleading for help, but with a leer Chanda lifted her foot and kicked her once again to the head. Her arm slipped down to the ground and she felt the pain subsiding as she drifted into unconsciousness. The last thing she saw was Chanda's face leaning over her and the last words she heard was her sister-in-law's voice screaming into the phone. 'There's blood, Gary; I've killed her, I think I've killed her.'

chapter twelve

Patrick Ambler and George Midgley had been waiting half-an-hour when John Handford walked into the interview room. George Midgley, well-built and balding seemed to fill the room – not unlike Maurice Ingleby in many ways, although Handford doubted he would have been flattered by the comparison. He introduced himself to Ambler, the very opposite of Midgley, small and rounded, with a jaded expression in his eyes. That might have been the stress of the election campaign or because he was in an interview room in a police station; he was probably far more at home in a political meeting. Whatever the reason, he had preferred the company of his election manager to that of a solicitor.

'I'm sorry you've had to wait, Mr Ambler,' Handford said, 'but Sergeant Ali has been held up. So rather than keeping you any longer, we'll make a start.' Without waiting for a reply, he unwrapped the tapes from their covering and pushed them into the machine. 'I will be recording the interview; it's as much for your benefit as it is for ours. When we've finished you will be given one of the tapes, which if it becomes necessary you can hand to your solicitor.'

Before Ambler could speak, George Midgley said, 'I can't see *any* of this is necessary. You are treating him like a criminal.'

Handford took off his jacket, hung it over the back of his chair and smoothed out the creases with quiet deliberation. When he was ready, he looked up. 'You are very welcome to stay, Mr Midgley, but I would ask you not to interrupt or to make any other comment unless you are specifically asked to do so.'

Midgley's face reddened in anger. 'As far as I know this isn't a police state yet. If I wish to exercise my democratic right to speak I shall and there is nothing you can do to stop me.'

Handford gave him a cold smile. 'I think you'll find there is. I shall ask you to leave and if you refuse I shall have you removed – forcibly if necessary. It's up to you.'

Midgley leaned back and crossed his arms. 'We'll see,' he muttered.

Handford sat down and faced Ambler. He switched on the machine. 'This is a taped interview with Mr Patrick Ambler timed at eleven thirty-five hours, Saturday the 22nd of May. Present are Detective Inspector John Handford, Mr Patrick Ambler and Mr George Midgley, Mr Ambler's political agent. Before we begin, Mr Ambler, I must remind you that you are not under arrest and that you are free to leave at any time. I must also caution you that you do not have to say anything. But it may harm your defence if you do not mention when questioned something which you later rely on in court. Anything you do say may be given in evidence. Do you understand?'

Ambler nodded.

'Would you answer for the tape please, sir?'

'Yes I understand.' There was a coating of anger to his voice that most would have missed.

These two men were forces to be reckoned with. Handford was not surprised Ali had fallen foul of them. 'Are you sure you wouldn't like your solicitor present or the duty solicitor?'

'Yes, I'm sure.'

Handford held his gaze. 'If you change your mind, sir, you only have to say and we'll stop the interview until he or she arrives.'

He opened the file in front of him. 'I believe you are currently conducting an election campaign, Mr Ambler?'

'Yes. I'm standing for Keighley West.'

'I imagine it's quite hard work?'

Ambler frowned, obviously at a loss as to where this was going. 'It tends to get frantic, what with meetings and canvassing. I have a day job as well, so most of my political work has to be done in the evening and at the weekends.'

'What is your work?'

'I own an IT business – well it's a shop really. I build and fix computers, give advice, sell toner, paper, that sort of thing, and I visit customers' homes if they have a problem. Most people use computers but don't really understand them; I'm there for them when they need help.'

'Describe for me how you conduct your election campaign.'

'I hold meetings, deliver pamphlets, talk to people, and explain what I stand for and what I will do if I'm elected.'

'Tell me about your movements on Thursday night?'

George Midgley sighed and altered his position. 'We went through this last night. Surely Sergeant Ali has told you.'

Handford allowed his eyes to remain firmly on Ambler, but his words were directed to the agent. 'And I want to go through it again, Mr Midgley. I want to hear it from Mr Ambler. You said last night that you were out canvassing?'

'Yes.'

'Where?'

'Out and about, within the ward.'

Handford frowned. 'Can you be more specific? Where in particular?'

'All over the Guard House Estate.'

'Did you talk to people or push leaflets through letter-boxes?'

'Both. I have to cover as many constituents as possible, so I can't waste time waiting for someone to answer the door. You'd be surprised how many pretend to be out.'

No he wouldn't; he'd done it himself when he didn't want to be disturbed. 'What time did you finish?'

'About eight o'clock, half past maybe. I didn't look at my watch; my feet were telling me I'd had enough so we had a quick drink in a pub and then we went on to George's place to discuss strategy for the meeting last night.'

'Where do you live, Mr Midgley?'

'Arctic Street in Beechcliffe, part of Keighley East.'

Did the man always talk in electioneering terms?

Handford turned back to Ambler. 'So from, let's say, nine o'clock onwards you were with Mr Midgley?'

'Yes.'

'Can anyone verify this? Did anyone call or telephone?'

'No.'

George Midgley broke in. 'Actually yes, we sent out for a pizza. It was delivered round about quarter past ten. I didn't have enough change and Patrick came to the door to help out.'

'Good. If you tell me where you ordered it from I'll get it checked.'

'It was the Pizza Hut in Cavendish Street.'

171

Handford opened the door and asked a passing officer to check the details for him. Five minutes later he came back with the information that they had indeed delivered a large meat-feast pizza together with garlic bread to a Mr Midgley in Arctic Street at ten fifteen. That was that. Even supposing Ambler had eaten his pizza in the car, it would have been difficult for him to be in place to kill Dianne Ingleby at ten forty five. If nothing else Karl Metcalfe would have seen him drive up and park. The only other possibility was that Ambler had tasked someone else with the killing. His known associates, specifically those who hated the BNP, would probably do anything to prevent them from operating, including murder; but for the moment it wouldn't harm him to think he was in the clear.

When Handford gave them the information, Midgley pushed back his chair. 'So now you know he couldn't have killed Dianne Ingleby, can we go?'

'I'm afraid not, Mr Midgley. I said we don't need to proceed any further with this line of enquiry. That doesn't mean I don't have other questions. While it's unlikely that Mr Ambler actually pulled the trigger, there's no proof yet that he wasn't somehow involved. You guessed last night that the bullet may have been meant for Maurice Ingleby, and you also made it quite clear that Mr Ambler hated him and why.'

Midgley's anger was matched by Ambler's. 'So, we're back at those bloody letters again?' he said. 'I told Keighley police, I told Sergeant Ali and I'm telling you, I didn't send them and you have no proof that I did. That case is closed.'

Handford made no reply. He let the silence drag on; there was more to come and someone had to fill it. He was fairly sure it would be Ambler. Silence hurt. The suspect couldn't second-guess his interrogator's thoughts and he would therefore feel the need to justify himself.

'Not that anyone would blame me,' Ambler said finally. 'That man deserves everything he gets. Because of him, I've lost my wife and his tainted money could make sure I lose the election. What do you think will happen to the town if the BNP gain even more seats?'

Handford was not to be drawn. Neither of these men cared that Dianne Ingleby was dead. Like Ray Braddock they cared only about how much hurt could be poured on her husband.

While he was sure neither of them had fired the bullet that had killed her, he was just as sure that one or both had been involved in the death threats. 'Tell me, Mr Ambler, where did you get your information that Mr Ingleby was funding the BNP?'

'He spends a lot of time with Lawrence Burdon, leader of the BNP in this area. Why would Ingleby want to do that unless he's of the same political persuasion? It's not rocket science, is it?'

'No, but neither is it evidence that he's helping to fund the party. Laurence Burdon is a master builder; it's hardly surprising the two would meet at functions or even work together. Circumstantial evidence is not a good enough reason to send Mr Ingleby death-threat letters.'

This time frustration got the better of Midgley. 'You seem to be making use of circumstantial evidence when you accuse Patrick of sending them. Instead of bothering us why don't you check Ingleby's bank balance? You'd find out soon enough then what he's doing with his money.'

'Because I have no reason to. As we have said over and over again, it's not an offence to fund political parties. And like it or not, the BNP is not a criminal gang.'

Midgley snorted. 'That's a matter of opinion.'

'No sir, until they are outlawed by Act of Parliament, it's a matter of fact. I did ask you not to interrupt Mr Midgley, and I think I have been very patient with you. But I'm telling you now that the next time you do so I *will* have you removed.'

He pushed back his chair. 'In that case, Inspector Handford, I will remove myself. You did say Patrick was free to go at any time?'

Before he could answer, there was a knock on the door and Ali walked in. He smiled, nodded at Handford and handed him an envelope out of which he withdrew a paper which he unfolded and read slowly. 'You're right Mr Midgley,' he said, 'Mr Ambler is not under arrest and can leave at any time. However before he does so, perhaps we can clear this up once and for all and ask if we can examine your computers.'

'For God's sake. No you bloody can't. There's sensitive stuff on them.'

I'll bet there is. 'Mr Ambler?'

'No, Inspector you can't. I consider this police harassment,' Ambler babbled. He had begun to sweat. As he had so rightly

173

said, most people didn't understand computers, but he did and he knew what examining them meant. Nothing was ever truly deleted; files were always there to be opened up and reveal their secrets.

Handford pushed back his chair and stood up. He walked over to the door and clasped the handle. 'In that case gentlemen I have to inform you that this piece of paper is a magistrate's warrant allowing me to seize your computers as well as your records, Mr Ambler. There are warrants also for Mr Hobson, for Mr Sugden and for you, Mr Midgley.' He pushed down the handle and opened the door. 'This is a murder enquiry, and although you may not like it, I'm sure you appreciate we have to be thorough.'

Back in his office Handford updated Warrender on his interview with Rebecca Ingleby. 'She agrees she bought the car for Ray Braddock to use. The house, she says, is to be turned into a holiday cottage and Braddock is doing it up. It gives him something to do apparently. She also insists she can't possibly afford to make trips abroad, and certainly she appeared surprised when I told her – but she could be bluffing. I couldn't push it because we only have Miah's friend's word for it that he is. Stick with Ray Braddock; see if we can tie down these trips. I want his alibi for Thursday night scrutinised again as well. Sergeant Ali can have a go at Darren Armitage; it's not the first time he's used him as his clubbing mate. I want to know if he had the opportunity to kill Dianne Ingleby; but more than that I want to know why he would. It has to be more than revenge on Maurice.' Handford allowed a deep sigh to escape.

Warrender sat forward. 'This case is worrying you more than usual, isn't it, boss?'

He was right. Handford felt as though it had become an intolerable burden. It was wrapped up like a parcel in the children's party game. Each time the music stopped and a layer was taken away, HMET or Russell or politics or confidentiality or secrets were there to prevent him from getting to the centre. 'If we accept Dianne Ingleby wasn't the intended victim, Warrender, I can't see him as our killer. He wouldn't have missed. But at the same time I don't know who else it could have been, unless it has something to do with Maurice's supposed involvement with the BNP and to be honest I doubt that. Not unless we have descended into killing to get our political will – and that doesn't bear thinking about.'

'Then don't. You know as well as I do that where there's an intended victim there's a trail of evidence and there *was* an intended victim, that first bullet was meant for one of them, the other three were panic or recoil shots. Murder's a sloppy business, guv; it's not even well thought-out most of the time. It's kill 'em and get the hell out of there. It's not a private business either. Somewhere someone has the knowledge of what our man is capable of – what his intentions were. It's just a matter of finding that person, and we will because he or she will be part of his world, you'll see. And stop worrying about HMET and Mr Russell ...', Handford glanced up at him. 'We're not stupid in CID, we know the DCI doesn't want you to go – you're the best DI he's got. But the bosses aren't stupid either, you'll be in there with the rest of us, don't you fret.' He grinned. 'There you are boss, my thoughts for the day.'

Handford wasn't quite sure what to say. Here he was being put back on track by a DC, and not any DC, but Warrender. He could have expected it from Clarke, the mentor of the team, but not Warrender.

Before he could formulate a reply, Warrender's smile widened. 'If Braddock goes to Europe, can I follow him? I could do with a few days away.'

The tension slipped from Handford. 'We'll see,' he said. 'Now get on and ask Clarke to pop in will you?'

'Yes, boss.'

'And Warrender, thanks.'

Warrender gave him a salute and another grin, and disappeared.

By the time Clarke arrived, Handford was feeling better. He handed over the diary. 'I want you to read this and tell me what you think. Then I want you to check out a case about five or six years ago when an assistant bank manager was found guilty of fraud and subsequently committed suicide in prison. I don't know his name or the bank he worked for, but it is likely it was in Bradford because Peter Redmayne – at least I think it was Peter Redmayne – felt there had been a miscarriage of justice. The manager of the bank was a James Gould. He left the area soon after the trial. And see if you can locate the Emma mentioned in there. She may well be Emma Crossley who lives somewhere in the Queensbury area or at least on the bus route through the village to the city and probably works at the Royal, but I don't know which department.'

Clarke took the diary. 'Let me get this right. You're not sure of the date of the case, the name of the defendant, the bank he worked for or even where that bank was, but the manager's name was James Gould and he left after the trial, but you don't know where he went. And Peter Redmayne might, just might have got himself involved, although you're not certain. You're equally not certain who Emma is but she might be called Crossley and probably lives somewhere on the bus route that goes through Queensbury into the city and might work at the Royal, but you don't know which department. Can I ask John, when you want this miracle?'

The corners of Handford's mouth twitched. 'As soon as possible. Start at the Royal. Get a list of all employees with Emma in their name.'

Clarke's eyes widened. 'Even if I can get over their arguments about the Data Protection Act and they give me this information, do you know how many people work there? Three to four thousand. That means there are likely to be a few hundred Emmas. It will take days.'

'I know, but do your best. Get some uniforms to help you. Come on Andy, I *need* this information.'

Clarke flicked through the pages of the book. 'Is it anything to do with Dianne Ingleby's murder?'

'I don't know, but I think it might be. Just read it and get back to me.'

As Clarke closed the door the telephone rang. Handford grabbed the receiver; would they never leave him alone? 'Yes.'

'John, it's Bob Milsom.' Bob was duty inspector. 'We've just taken a woman to the Royal; she was found up in Bradford Moor Park off Killinghall Road; she's probably been mugged.'

Handford was about to ask what a mugging was to do with him, when Milsom said, 'She's Parvez Miah's wife, John, and it doesn't look good.'

The Scarborough weather was perfect. Wispy fingers of thin white cloud stretched across the sky and a light breeze peeled back the temperature enough to give some relief against the heat of the sun. Many families had had the same idea as Gill and Amina and the beach was busy, though not overcrowded. They had left the car in the parking area on the cliffs on the north side of the town and carried the picnic hamper, buckets and spades, towels and swimming costumes, down the long flight of steps to the beach.

Gill relaxed in the deckchair and breathed in the ozone; it was good to be away from the stifling heat and the pollution of the city if only for a day. She glanced at Amina and frowned. There was something wrong. She'd not been her usual placid self on the journey, but each time Gill had asked if she was all right, she had said, 'Fine'. She wasn't sure she believed her for even now she looked as though she had the worries of the world on her shoulders.

Hasan ran over to them screaming with delight. 'Look Mummy,' he cried pulling at her sleeve, 'look at the sandcastle; it's the biggest ever already, but Nicola thinks it can be even bigger.' He ran back to continue digging.

'Your girls are wonderful with my two,' Amina said. 'I was afraid they might find it too much being with children so young.'

Gill squinted at them, at the moment they seemed to be enjoying themselves. 'They might eventually, and if they do we'll take a bus round the cliffs to the south shore after lunch and Hasan and Bushra can play in the sand again or go to the pleasure beach, and the girls can do their own thing. But while they're happy doing what they're doing, let's make the most of it. I'm just relishing not having to think about school or marking or examinations for a day.' She sat up. 'I'm not sure about you though; you don't seem as relaxed as you usually are. There's nothing wrong is there?'

Amina leaned over to pick up a handful of sand which she let trickle through her fingers. 'I'm fine, just a few things on my mind. I'm not sleeping very well. You know how it is?'

'No, I don't. Tell me; I might be able to help.'

Amina shook her head. 'It's not worth it; I'm worrying over nothing. So is Khalid. I keep telling him not to fuss so and that until we know for certain there's no point bothering anyone.' She stood up. 'I'll go and check on the children.'

Gill caught hold of her hand. 'The children are okay. And you're not making any sense. I don't know about you worrying, you're beginning to worry me. For goodness' sake, Amina, sit down and tell me. Is it Khalid's application to join HMET? I know he really

177

wants to be accepted and I'm sure he will be. At least Russell will be backing him which is more than he is for John.'

'No, it's nothing like that.'

'Then what is it? I swear I'll not take you home until you tell me.'

A frown formed a deep vertical furrow in the middle of Amina's forehead. 'I didn't want anyone to know until I was sure one way or the other, but I've got to talk to someone.' She sat down and attempted to keep her emotions and the tears building in her eyes under control. 'I've found a lump – in my breast.'

'Oh Amina, are you sure? Have you been to the doctor?'

'Yes, straightaway. He sent me to the hospital and I had a biopsy last week. I'm waiting for the results. It's just a bit worrying that's all.'

Gill crouched down in front of her. Suddenly the day had lost its sunlight and all sounds had receded into the background. It seemed as if there were only the two of them on the beach. 'Of course it's worrying, it's every woman's worst nightmare, but at least you did the right thing.'

'They wouldn't have sent me to the hospital if they didn't think it might be ...' Amina hesitated before saying the word, 'malignant.'

Gill didn't know, you heard so many stories. 'And you've had this on your mind for a couple of weeks. You should have rung me; I could have been there for you. Do your parents know?'

'No, no one does except for Khalid of course – and John.'

'John knows?' Compassion turned to fury. How could he have kept it from her? 'I'll kill him; how dare he not tell me.'

'Don't blame him, Gill; he was only given the information because he's Khalid's line manager and needed to be aware that he might want some leave if I have to go into hospital. I was the one who insisted it stayed confidential. I don't want any fuss until there's something to fuss about.'

'Yes, well, there are some secrets you keep and some you don't and this was one of them. When do you get the results?'

'Next week. They said they'd ring me with an appointment.'

Gill regained her seat on the deckchair. She grasped Amina's hand and squeezed it. 'Then let me know the minute you do.'

For some time they sat in silence. There was nothing Gill could say that wouldn't sound trite. She would like to have told her not to worry, but the words would have been meaningless. A few metres away Amina's children were playing, oblivious of everything but their sandcastle and the task of making it the biggest and best ever. She smiled as Clare ran back from the sea with a bucket of water which she poured into the moat. It sank into the sand and Bushra squealed and pleaded with her to get some more. There was a lot to be said for being young and invincible because once life took over it could be a swine.

Handford drove Parvez Miah to the hospital. Aisha was in a cubicle in the resuscitation room when they arrived. 'We've stabilised her,' the sister said, 'but she keeps drifting in and out of consciousness, so you'll not get much from her for a good while. She's got some nasty injuries, particularly to the head. There might be some swelling of the brain and there's always the danger of a blood clot forming. As soon as there's one free, she's going up to theatre. It shouldn't be long now.'

She pulled back the curtains. Aisha Miah lay propped on a pillow, an oxygen mask over her nose and mouth. Heavy bruises contrasted against the pallor of her skin which seemed to have been drained of all pigmentation. Cuts to her face and lips had either been stitched or taped, and one gash had a row of small but ugly black stitches running from her cheekbone to her nose. The police officer who was sitting beside her bed stood up to let Miah have the chair. 'I'm sorry mate,' he said. He glanced at Handford, then turned back to Miah. 'We'll get whoever did this to her, don't you fret.'

Miah nodded, not taking his eyes from her. 'Where was she found?' he asked. 'I know it was Bradford Moor Park, but where exactly?'

'One of the wardens came across her just inside the gates.' The officer seemed uneasy. 'We don't really know anything else. She might have been attacked in the park or on Killinghall Road or Silverhill Road or even Leeds Road and crawled through the gates for some reason. We haven't found a bag or anything. They'll have taken that; it's what they'll have been after. We're checking the park as well as bins and gardens to see if we can find it.'

'And no one saw or heard anything? It's Saturday, there must have been people around; how could they not see anything on a Saturday?' Parvez grasped his wife's hand. Aisha stirred and moaned slightly. He turned to Handford. 'What was she doing out there, sir? I don't understand it; it's a long way from home. Why would she be so far from home?'

'I don't know and it's not for you to worry about at the moment. You stay with her; take as long as you need and I'll see what I can find out.' He walked towards the uniformed officer and indicated he should follow him into the reception area. 'You were keeping something back in there; what was it?' he said.

'Well I didn't want to say anything to Parvez, sir,' he said. 'As the sister says Mrs Miah has been drifting in and out of consciousness, but when she came round for a while I did manage to get out of her that she knew her attacker and it wasn't a mugger. It seems she was kicked senseless in her own home by her sister-in-law. She even took photographs of her on her mobile phone. What kind of a sister-in-law does that to you?'

'I don't know. One who's jealous of her good looks or her freedom?' Certainly one whose jealousy turns to aggression. There was a lot of anger in the bruises he'd seen.

'I suppose when she realised how much damage she'd done she took her to the park and left her there. Well she wouldn't want her found lying on the mat would she?'

'Did she say how they got to the park?'

'In a car, apparently. She couldn't tell me anything about it. As I said, she kept drifting off and the nurses didn't want her bothered with questions. But there's something else as well. According to the doctor there's a considerable amount of older bruising. He thinks she might well be a victim of domestic violence. I can't see it myself, can you? Parvez is a nice chap; surely he can't be beating his wife up.'

Handford hoped not. 'I wouldn't have thought so but it's difficult to tell – wife-beaters often have two personalities, one for the outside world and one at home. It could be her sister-in-law, of course. If she's done it this time, she may well have done it before. Have you passed all this on to the duty inspector?'

'Yes sir. He's sending someone up to the house.'

'Do me a favour, constable, keep it to yourself until we know more. Don't turn it into canteen gossip.'

'No I won't sir.'

'Do you have a name for the sister-in-law?'

The officer flipped the pages of his notebook. 'Yes sir, it's

Chanda Hussain,' he indicated back towards Parvez. 'She's his brother's wife.'

'Are you sure – of the name, I mean?'

'Yes sir, that was the name Mrs Miah gave me.'

Handford stemmed his desire to pull Miah out of the cubicle and tell him what he thought of him. How dare the man lie to him? How dare he make him believe he was unable to find a girl called Chanda? Handford had soothed his embarrassment by telling him not to worry about it and to keep on trying; he'd even offered him a coffee for God's sake. Miah must have been aware the Asian girl involved with Darren Armitage, an associate of Gary Marshall but more importantly, Ray Braddock's nephew, could well be his sister-in-law and he had no right to keep it from his senior investigating officer. It was information that may or may not be important to the enquiry but whatever the situation it certainly wasn't his place to make the decision. Iqbal Ahmed was at the back of this, of that he was certain.

Handford would leave it until Aisha was out of theatre and hopefully out of danger, but Iqbal Ahmed or no Iqbal Ahmed, he was going to have to have a serious talk with Trainee Detective Constable Parvez Miah, and soon.

chapter thirteen

Jason Lake stood in the sitting room of his sister's house and fought to imagine what she could possibly be mixed up in to induce someone to do this to her. Kathie had insisted to Emma that it wasn't a burglary gone wrong and looking round, it was obvious the place hadn't just been trashed; it had been searched as well. Every drawer, every cupboard had been turned over and its contents scattered – the search had been systematic, the damage fanatical. He made his way through the hall and into the kitchen; it was the same scenario, as it was in the bedrooms. Everything had been turned over; nothing had been spared. So much was broken, not just ornaments, but furniture as well. Yet she hadn't told the police. Why?

He returned to the sitting room and sat down. Judging by the security measures: the locks, the bolts, the spyholes, she had been expecting this. Kathie was an auditor – one of the most boring jobs in the world in Jason's book – so what was there in her life that demanded such an outburst. Boyfriend trouble? Possibly. If it was, not only must it have been a tempestuous relationship, she must have had something he desperately wanted back. There was one, Ray someone or other, he couldn't remember his surname. That had been stormy. He flicked through the post he'd picked up from the mat in the hope it might give him a clue. Junk mail and bills mostly, bills that would need paying: telephone, electricity and credit card – he could do that for her on Monday – as well as one or two letters, including one from him. He pushed them into his pocket.

On arrival he had rushed to the hospital to find Kathie had been given a sedative and was sleeping. There was no chance of talking to her for some time the nurse said nor did they want her upset again. He was her brother; how could he upset her? The nurse was kind, but warned him that she hadn't wanted him told, although when she saw him, she was sure Kathie would think differently. 'Stay as long as you want,' she had said.

He had sat with her for a while, holding her hand and staring at the fading bruises on her face. Whoever had done this to her wouldn't get near her again; he would see to that. He was here now and he would look after her, whether she liked it or not. As he took in the damage he knew one thing for sure, she couldn't come back to the house in the state it was. His first job would be to make it habitable after which he would move in himself. But before he did any of that he needed to know what was going on, why she hadn't notified the police and, more importantly, why she had lied about contacting him. He needed to talk to Emma.

Gary Marshall was becoming tired of driving round. He needed to dump the car before it was called in stolen and the police nicked him for it. Chanda had been in a right state when she'd rung him, but she was calmer now that she knew the woman she thought she'd killed was still alive. It had been his idea to hang around until she was found and luckily one of the wardens on a motor bike had ridden into the park. They'd heard the engine stop, so they knew he'd seen her. It hadn't been long after that that the ambulance had arrived. It had stood outside the park for quite a long while and there'd been some people who'd been passing who had stopped to watch, so that Darren had had to get out of the car and join them. When he came back, he had said the paramedics had only put the blanket over her body, and they wouldn't have done that if she was dead, they'd have covered her head as well. And anyway when she'd been taken into the ambulance, one of the men had been carrying one of those bags of water or whatever it was. They wouldn't bother with that either if she was dead. Chanda had quietened down after that.

Then it was a question of what to do for the best. Aisha had been told to look after Chanda, so what they needed was to make it look as though it was she who hadn't done as she was told. They'd stopped off at the chippy for some pickled onions because Darren said they made him think more clearly. Chanda hadn't wanted any so she'd had chips instead. They'd decided in the end to take Chanda back to her house before her father-in-law came

183

home and found her missing – although what it had to do with him, Gary couldn't imagine. He wouldn't let his father boss him around like that let alone his father-in-law, but Chanda said he didn't understand so he'd shut up. What they had to do was to make Iqbal Ahmed think it was Aisha who had left the house and Chanda who had stayed there as she had been told to, then it would be Aisha who was in the wrong not her – and serve her right too, the stuck-up cow.

But things hadn't gone according to plan and as they had driven up the road towards the house they'd seen a police car standing outside. Chanda had started screaming again and Gary had had to turn down another street and drive away. Now they were coasting around in a nicked car trying yet again to decide their next move. They'd managed to calm her down by saying the police always go to the house when they find someone beat up like that; they have to tell the relatives. But she'd said she wasn't there as she was supposed to be and then that there was blood on the carpet from Aisha's head wound. He was getting a bit fed up with her now and told her not to be so stupid. They'd found her in the park so they wouldn't be looking for blood in the house and she could clean it up when everyone had gone.

But Chanda was stalling. She said she daren't go home because Iqbal would beat her for not being where she was supposed to be. Gary said not if she told him she couldn't find Aisha and had gone out to look for her. That would work. Gary would drop her off at the end of the road and if Chanda walked back in as though she was exhausted, they would have to believe her. Once they'd done that, Gary could dump this bloody car. It was beginning to feel too hot in his hands. They'd all agreed until Darren had said that since Aisha was alive she could have told the police what had happened and who were they going to believe, Chanda or a solicitor? Gary told him to shut up, but Darren had said they'd believed Chanda last time, but that was only because the other women had agreed that Aisha had fallen down the stairs and that Chanda had come up behind her to help her. This time was different, the police were there, so she could have told them. And there was no one to back up her story.

Chanda panicked again. 'You can't take me back, not while the police are there. I've got to go somewhere else. I can stay with you, Gary.'

Gary liked Chanda, she was fit, but not fit enough to stay with him when the police were involved. He wasn't off the hook with the old lady yet. 'I don't think so, not with you about to drop any minute.' He glanced over his shoulder at her. 'The old man isn't going to beat you up when you're about to drop; the police wouldn't let 'im. And anyway they'll take you in so you'll be safe.'

The thought of being taken to the police station made things worse.

'Then I'll stay with Darren.'

Darren wasn't any happier with that than Gary had been. 'No, you've got to go home. Say what Gary told you to say; they can't argue with you 'cos they won't know. We'll go back, wait until the cops have gone and you walk in and tell them you've been out looking for Aisha. And if they say anything about the blood, you say you know nothing about it. And if she has said it was you who beat 'er up, tell them she's lying and she's always had it in for you.'

'That's right,' Gary added. 'And if you think about it, she was found miles away from where you live. If you'd done it, how would you have got her there; she couldn't have walked, and you haven't got a car, and they don't know about us. And anyway, we haven't got a car. Well we won't have if I can ever manage to dump it.' He glanced back at Chanda again. She was beginning to crack. He took his hand off the wheel, thumped Darren's arm then glared at him, in the hope he would cotton on and back him up.

Darren rubbed his arm and glared back. 'Yeah, that's the best,' he said.

Gary was becoming impatient. 'You've got to go, Chanda. We can't sit here all day.' He fought to give her a better reason than that. 'If you leave it too long they won't believe you. Tell them that after she'd gone you started to have stomach pains and you got frightened and, when she didn't come back, you went out to look for her.' He turned to Darren and winked. 'They can't prove nothing one way or another, not with you pregnant like this. If you say you've got stomach pains then you've got stomach pains; they'll 'ave to believe you. They'll probably put you to bed and not let the police talk to you.' He could see Chanda half-believed him, but she was still not moving and if she didn't they'd all be

185

down at the cop shop anyway for nicking a car. 'Look,' he said. 'It'll be her fault she got beaten up. I'll bet that when she comes 'ome from hospital your father-in-law'll probably do it again to 'er – or send 'er back to Pakistan.'

This was something Chanda understood. 'Yeah, and it'll serve her right.'

She pulled herself out of the car and walked hesitantly towards the house looking over her shoulder as she went. Gary waved her on. She had to do this, if she didn't he had no idea what he was going to do with her. She was too near having the baby for a squat, and anyway her father-in-law would send the police out looking for her and Gary didn't feel like having to dodge the cops over a missing person – mugging was one thing, he was used to that, but this was something else.

Even so, he was worried for her. A frown wrinkled his forehead. 'Do you think she'll be all right?'

'Dunno,' Darren said. 'Depends on whether they believe her or not.'

'I suppose so.' Gary put the car into gear. 'I got to get rid of this,' he said. 'There are too many cops around here for my liking.'

Handford stayed at the hospital until Aisha Miah was taken to theatre. He spoke to Parvez only to say he hoped the operation would go well but as he and the trolley carrying his wife disappeared into the lift he asked the uniformed officer to ring him when it was over to let him know how Mrs Miah was. He couldn't do anything about the trainee detective while his wife was in danger, but he could settle the question of the twenty thousand pounds Ingleby had given to Braddock. Get their separate sides of the story. He drove to Queensbury first.

'What do you want?' Braddock said as he opened the door. He was dressed but hadn't yet shaved.

'I have a few more questions, Mr Braddock. Can I come in?'

'Do I have a choice?' Braddock said as he stood to one side to let the detective through.

'Yes you have a choice, but I'm going to have to ask them at some point. You can come down to the station if you'd rather, but it might be easier here.'

He had been watching television – an old black-and-white film as far as Handford could see. The room smelt of stale cigarettes. Little had been done in the way of housework; the waste-bin was overflowing with empty beer cans and the ashtray filled with butts. Braddock moved some papers and letters off the chair. 'Sorry about the mess, I haven't had time to tidy up.' He turned off the television. 'Unemployment doesn't give you much time to do anything but to watch the box.' Or renovate a house for Rebecca or trip off to Europe. But these were things better discussed under caution at the station.

Braddock sat down and picked a mug off the floor. He took a drink. 'What do you want?'

'Why did Maurice Ingleby lend you twenty thousand pounds?'

Braddock looked up and then away, contempt creeping into his eyes. 'He didn't lend me twenty thousand pounds, he gave it to me and now the bastard wants it back.'

'He *gave* it to you? Why?'

The contempt turned to sarcasm. 'Because he felt sorry for me. Well that's what he said at the time.'

'What do you mean "he felt sorry for me"?'

'My father drank most of the profits of the business and when he died he left a load of debts, only he hadn't thought to tell me about them, so I copped for the lot and had to declare myself bankrupt. Maurice Ingleby said he was giving me the money to help me start up again. It wasn't my fault he said; I needed someone to give me a break.'

'I didn't think a bankrupt could start a new business?'

'He can't, at least he couldn't then, not until five years after he'd been discharged.' He smiled and the derision returned to his voice. 'But there are ways round anything if you know what they are, and Maurice Ingleby knows them all.'

It seemed to Handford that the two men probably deserved each other. 'Tell me.'

'The money was a gift to me he said, but the new business would be under his wife's name. She had nothing to do with the running of it; I did that, but officially I was one of the employees, so I had to go cap in hand if I wanted to do anything – anything at all and not to her, but to him. I suggested once that we should become a limited company, but Maurice wouldn't have it. Now I know why.'

'Why?'

'It made it easier for him to ruin me.' Again Handford caught the venom in his tone. 'All the business debts were mine, so when he refused to pay me it wasn't just the company that went bust, it was me as well.'

'When did the business become yours?'

'After the five years were up Dianne sold it to me for a pound. I wanted to register as a limited company straightaway, but since I had to have a company secretary and Ingleby put the word around that it wouldn't be a good move to work for me, and I couldn't afford to pay anyone the going rate anyway, I would have been stuck with being company director and Darren as company secretary. Darren would have been useless and I couldn't have coped with the paperwork on my own, so I didn't bother. At first it didn't matter; the firm was more than solvent when Ingleby backed out. Then the conglomerate opened up and undercut my prices. I think he knew this was on the cards – he has friends in high places you know.'

Handford did know – his DCI for one. 'You say it was Mr Ingleby who suggested you wouldn't be the best person to work for? How do you know this?'

'He's not the only one with friends, mine are not in the same high places, but they kept me in the loop. It was him all right.' Braddock was trembling as he stretched over to the table and reached for the cigarette packet. He flipped it open and took one out, lit it, pulled on it and blew the smoke into the air. It seemed to calm him. 'I tried to keep up, but Ingleby put the word about that my goods were inferior and either builders stopped buying from me, or they held on to payment, or like Ingleby refused to pay me at all.'

Handford let his gaze wander over the man opposite. Big, beefy, more like a prop forward than a builders' merchant yet at this moment, defeated. If what he claimed was true, it said a lot about what one person would do to another in the name of business – if it were true. He leaned forward, his elbows resting on his knees and his fingers steepled under his chin. Eventually he said, 'What I don't understand, Mr Braddock, is why Mr Ingleby would do that. You weren't in competition with him; why after giving you such a large sum of money would he want to ruin you, and why then would he ask for it back?'

Anger spread like a slow bruise across Braddock's face. 'Oh, that's easy to explain,' he said. 'Rebecca.'

'Rebecca? I thought he didn't know about the relationship you and she have.'

'He doesn't, but he found out about the one we did have. She was seventeen and he didn't approve. No one touched his little girl and got away with it, particularly not at seventeen and not a man going on thirty. He had higher things planned for her and they didn't include a bankrupt.'

'Or a man who puts it about a bit?'

For the first time Braddock grinned, but it was a grin of satisfaction rather than humour. 'If you like.'

'I understand Rebecca Ingleby bought you a car.'

He seemed surprised. 'You have been busy haven't you? But actually you've got that wrong, Rebecca bought herself a car and I have use of it.'

'That isn't what she says. She says her aunt died and left her a considerable amount of money, part of which she used to buy you the car. Who pays the road tax, the insurance and the MOT?'

'She does. It's her car.'

'It's garaged in Queensbury.'

'I know.' Braddock's eyes sparkled. 'And when he finds out, there's not a bloody thing Maurice Ingleby can do about it.'

'You're going to tell him are you?'

'Why not, I've got to have some pleasures in my life. In fact now you mention it, I might even drive up to the house in it. Offer him my commiserations on the death of his wife. Drip, drip, drip. What's it called? Chinese water torture?'

Handford couldn't contain his disgust. He stood up. 'I have to ask myself Mr Braddock if there is anyone you wouldn't use or anything you wouldn't do to get your revenge on Maurice Ingleby.'

Braddock pulled himself out of his chair and came towards him until he was no more than a few centimetres away. He held Handford's gaze. 'Yes copper,' he said evenly. 'I wouldn't kill his wife. So don't even try to pin it on me.'

As Handford drove towards Ingleby's house he was shaking with anger. When he came to a lay-by he pulled in. He was angry he had let Braddock get to him and angry that he couldn't stop

189

himself from being angry. But what was worse – at one point he had actually found himself feeling sorry for the man. He had been failed by his father and used by Maurice Ingleby, and he hadn't been aware of it until it hit him in the back of the neck. He could even understand why he should want his revenge, but whether that revenge stretched as far as waiting in a multi-storey car park, pulling out a gun and shooting Dianne Ingleby was questionable. His need to settle scores was steeped in vengeance, but he was also quite calculating enough to carry it out. Did Braddock have that kind of personality? Probably. From what he'd seen today, very likely. Did James Mossman or Patrick Ambler or anyone else had done he needed to be passionate enough to want to do it, but cool and Maurice Ingleby had made an enemy of? Or even the unknown who beat up Kathie; did he have that kind of personality?

Handford sighed and stretched over to push a cassette in the player. He needed his brass band to calm him down before he spoke to Maurice Ingleby. He listened in silence, allowing the music to flow over him. There was nothing like a good brass band giving their all. He ought to have a CD player, but at the moment while he was saving every penny to keep the girls in university over the next few years, it seemed like an extravagance to change a perfectly good cassette player. He smiled – by the time he could afford it, CD players would be old-fashioned. Perhaps if he became a DCI …? He didn't want to think about that. For a while he immersed himself in the rich sounds of the band, allowed them to clear his mind until they faded into the background and the investigation took precedence.

Warrender had reminded him that where there's an intended victim there's a trail of evidence, and it was looking more and more likely that the intended victim was Maurice Ingleby. The question was to whom did that trail of evidence lead, and how much of it was hard evidence and how much circumstantial? There were plenty of suspects, but then generating suspects in any case was easy – the hard part was reducing them to one. That said, except for his alibi, the obvious suspect was Braddock. To put him in pole position they needed to break that, find the car, place him in it and trace the gun – a much harder prospect. He pulled out his phone, turned down the music and rang Ali. 'Bring Darren Armitage in and have a go at breaking Braddock's alibi.

And while you're about it, ask him about Chanda Hussain. We need to know where she is. Oh and by the way, she's married to Miah's brother.'

'Are you sure?'

'Oh yes. She's Aisha Miah's sister-in-law, which also makes her Parvez Miah's sister-in-law.'

'But Miah said he'd never heard of her. You asked him to find her for us. You mean he was lying?'

'He was and I will speak to him about it – but not now. He's enough to cope with. It's probably a family thing so you're not to discuss it with him.'

'You mean as one understanding Asian to another?'

'No, I mean as my sergeant to a trainee detective. It's not as straightforward as it seems, Ali. Apart from anything else, Aisha says it was Chanda who assaulted her and according to the doctor there is a significant amount of older bruising. It could be we have a case of domestic violence here and it's likely the family were hiding it. Parvez is bound to be questioned at some time, but for the moment I would rather he came to us than we go to him. If we have to go to him, then I will be the one making the journey. Is that clear?'

'Yes, perfectly. In fact I'd rather it was you than me.' Ali paused for a moment then said, 'I'll get on to Darren Armitage.'

Handford closed his mobile, switched on the car's ignition, turned up the volume of the cassette player and drove to Maurice Ingleby's house.

Chanda's arrival back at the house was not greeted as favourably as Gary Marshall had predicted. Iqbal was furious she had been out, and when she tearfully tried to explain how Aisha had left her on her own and how she had developed stomach pains and had been frightened so she had gone out to find her sister-in-law, the policeman hadn't believed her and she was not sure Iqbal had either. The policewoman had been more sympathetic. She sat her down and asked if she was still having pains, because if she was they ought to get her to the hospital. The question surprised Chanda and at first she thought about saying yes, going to the hospital would get her away from here, however one look at her father-in-law's expression had decided her to shake her head. 'No, not now.'

'Then they were probably early pains,' the policewoman said. 'They're like practise ones, nothing to worry about. They're called Braxton Hicks contractions.'

'Oh.' Chanda smiled weakly and blew her nose.

Iqbal wasn't so kind. 'Aisha has been assaulted,' he said. 'Did you hurt her, Chanda?'

'No,' she said plaintively. 'No, I didn't; I went out to find her.'

'Then, officer, if Chanda says she didn't hurt her then she didn't. Members of my family do not lie. I suggest that rather than questioning a young woman who is heavily pregnant, you go out and find the person who mugged Aisha.'

The officer turned to him. 'Mr Ahmed,' he said, 'we are looking for anyone who could have robbed Mrs Miah but she has made an allegation that she was not attacked by a stranger but by your daughter-in-law here. She says it happened in the house and she was taken by car to the park and left there.'

'Then you cannot possibly accuse Chanda. She has no car, indeed she cannot even drive. You saw her walking up the street only a few minutes ago.'

'I'm sorry sir, we are bound to investigate her allegations.' He sat in a chair opposite Chanda and took out his notebook. 'What time was it you say she left the house?'

'I don't know. Everyone was out but her and me. I was upstairs listening to my music and she went into the garden to use her mobile.'

'You saw her do that?'

'Yes, I can see the garden from the bedroom window. After the call she disappeared and I thought she was back in the house. About a quarter of an hour later I came downstairs to tell her I was having these pains, but she wasn't there. I got frightened and went to look for her.'

The policewoman said, 'Why go out? You could have called her on her mobile, found out that way.'

For a brief moment Chanda thought about crying, but decided it wouldn't have any effect on the police officers. Instead she held the woman's gaze and said, 'I did, but she'd turned it off – the cow. She didn't want me to find her.'

'Why wouldn't she want that?'

'I don't know, ask her.'

'How far did you go looking?'

'All over. I thought at first she might have gone to the shops and had shouted up to tell me, but I couldn't hear her for the music. Then when I couldn't find her I thought that she might have gone to see whoever had rung her on her mobile, but I didn't know who it was so I couldn't ring them and ask. I wasn't worried at first because her car was still there, so I didn't think she could be far away.' Chanda was warming to her story. 'I looked everywhere, even as far as the main road. She was nowhere so I came home.'

'Did you go as far as the park?'

'No, why would I go there, it's miles away.' She became indignant. 'You might not have noticed but my baby's due any time; I daren't go too far in case my waters break. It's her fault, she shouldn't have left me.'

The officer closed his notebook and stood up. 'We'll like your shoes, Chanda.'

'Why?'

'Mrs Miah was kicked about her body and head. We'll send them to the forensic people and they'll be able to tell us whether any of the bruises match the toes of your shoes, and whether there's any trace evidence – blood, hair, that kind of thing on them.'

Chanda began to cry. This hadn't occurred to her; she appealed to her father-in-law but the woman officer took hold of her. 'Come on love, give us your shoes or we'll have to arrest you, and I don't think in your condition that's a very good idea, do you?'

Trembling Chanda bent down and took them off. She handed them to the officer who put them in a large brown paper bag which he sealed. He picked up his cap. 'That's all for now,' he said, 'but a scene-of-crime officer will be here soon to check over the area Mrs Miah said she was in when she was attacked and we may have more questions to ask Chanda.' The two walked towards the door. The policeman hung back. 'Mrs Miah was badly hurt Chanda, she's having an operation as we speak; it will be a charge of actual bodily harm at the very least, could even be considered attempted murder. So what I find difficult to understand is that you haven't once asked about her.' He looked at Iqbal. 'Thank you for your cooperation, sir. You don't need to see us out; we'll find our own way.'

There was silence in the house until they heard the police car move off. Chanda stood up and stared up at Iqbal who was walking slowly towards her. She backed away from him. 'No,' she screamed. 'No.'

The blow when it came flung her into the chair. Her cheek stung her and her head reeled as though she had been spun round a thousand times. He leaned over her. 'Be thankful you are in no condition to be given the beating you deserve. But don't think you will escape your punishment. Once that child is born it will be handed over to the women and you will go to Pakistan where you will remain until you learn the ways of Islam; and believe me, Chanda, you *will* learn them – one way or another. Now, go to your room and stay there until I say you can leave it.'

chapter fourteen

John Handford found Ingleby in his study. Papers were spread out over the desk and the computer was on. As he walked in Ingleby raised his head, an expectant look on his face that turned almost immediately to one of sadness. He looked even more haggard today. 'I thought it was Dianne,' he said. He threw the pen he was holding on to the desk. It bounced and rolled on to the floor. Handford bent down to pick it up.

'Will I ever get used to it?' Ingleby said.

'It's only two days.'

'Is it? It seems like for ever. I don't think I've ever known time go so slowly. Except when I look back it was only yesterday we were walking down that aisle.' His eyes filled with tears. 'She was so beautiful, you know, not just on the outside but inside as well.' He picked up the papers. 'Work is the only thing that keeps me sane.' He allowed them to drop back on to his desk then stood up and walked over to the window. 'I've spent a lot of time since she died looking out on the garden; seeing her in my mind, wishing she was with me.' He faced the detective. 'I didn't deserve her, Handford; I was a real bastard to her. I cheated on her more than once.'

'I know.'

Suddenly the man laughed. 'I expect you do,' he said. 'You're bound to have been checking up on me.' He poured himself a whisky from the bar, lifted the bottle to ask if Handford wanted one.

'No thank you, I've got a long day to get through yet.'

Maurice Ingleby carried his drink to one of the settees where he made himself comfortable and indicated Handford should do the same. 'You never asked me about my affairs.'

'I would have done eventually. The husbands of those I know about have alibis for Thursday night, and to be honest there are people with better motives for killing you. You have to have a powerful one to wait in a multi-storey car park and then calmly fire a gun. You could tell me though if there is anyone recent.'

He shook his head. 'No. As hurt as she was, my wife would always forgive me. I don't know why; I doubt I would have been as accepting.' He took a deep sigh. 'But she did and she was and I promised her after the last one I would never do it again and I haven't. I only wish I could erase all the others.'

'We would all like to erase things we're ashamed of, Mr Ingleby. But if it's any comfort to you, I don't think your wife's murder has anything to do with your affairs.'

'But it may still have something to do with me?'

Handford sighed. 'It may; I wish I knew. It would make my job a lot easier if I was sure.' He held Ingleby's gaze. 'We have suspects who would like to see you gone, we have suspects who are too good a shot to have hit the wrong person, and we have suspects who could quite easily have done so but who have strong alibis and witnesses coming out of their ears.'

'So what you're saying is that you have nothing?'

'No, I'm saying we have a lot, but little of it taking us anywhere yet. There is a possible link – and I stress it is only possible – with your wife's work as a volunteer with Victim Support and a young girl she was helping. She left a diary describing the time she spent with her, but we don't yet actually know who she is. Dianne was obviously concerned about her, but apart from her notes, there is little to go on and Eileen Leighton is stuck to the concept of confidentiality with superglue. She flatly refuses to open up her books to us or to say who the girl is.'

'Even though Dianne has been murdered?'

'Even then.'

'Can't you get a warrant or something?'

'I haven't got enough yet for a warrant; it would be turned down. People have the right to confidentiality even in these circumstances.'

Maurice Ingleby picked up his glass and walked over to the bar. He poured himself another whisky, 'Are you sure you won't have one?'

Handford changed his mind. Why not? 'Just a small one.'

When he had finished here he had a meet with Russell to bring him up to date and the chances were that breathing whisky over him would only give him another reason to suggest his DI wasn't suitable for HMET. But what the hell, Handford was tired of having his life and his future ruled by that man, and if necessary he could suck mints on the way back to the station.

Ingleby handed him the glass and sat down again. Handford took a sip. The time for chat and keeping the family in the loop had come to an end. 'I have two questions I need answering. Do you donate money to the BNP?'

'So that's rearing its ugly head again is it? No, Inspector, I *do not* donate money to the BNP. I do not donate money to any political party. I'm not a political animal. When it comes to elections I'm what is known as a floating voter, I make my mind up at the time. Not that my political leanings are anyone's business but my own – not even yours.'

'I appreciate that, but last year you were sent a series of death-threat letters and now your wife is dead. I have to be sure they are not part of the investigation.'

'You know who sent them?'

'Almost, but I'm equally sure they didn't kill your wife, or at least not personally. Whether they persuaded some hothead to do it for them is another matter.'

For a few moments Ingleby seemed to detach himself from the exchange, leaving Handford to wonder if there was something he was holding back. Eventually he said 'You had two questions.'

Handford placed his glass on the small table next to the settee. 'Why did you give Ray Braddock twenty thousand pounds, Mr Ingleby?' he said, fixing his eyes on the man opposite.

'Is that what he told you?'

'He told me you had given him the money to start up in business after he went bankrupt when his father died. He said it was set up in Dianne's name but he ran it, although he had to come to you if he wanted to do anything other than normal day-to-day trading. When the bankruptcy was discharged, Dianne sold it to him for a pound.'

'Yes, well, what he said is more or less accurate. He missed out one vital point though.'

'Which was?'

'The money wasn't a gift, it was a bribe.'

197

Handford raised an interrogative eyebrow. 'A bribe?' A hell of a bribe.

'Yes, a bribe.' Ingleby's tone was unremittingly matter of fact. 'I gave him the money to stop him seeing Rebecca. She was seventeen, he was going on thirty, he had women by the score and he didn't care how young they were. I wasn't having him involved with my daughter. I didn't even know if he was clean. I offered him twenty thousand to stop seeing her and he took it, didn't even have to think about it.' He stood up again and walked over to the window.

Everything in these two men's lives came back to Rebecca. To Ingleby the money was a bribe to stop him seeing her; to Braddock asking for it back was revenge for him having seen her. Did she realise that? Did she care? Handford doubted it. She was her father's daughter. She wanted Braddock and she kept him with money. The car for instance, even the house in Station Road – were they bribes as well? Didn't she realise that what her lover wanted was the business? The likelihood was that he would marry her to get it and then let her go as soon as he had what he wanted. But to do that he would need Maurice out of the way because there was no way he would accept him marrying his daughter. Even if he retired, he would make damn sure Braddock didn't get a sniff of it. The only chance Braddock had was for her father to be out of the picture. Perhaps Dianne Ingleby's death was the start of it. One down, one to go. For him to kill Maurice would have been too obvious. But to kill Dianne, would not only take suspicion off him but it would also give him the satisfaction of watching her husband suffer. What had he said? *Drip, drip, drip.* Perhaps he was in the frame after all. And perhaps Ali was right – Maurice Ingleby was in danger – not yet, not immediately, but eventually.

Maurice Ingleby turned back to face him. 'I know what you're thinking, Handford. Pot, kettle and black and all that, but she was my daughter and I wasn't having him anywhere near her.' *If only.* 'You have daughters?'

'Two.'

'Then you'll know how I felt.'

Handford didn't want to follow this line. It was becoming too personal. He wasn't one of the 'friends' Ingleby had secured over the years; he was investigating his wife's murder, a murder which could well have something to do with the man he had bribed and then ruined. 'Why when Mr Braddock was made bankrupt, did you name yourself one of his creditors and ask for the twenty thousand back?'

'A token gesture because he didn't keep to his side of the bargain. He tried it on with her again. She pushed him off, so he bragged to everyone about bedding her, about her wanting him and about how one day he would have my business, and I wanted him to know that he couldn't mess with me or my family or, more particularly, with my daughter.'

Jason Lake knocked on Emma Crossley's door at two thirty in the afternoon. As soon as she saw him, her heart missed a beat. His dark hair was shorter but otherwise he was exactly as she remembered him: tall, good-looking and serious. Although almost two years younger than his sister, he could have been her twin they were so alike.

He hugged her. 'It's good to see you, Emma.'

She clung on to him and for the first time since Kathie had been assaulted she made no attempt to stop the tears.

'Come on,' he said, 'I'm here now.' He held on to her until the sobs subsided, then she pulled herself away and wiped her eyes with the back of her hand.

'I'm sorry,' she said. 'I've tried so hard to hold it together since she was attacked. It's just such a relief to have someone else.' She was embarrassed. Anger came easily to her as it had with Ray Braddock, supporting others came easily as it had with Kathie, but she wasn't used to being the one being supported and she didn't know how to deal with it. 'I'll make us a cup of tea,' she said. She knew it was crass, but it got her out of his presence and gave her time.

When she returned to the room with the tray he was sitting on the chair next to the fireplace. 'It's nice here,' he said.
'I try.'

He looked round. 'Where's the little one?'
'With my mother.' She was on safer ground now. 'It would be impossible to talk with him running round and she loves having him. She spoils him rotten.'
'That's what grandparents are for.'

'I suppose.' She handed him a cup of tea. Milk and two sugars, she remembered. 'Have you seen Kathie?'

'Briefly. She's not coping well with Dianne Ingleby's death. She hasn't slept much since it happened and doctor had given her a sedative. I sat with her for a while and then went up to the house to see what sort of a mess it was in. You did warn me, but I never expected so much damage. Who the hell would do that to her?'

When Emma had spoken to Jason on the phone, she'd denied any knowledge of who it could be; now, seeing distress cloud his eyes, she said, 'I think it might be Ray Braddock.'

'Jack's father?'

'Not according to him.'

'Why do you think it might be him?'

'Because of what she knows about him. He's scum. He's a bankrupt but he always has money, although he pretends he hasn't. Whatever he's doing it's bound to be illegal. I don't know what he's into and I'm not even sure Kathie does, but at one time she taunted him about his extramural activities, and with having written evidence which she will use if he doesn't do the decent thing by Jack, and he's never forgiven her. I know he frightens her, particularly when he goes to the house and threatens her about what she can expect if she shops him. I know he's slapped her around and broken some of her things like he does with me. It's what he's good at. But this time I think he lost it big time and she's so frightened about what he might do next that she's not prepared to shop him. Perhaps she does know more than she's saying; if she does, she hasn't told me. In fact the nearest she's come to confiding in anyone is with Dianne Ingleby, the woman from Victim Support. She was about to tell her who it was, of that I'm sure. I warned Ray, but then Mrs Ingleby was shot, so he's off the hook. There's something else though.' She walked over to the cupboard in the alcove and took out the envelope. 'Kathie asked me to go to the house and take this from a chest in the loft. She wanted me to look after it for her. I think it's what he was after. I tell you Jason, I was really scared going into that house on my own and it took me ages to find it.'

Jason put down his cup and took the envelope from Emma. 'She gave you no idea what was in it?'

'No, just that it was marked "Personal" and asked me to keep it for her but not to tell anyone, not even Ray.'

200

He slit it open and slid the contents on to the table. In it were newspaper clippings, another sealed envelope and a couple of sheets of paper on which were handwritten lists. Jason rifled through the clippings. 'The stupid, silly woman,' he said almost to himself. He looked up at Emma. 'I tell you she's paranoid. Why can't she just let it go?'

'What? I don't understand, Jason. Let what go?'

'This.' He waited for a few seconds. 'This is nothing to do with Ray Braddock; these are clippings of my father's trial.'

'Your father's what?'

'His trial. He was found guilty of fraud six years ago, but Kathie would never believe it. She thought – and obviously still does think – that he was set up by the manager of his bank.'

'I'm sorry Jason, I don't understand any of this.'

Slowly and painfully, it seemed to Emma, Jason explained. Finally he described his father's suicide and his mother's fatal asthma attack. 'We buried them together, at the same time, in the same grave,' he said. He let a few seconds pass. 'Kathie always blamed the manager, James Gould, for what she describes as my father's murder. My father was aware of customers' passwords and he was brilliant with computers; he was perfectly capable of using the electronic transfer system to steal the funds. Mr Gould insisted he wouldn't have known where to start, and anyway he had no motive the police could find. But Kathie is convinced he set up my father and that he was lying when he said he wouldn't know how, and nothing has moved her from that. One of the reasons I went to work abroad was to give myself a chance to forget, or at least if not to forget then to lay it all to rest. Kathie stayed here because she said it was the only place she would learn the truth. Now, it appears James Gould is back in the district and she has met him and spoken to him.' He picked up the hand-written list of dates. 'According to this he has been back about three years and she first realised who he was a couple of years ago. Since then she's been stalking him at every opportunity; she's got every single time down with the dates. My God, she even tackled him about it, called him Mr Gould …'

'Instead of?'

'She doesn't say.' He ran his fingers through his hair as if in desperation. 'What the hell was she thinking of? Why can't she leave it alone?'

'Is there a picture of James Gould? Perhaps I might know who he is.'

He flicked thorough the cuttings. 'No, just of my father. There's a newspaper comment on the trial by Peter Redmayne.' His eyes skimmed it. 'The gist is that the police had relied too much on the evidence from the bank's investigative branch, instead of running their own enquiry from scratch and thus the verdict he believed was very much in doubt.'

'Was he right?'

'He might have been, electronic crime wasn't something many people understood, but my father was refused an appeal, so obviously the judges felt the conviction was secure.'

'What's in the other envelope?'

Jason ripped it open and scanned the contents quickly. 'It's a statement from a bank employee who was a junior teller at the time. He maintains that Gould was lying when he said he didn't understand computer systems and also that he had seen him working in my father's office when he was not in the bank. After my father had been charged he told a friend on the force who passed it on to the senior investigating officer who said they were sure they had the right man and were not prepared to open up the case again.' He threw down the statement. 'This is so thin it's ridiculous. I'm not surprised they didn't reopen it.'

Emma sat back and rested her head on the cushion of the chair.

'So what do we do?'

'We go to the hospital and tell Kathie she's wrong. My father committed fraud and when he couldn't take prison he killed himself. That's the reality of it.'

'And the other reality is that Kathie was the victim of a vicious assault that nearly killed her, that she was too frightened to tell anyone who it was and when she was almost ready the woman she was talking to was shot. Don't you think that's just too much of a coincidence? Don't you think we ought to go to the police and take these with us?'

'And have them laugh at us? No, I don't.' Jason picked up the cuttings and slid them towards her. 'These are no more than the yearnings of someone who cannot accept her father was a crook. He *wasn't* perfect, even though she thought he was. He was an expert in IT and was mad about the sea; he wanted to spend his entire retirement sailing; it was all he ever talked about.'

'But that doesn't make him a thief.'

'Oh, come on Emma. I saw the pictures of the yachts. Have you any idea how much those things cost? My father couldn't have even begun to have afforded one.' He pushed everything back into the envelope. 'You asked me what I was going to do. Well I'll tell you. I'm going to see Kathie, find out when she can leave hospital. Then I'm going to sort out the mess in her house, throw away what's beyond repair, buy any essentials she will need, plus perhaps the odd extra like a television and then I'm going to look after her until she's well enough to travel, when I will take her back to Brussels with me for a holiday, and try and persuade her to see sense.'

Parvez Miah wasn't sure just how long he had been sitting by his wife's bedside. He was stiff and needed to take a walk. The sister suggested he should go to the canteen and have a coffee, but he said he would wait until she came round. He didn't want her to wake up and find herself alone. He looked down at her. Where her face was not discoloured with angry bruising it was ashen, and there was a crust of blood shielding the gash over her eye. At least they hadn't had to shave her hair; she would have found that difficult to bear; she was so proud of her hair.

The surgeon said the operation had been long but had gone well. The injuries to her head were not as severe as first thought; she had suffered a hairline fracture to the skull, but little or no damage to the blood vessels beneath it. The blows to her abdomen however had caused tears in the internal organs, especially the spleen and the liver, but also the intestines. She also had three broken ribs. 'We've stitched her up and in time we expect her to make a full recovery. She could be in some pain for a few days and we'll keep a close eye on her, but on the whole your wife has been very lucky.'

Parvez had thanked him but instead of walking away, the doctor had taken a step closer to him. 'It's not my place to say anything, Mr Miah,' he said quietly. 'I'm just here to patch 'em up, but whoever did this to Aisha needs putting away for a long time. You know and I know it's not the first time it has happened, there is old bruising to prove it. At best, if your sister-in-law is the attacker she needs help, and at worst, she is so dangerous she is beyond it. I hope your wife is not one of these people who won't make a complaint, because if she is I'm willing to bet my pension this will not be the last we will see of her – only next time it will probably be on a mortuary slab.'

The surgeon's words hurt like a physical pain which no analgesic would cure. This was his fault, his, his brother's and his father's. They knew what Chanda was like but had been too afraid of shame being heaped on the family to do anything about it. Every time she had been in trouble at school her father, helped by Iqbal as the senior and most influential member of the community as well as her prospective father-in-law, got her out of it. Then later after her marriage turned a blind eye to what had been happening at home. They had tried to tame her with marriage and pregnancy, but it hadn't worked. If anything it had made her more rebellious. She had made dubious friends and although expressly forbidden, she had continued to spend time with them. Warrender had said Darren Armitage and Gary Marshall were known petty criminals who hung around with an Asian girl called Chanda. And what had he done? Lied about it to the DI and then gone to his father for advice. She was mixing in bad company, which in her mind added credibility to her depraved view of the world and they hadn't done much to stop her. Gary Marshall in particular could be brutal. He purposely stole from vulnerable pensioners because they were more likely to have poor eyesight and hearing. Defence lawyers used it to suggest they had mistaken their client for the attacker so that a not guilty verdict would be brought in; he'd seen it happen in court more times than he cared to remember. Marshall would always get away with it as would Chanda. Parvez wasn't a fool. He'd been a police officer long enough to know how it worked. Chanda, the defenceless pregnant girl, chose the victims then watched and enjoyed the drama until finally she slid away unnoticed.

As he looked down at his sleeping wife he heard again the disgust in her voice: '*I thought police officers were supposed to uphold the law. If you were any sort of a police officer, you would do just that.*' This time he would; this time he would see Chanda brought to court. There would be forensic evidence on her shoes, probably even on her clothes – fibres and Aisha's blood and skin. There was no way she was going to get away with it. He would ask if he could arrest her, although he doubted DI Handford would allow it. As he thought of his boss his stomach curled and his nerve endings thrashed, making him feel sick.

'Anything on Chanda?'

'No sir, not yet.'

'Don't worry about it, she's probably not important. Let me know when you have.'

Mr Handford had trusted him and tomorrow, whatever his father said, he would go to see him, admit that he had lied and accept the consequences. He owed that to Aisha, to the DI and to Dianne Ingleby.

Aisha stirred. As she opened her eyes a frown of pain slipped across her forehead. He grasped her hand. 'How are you feeling?'

Her tongue flicked over her lips. 'Awful. Can I have a drink?'

'The sister said not yet.' He picked up a sponge, dipped it into the water on her bedside table and ran it gently over her lips.

She closed her eyes again. When she opened them she turned her head carefully towards him. 'It was Chanda,' she said.

He squeezed her hand. 'I know.'

'Will you arrest her?'

'Not me, but someone will.'

'Good.' Her eyes closed again and he could hear the regular breathing of normal sleep, not one induced by anaesthetic. He kissed her forehead and tiptoed out of the room.

The meeting with DCI Russell had been long and painful. Everything Handford had done, every step he had taken so far in the investigation had seemed wrong in his boss's eyes. Forty-eight hours in and they were no nearer a result, he said. The press would have a field day. Was he sure yet who the intended victim was? No, not yet. It was looking more and more likely that it was Maurice, but he had some concerns still about the contents of the diary. Russell was unsure. Why should an attack on a young woman, as vicious as it was, lead to the shooting of Dianne Ingleby? It seemed a poor motive for murder. Handford agreed – on the face of it, it did, but there was always the possibility that the killer thought Dianne knew more than she actually did. Once he was able to interview Kathie or even Emma he could clear it up one way or another. He was fairly sure she was in Ward Eleven at the Royal and he would visit her tomorrow.

He went on to brief him on what he had learned about Ray Braddock.

'It seems to me that he's your main suspect,' Russell said. 'Stop worrying about diaries and death-threat letters and bring him in, question him, break that alibi of his. At least be seen to be doing something, John.'

The confiscation of the computers of three would-be councillors and a political agent, however, was a different matter. The DCI was furious. They'd never be able to keep that from the press. The BNP would love it. 'We managed to maintain secrecy with the last complaint by handing it over to Keighley, now you've put it squarely back in our laps.'

'I'm sorry, sir, but I wasn't the one who brought in Peter Redmayne.'

Russell opened his mouth to argue, but before he could say anything, Handford interrupted. 'And nor did Sergeant Ali.'

'Perhaps not, but neither was he discreet in his choice of venue for questioning Patrick Ambler.' When Handford made no attempt at a reply, he went on, 'You are aware I suppose that there is an election the week after next. It's not going to look good if we charge local politicians with making threats to kill.'

'Not even if they have carried out their threats?'

'Did they?'

Handford had to admit none of them could have pulled the trigger.

'Then leave it.'

'Even if we find evidence of the letters on their computers?' Russell sighed. 'It doesn't prove they were the people who typed them in.'

'No, except that their PCs are protected by passwords and it's unlikely that anyone else could find their way in. George Midgley insisted they had sensitive political information on them so they're hardly likely to give out their passwords. Once I know one way or another I *will* have them back in for questioning. I am ninety-nine point nine per cent sure they were involved in the death threats and I'm waiting only for confirmation from the scientists.'

'So you will charge them; you're not prepared to wait until after the elections?'

'No. I can't see the point.'

'The point is they may well have to forfeit their candidatures and at this late stage it won't give their party time to bring in anyone new. Some people might consider the police are letting the BNP in.'

'I don't see why. One or more of these men may well have made threats against a man whose wife is now dead. How can that be seen as letting in the BNP?'

Russell's barometer had swung all the way round from angry to calm. It was when he was like this that he was at his most dangerous. 'Don't be so naïve, John,' he said softly. 'For most people it won't be, but the BNP will make political capital out of it; that's what they do, and those opposed to them will blame us.' Each word was articulated carefully. 'It might be better to wait until after the election; let feelings settle.'

Handford had had enough of this. He was not a schoolboy to be reprimanded by his headmaster; he was an experienced detective, with more years under his belt than Russell. If the man felt that his DI didn't understand the fundamentals of police politics, then why did he want him as his DCI when he was promoted? 'A few minutes ago you were complaining I'm forty-eight hours in and getting nowhere; now you're telling me I should wait. These men are suspects with a motive for killing Maurice Ingleby, waiting is not an option.'

'You agreed they couldn't have pulled the trigger themselves.'

'But I'm not ruling out that someone did it for them. There are enough hotheads in this city who would want Maurice Ingleby out of the way. They think he's giving money to the BNP; he says he isn't and they don't believe him. For one or two of the extremists it's a motive for murder.'

'From what you've said, I would have thought Ray Braddock had the clearest motive.'

'Yes, and I would agree, but as you know there are always as many motives as there are suspects in this kind of crime and all – all – have to be followed up whether senior officers and politicians like it or not. It's not on, Stephen, that we're expected to choose which suspects we investigate and which we don't for no other reason than a need to cover our own backs. I will not go along with that, and if you think I'm wrong then hand the case over to someone who will.'

'Is that what you think I'm doing – covering my back?' Russell was straining to maintain his composure.

Handford made no reply; he'd said too much already.

'Because if you do, John, then perhaps you're not ready to be a DCI.'

Handford lifted his eyes and looked squarely at Russell. 'Perhaps I'm not, Stephen, and perhaps I don't want to be if it means I'm more important than the case I'm investigating.'

Russell's face was impassive and his voice cold when he suggested Handford should go home and think about things, but as much as he stood by what he had said, as he walked out of the station he glanced up at the DCI's office. Russell was looking down at him and in that brief moment Handford saw HMET and his future fly out of the window and soar into the sky.

chapter fifteen

John Handford woke on Sunday morning with a blinding head-ache and the distinct feeling he had put the noose round his own neck in his meeting with Russell. It was all very well standing by his principles, but to suggest the DCI considered himself and his career was more important than the death of a woman like Dianne Ingleby was probably a step too far. Perhaps he ought to go grovelling to him – to apologise? But if he did, what would he be apologising for? The complaint that his investigation was deliberately being hampered for political reasons or that he hadn't kept his observations to himself?

He turned his head to look at the clock radio. The time flipped from 6.29 to 6.30. He could stay where he was and go into the office at nine o'clock like everyone else, but he doubted he would sleep again and if he did it would either be fitfully or deeply – neither of which would do him any good. He slipped out of bed as carefully as he could so as not to disturb Gill. She hadn't been pleased with him last night either. As soon as he'd walked into the kitchen she'd rounded on him. 'Why didn't you tell me, John?'

He hadn't had the vaguest idea what she was talking about. 'Tell you what?'

'About Amina.'

He made a clumsy attempt at an apology, 'It wasn't that I'd forgotten, it was because Khalid said she didn't want anyone to know until she was sure.'

'And you think that meant me? You should have told me, John. She's terrified and I could have been there for her.'

'I couldn't go against her wishes.'

Gill closed the lid of the picnic basket. 'There are times when you are a law unto yourself, do you know that?' It seemed his wife and boss were in collusion – same message, different words. 'You complained last night that Eileen Leighton was keeping things from you in the name of confidentiality, and now here you are doing the same thing to me.'

He attempted to defend himself. 'It's not the same.'

'Yes it is, it's exactly the same.' And she was right.

He shuffled into the bathroom and studied his face in the mirror. Dull grey eyes stared back at him. His hair was becoming flecked with grey and he was sure he could count extra wrinkles. He looked like he felt: an ageing police officer past his sell-by date. He took a couple of painkillers then turned on the shower. The stinging flow of water went some way to refresh his body and when he was finished he turned the water to cold to persuade his brain into gear. He shivered as the last droplets of water pinched at his flesh, and stepped out of the cubicle to wrap himself in his towelling robe and shave before dressing and making his way to the kitchen, where he switched on the kettle and put a slice of bread in the toaster. At the sight of him Brighouse and Rastrick stretched their way out of their respective baskets and demanded to be fed. The cats named after his favourite brass band curled round his legs as he cut open the pouches and squeezed the food into their dishes. Everything was so simple for a cat – eat, sleep and catch the odd mouse. They had more sense than human beings; they deliberately made life simple.

As he ate his toast and drank his coffee, he pondered on how he would deal with Parvez Miah. Aisha's injuries, though bad weren't as severe as first thought and she had come out of the operation well. There was no reason why the trainee detective shouldn't be in work today, at least for a few hours. When he did come, Handford ought to bollock him good and hard and throw him off the team, and although he would do the first he doubted he'd do the second, partly because it would need Russell's agreement and, although it shouldn't make any difference, the boss would recite Iqbal Ahmed at him as a reason for allowing Miah to stay. Like it or not, keeping the peace with the community meant keeping the peace with that man.

There was no doubt it would make the situation easier to deal with if Miah came to him; then he could threaten him with the sack if he ever did anything like that again – plead guilty and the sentence is reduced. But if nothing else he would make him understand the knock-on effect of his lies. If he hadn't denied knowing Chanda, the attack on his wife may have been prevented. No guarantees, but it may have been.

The roads were quiet on a Sunday and he drove into work on automatic pilot so that when he arrived at Central, he couldn't remember anything of the journey. Russell's car was not in its usual spot in the underground parking area, but further along the line he could see Parvez Miah's, although there was no sign of him. On his way to CID he bought a coffee from the machine; he didn't really want one but it was a mechanical response to weekend working and since he knew the day was probably going to get worse rather than better, he needed the caffeine to sustain him. He carried it carefully to his office and set it down on his desk. He settled himself in his chair and stretched over to his in-tray. It was piled with reports, statements and memos. On top was a note from Warrender to say that after Handford had left Braddock yesterday he had had three more visitors; Darren Armitage and Gary Marshall who had stayed no more than half an hour, and another man he didn't know, small, stout, and well-groomed. Braddock had taken him to the house on Station Road where they'd remained for more than an hour. On exiting they had shaken hands as though they had completed a business deal and then returned to the cottage. Shortly afterwards a BMW had picked up the man and driven him to Manchester airport where he caught a flight to Prague. On a hunch Warrender had followed him (expenses claim later) rather than stay with Braddock. He hadn't yet been able to ascertain the man's identity but DC Elliott had agreed to check out the photographs he had taken of him on the national computer. If it was all right by Handford, he would spend more time in Queensbury today (Sunday). He had a feeling something might be about to kick off.

Handford chuckled at Warrender's idea of report language. Nevertheless he had respect for the man's 'feelings' and there was little doubt that Braddock was up to something, probably in the house Rebecca Ingleby was hoping to use as a holiday let. The question was, was it some scam of her lover of which she knew nothing, or was she a part of it and was it in any way linked with Dianne's murder? Russell was right, though for different reasons; he needed to bring Braddock in but he didn't want to waste the precious hours the Police and Criminal Evidence Act allowed him until he was sure of the way questioning should progress. If only they could get into that house. The obvious person to ask was Rebecca Ingleby, but at the moment he had no good reason he could give her for doing so, and after yesterday she would be likely to assume his request was nothing to do with her mother's death and a lot to do with her lover. He didn't want to go down that path again, not yet.

A knock on the door broke into his thoughts. Andy Clarke peered in. 'Are you busy, John?'

Handford beckoned for him to come in. 'What can I do for you?' He indicated the chair.

'I've read the diary and I think you're right; it's worth following. Dianne Ingleby wouldn't have written up her sessions with Kathie in such detail if there hadn't been a good reason. Although I have to say it's going to be difficult to link it with her murder. We haven't got a suspect, for one. I'll make a start on what you want checked out if you still need me to.'

Handford nodded.

'You didn't mention the Reverend Iveson; do you want me to look into his background as well?'

Handford pondered for a moment. 'He's got an alibi, Andy; he was with a dying woman when Dianne Ingleby was shot. I can't see him being involved in this as anything more than the minister of the chapel she attended or as a hospital chaplain, but go on, I suppose we'd better be thorough. Yes, check on him as well. I don't know much, but according to Maurice he came to God late, so you'll need to find out where he was previously. He has a sister; she might be worth talking to ...' Handford's lips twitched. 'Although I don't know who she is or where she lives, but she does spend time at the manse acting as his would-be minister's wife so to speak.'

'Right. I'll add her to your list of uncertains then, shall I?' Clarke stood up. 'Have you run this past Mr Russell?'

'He knows about the diary and Kathie, but he's told me to stop worrying about it and concentrate on Braddock.'

'It might be good advice, John,' Clarke said seriously.

'I know.' Suddenly Handford needed someone to talk to. 'Do you fancy a drink tonight? I could do with a chat away from here.'

'Why not? The Globe at seven?'

'Fine.'

Clarke made for the door. 'Oh, Miah asked if you'd see him when I'm finished.'

Handford sighed. It had to be done and at least the detective was making the first move. 'Yes, tell him to come through.'

'Go easy on him, John. He's feeling guilty enough as it is.'

Handford smiled his agreement.

At first sight Miah looked terrible, as though he had been up all night. But it was more than that for a multitude of emotions swathed his exhaustion: remorse, apprehension, anxiety.

Handford wished he didn't feel sorry for him, but he did. 'I think you'd better sit down, Miah, before you fall asleep on your feet.'

The trainee slumped into the chair Clarke had vacated.

'How's your wife?'

'She's still in quite a lot of pain, sir. I stayed at the hospital last night with her; I think she probably got more sleep than I did.' He made an attempt at a smile.

'Are you sure you're fit enough to be here?'

'I have to be, sir; I need to do this.'

Handford grimaced. He was no bloody good at this. 'Do what?'

'Sir.' Miah's voice cracked and he cleared his throat. 'Sir …' His gaze was fixed on his hands, but suddenly he made eye contact. 'Chanda is my sister-in-law, sir. I lied to you when I said I didn't know her.' The words tumbled out as though the speed at which they were spoken would make them more palatable.

'Yes, I know.'

Miah raced ahead as though he hadn't heard. 'She's been abusing my wife for some time.'

'I know that too – at least I know someone has.'

'And it's also likely she's involved with Darren Armitage and Gary Marshall, but I don't know whether she's acquainted with Ray Braddock.' He returned to scrutinising his hands.

To give the young man time to pull himself together, Handford picked up his coffee. He replaced it without taking a drink – it was more than likely cold anyway. What should he say? 'Thank you for telling me, but I doubt Chanda was important anyway.' It would be the kindest thing to do given the current circumstances.

But the fact was Miah had lied to him and to the team, and he couldn't let that pass.

'You do realise by lying and by keeping this information to yourself you've let everyone down, don't you? Me, the team, the Inglebys, your wife, even yourself.'

'Yes sir.'

'I think you owe us an explanation as to why you decided not to tell the truth.' Handford was sure he knew the answer; it was always the same one in a situation like this. Family. And that was why he was doing this – because Miah had a lesson to learn. Family affected most officers at sometime or other, but particularly the Asian officers. Ali had had a difficult time coming to terms with exactly where his allegiance lay as a detective – even Handford had fought his own sense of loyalty in an investigation in which through no fault of her own, his wife had become involved.

'We've had a lot of problems with Chanda, sir. My father said if she was involved with Armitage and Marshall we would deal with her within the family.'

'Would you have passed on the information to me?'

Miah shook his head. 'My father …'

Handford tried to stop his voice from rising, but didn't succeed. 'Never mind your father,' he said angrily. 'He has nothing to do with this. He has no right to interfere and you know it, Miah. When you're on my team, you obey my orders not your father's. Do you understand?'

'Yes sir.'

'And I shall make my feelings plain to him …'

'No sir …' The words came out as a half-strangled cry.

'Yes sir,' Handford affirmed. He leaned over the desk towards him. 'He's lucky I'm not arresting him for obstructing a police investigation.' At his words Miah's features became even more strained. Handford waited for a few moments, then said, 'Now you listen to me. I could have you disciplined and off the team.' He watched again as Miah winced. To have to go home and tell his father he had been put back into uniform would be a much worse shame. 'This time I'm not going to, more for your wife than for you. She needs every ounce of strength to recover and you on a charge will not help her, but one more step out of line and I will, Aisha or no Aisha. You remember this, Miah, when I give you an order you obey it to the letter. You do not go to your

214

father to seek his permission. You do this once more and I will have you out of CID. Do you understand that?'

'Yes sir,' Miah whispered.

'Right. Now I want you to go home and get some sleep; I'll see you this afternoon. You talk to no one – and that includes your father – about the investigation into Mrs Ingleby's murder. Nor do you discuss the assault on your wife; you leave that to the investigating officers. You remain professional – one peep that you haven't and I *will* have you disciplined.'

Silence stretched as taut as an elastic band until suddenly the telephone rang, startling both of them. Handford reached out and put his hand on the receiver. 'You go, Miah, and remember what I've said.' As the trainee detective stood up, Handford picked up the handset. 'Detective Inspector Handford.'

'Inspector, this is Iqbal Ahmed.' He sounded worried and Handford waved to Miah to remain where he was.

'What can I do for you, Mr Ahmed?'

'It's Chanda, Inspector. She's disappeared. Her bed hasn't been slept in.'

Chanda stirred and opened her eyes. Pain spread upwards from her cheek to her forehead and she lay still until it subsided. She was in a bed in a room she didn't recognise and she took a while to work out where she was. Slowly it came back to her. She was at Gary's – the only place she could think of to go. She glanced round in distaste; it was like a box on the top floor of a block of flats. Not what she was used to. The room smelled and the sheets on the bed were grey rather than white. But none of that mattered, because when she needed him, Gary had been great. She had knocked on his door and he hadn't argued. He had let her in and when she had explained he had said immediately she could stay with him. Even Darren sprawled on the settee with a can of beer had said she couldn't go back. And she couldn't; but neither could she stay, as much as she would like to. Apart from anything else there was the baby. Gary wouldn't want her there with a kid, even if the council would allow it – and as Darren had said, she wasn't safe in Bradford, not from the police and not from her family. Iqbal had told her they would take it from her when it was born. Over her dead body. She might make out she didn't want it, but she did; it was hers and she loved it already

– at least she thought what she felt was love; she'd never loved anyone before so she couldn't be sure. Iqbal had also warned of his intention to pack her off to Pakistan. No way; she wasn't a parcel they could shunt half-way round the world. She was staying here with her baby, but not in Bradford. Everyone knew everyone else in Bradford, and Iqbal would have put the word round already that she was missing. The cops would be looking for her as well. The thought of the police turned her insides cold. They had her shoes; they'd find blood and hair on them from Aisha where she'd kicked her and she knew they'd need only the smallest amount to trace it back. No way was she going to prison for her. Did they let you keep your baby in prison? She didn't know.

She pulled her hand from beneath the sheets and fingered her cheek. It was sore; Iqbal had hit her hard. Tears welled; he had no right to do that; she had explained what had happened. Why would he not believe that cow over her? She struggled into a sitting position. The light in the room was muted by the curtains except where they did not meet, and through the slit a shaft of sun shone on to the bed. She had no idea of the time, but she could hear traffic so assumed it was at least mid-morning. Not much happened until mid-morning in Bradford on a Sunday. Nothing much happened in Bradford at the best of times, particularly now she was married and expecting. They had done that to her. She hadn't wanted to be married – not yet. She hadn't wanted to be pregnant. She didn't even like her husband very much; Parvez was much nicer, but he was married to *her* and they had been allowed to marry because they loved each other. No one gave Chanda the choice.

She wondered where Parvez was now, probably at the hospital with Aisha. Her own husband was on his way to Pakistan to organise her stay there. It wasn't fair; why should Aisha have everything she hadn't? She deserved the kicking. Chanda felt again the impact of her shoe as it connected with Aisha's head and reverberated back through her own body, and concern took over from anger. Was she all right? She hadn't died during the night? It wasn't that she cared one way or another; it was just that she needed to know so that she could work out when to go. She could ring the hospital, say she was her sister-in-law and ask how she was. She picked her bag off the floor and hunted for her mobile phone. It was right at the bottom. She grabbed it and turned it on. As she pressed the photo button, pictures of Aisha lying on the floor of the sitting room filled the small screen. She could just see the pool of blood. She had to delete them. As she did so, she heard the policeman telling her she could be charged with actual bodily harm, even attempted murder. She wasn't sure exactly what actual bodily harm meant, but she understood murder.

Frantically she pulled herself out of bed. She had to get out of here. She'd go to Birmingham or London, now, today, before the baby was born. She'd need money and Gary and Darren had promised to help her with that. They would go tooled up and rob the corner shop as they had intended. Chanda had looked for a decent knife, but there wasn't one, not one that would frighten the shopkeeper anyway. Then Darren had said to forget the knife; he had a far better idea. She and Gary had demanded to know what, but he had refused to tell them, he'd just said he'd sort it tomorrow. And that meant today.

Satisfied, she patted her tummy. 'We'll be out of here by tonight you and me baby; somewhere no one can touch us.'

Warrender was tired of waiting for something to happen. Following Braddock's meeting with the well-groomed man yesterday, he had been sure something was about to kick off. But so far nothing. The cottage was in darkness and the curtains still drawn. To add to the boredom, Queensbury was about as dead as it could be. Even the pub wasn't open. He stretched over to the glove compartment and pulled out a packet of crisps. As he chewed, he decided that if he wasn't to lose the will to live he had to force the issue and make something happen. It wasn't in his nature to hang around watching nothing. Elliott hadn't managed to track down the man Ray Braddock had met, but whoever he was, they had done a deal, and it was at the house on Station Road in which they'd done it. So it was Station Road where he had to be. He poured the last of his crisps into his mouth as though he was drinking them from the packet and climbed out of his car.

It took him no more than five minutes to walk to the house and as he rounded the corner at the end of the lane it came into view. He stopped to contemplate the exterior silhouetted in the morning sunlight. Looking at it from this distance he had to admit it had potential as a holiday cottage, though at the moment it was in much too poor a state of repair to demand any kind of rent, let alone one that would satisfy the likes of Rebecca Ingleby. It had been hers for almost a year now and Braddock had been charged with renovating it yet it seemed to Warrender little was being done; it hadn't even been given a lick of paint. Nor was there any equipment that would suggest a builder was working there – no ladders, no supplies, nothing. He wondered if Rebecca ever came down here to see how work was progressing. But then, perhaps she didn't need to and the story about letting it as a holiday cottage was no more than that – a story.

He pushed his way through the gate and followed the path round the house. The front of the building was catching the rays of the morning sun while at the back the garden, such as it was, stood in the house's shadow. Each gable was obscured by mature chestnut trees. It was not a place most people would look at twice, let alone buy. But Warrender was trained to look twice. And what he saw suggested a more than conscious effort at security. The windows, though filthy were double glazed with toughened glass, and those away from the road had the added protection of iron grilles on the inside. The rooms were concealed from view by curtains and high above on the front wall was a security alarm. He made a note of the firm's name; it was not local. There were two doors to the house. He pushed at them. Both were securely locked and, he decided as he rubbed his shoulder, heavy. Why, if all that was going on in there was a refurbishment, would Rebecca need iron grilles, heavy doors and an up-to-date security alarm? Queensbury wasn't exactly crime-ridden.

The sound of a car's engine started him. It had to be Ray Braddock, no one else came down here. Warrender held himself flat against the side wall and peered cautiously towards the road. The vehicle had stopped on the other side of the road and a young man was getting out. It wasn't Braddock nor was it the Volvo Estate. In fact, unless he was very much mistaken it was Darren Armitage. He was carrying what looked like a sports bag. Without so much as a glance round, he opened the gate, dashed up to the front door, pushed a key in the lock and went inside, leaving it ajar. Careless.

Warrender called in the vehicle's registration and waited impatiently for the reply. When it came it was exactly what the detective wanted to hear. It had been reported stolen some half-hour ago and that gave him a legitimate reason to enter the house. By the book Handford had said, and by the book was what he was getting. He tiptoed to the front door and pushed it open. It led into a large room. An overpowering smell caught at his nostrils, a smell heavy with grease and metal rather than the sweetness of wood and sawdust. The curtains over the windows filtered the sunlight, but even in the murkiness he knew he was in some kind of a workroom. He could make out the figure of Darren Armitage crouched against a box in one corner. Warrender felt along the wall for a light switch. When he found it he pressed it down and, as light flooded the room, Armitage spun round. A long trestle table stood between them in the centre of the room, behind it a couple of wooden chairs. Against one wall was a bench on which there was a kettle, several mugs and various tools, none of them much to do with joinery, and some of them the detective was fairly sure he recognised. He hoped he was wrong, but if he wasn't, what was going on in this house would account for the trips to Europe not to mention Braddock's undeclared finances. It might also account for the possible business deal with the man yesterday.

Once over his surprise, Armitage made a dash for the door. Warrender was quicker and barred his way.

'Sorry, Darren, you're not going anywhere,' he said with a smile. He showed him his warrant card. 'I'm Detective Constable Warrender and that car you drove up in has been reported stolen, so I'm going to have to arrest you.' He cautioned him to prove he was serious, then pointed to the box. 'You stealing from Miss Ingleby as well?'

Darren said nothing. He knew better than to tell a copper anything.

'So what were you doing?' When Darren continued to remain silent, he said, 'Let's have a look shall we? Let's see what's in the box.'

Again Darren tried to make a bolt for it, but Warrender caught him by his collar and pushed him into one of the chairs. 'Stay there,' he said, emphasising each word. He held out his hand. 'Keys.'

When Armitage made no move, Warrender leaned over him

and barked again, 'Keys.' He stood back. 'It's either that or I'll tie you to that chair.'

Morosely Armitage pulled a keyring from his pocket and handed it to him. There were three in total, two for padlocks and one which he assumed was for the outside door. He tried it, turned it and pocketed it. There were times when getting out could be as difficult as getting in. He wondered if Braddock had thought about that. 'You can't lock me in,' Armitage bluffed.

'Sorry mate, I've done it. Move a muscle and I promise you I *will* tie you to the chair. Now let's have a look shall we?'

The box was heavy and it took some strength to drag it across the floor. Armitage had already opened up two of the flaps; Warrender pulled at the rest. On top was a coating of polystyrene chippings. He pushed them out of the carton and on to the floor to reveal what he feared. Wrapped in waxed paper and nestling among the chippings was a revolver. He picked it out and felt round. His fingers counted twelve similar parcels. The other boxes would no doubt contain the same. Braddock was dealing in guns and, by the look of the tools, was more than likely modifying, converting or even reactivating them. A dangerous game.

He took out his mobile phone. 'I think you'd better get up to Queensbury, guv,' he said when Handford answered. 'I'm at the house in Station Road. And I think while you're about it you'd better arrest Ray Braddock and Rebecca Ingleby before they realise we're here.'

Chanda was becoming frightened. Where was Darren? He'd said it would take no more than an hour and he'd been gone much longer than that. Gary tried his mobile but although it rang, he didn't answer it. Instead a disembodied voice said he could leave a message, but there was no point; it wouldn't tell him where he was.

They'd have to go and look for him Chanda said, but Gary pointed out they'd no idea where he was. 'He probably had to nick a car and that can take time.'

'Do you think he's been caught?'

Gary was becoming impatient 'How the fuck should I know. We'll just have to wait.'

Chanda switched on the television. She flicked through the channels. Nothing, at least nothing that was of any interest to her. 'There's nothing on here; don't you have Sky?'

'How the hell am I supposed to afford Sky? I can't even afford the licence.'

A hand squeezed at her tummy. She caught her breath; it must be one of those practise pains the policewoman had talked about. She shifted uncomfortably.

Gary hadn't noticed. 'You want some fish and chips?' he said.

The thought made her feel sick. 'No, I don't want anything, I'm not hungry.'

'I think I'll go and get some.'

'No, Gary, don't leave me.'

'Chand, me stomach thinks me throat's cut. I need something to eat and the shop's only down the road.'

'What if Darren comes back?'

'Then tell 'im to wait 'ere. I'm not going to be away for ever.'

He gave her a sideways look. 'You all right?'

'I don't know. I feel funny, a bit sick.'

'It's the crack on the 'ead that maniac gave you. It's still swollen you know.'

The hand squeezed harder. That didn't feel like it was practising; that felt like it was real. She wished now she'd been to the classes which explained about having babies; she'd have had some idea of what to expect. She hadn't gone then because she hadn't seen the point. Instead she'd used them as an excuse to get out of the house and spend the afternoon hanging round with Gary and Darren.

Gary got off his chair and walked to the door. 'I'm going to the chippy and I'll be as quick as I can. Probably Darren will be back by then. You sure you don't want anything? Some food might help.'

She shook her head. 'Please don't be long,' she said. She didn't want to be alone any longer than she had to be. He slammed the door and she heard his footsteps on the concrete stairs. She switched on the television again. Still nothing, but the sound broke the silence and took her mind off her fear. She shifted her position again. It didn't matter where she was, standing, sitting, lying, she couldn't get comfortable. She struggled off the settee and began pacing the room, but that made her back ache. Where was Darren? He ought to be back by now; they needed to get on with the job; she needed the money from the off-licence; she couldn't get way from Iqbal Ahmed without it. She opened the door to the small balcony and looked over it into the street. There was no sign of either of them. The flat was ten floors up, and seeing things from this height made her dizzy. For a moment she thought she would faint, but once she lifted her head towards the horizon she felt better.

The programme on the television finished. There was a film on next – one she'd never heard of. They didn't watch English or American films at home. Iqbal wouldn't allow it. The television was there for the news and the Asian programmes. That was the only reason they had Sky, for the programmes he approved of. When she lived on her own she would watch what she wanted and so would her baby.

The hand squeezed again, even harder. She knew now this wasn't practise, it was for real. Tears ran down her cheeks as panic took over. Where was Gary? She looked towards the road again, but her head spun and she had to come off the balcony. If only the women were here; they would know what to do; they would look after her. Perhaps she should ring Iqbal, say she was sorry and ask him to let her come home. He wouldn't deny her if the baby was on its way, but then afterwards he would take it from her and send her to Pakistan. And what if the police had come back? Pictures of babies, police cells and the crowded streets of Islamabad flooded her mind. She tried to watch the film, but her fears took precedence and she couldn't concentrate.

It must have been fifteen minutes later when she heard the footsteps on the stairs and the door open. Gary came in munching a chip. The smell of them made her retch.

He hardly noticed. 'Sorry I've been so long,' he said. 'It was busy and I met a couple of mates and we got talking. I asked if they'd seen Darren, but they hadn't.' He pushed at her legs. 'Shove up.'

The hand squeezed as she moved but so much harder that it hurt and it lasted longer.

When it was over she looked at him, 'Gary, I think the baby's coming,' she said.

chapter sixteen

As soon as John Handford received Warrender's call he drove up to Queensbury. By the time he arrived Station Road had been cordoned off and scene-of-crime officers plus a couple of firearms experts were carrying out an examination of the house and its contents. It seemed the potholed lane had not been so popular since trains ran from the village to Keighley, Bradford and Halifax during the nineteen thirties and forties. A small crowd gathered at the cordon tape together with several on-duty journalists. They threw a few questions at him as he passed them, which he answered by saying he knew very little but would make a statement when there was something to tell and with that they had to be satisfied.

Warrender met him by the gate with the news that there were six boxes containing various weapon types in the house – all, according to the experts, had been reactivated. Six were Lugers – the kind as used in Dianne Ingleby's murder and they would be examined against the bullets retrieved from her body and the multi-storey car park. There was also a box of ammunition. At the moment the find didn't point directly to the identity of the killer, but it did suggest that either Ray Braddock or Rebecca Ingleby or both could have been involved. It also brought Handford a possible step nearer to the attack on Kathie. The link was there. If she had known about the guns and threatened to shop Braddock, the assault would have been his warning to her, and then if he thought she was about to tell Dianne Ingleby, he would have had no alternative but to silence her as well, only this time to make it permanent.

'Take a PC with you and wake him up and arrest him, Warrender.'

'It'll be a pleasure guv.'

'Cordon off the cottage and get someone in to search it thoroughly.'

'I won't.'

As Warrender disappeared up the road, Handford rang Ali, explained what had happened and told him to bring in Rebecca Ingleby. 'It's not going to go down well with Maurice, but don't let him intimidate you.'

'He'll more than likely demand his own solicitor and since it's Sunday it could take a while to get hold of him. Darren Armitage is on his way down to the station shouting the odds about police brutality and being held hostage by Warrender. You and Clarke interview him; we need to know what he knows about the gun in Station Road. Find out too why he wanted the gun. If he and Gary Marshall are thinking of branching out into armed robbery, we need to stop it now and while you're about it check his movements on Thursday night; see if they tie up with Braddock's.'

'Right. Do you think it was Ray Braddock who killed Dianne Ingleby?'

'I don't know, Khalid; maybe. To be sure we need to break that alibi. Let's see what we get when we question him.'

'Before you go, John, the IT people have found the death-threat letters on two of the computers seized: the first three on Patrick Ambler's and the fourth on George Midgley's.'

That was good news. For the first time since the murder, cracks were forming; all they needed now was for one of them to open up. 'We'll have to leave them until tomorrow. Organise for someone to pick them up in the morning. I'm coming back to Central now so I'll see you later.'

As he walked into the foyer some quarter of an hour later, the civilian behind the counter beckoned to him. She pointed over to Iqbal Ahmed. 'He's been waiting a while,' she said. Handford groaned. It had been a long morning, the afternoon promised to be even longer, and the last thing he wanted was to enter into discussion with the man. Chanda's case was nothing to do with him and nor was he in the mood to discuss Parvez Miah. He walked over to him. 'What can I do for you, Mr Ahmed?'

'I need to talk to you, Inspector. I will not detain you long, but it is important otherwise I would not have waited.'

Handford could have used his own office but decided instead

to take him into a small one beyond the foyer. Officially it was a press office but was hardly ever used as such. Its dingy decorations and limited furnishings were designed to put off any journalist who wanted an interview and they had got wise to it, preferring instead to conduct their discussions by phone. This in turn suited the officers involved, who could cut the conversation short by saying they were wanted for something urgent (usually having been called by a non-existent sergeant named Frank) and the reporter was none the wiser.

He opened the door and switched on the strip light. It flickered, but eventually settled into a yellowy dimness. Ahmed seemed not to notice. 'What are you doing to find Chanda?'

Handford pulled out a chair for him and sat opposite. 'I'm not involved in Chanda's case sir, uniformed officers are looking for her. If you want me to pass you on to the duty inspector, I can do so and he will put you in the picture.'

'I don't wish uniformed officers to be looking for her,' Ahmed said. 'I wish her disappearance to be passed to the investigative branch, particularly as I hold you personally responsible.'

Handford opened his mouth to protest, but Ahmed cut him short. 'If you hadn't sent in your officers to frighten her, she wouldn't have run away.'

'Mr Ahmed, I didn't send anyone in. Uniformed officers were dealing with the attack on Aisha. She had made a complaint against Chanda and they were bound to investigate it. If they frightened her, then it was because she had something to be frightened about.'

'If she had, and I repeat *if*, then it was something to be dealt with within the family, not by the police.'

Handford could see why Miah lied. 'No, sir, it became a police investigation as soon as Aisha made her complaint. The attack on her is not a family matter. She was very badly beaten and according to the doctors this isn't the first time it has happened.'

'So they say.'

'So the old bruises say.'

At that Ahmed paused then changed the direction of the conversation. 'You told Parvez you wanted to speak to her about the murder of Dianne Ingleby.'

'I said I wanted to speak to an Asian girl called Chanda who may have known one of our suspects, no more and no less. I never thought for a minute she was involved in the murder, but she could have been aware of something we weren't. You forced your son into lying about her existence. You had no right to do that, Parvez is a police officer and you put him in an impossible position. This time all I have done is warn him about his future behaviour, next time I will make sure he goes back into uniform and is never allowed in CID again, and that would be a pity, Mr Ahmed because he has the makings of a good detective, but to become one he has to accept that while family secrets are all right in their place, a police investigation isn't it.'

He paused to let his words penetrate and wondered what Russell's reaction would be to what he was saying. This was the difference between him and the DCI. He would polish over the situation to cleanse it before discussing it, Handford told it as it was, dirt and all, because sometimes that was the only way.

'Please don't do this to him again, Mr Ahmed. Not only are you putting your son's career at risk, you are also at risk yourself of being arrested for obstructing the police. This time I haven't gone down that path because the harm is to your family and not to our investigation, but remember this, had it been the other way round, I wouldn't have hesitated.' Handford stood up. 'Now, if you will excuse me, I have work to do, but if you want here, I will have someone take you to the duty inspector.' And with that he opened the door and called a passing constable.

He made for CID diverting only to pick up a sandwich and a tea from the canteen. He could just about have these while he was waiting for the solicitors to finish meeting with their clients. The phone was ringing as he reached his office. He pushed open the door and managed to reach the desk without spilling the contents of the Styrofoam cup. 'Handford,' he said as he picked up the receiver.

'I've got a Mr Ingleby in the front office, Inspector; he would like a word.' It was the same woman who had pointed out Iqbal Ahmed to him. Her voice slumped to a whisper. 'He's very angry,' she said. 'Do you want me to send him up, or shall I say you're not available?'

They were forming a queue – first Ahmed, now Ingleby. He had expected a difficult day, but this was turning into a nightmare. The chances were Ahmed would go to Russell when he'd finished with the duty inspector and Ingleby would follow him, but that was no reason to turn the man away. He deserved an explanation. 'No don't do that, have him brought up.' He put his sandwich in his desk drawer. A few moments later there came a knock on the door and a constable showed in Maurice Ingleby. Yesterday his features had been haggard; today they were purple with rage.

'What the hell do you think you're doing, Handford, arresting my daughter?' he bellowed almost before the door had closed. His voice bounced round the room.

He had told Ali not to let the man intimidate him, and he had no intention of allowing him do the same to him. 'She has been arrested together with Ray Braddock on suspicion of importing and dealing in illegal firearms,' he said quietly as he indicated the chair.

Ingleby refused the offer. 'What do you mean importing and dealing in illegal firearms with Ray Braddock?'

'We found a supply of reactivated revolvers in the house she owns in Queensbury. Now, please Mr Ingleby, sit down.'

Deflated, the man collapsed into the chair, his eyes screwed up like a child attempting to make sense of what he had heard. Handford pitied him. For the first time, he looked small, grey and not the hard business man he was considered to be: the one who got what he wanted, whether it was the best contractors, the best materials, or the most beautiful and successful women in his bed. The element of control he had had when he had marched into the office had gone. 'You've got this wrong, Handford. She doesn't have a house in Queensbury.' The words were there but not the assurance.

It was startling how when the skittles began to tumble they did so at an alarming rate. First Dianne, now Rebecca. There was a lot Ingleby didn't know about his daughter, a lot she hadn't wanted him to know and for the second time in almost as many days Handford was about to rip his world apart like a piece of old rag. 'I assure you sir she does. It's down Station Road. She bought it almost a year ago with money left to her by an aunt. Her intention was to renovate it and turn it into a holiday let. Apparently Mr Braddock was doing the renovation for her. We've had him under surveillance for a few days now and this morning we were able to gain entry into the house where we found a supply of handguns, together with tools used to reactivate and modify them. I can't see how she didn't know what the house was being used for because I find it hard to believe she never once went down there to see how work was progressing. She's a builder, trained by you; surely it would be a natural instinct for her to do that.'

Ingleby sank deeper into himself. 'I don't believe she's involved with Ray Braddock. She wouldn't do this to me.' He was clutching at anything that would return to him the daughter he thought he knew. 'She's had nothing to do with him for a long time. She knows what a loser he is, and how against him Dianne and I were.'

'I'm sorry Mr Ingleby, but your daughter has been having a relationship with him on and off since she was seventeen, and an intimate one for more than a year. After the bankruptcy she even bought him a car, a silver Volvo Estate. It's registered to her, but it's for his use.'

The truth hung over him like a cloud. 'You're telling me she's been lying to me all this time?'

Handford tried to minimise it. 'As you said yourself, she's twenty-five; she wants her own life.'

'She hasn't always been twenty-five,' Ingleby said bitterly. He leaned forward resting his elbows on his knees and covering his face with his hands. When he recovered his composure his gaze met Handford's. 'Why? Why would she do this?' As overpowering as it was, he was beginning to accept the reality of the situation.

'I don't know. Money perhaps, or excitement, even love I suppose.'

The next question was harder and for a while Ingleby played with it. 'Did she – did they have anything to do with Dianne's death?'

'I don't know Mr Ingleby. It's always possible your wife had found out what they were doing and it was necessary to . . .' he sought for words that wouldn't hurt too much, 'silence her.' He paused again. Connie Burns had said she was sure Rebecca had more on her mind than her mother's murder; she had described her as panicky when she learned Handford was coming to the house to question her. He had thought it was because he knew of her relationship with Braddock, but perhaps it was more to do with what was going on in Station Road. 'All I can say is I've never had your daughter down as a suspect.'

Ingleby pushed himself from the chair and stepped to the window. For a moment or two he looked out then he leaned forward until his forehead was pressing hard against the glass. Finally he turned round. 'Can I see her?'

Handford shook his head. 'No, I'm sorry. We're waiting for her solicitor and then we're going to interview her.'

'Can you pass a message to her?'

'I can do that.'

'Tell her I'm here for her.'

Handford had been right. When it came down to the bottom line, Maurice Ingleby would support his daughter no matter what she had done. Just as Handford knew he would support his. That's what fathers did.

When Handford and Warrender walked into the interview room, Ray Braddock was leaning back in his chair adopting an air of disinterest. It was designed to make the detectives think that either he had nothing to hide or the police had nothing on him. Either way Handford had seen it all before. The man had taken advantage of the services of the duty solicitor; he was too astute to ask for someone he would have to pay for; after all he was an unemployed bankrupt with no money except what the State handed out to him, and no doubt if and when he was charged he would demand Legal Aid.

Handford nodded to Warrender to go through the preliminaries and when they were over he said, 'You understand why you are here, Mr Braddock?'

'Oh, I understand all right. I'm here because I've been set up by that bitch Rebecca Ingleby. When it comes down to it, she's no different from her father. He set me up, now she's doing the same, probably because he told her to.'

It was an interesting thought and Handford smiled. 'Would you like to explain how you think she has done that?'

'I know nothing about what goes on in that house. She bought it, it's hers, it's nothing to do with me.'

'You haven't been involved in renovating it?'

'Why should I? Her father owns a building firm. If she wants it renovating there are plenty of people there to do it for her. Why should she ask me?'

'To give you something to do; start you off again.'

'Is that what she says? And where am I going to get the money to do that? She's never given me any and no one is going to give me materials on credit are they? I'm a bankrupt. I needed cash.'

'She says she gave you cash.'

'She's lying. I told you, her and her father have set me up.'

'When I spoke to Mr Ingleby he didn't seem to be aware of the house in Queensbury.'

'Then he's lying as well.'

'Let me get this straight, Mr Braddock. You're telling me that you know nothing about the house and you've never been there.'

Braddock turned to the solicitor. 'Do I have to keep answering the same question?'

The solicitor agreed. 'I think my client has made his point Inspector.'

'We'll leave it for the moment then. You've been having a relationship with Miss Ingleby for the past few years, I understand?'

Braddock sighed as though he was bored by the question.

'Yes.'

'Can you describe that relationship?'

He smirked. 'What everything?'

Handford ignored the implication.

'We are a couple. We sleep together and we have been for quite a while.'

'You told me you intend to marry her.'

'If I have to.'

'What does that mean?'

He grinned. 'No comment.'

'You have the use of a car that Miss Ingleby claims she bought for you?'

'I suppose.'

'Can you tell me what make and model it is?'

'It's a 2003 silver Volvo estate.'

'Do you use it often?'

'When I need to.'

Handford turned to Warrender. The detective pulled a photograph from the file in front of him. 'This is exhibit CW1. It is a photograph of a silver Volvo estate car. Is this the car Miss Ingleby bought and which you use?'

There was little point in denying it and Braddock nodded. 'For the benefit of the tape, Mr Braddock nods a yes.'

'Can you give me some idea of the location of the photograph?'

Braddock swallowed hard. 'I'm not sure, at the edge of a road, next to a fence.'

'Do you know which road?'

'It's just a road.'

'Would you accept that the car is parked in Station Road in Queensbury?'

Braddock shifted his position. 'If you say so, one road is very much like any other.'

'Is there anyone in the car?'

'There might be.'

'Do you know who?'

'Should I?'

'Can you look at the date on the back of the photograph?'

Braddock turned it over. 'It's the twenty-second of May 2005.'

'Yesterday?'

'Yes.'

'And the time?'

'Twelve thirteen and twenty seconds.'

'Right – now I want you to look at this next photograph, exhibit CW2. Give me the date and the time on that.'

'Twenty-second of May, 2005, twelve thirteen and fifty-five seconds.'

'You would agree these two photographs were taken one after the other?'

'Yes.'

'Now look at the photograph. Is that you locking that car?'

Braddock slumped. 'No comment.'

'It looks very like you to me.'

'No comment.'

'Now this one, exhibit CW3.' Warrender put it in front of him. 'Same date, almost a minute later. This is you again unlocking the door of the house you say you have never visited. Would you agree?'

'No comment.'

'All right, let's have a look at this one, exhibit CW4. It has

231

the same date again and was taken approximately an hour later. You're shaking hands with a gentleman outside the house in Station Road.'

'No comment.'

'Who is that gentleman?'

'No comment.'

Warrender leaned forward. 'You can give as many 'no comment' answers as you want, Mr Braddock, but I think these photographs tell a different story. Do you still say you have never been to the house on Station Road, that you have no idea what is going on in there, and that it is Miss Ingleby who has set you up?'

Braddock smiled. 'No comment.'

Rebecca Ingleby's features were strained as she was brought into the interview room accompanied by her solicitor. As expected he was one of the priciest and most experienced in the city. Handford shook hands with him. 'Thank you for coming, Mr Sullivan. I'm Detective Inspector John Handford and this is Detective Constable Warrender.'

Sullivan acknowledged Warrender. 'I hope you know what you're doing Inspector,' he said.

'I do, sir.'

Except when he was blaming Rebecca for setting him up, Braddock had given a no comment interview. The time came when they were getting nowhere and there was little point in continuing, so he had been taken back to his cell. What Handford didn't want was to let him go and have him disappear to Europe. He needed something from either Rebecca or Darren Armitage which would put him firmly in the frame, if not for the murder, then at least for the trade in illegal firearms. He didn't expect anything much from scene of crime, although fingerprints may come through with something later today. Modern technology made it so much easier and quicker to get a match.

'Perhaps we can make a start,' Sullivan said. 'I left a game of golf halfway through and I would like to get back to it.'

So much for his concern for his client.

Warrender put the tapes in the machine and switched it on. At the bleep, he went through the day, the time, those present and cautioned Rebecca Ingleby.

Handford asked her the same question he had put to Braddock. 'You understand why you are here, Miss Ingleby.'

'I understand what you have said; I do not understand why you've said it.'

'Then let me explain. This morning we found a number of boxes containing firearms in the cottage you bought down Station Road in Queensbury. All of them have been reactivated, which is illegal. There were also a number of tools used for such a task. Mr Braddock says he knows nothing about them, in fact he says he has never been near or in the house. Perhaps you could furnish us with a reason as to why they are there.'

'You don't have to answer that, Rebecca.'

She looked at him wide-eyed. 'I can't answer it; I don't know. Ray is refurbishing the house for me. I never go down there.'

'Why don't you go down there? I would have thought you would have wanted to know how the work was progressing; after all you are hoping to open it up this summer.'

'Ray fills me in as to how it's progressing. I don't need to go there.'

Was she really as naïve as she sounded? 'Your father informs me she is unaware of the Queensbury house.'

'I don't tell him everything. What I do with my own money is none of his business.'

'Nor was he aware of your relationship with Ray Braddock.'

'But I imagine he is now. You said you wouldn't tell him.'

'I said I wouldn't unless it impinged on your mother's murder.'

'Inspector, really.' Edward Sullivan's tone was tinged with distaste. 'Are you suggesting Miss Ingleby was responsible for her mother's death?'

'No sir, I'm not suggesting that because at the moment I don't know. What I do know however is that several boxes of illegal firearms were found in a house Miss Ingleby owns, some of which were of the type used to kill Mrs Ingleby. I also know that Mr Braddock, who agrees he is having an intimate relationship with your client, insists he knows nothing of the house or of the renovations or of anything that may be in there. Indeed he says he has never been asked to do any work, nor has he been given money for materials.'

Rebecca remained quite still, her expression one of disbelief.

'I don't believe you. Ray wouldn't do this to me.' She began to panic. The coolness and assurance she exhibited at her parents' house was gone. Suddenly she was losing the lover she thought was faithful to her and she wasn't prepared to believe it. 'It's a trick; my father has put you up to it.'

'I can assure you he hasn't,' Handford responded quietly. 'But what I can assure you of is that the house in Queensbury is being used as a gun factory either by you, or by Mr Braddock or by both of you.' He leaned forward. 'I'm sure your solicitor understands how serious this situation is; it would be in your best interests to cooperate with me.'

She turned to Edward Sullivan. He gave her an encouraging smile but made no comment.

Handford pulled one of the photographs from the folder. 'This is exhibit CW4. Do you know this man with Mr Braddock?'

She glanced at it. 'No, I've never seen him before. Who is he?'

'Take a good look, Miss Ingleby. Are you sure you don't know him?'

She let her eyes fall on to the picture in front of her. 'Quite sure, I've never seen him before.'

'I talked to you yesterday about Mr Braddock's frequent trips to Europe. Do you ever go with him?'

'I've already told you that that is impossible. He can't afford to go to Europe at all and certainly not frequently.'

She was still clinging on, remaining faithful. Until he gave her something that would force her to let go of Braddock, Handford would get nowhere. 'How often do you meet?'

'As often as we can.'

'What does that mean? Once, twice a week, more often?'

'More often, except ...' She stopped.

'Except?'

'Except when he has to go away for a few days. To see his mother, he says.'

She was beginning to doubt; the last two words said so. He was about to clinch it for her. 'His mother is dead Miss Ingleby. She drowned when he was fourteen. Wherever he has been going it hasn't been to see his mother.'

Rebecca looked round wildly, first at her solicitor, and then at Handford and Warrender. The self-assured twenty-five-year-old disappeared, and a young girl who was already hurting began to sob uncontrollably. Everything she was feeling about her mother's death and her boyfriend's faithlessness poured out with the tears. There were times when Handford hated his job.

'I think we need to take a break, Inspector, don't you?' Edward Sullivan said.

Handford pushed back his chair. 'We'll leave you for a while. I'll send someone in with a glass of water for Miss Ingleby.'

The interview with Darren Armitage did not begin well for he gave the same 'no comment' answers his uncle had given. After fifteen minutes Detective Sergeant Ali and Detective Constable Clarke were becoming bored. Ali wished they had used the press room; the atmosphere there would have worn him down more quickly.

Finally, more in desperation than in anger, the sergeant leaned towards him. 'You can continue answering our questions with a "no comment" if you wish, but I have to warn you we have DC Warrender's statement which says you were in the house in Station Road. It's very likely we have your fingerprints on the carton you were opening and forensic evidence in the car you stole. So stop wasting my time and do yourself a favour, because if you don't you could find yourself going down for a lot more than taking and driving away and being in possession of a firearm.'

As his tongue flicked over his lips Ali didn't doubt Armitage had got the gist of what was meant. Fear had taken the place of bravado. 'What were you doing in the house Mr Armitage, and why did you want that gun?'

Armitage thought for a while. 'It was for Chanda,' he said finally.

'Chanda?' The two detectives glanced at each other.

'Her father-in-law hit her last night; she has a big bruise on her face and he's threatened to take her baby away from her when it's born. What kind of a person does that? Anyway, she needs to get away from him, but she needs money. We were going to get it for her. We were going to do the off-licence.'

'And the gun?'

'We weren't going to use it, just wave it about a bit to frighten the owner.'

'Who are we?'

235

'Me and Gary and Chanda.'

'Where is Chanda now?'

'She's at Gary's place. Look, I think you ought to let them know where I am. Chanda's in enough of a panic as it is.'

Clarke pushed back his chair. 'I'll tell Parvez,' he said. 'He can pick her up.' He returned a few minutes later. 'Miah and a female officer have gone up to the flat.'

Ali nodded then turned back to Armitage. 'You say you wanted the gun for this job you were going to do. As far as I understand it you haven't used a gun before; there's nothing on your record. How did you know where to get one from?'

'I just knew.'

'Come on, Mr Armitage, you didn't just know. You went to the right house and were in the process of opening the right box. Someone must have told you there were guns there.'

Armitage made no reply.

'Ray Braddock's your uncle isn't he?'

'Yes.'

'He's working at the house?'

'He goes down there sometimes.'

'Why?'

'Ask him.'

'Do you go there at all?'

'Sometimes.'

'Why?'

Armitage shrugged again. Obviously he wasn't prepared to grass on his uncle.

'Then let me help you. Your uncle is dealing in illegal firearms and you are helping him. I know it and you know it, otherwise you wouldn't have stolen a car and gone there to pick up a gun. You can keep your uncle out of it if you want; I doubt he will be so accommodating towards you. But if you want to take all the blame that's up to you. We can end this interview now.'

Clarke made to turn off the recorder.

'No wait.'

The detectives waited.

Armitage began to pick at the Styrofoam cup in front of him. 'What my uncle does there is nothing to do with me. I don't know anything about reactivating guns or about selling them. That's down to him and I'm not going to serve time for it. He

236

pays me for shifting them down to the tunnels and for bringing them back up, but that's all I do.'

'Which tunnels?'

Clarke brought out a map of the area.' Show me,' he said.

Darren Armitage scrutinised it for a while. 'That's where the old station was, and if you go that direction,' he indicated to the east, 'there's an old tunnel. If you go the other way there's another one. He keeps his stuff in those.'

Clarke picked up an evidence bag in which was the set of keys Armitage had with him. 'That's what the two padlock keys are for?'

'Yes. Go and see for yourself if you don't believe me.'

'Oh we will, Mr Armitage, you can be sure of that,' Clarke said.

'Now that we've cleared that up,' Ali said. 'I've got another couple of questions. Can you tell me what you were doing last Thursday evening?'

The solicitor intervened. 'I fail to see what this has to do with the firearms found today.'

'Probably nothing, but if Mr Armitage could clarify his movements for us, I'd be grateful.'

The solicitor nodded.

'So, what were you doing on Thursday evening?'

'I was out. Ray and I went into town. It was his bird's birthday and he was a bit fed up because she was spending it with her family, so I suggested we went out.'

'Where did you go exactly?'

'We caught a bus into Bradford, did a few pubs and then on to a night-club.'

'Which pubs?'

'The Speckled Hen, the Shoulder of Mutton and the Cock and Bottle.'

'And the night-club?'

'The one up by the college – the Copper Coin I think it's called. We left about half past one. I have a mate who drives a minicab; he brought us home.' He searched in his pocket and pulled out a crumpled card. 'Why don't you ask him.'

Gary had gone and Chanda didn't know where he was. He stayed for a while until the pains became so strong that she screamed out that they hurt, and then he said the noise was doing his head in and left.

They were coming closer together now and a few moments ago her waters had broken. She was wet, everything was wet, and she was cold. She didn't know what to do. She couldn't have the baby here, and she couldn't ring Iqbal. He would take it away from her. If she went to hospital they would tell him where she was and he would come and take it.

She'd never been so frightened. Surely Gary wouldn't leave her alone, not after she'd helped him with his muggings, told him which old women to rob. He had to come back; he had to help her. She picked up her phone and thumbed in his number. It was turned off. The bastard. The fucking, fucking bastard. Another pain came, stronger and longer than the last. Tears ran down her cheeks as she tried not to scream, but she had to; it was the only way she got some relief. She wanted to run away from them, but there was nowhere to run and even if there was they would go with her. She couldn't do this, not on her own.

She lay back in the chair and waited. Another one would come soon. She closed her eyes and for a moment she thought she heard footsteps on the stairs. She lifted her head. She had; she had heard them; they were running. Gary. She screamed his name, 'Gary.' But there was no answer. The footsteps passed by. A woman's voice said, 'I'm sure it's this one.' It is, it is. Chanda didn't care who was out there, whether they had the wrong door or not; it was someone who could help her.

'Chanda.' A man's voice.

'Gary?'

The door rattled. Someone was trying to get in. Perhaps Gary had sent for an ambulance.

'Chanda, it's Parvez. The lock seems to have slipped. Open the door.'

She pulled herself off the chair as another pain struck. She bent over and clutched at her stomach. And she screamed, long and loud. As the pain subsided, she heard her name again.

'Chanda what's the matter? Are you having the baby? Can you open the door?'

She stretched over to release the lock and as the door was pushed back she slid down the wall to sit on the cold linoleum flooring.

238

Parvez crouched down beside her. 'Is it coming?'

She nodded.

He turned to the woman next to him. 'I think we need an ambulance,' he said.

chapter seventeen

The Globe car park was almost full when Handford drove in. The good weather was bringing out the drinkers and most of them were in the garden. He was looking forward to a beer and a chat with Andy Clarke. They had been friends for a long time and Andy was godfather to Handford's daughter, Nicola, but promotion prevented them getting together too often. Too much fraternisation between ranks was frowned on – a throwback to the time when the police were a military force as opposed to the public service they were meant to be today.

Clarke was in a corner booth. 'We can go outside if you'd rather,' he said as Handford walked over to him. 'But I thought it might be easier to talk here.'

'No, here's fine. What do you want to drink?'

'I'll have a pint if you're buying.'

As Handford waited at the bar to be served he let his mind wander. The first time he had come here was to meet Peter Redmayne; now it was almost his local. It was a free house with a variety of beers including real ale, a passable restaurant and bar menu, and a congenial atmosphere. The furniture was dark oak and the carpet deep red. Along the length of the beamed ceiling hung four large, eight-spoked wheels holding, where the spokes met the rim, small candle-shaped light bulbs and their shades. The garden area too was immaculate, for the owner had taken as much care with the external design as he had with the interior. Perhaps he had the same talent as Rebecca Ingleby – he could see potential and put it into practice. The problem for Rebecca was that thanks to Ray Braddock, she hadn't had the chance to do the latter. Handford felt sorry for her. She was a naïve twenty-five-year-old desperately trying to grow up and, as such, was vulnerable to men like him. She had believed everything he had told her, about how he felt, about the renovations to the house, everything. Never once had it occurred to her to question him. And Ray Braddock didn't care; he lived by one code only and that was look after number one. Everything centred round him and he didn't give a toss for anyone else. Rebecca, on the other hand, had been an only child whose parents doted on her and although she appeared independent to the onlooker, they hadn't given her the rein she needed to make her own mistakes. Even the deposit on the house in Denholme had been a present from her father and he had made sure she earned enough to pay the mortgage as well as enjoy a decent lifestyle. The past few days were probably the only time she had ever had to struggle. Handford had let her go without charge – there wasn't a law against gullibility.

He paid for the drinks and took them over to the table.

'You don't think Braddock killed Dianne Ingleby then?' Clarke said.

'Do you? You say you believe Darren Armitage's account of the events of last Thursday night and to be honest I can't see any grounds to argue with that. He was right about the tunnels; I have no reason to suppose he wasn't right about Thursday evening,'

Clarke took a drink. 'I gather there's quite a cache.'

'More in the Clayton Tunnel than in the Queensbury, but yes, the street value will be somewhere around a million, more even. You've got to hand it to Braddock he's found two clever hiding places. We'd never have found them without Darren Armitage's confession, and it will take us a long time to move and check everything. I hope to God the magistrates remand him.'

'But it means we've lost our prime suspect?'

Handford nodded. 'And I doubt it had anything to do with Patrick Ambler or George Midgley either. Their intelligence level stretches as far as writing death threats and that's more to do with winning an election than it is to do with the BNP's funding. They don't know any more than I do whether Maurice Ingleby is the money behind the Party. They've seen him with Lawrence Burdon who is the leader of the BNP in this area, and they've put two and two together and made five. The fact that he's also a master builder and is likely to meet up with Ingleby from time to time has completely passed them by. We've been through their associates and unless we've missed something, not one of them would to go as far as killing the BNP's money-man. We'll charge them with issuing threats to kill and leave it at that.'

Clarke took a long drink. 'So what are we left with?'

'Not much. Braddock is in the bottom corner of the frame ready to slip out, closely followed by Ambler and Midgley. We've gone through every man we know of whose wife has had an affair with Ingleby, and for one reason or another not one of them could have done it. Then there's Mossman …',

'No, sorry John, he's out too. When he realised we were still checking into the missing three-quarters of an hour, he came clean. He'd slipped out of the party to meet up with a lady of his acquaintance – Jade –.'

Handford's eyes widened. 'Jade? The prostitute?'

'Yes. Apparently he doesn't get much chance to go with women since his wife left him. He's out on the road a lot and he tells me these salesman conferences aren't all they're cracked up to be. He's one of her regulars, but he took great pains to tell me that she's the only one; he doesn't sleep around.'

Handford tried to keep his face straight. 'There's nothing like being faithful. Have you checked it with her?'

'Absolutely. She corroborated his story one hundred per cent – even gave me one of her cards.'

Handford's attempt at seriousness failed and he laughed out loud. 'Don't let Janice see it, Andy.'

'You may mock, John, but let me tell you my wife trusts me completely, and anyway I shredded it as soon as I got back to the office.'

Handford looked at his friend with affection. 'You have no idea how much good you do me,' he said.

'That's because I don't take myself too seriously. You let cases get to you and this one more than most. We're doing a job, John, that's all – a job. Sometimes we do it well, sometimes we don't. But you've got to trust yourself more and not let Russell wind you up.'

'Is that what you think I'm doing?'

'That's what we all think you're doing. You want to join HMET, he doesn't want you to, and the reason he doesn't want you to is because you're too good a copper to lose.'

Handford put down the pint he had just lifted to his mouth.

'Are you telling me I'm the talk of CID? Have you taken bets on whether I'll make it or not?'

Clarke sighed as though he was dealing with a teenager with attitude. 'No, of course not, you're too well-respected for that. But think about it, would. it matter if we had? There are two things you need to do, John: one is to trust yourself more and the other is to like yourself more.'

Gill was always telling him that. He wasn't sure why he couldn't. Somewhere along the line his confidence had been sapped, probably during the enquiry into his alleged racism. He didn't know. He drained his glass. 'Do you want another?'

Clarke handed his over. 'Yes, but just a half. I don't want to be pulled up for being over the limit.'

As Handford was sliding from the booth his mobile rang. He groaned, put down the glasses and lifted it to his ear. 'Russell,' he mouthed a moment later.

'Sorry to bring you back in, John,' the DCI said, 'but we've found the body of a young man; he's been shot in the back. The SOCOs think it likely it was the same gun used to kill Dianne Ingleby. He was in a house belonging to his sister – Kathie Lake. The neighbour heard a commotion then a shot, and rang us. She said she knew it was empty because Kathie is in hospital. According to the victim's driving licence and a letter in his pocket he's her brother, Jason Lake. Perhaps we've found Dianne Ingleby's victim.' He paused briefly. 'And perhaps you were right to consider the diary as important.'

Handford arrived in the office the next morning angry at himself for not insisting the information given him by Dianne Ingleby was important. He might have been able to prevent this had the question of the intended victim, Russell and HMET not got in the way. He shouldn't have allowed them to. He should have done what Clarke suggested and trusted himself more, but he had been so busy trying not to be seen to fall and so give the DCI something that would suggest he wasn't right for the serious crime team that he had fallen big time. Jason Lake was probably dead because of him.

He read through the diary again; there were three other people mentioned apart from Kathie's family: Emma Crossley, James Gould and Michael Iveson. James Gould was the mystery man

243

and had to be found. According to Kathie he was in the area; she had to tell him who he was and where he was, the only other person who had that information was Peter Redmayne. He rang him.

'John, I'm surprised you're ringing. My editor says you've been given the hard word and ordered not to contact me.' There was a chuckle in his tone.

Handford wasn't in the mood for chit-chat. 'I need information on Kathie Lake,' he said. 'The investigation into her father, the trial, his suicide, James Gould – everything you have, I shall be out for the next couple of hours, so shall we say Central at eleven?'

He also wanted Emma Crossley and Michael Iveson brought in. He left that to Ali and Clarke. He pulled Connie Burns away from the Ingleby house and told her to meet him at the hospital. She was the best there was in this kind of situation, and Maurice and Rebecca needed space to sort out what had happened. She could go back later. In the meantime he intended to visit Victim Support to make his feelings clear to Eileen Leighton. If he was to blame for Jason Lake's death, then so was she.

'John,' she said as he was shown into her office, 'how's it going?'

He sat down. 'You haven't heard then?'

'Heard what?'

'Kathie Lake's brother was murdered last night and I've had her moved from the ward and put under armed police guard.'

She pulled together the papers she was working on and placed them in a drawer. 'She'll need some support; I'll go up there.'

'No way. Apart from the hospital staff only two people are going anywhere near Kathie – me and Connie Burns, our family liaison officer.'

Eileen Leighton looked as though she was about to argue, but thought better of it. Eventually she said, 'Perhaps later when she's ready.'

'Not ever Eileen. You are as much responsible as I am for Jason's death.'

She frowned, obviously puzzled as to the meaning of his words. 'Me? How do you come to that conclusion?'

'Didn't it occur to you that Dianne Ingleby had written down her fears for a reason? Didn't it occur to you that she was worried?'

For the first time there was an unmistakable nervousness in her manner. 'Of course it did, but I am bound by our code of …'

'Confidentiality, I know. Shall I tell you something, Eileen, this case has been hampered from the beginning by secrets. Every way I've turned people who should know better have kept information hidden from me. Some hide behind confidentiality and think they're being righteous, others insist I don't investigate because it will look bad for them or it will bring shame on their family, and none of you really care about the dead woman. And one of these persons might – just might – be hiding behind that code or that secret because he or she is the killer. It's a good place to hide don't you think?'

'You surely don't think …'

He stood up and with his knuckles on the edge of the desk he leaned over it, his face close to that of the Victim Support coordinator. 'I've stopped thinking, Eileen,' he said, his voice controlled, but with a hint of threat. 'Instead I'm going to investigate and in the process I'm going to turn every one of you over until there's nothing I don't know about you.' By now he was shaking with the heightened adrenalin fuelling his anger. 'So what I want now is Emma's full name and address and, if you have it, her place of work, and if you refuse to give this information I'll get a warrant and then have you charged with obstruction or even conspiracy to pervert the course of justice, if I can make it stick. And just in case you want to make a complaint DCI Russell's extension is 743.'

Handford met Connie Burns outside Kathie's room. She was chatting to the officer on guard. 'Anything?' he asked.

'Nothing sir, it's all been very quiet.'

He turned to Connie. 'Are you ready?'

'Yes sir.'

'Remember I do the talking, you are there if there is a problem.'

'Sir.'

It seemed odd to Handford that he was nervous; he'd done this kind of thing so many times before that he ought to have been immune to it by now. But it was an unusual situation. He already felt he knew Kathie, but didn't know her at all. The doctor he'd spoken to said she seemed to be in denial, not accepting her brother was dead. He expected her to be in bed, but she was sitting on a chair next to the window, looking out. He wondered how much she was actually seeing.

She turned as he walked in. He wasn't sure what he expected, a voice can sometimes give clues to appearance, but he'd never heard hers except through the diary, and from that he had imagined a frothy but frightened young girl. She was nothing like that. She was pale and tear-strained but that wasn't surprising. Her short hair was black and worn like a cap. Her eyes too were dark and when they looked at him, they penetrated his and, like a seasoned detective's, they hardly flinched. Her features were sculptured and she was anorexically thin. No one would have described her as attractive, but she had an angular beauty difficult to define. She was also the image of her brother, but whereas in her the features were not so appealing, in him they bordered on the handsome. If there had been any doubt as to the identity of the body, it was surely dispelled now.

'It looks a nice day out there,' she said.

'It is.'

'You're the police?'

He took out his warrant card. 'I'm Detective Inspector Handford and this is PC Connie Burns.' He pulled up a chair to sit next to her. 'I'm sorry about your brother.'

'It's not your fault.' He wished he could be sure about that.

'Do you mind if I ask you some questions?'

'It doesn't matter now, does it?'

'I think it does; we need to find out who killed Jason.'

She said nothing. What was going on in this young woman's mind? Was it like the doctor had said – that she was pretending he wasn't dead? That he was still in Brussels, unaware of what had happened to her?

'Tell me about the attack on you.'

'What is there to tell? A man came into my house and beat me up.'

'He almost killed you, Kathie. Why did you insist on no police?'

When she didn't reply, he said, 'Do you know who it was?'

'Would you take my word for it if I told you?'

'No.'

'I didn't think so. The police and the courts didn't take my father's word.'

'But I'd investigate.'

'That's what *they* said, and when they investigated they came up with the wrong answer, and as a result my father committed suicide.'

So that was it, she wouldn't say who it was who attacked her because she didn't trust the police or the courts to investigate fairly. And if it was James Gould, or the man he had become, was it her intention to get her revenge in her own way? Dianne Ingleby had portrayed her as a frightened young woman – too frightened of the man who had attacked her to say who it was. But was that true? Had Dianne got it wrong? Was Kathie in fact someone much stronger than that? Someone who in the end wanted revenge in her own way? Because if she was, she was playing a very dangerous game. He cast his mind back to the beginning of the diary. Dianne had been unsure as to why she was so concerned for her, why she was uneasy, but rather than going with the unease, she had assumed it was because Kathie had refused to tell the police. Or perhaps she was unable to articulate properly what she felt. And Kathie had been clever; she had played on it by showing fear towards Ray Braddock, so much so that Dianne had been sure the attacker was him.

'Who was the man who attacked you?'

Kathie shook her head.

Perhaps it was time for some truths. He hadn't wanted to betray Dianne Ingleby, but she was dead and it couldn't hurt her now. 'I know about your father,' he said, 'and about James Gould and Ray Braddock.'

Her eyes widened; this was something she hadn't expected. 'How?'

'Dianne wrote everything down. We have her diary.'

'She had no right; she promised me it would be confidential.'

'And it would have been had she not been killed.' Handford leaned forward. 'Kathie, your brother was killed by the same gun used to shoot Dianne Ingleby. We know that. All through this investigation our prime suspect has been Ray Braddock. But now we know it wasn't him, because he has an alibi for the night of Dianne's murder and he was in our custody when your brother

247

was killed. It could have been him who assaulted you, but I don't think it was, and you know it wasn't otherwise I think you would tell us. So either it was a complete stranger or it was James Gould. You told Dianne that Gould is in Bradford under another name. Who is he, Kathie?'

Again she made no reply. She would have stood with Dianne, but not with him, she would have worked out by now just how far she could go with him. 'You don't want us to catch your brother's killer?'

Tears filled her eyes. 'Yes, of course I do. But no matter what I said to him, Jason believed my father was guilty. He didn't think James Gould had anything to do with it; he wouldn't even let me talk about it and you'll be the same if I tell you; you'll do what the others did and not investigate properly. Just like you didn't with my father.'

'I didn't investigate your father at all; that was someone else. Don't assume all police officers are the same.' He stood up and replaced the chair next to the bed. 'I will investigate this with or without you, Kathie, and I will do it properly. It would be easier and quicker if you helped, but if you won't then so be it.'

He beckoned Connie Burns to follow him out. 'What do you make of her?' he said.

'Weird is the word that comes to mind.'

He smiled. 'And after that?'

'I think she wants to exact her own form of revenge on James Gould but she needs to be careful. If it is him, he has attacked once and killed twice. He has absolutely nothing to lose by making an attempt on her life. And if I'm really being honest, I think she would welcome it. Her parents and her brother have gone; she has nothing else to live for. He would be helping her commit suicide; you know a bit like luring the police to kill the man who holds kids hostage. He comes out waving a gun and the police shoot him.'

He hadn't thought of it like that before, but she was right and it made the situation all the more dangerous. 'Stay with her, Connie. See what you can get out of her. And be careful but don't worry, there'll be armed officers outside her room day and night. In the meantime I'm going to find Gould.'

When Handford arrived back at Central Peter Redmayne was

waiting for him. 'We'll use my office,' he said. 'I've just got back from meeting Kathie.'

Redmayne chuckled. 'What do you make of her?'

'I think the FLO best described her, when she said she was weird.'

'She certainly is, but I have to say in all honesty she is probably right about her father and the investigation.'

As they passed the incident room, Handford put his head in. 'Andy, you're back. Can you join us and bring some coffee with you?' He cocked an eyebrow at Redmayne.

'Yes please, milk and two sugars.'

A few moments later Clarke appeared balancing three mugs of coffee. He edged the door shut with his foot and placed the drinks carefully on the desk. 'Thanks for Emma Crossley's address,' he said. 'Did you use an arm lock to get it out of Eileen Leighton?'

Handford smiled. 'Something like that,' he said.

'I finally got hold of Emma on her mobile. She's at the hospital at the moment and I've arranged to meet her during her lunch hour. She said she was intending to come into the station after work anyway.'

'Was she? It's a pity she didn't come to us earlier when Kathie was attacked. She didn't have the excuse of confidentiality.'

'No, John, just the excuse of friendship.'

Handford sighed. 'Yes, all right Andy; I'm being too hard on her, but I'm sure you won't be. Now, what about Michael Iveson? Have you found him?'

'Not yet. He wasn't at the manse; probably out on his rounds or whatever ministers call them. I'll try again later.'

Handford turned to Redmayne. 'You said you think Kathie's right about her father and the investigation. Why do you think that?'

Redmayne pushed his glasses up his nose. 'Before I answer that can I ask how you found out about Kathie?'

Handford had debated with himself on the way back from the hospital whether or not he should tell Redmayne about Dianne and the diary. He'd decided in the end he would do so, but ask that he kept it quiet until such time as it wasn't possible. If and when there was a trial it would come out, but for the moment he didn't want people to be concerned that Victim Support would automatically break confidences. In spite of what he had said to

Eileen Leighton, he did believe in what they were doing, and that clients had to be able to go to them and say anything they wanted without it ever being broadcast. This was an unusual case and he didn't want the local branch to be damaged by it.

'If I tell you, I want you to promise you won't print it – not yet at least. I don't want letters to the press and editorial comment, and I don't want Dianne Ingleby's name pulled through the proverbial; she wasn't doing anything but what she thought was right.'

Redmayne smiled. 'That sounds intriguing. If I'm to agree I shall want something in return.'

Always the journalist, never the compassionate man. 'How about I'm going to charge Patrick Ambler and George Midgley this afternoon with issuing threats to kill Maurice Ingleby?'

'That'll do for starters, but what I really would like is to visit the tunnels where Ray Braddock stored his illegal firearms.'

How did he know about that? Handford had always said the man was in the wrong job; he should have been a detective. As an investigative journalist he had more informants than the police had. But then he probably paid more.

He looked at Clarke who raised his eyebrows and shrugged. The press were already making noises and a statement would have to be made sooner rather than later. What were a few scoop pictures once the area had been examined? 'I won't ask you how you got the information, Peter, and it seems to me you are getting more than you're giving, but when we're ready you can have the exclusive. Do I have your promise?'

Redmayne nodded and Handford described the diary and the information in it. 'Now you.'

'Such as?'

'You have to remember that Kathie is obsessed with the belief that her father is innocent, but that apart she was right about one thing, the whole case was badly handled. The SIO took too much notice of the bank's investigators and to be honest there were big holes in what they came up with.'

'Much of their evidence relied on the fact that Lake was a brilliant IT specialist and that Gould wasn't. The trouble was not much was known about electronic fraud at the time, and they didn't know what they were dealing with or understand how it was done. Nor did the jury when it came to trial. The prosecuting barrister blinded them with scientific language as did their experts, and the defence wasn't able to break through it. It's not an unusual ploy to use easy language when you want the jury to understand and technical language when you don't. That and the pictures he had of the yachts clinched it for them.'

'Has the money ever been traced?'

'No and that's another thing. Kathie is convinced that if he had done it and it had been his intention to commit suicide he would have let her mother know where it was. I'm not so sure, but there you are.'

'She mentioned a new witness.'

'Yes. Matthew Outhwaite was a junior teller at the time. After Lake had been charged he told the police Gould was lying when he said he didn't understand computer systems, and that he had seen him working in Lake's office when he was out of the bank. It's thin and the police weren't prepared to accept it, but he took the time to find Kathie and tell her what he knew, so it must have been worrying him. If it's true and I have no reason to doubt Outhwaite, then at best it suggests Gould was not telling the truth, and at worst that he wasn't doing so because he was the person carrying out the fraud and deliberately setting out to implicate Lake.'

'What do you think?'

'I think it's worth opening the case again.'

'What about Gould?' Clarke asked.

'He disappeared shortly after Lake's suicide – left banking and completely disappeared. Even I haven't been able to find out where he went.' He stirred his coffee with a pencil he picked up from Handford's desk. 'I must be slipping,' he said.

'Kathie says he's back in Bradford under another name and has been for about three years.'

This was news to Redmayne. 'Has he? I wonder why she didn't tell me.'

'I think she'd decided to tackle him herself.' Handford said nothing about Connie Burns' theory. Let Redmayne work it out for himself; he'd been given too much already. 'Do you have a photograph of him?'

'Just one. It was taken outside the court. He wasn't prepared to let us have one of his own, so we had to snatch them so to speak.' He pulled it out of an envelope and passed it over.

Handford picked it up. James Gould walking up the steps into the court building. Small and slightly built he was clean-shaven and smartly dressed – the typical bank manager. But to Handford there was no mistaking him. He slid the photograph over to Andy Clarke. He stared first at it and then at his DI, holding his eyes for a long moment. 'Give me a minute,' he said and dashed out of the room. It wasn't long before he returned, clutching the original and a photocopy. He passed the latter to Handford. He had scribbled a beard on it and fattened the man up a little. 'It is, isn't it?'

'Yes it is,' said Handford grimly, 'This is the Reverend Michael Iveson.'

When Peter Redmayne left, promising to check into both James Gould and Michael Iveson's background more thoroughly, Handford sent for Ali. He told him what had happened and showed him the photograph as well as the photocopy Clarke had scribbled on. 'I'm having it aged properly, but I don't think there's any doubt that Iveson and Gould are one and the same.'

'I haven't met Iveson, you have,' he said. 'Do you think he's capable of beating up a woman, then killing two people?'

Handford leaned back and clasped his hands behind his head. 'If you'd have asked me that yesterday, Khalid, I would have laughed at you, but yesterday we were sure it was Ray Braddock, and yesterday it hadn't occurred to us that each time Dianne Ingleby wrote up her diary, Iveson figured in it. It didn't mean anything then, because he's a hospital chaplain, but if you read it carefully, it's clear that when she mentions him, he is either attempting to persuade her to leave Kathie alone or he is fishing for information.' He sat up again. His head was reeling and, if the truth were known, he wasn't sure of anything, except that they couldn't afford to take the risk that Iveson wasn't the killer, any more than they could have taken the same risk with Braddock. He had to be brought in, and he had to be questioned. If only they could find that damned car; they might be able to link it to him.

The other thing Handford was sure of was that the Kathie he had met wasn't the Kathie described in the diary. 'I'll tell you what I do think, Khalid. I think Kathie Lake has been fooling everyone,' Handford related his meeting with her. 'According to Dianne Ingleby's diary she's a meek, frightened young woman, but that wasn't what I saw. I saw a determined, strong and inflexible lady who had no intention of helping us find her brother's killer; she wants him for herself. She knows who he is, and he knows she knows.'

'And you're absolutely sure it's Michael Iveson?'

'No, not yet, but I can't take the risk it isn't. What I am sure of is that Michael Iveson was once James Gould, the bank manager who may have committed the fraud Mr Lake was found guilty of. If he did, the last thing he would want is to be denounced as a fraudster. He's a born-again Christian who has a reasonable living with three or more chapels under his wing. He considers himself a good man and is strong in his faith – I've never seen so many crucifixes in one room as there are in his study. There's no doubt he's respected, loved even. Ministers are like doctors, they tend to be both, so he's not going to give that up without a fight. If we assume the police got it wrong and there was a miscarriage of justice and Kathie has harassed him over the past two or three years, and then appeared to be about to tell Dianne Ingleby the identity of her attacker, he may feel he had to do something about it, he may even feel God was ordering him to do something about it.'

He stood up and walked over to his filing cabinet. 'Peter Redmayne will find out all he can about him, but we need to do a thorough background check ourselves, we can't let the press do all our work. Put Warrender on to it. Get Miah to work with him. He used his initiative with Braddock, tell him to do the same with Iveson. How is he, by the way?'

'Exhausted. He was up most of the night in the maternity department. Chanda had a girl at four o'clock this morning.'

'What's going to happen do you think?'

'I don't know. Aisha is still determined to go ahead with the complaint and for what it's worth I think she's right. A lot depends on how Chanda is sentenced, and whether Iqbal Ahmed carries out his threat to take the baby from her.'

'Can he do that?'

'Again it depends on whether she's given a custodial. If the magistrates can be persuaded to give her community service with supervision, then the probation service will make sure she is able to care for her own baby. Unless of course Mr Ahmed decides to take the child over to Pakistan and leave Chanda here.'

Handford returned to his desk. 'Wouldn't that be kidnapping?'

'Probably. I've told Parvez it's up to him to make sure it doesn't happen, to talk some sense into his father. But it's difficult, John.'

They sat in silence for a brief while, each deep in their own thoughts, until eventually Ali said, 'Is Kathie Lake in danger?'

Handford stirred. 'Oh I think so, don't you?'

'And Connie?'

'Probably. I've already asked Russell if we can double the guard. He needs Mr Slater's permission, but I think he'll get it. The superintendent is too near his retirement to risk a police death.'

Ali smiled, 'You're very cynical, John, do you know that?'

'It comes with old age and experience, Khalid.'

Ali walked to the door, 'I'll brief Warrender and Miah.'

As he was about to leave, Handford said, 'Make sure they understand the importance of speed here. I don't like to think we're on the tip of another murder, but I've got a nasty feeling if we don't find Iveson soon, that's exactly what will happen.'

chapter eighteen

It was shortly after one when Clarke finally met up with Emma Crossley. She was pale and drawn, and there was a hint of fear in her eyes. It was obvious she wasn't looking forward to his visit. In an attempt to put her at her ease he smiled as he shook her hand. It was a delicate hand, but cold. 'It's like a warren down here,' he said.

'It's not very nice, but we don't often have visitors so it doesn't much matter.' She stopped at a regulation green door. 'This is my boss's office; he said we could use it.'

She stepped in first, and he smiled to himself when she took the chair behind the desk and offered him the one opposite. Perhaps it gave her a feeling of being in control.

She came to the point – to what was worrying her. 'I ought to have come to you earlier,' she said, 'when Kathie was attacked.'

He didn't reply. There was no point making her feel worse than she already did.

'Is it my fault?'

'What?'

'That Mrs Ingleby and Jason are dead. If I'd gone along with what Kathie wanted, hadn't interfered, they might be alive now.'

'You can't know that, Emma. It's like saying if Kathie had come to us in the first place they wouldn't be dead. You're a scientist, you understand hypotheses – both of them could be true, or just one of them, or neither.'

She nodded. 'As a theory it doesn't seem to work when emotions are involved.' Her voice faltered. 'Is she in danger?'

He couldn't pretend. 'She could be, but we have officers with her all the time. Try not to worry about her.' He leaned forward. 'You said on the phone you had something for me.'

Emma picked up her bag and took out a brown A4 envelope marked 'Personal'. It had been opened. 'Kathie asked me to get it for her from the house.' He pulled out the clippings and skimmed them. There was also a lengthy comment on the case by Peter Redmayne, a statement from the junior teller, Matthew Outhwaite, and a handwritten list of dates when she had seen or spoken to Michael Iveson. Everything in the package suggested Kathie had been determined to avenge her father.

'Who knows you have these, Emma?'

'No one except Kathie – and her brother. I showed them to him. He was furious with her. He said she was denying the truth of what their father had done and was obsessed with proving him innocent.' This was more or less Redmayne's belief. 'Jason didn't believe he was; he believed his father was guilty. When she was better, he said he was going to take her back to Brussels where he works.' Her voice dropped to a whisper. 'Worked.'

'And you're sure no one else knows you have them?'

'No, I'm sure they don't. It took me ages to find it, so if it was well-hidden I can't see Kathie telling anyone else, can you?'

Clarke shook his head. 'No, I can't. Do you know James Gould?'

'I'd never heard of him until Jason told me about the bank and the fraud.'

'What about Michael Iveson?'

She seemed perplexed. 'The minister?'

'Yes.'

'Yes, I know him. Not well, but I know he's been visiting Kathie since she's been in hospital. Not that she's pleased about it, because she doesn't like him much.'

'Why do you think that is?'

'I don't know. She did once say he was an evil man, but that never stopped her from going to the chapel when he was preaching there. She used to sit at the front and stare at him; she never took her eyes off him. I told her once she was spooky, but she just laughed and said it was something to do in his sermons.' She thought for a moment. 'If I'm honest, I think it was more than that. I got the impression he'd upset her somehow and she was getting her own back threatening him in a way that only she and he understood. I know Kathie's my friend, but I wouldn't want to cross her; she's a great believer in revenge. I've seen her settle a few scores with Ray Braddock. Not that it's made any difference to him; he's too thick-skinned to see what she's doing for what it is.' She paused for a moment, then said, 'Did he kill Mrs Ingleby?'

'I can't tell you that, Emma.'

She let her eyes wander over Clarke's face as if she was trying to read meaning into what he had just said. 'I hope not,' she murmured. 'I wouldn't like Jack to have a father who was a murderer.'

When Peter Redmayne left him, Handford settled down to read statements and bring his action reports up to date. At two thirty Patrick Ambler and George Midgley were charged under the Malicious Communications Act and bailed to appear at the magistrates' court in two days' time. While Ambler said nothing, Midgley was more garrulous. He insisted someone had to stand up against the BNP and those who worked for them, and that Handford ought to understand that.

'I warn you, I'll hold you responsible if they take the seats,' he thundered. 'And if we're made to stand down because of this ludicrous charge …' He left the threat hanging in the air.

Handford listened to him in silence. There was little point telling him it shouldn't happen – in law they were still innocent, but now they had been charged most would assume guilt, and some would demand his and Ambler's withdrawal. Nor could he deny there weren't tensions in certain quarters of the city or that Midgley wouldn't take every opportunity to exploit and heighten them – he was fighting for his political life, such as it was – or indeed that once their arrest and subsequent charge hit the newsstands the BNP wouldn't make capital out of it, adding to the pressure. Bradford may well be in for a difficult time until the elections were over.

He asked a constable to show them out, but Midgley hadn't finished and at the door turned to face him. 'I'll make sure everyone knows what Ingleby is doing to this city and that the police are making no attempt to stop him. And if you and he don't like it, you can sue me,' he ended triumphantly.

Handford shook his head and walked away. When it boiled down to it, petty thieves like Karl Metcalfe had more morality in their little fingers than the likes of Midgley. At least he'd cared about what had happened to Dianne Ingleby. He climbed the stairs up to his office; he had more important things to worry about than the ranting of a minor political agent – the whereabouts of Michael Iveson for one. He hadn't turned up at the afternoon meeting, much to the concern of the Ladies' Friendly Society, nor was there anything back from either Peter Redmayne or Warrender to give them a lead. He had to be hiding somewhere, although where, Handford had no idea. There was the sister of course, he could be with her – a call to the Methodist circuit superintendent should tell him where she lived.

Then there was Kathie. If Iveson was the killer, she had to be his next victim. As far as he was concerned, she was the only one who knew the full story. In his warped mind he would realise that if he was to survive intact, he couldn't allow her to live. Threats and intimidation were no longer enough. Handford would have liked to have moved her to another hospital, or even to a safe house, but she wouldn't hear of it. Only the psychiatric consultant could force the issue by sectioning her, but he refused, insisting she was grieving, not suffering from mental illness. Handford wasn't so sure; he was inclined to agree with Connie Burns – that it was Kathie's intention to commit suicide at Iveson's hand.

All that was left to them now was extra armed protection. He put it to Russell and Slater. The superintendent had approved the request immediately. It was as Handford had inferred, he couldn't run the risk of a police death at this stage of his career and nor it seemed could Russell. The last thing he wanted was to walk into the post of head of CID and have to explain why, when there was obviously a problem, all precautions hadn't been taken. For once Handford was on the right side of his DCI.

Finally, when he could concentrate no longer on his paperwork, he stashed it in his briefcase, left a message to say if he was wanted to ring him on his mobile and drove to the hospital. Connie Burns was about to go off duty. She hadn't had any result with Kathie. 'She's not prepared to talk about it. In her own way she's distressed, but there's a core of something else there and it's deep. She needs help to come to terms with what happened to her father before she can even begin to move on. The doctor has suggested psychiatric counselling, but she won't hear of it.'

258

From Kathie's room Handford went into the ward to see Aisha Miah. He wasn't sure whether he ought to, but he needed to know how she was, and to talk to her about Chanda. Apart from anything else, he was worried Iqbal Ahmed might carry out his threat and send her to Pakistan, and as things stood it might need the law to stop him.

She was sitting by the side of the bed when he walked in. It was only a couple of days since the attack, but she looked better than he expected.

'How are you?' he asked.

'Not bad. Have you heard about Chanda?'

'Yes, a little girl, I believe.'

'Seven pounds four ounces. She's going to call her Salma; it means peaceful.'

'Then let's hope she has a more peaceful life than her mother. Do you still intend to continue with your complaint?'

'I think I have to. No matter what she's gone through, she can't be allowed to get away with it. That's happened too often. No, I'll go through with it. Parvez agrees, although his father doesn't. I'm not interested in family honour or shame, Inspector; I'm interested in law and justice. If she will give a statement against Gary Marshall, then I'll put in a good word for her, ask the magistrate not to pass a custodial sentence. Chanda was the girl in the background at Mrs Shaw's mugging, and since I gather he left her to go through her labour alone and didn't even ring for an ambulance, I think she might just want to get revenge on him. I might as well make use of her worst traits if I'm to see justice for the old lady.'

Handford smiled at her. 'Couldn't that be considered in some quarters as blackmail?'

She laughed, wincing as she did so. 'Well, I won't tell if you won't.'

He became serious. 'Off the record, I think we may be able to prevent Mr Ahmed from sending Chanda to Pakistan. I've been talking to the officers investigating the case and they can't charge her until the forensics on the shoes are back. I know they have the pictures on the mobile, but it doesn't mean to say she took them and you know as well as I do that a good lawyer will suggest it could have been anyone. It concerns me that while they're waiting for the lab report Chanda could be packed off abroad.

What I'd like to suggest is that you ask Parvez to get Chanda to give him her passport. We can't demand she relinquishes it until she's charged, but as her brother-in-law he might be able to persuade her.'

Aisha thought for a moment. 'It's a bit unorthodox, but yes, I'm sure we could get her to agree. It could be put to her that her choice rests between prison, probably with the baby, or Pakistan without it. It will do her good; it's time she was forced into making a serious decision. I'll ask him, Inspector Handford.' She smiled. 'I'll tell him he owes you one.' She became silent for a moment and then said, 'Thank you for keeping Parvez in CID. He deserved the reprimand, but it was difficult for him. Iqbal is a strong man. As head of the family he takes his responsibilities seriously. Few people disobey him.'

'That's as may be, but he can't interfere in police investigations, however much he feels they cross the boundaries of family. What he forced Parvez into doing could have affected the case quite significantly. I had said I didn't for a minute believe Chanda was involved in Dianne Ingleby's murder; she was simply a possible route round to finding out more about a suspect. I suppose in the end it was thanks to her that we did, but a lot of people had to suffer for it to come to that; talking to me would have been much easier on all of you.' He pushed his chair back and stood up. 'What are you going to do now? It won't be easy for you to return to the house.'

'I'll have to for a while; but Parvez has promised to look at properties for us. It will be easier with our own home, and it's not as though we can't afford one.'

He held out his hand. 'Then I wish you all the luck in the world and don't worry about Parvez; he's going to make a fine detective.'

She shook it. 'And don't you worry about Chanda. She'll be with her baby; one way or another I'll see to that.'

'I don't doubt it,' he said. Iqbal wasn't the only strong one in that family.

The evening was drawing in as he left the hospital to drive home. The sun was low in the sky, but the air was balmy. He took off his coat and threw it in the back of the car. This morning it had seemed that they would never know the intended victim, let alone track down the killer; this evening they were nearing a

260

conclusion. But until they could question Michael Iveson, locate the gun and the car he used, they didn't have much in the way of hard evidence against him – even his alibi for that night would be difficult to break. The gun was vital to both murders and Handford was sure it wasn't, as Jane Charles had suggested at the multi-storey car park, on its way back to Manchester or Liverpool – or even to Ray Braddock. It was Iveson's own, and it had been, and still was, his protection against Kathie Lake should it become necessary. What he probably hadn't expected was that she would confide in Dianne Ingleby, or that someone would contact her brother and he would turn up. That had thrown him off-track for a while, but after ridding himself of the two of them he was back on it now and Handford was sure that the track led direct to Kathie

He accepted it wasn't over yet; there was still much to do but, unless uniforms found Iveson, there was nothing that couldn't wait until tomorrow. The important thing was that now at least he wasn't floundering; he was aware of the direction of play. As he pushed a tape in the cassette recorder he felt more at ease with life than he had for days. He hummed to the Brighouse and Rastrick brass band, tapping his hands on the steering wheel as he did so.

Twenty minutes later he put his key in the door to be met with the aroma of a meal cooking. It smelt good and he realised how hungry he was; he hadn't found time to eat the sandwich he bought in the canteen; it was still in his desk drawer. Gill met him with a glass of whisky and the news that Khalid had rung to say Amina had been given an appointment at the hospital the next day to get the results of the biopsy. He had said that since they were so busy he would arrange for her mother to go with her.

'You're not going to let him do that are you, John?' Gill said with a look that told him to argue if he dared.

'No, I'll give him a ring. Tell him to take as much time as he needs.' He was still feeling guilty about his comment to Ali earlier in the day. '*I know you're worried about Amina, but that's no excuse for sloppiness. Either take some leave or deal with it.*' It had been unfair, not to mention cruel. He couldn't take it back, but he could make sure that tomorrow Ali and Amina had all the support they needed.

*

By the time Handford left the incident room after the briefing the next morning, the case had taken on a fresh atmosphere. There was plenty to do and the team were ready to do it; they could smell an arrest. The major task today was to find Michael Iveson. The longer he was away and neglecting his duties, the more sure Handford was that he was involved in the deaths of Dianne Ingleby and Jason Lake. Warrender's trail of evidence was leading straight to the minister.

At eleven o'clock, Redmayne arrived at the station with a large envelope. It contained much of what Emma had passed over to Clarke as well as information and photographs of Michael Iveson / James Gould at various stages of his life. Redmayne had done a good job, but then nothing would be wasted; he probably had all he needed for the exclusive when the time came for him to go into print.

The age enhancement of the photograph was back and there was no doubt as to who James Gould currently was. Redmayne furnished further proof, 'It took a while, but eventually I found him. He was born James Michael Iveson-Gould. Iveson was his mother's name and Gould his father's. For them to hyphenate in those days was unusual to say the least and the family were probably considered snobs. I've talked to his sister, and I gather poor James Michael was badly bullied in school.'

'He told me his sister looks after him. She was certainly at the manse when I went up on Friday, although I didn't actually see her.'

Redmayne shook his head. 'I think "looks after him" is a bit of an exaggeration. She's not quite the type to "look after" someone. No, she pops up from time to time, and is there for him when his duties warrant it. But as far as looking after him, I think he does that himself. There's no mention of a daily or a housekeeper or anything.' He picked up a sheaf of papers and read from them. 'After he left school with good O and A-levels, he went to university to study mathematics and economics. From there for some reason he joined the army with a commission, but either he didn't like it or they didn't like him, and he left before his tour of duty was complete. I can't find any suggestion that he was thrown out, but I'll carry on digging. After the army he moved into banking and because of his qualifications he went immediately on to fast track. He was a manager within five years.

The branch at which both he and Simon Lake worked was a big one. The staff felt Simon ought to have been made up to manager, but you can't keep fast-track people down ...' Handford smiled grimly; he knew it only too well. The express line was the very reason why Russell was DCI, about to become a superintendent and he was still a DI. 'And James Gould, as he was by now,' Redmayne went on, 'got the job.'

'So there was friction between them from the start?'

'Oh yes, I think so. Gould had a particularly vicious streak in him; he had been known to reduce staff to tears – men and women. Lake on the other hand was well-liked and attempted to act as a barrier between the manager and the staff. This was a bone of contention as far as Gould was concerned, so there was much conflict between them, and it was well-known he wanted rid of his assistant manager. He'd attempted various things, like warnings about misdemeanours he decided Lake had committed, but had been at the bank a couple of years before the big one – the allegation against him.'

'Did this come out at the trial?'

'It was skimmed over, but neither the prosecution nor the defence made much of it and no witnesses were brought in. This was typical of the whole case which is why I'm inclined to go along with Kathie. Anyway after the trial James Gould stayed at the bank until Simon Lake committed suicide when he left. The staff thought that he had been moved to another branch to prevent further bad feeling towards him, but in fact he left banking entirely. After that I can't find anything referring to a James Gould. He probably reverted back to James Michael Iveson-Gould, to return eventually as Michael Iveson.'

'Where did you find Iveson?'

'He was living abroad when I caught up with him – backpacking from country to country like a student, except that he stayed in hotels and travelled first class.'

'On the proceeds of the fraud?'

'More than likely, but at the moment without evidence, I could be sued for saying so. It was when he was in New Zealand he became friendly with a minister of religion and apparently found his own faith. From there he came home, went to a Methodist college and trained as a minister. He came to Bradford three years ago. The rest you know.'

263

Handford leaned back and thought about what he had heard. 'Thank you Peter; as always you've done a good job. There's just one thing though.

'In Bradford. She's a widow – quite a wealthy one by all accounts; her husband owned a series of wholesale warehouses which she sold when he died. Not that you'd notice; she lives in a small semi, drives a second-hand car and rides around on a bicycle most of the time.'

Suddenly, Handford sat forward. *Lives in a small semi, drives a second-hand car and rides around on a bicycle* – he'd heard that before. 'What's her name Peter?'

'Sorry, didn't I say? It's Elizabeth Dutton.'

Handford was about to leave the station to visit Elizabeth Dutton when the civilian worker on the desk rang through to say she was in the foyer and would like to see him.

This was unexpected, there was no reason he could see as to why she would come here and ask for him. 'Did she ask for me specifically?'

'No sir,' she asked for the officer in charge of the Ingleby murder.'

Curious. 'Get someone to bring her up will you?'

Mrs Dutton was a younger version of her brother – small and slightly built, with the weight of the mature woman, but that was where the similarity ended. She might be living in a small semi and drive a second-hand car, but no one could say she was grey. Her style gave away her wealth. Her clothes and accessories had not been bought at Marks and Spencer, nor had her hair or her nails been groomed at the local salon. Her whole persona shouted Harvey Nichols and Vidal Sassoon.

Handford offered her a chair. 'What can I do for you, Mrs Dutton?'

'I want you to tell me the truth,' she said.

He was surprised at her directness. 'About what?'

'About my brother.'

For a moment he was thrown by her answer and he remained silent. How much did she know, and how much did she just suspect? He prevaricated. 'I'm not sure exactly what you mean, Mrs Dutton?'

'I mean that the car used in the murder of Dianne Ingleby was the same model as mine or very similar; I mean that mine has now been taken away for forensic examination, and I mean that my brother is missing. Those three things suggest to me that you have some evidence against him, and that since going missing is something he has done more than once when he has been in trouble, I'm concerned he may have been involved.'

'Has your brother been in touch?'

'I wouldn't be here if he had, Inspector.'

Handford ought not to believe her; he ought to tell her he couldn't discuss the case with her or his interest in her brother, but he wasn't used to such straight talk from those whose relatives might be in trouble, usually they kept that for the lies they told. Yet she didn't seem to be protecting him. There were times when you took a chance, and both Gill and Clarke had told him to believe in his gut instinct. He hoped this was the time when he should go along with it. If he was wrong it would backfire badly. Saying a prayer to whoever was listening, he picked up the phone and asked Clarke to come in. When he arrived, he introduced Mrs Dutton to him, explained what she wanted, and waited as he brought a chair over and settled himself in it.

'I'll tell you what we know, Mrs Dutton,' Handford said. 'We know your brother once called himself James Gould and now he has become Michael Iveson. We also know of the events at the bank that ended in a custodial sentence for the assistant manager, Simon Lake, and his subsequent suicide. Simon Lake's daughter has never believed in her father's guilt and when she realised who Michael Iveson was, she began stalking and threatening him. A month ago she was badly assaulted – we think by your brother, although she refuses to give us his name so we can't be sure. She's currently in hospital, and until Thursday was supported by Dianne Ingleby who was a volunteer for Victim Support. She left a diary on Kathie Lake and much of it included your brother. It wasn't until we learned he was also James Gould that we realised he knew just about everything that had been said at those meetings and that he was aware that Kathie was about to tell Mrs Ingleby the identity of her attacker. However, as you know, she never got the opportunity. I'm sorry, Mrs Dutton, but there is a chance your brother killed her and also Jason Lake whose body was found on Sunday, shot with the same gun as was used on Mrs Ingleby. But until we can talk to him we won't know for sure.'

While he had been talking Mrs Dutton had listened without comment, her lips tight together, her face paling. When he finished she said, 'Thank you for telling me the truth, Inspector.' She put her hand up to her head. 'I'm sorry, but I think I feel a little faint; would you be so kind as to get me a glass of water?'

Clarke left his chair and walked out of the room. He returned a few minutes later with the drink and handed it over.

Mrs Dutton took a sip and placed the glass on Handford's desk. She lifted her head and looked up at him. 'Now, Inspector, if you want to ask me any questions about my brother I will answer them just as truthfully.'

Handford glanced at Clarke, who gave the briefest of nods, and then he said, 'We know quite a lot about him, but perhaps you could tell us first why he left the army.'

'Left is not quite the word I would use. He struck an officer and only escaped a court martial when it became clear that the officer had been bullying him as well as other soldiers. It was suggested that rather than the publicity of a trial, they should agree to resign their commissions. A court martial would have given him a criminal record, and obviously he didn't want that, so he resigned and shortly afterwards joined the bank. Nothing was said at interview about the reason why he left the army, so I imagine they accepted his story whatever it was. I suppose the army wanted to keep the bullying quiet; they tend to close ranks with things like that, and in return for his silence he was given a good reference.'

'Since he was in the army I assume he is able to use a firearm.'

'Oh yes.'

'Does he have one that you know of?'

'If he does I haven't seen it. I don't think he brought one with him as a souvenir; I'm sure he would have shown it to me had he done so.'

'Has he been abroad recently?'

Mrs Dutton thought for a while. 'Not recently, not as far as I know, although he did spend a holiday in the Czech Republic about six months ago. Is it important?'

'It might be. How did he travel?'

'As far as I recall, he drove. He hates flying and will avoid it if he can. Actually, yes he did. He used my car; there was something wrong with his and the garage couldn't get it ready in time.'

'Does he often use your car?'

'Occasionally, particularly if I'm away; he says like all mechanical things it needs to be used. I don't know how true that is, but I don't cross him on something so petty.'

'So he has a key?'

'Yes and I have one for his.'

'Were you at home Thursday night, Mrs Dutton?'

'I went to a dinner at the golf club. It finished very late and I didn't get back until well gone two.'

'How did you travel there?'

'A friend picked me up.'

'Did your brother know this?'

'Yes, I told him sometime during the day. He said to go off and enjoy myself.'

'So your car was in the garage?'

'It was when I left; I didn't look when I got home. I'd had quite a bit to drink and all I needed to do was go to bed. It was certainly there next morning though because I thought about using it to go to the manse, but decided I was probably still over the limit, so I took a taxi.'

It was coming together, all circumstantial until the car had been examined and even then it might only show what they already knew – that he did sit in it and drive it. The real question was did he sit in it and drive it on Thursday night, and his sister wouldn't be able to answer that.

He changed the subject. 'Do you think your brother deliberately lied about Simon Lake's involvement in the fraud?'

'I have absolutely no idea. All I know is that after Mr Lake's suicide he gave in his notice and disappeared for a year. James has always done that. When he was little and he was in trouble he used to hide in the cupboard under the stairs, now he goes on a jaunt round the world. It's just that the reasons he has had to do it have become more and more serious over the years, and the time he spends away longer.'

'Were you surprised when he came back as the Reverend Michael Iveson?' Clarke asked.

'I wasn't surprised he'd used his other names, but I was surprised he had joined the church. He'd never shown any interest in religion until he went to New Zealand, but he came back obsessed by it. He still is.'

267

'Why do you think that is?'

She sipped at the water again. 'Probably because it has given him a fresh start; he can leave the bullying, the lies, the vicious streak and his past behind. The funny thing is that he's actually quite a good minister. He is loved by some, and liked by the rest of those who attend his churches, and if I'm honest he does his best by them. He wouldn't want to let them down. If it was likely that Kathie was intending to tell what she knew or thought she knew, then I think the James Gould in his character would come to the fore. It's not exactly a split personality he has, more a useful ally.'

'Can I ask why you're telling us this? After all he is your brother.'

'It's precisely because he's my brother that I have come to you. I hoped when he joined the church he would have also learned to live with himself. Perhaps coming back to Bradford was intentional – a means of erasing the past. If it was, Kathie hasn't allowed him to do that. Instead she has damaged him. I'm not blaming her, Inspector; she has a right to attempt to get her father's conviction quashed. It's just that to do that she will ruin Michael and I'm worried he feels he can't let that happen; that he has already made sure it won't.'

The silence in the room was palpable. If what Iveson's sister was saying was true, then he had to be picked up, and quickly, or else Kathie would definitely be the next in line.

'Just one last question, Mrs Dutton, are you sure you don't have any idea where he can have gone?'

'I only wish I had. All I can say is that sometimes he returns to where he feels safe and in this city it's the manse. I'll stay there for a while and I promise you if he returns I will let you know.'

The armed officer saw him first as he looked through the window of the door at the end of the corridor. The man in the dog collar. Where the hell was Paul? He was supposed to be protecting the area. No one should have got anywhere near. Not that he could get in; there was a new combination and that had only been given out on a need-to-know basis.

The minister rang the bell then he pushed at the door. It rattled but stayed shut.

Slowly the officer approached it. As he got closer he recognised the face as that of the photograph – Michael Iveson's, the batty minister. What to do? He'd obviously come for Kathie; he was more than likely armed. It could mean he had to shoot him; the thing he had always dreaded. It was one thing training, but quite another faced with the real thing. For God's sake Paul, I can't do this on my own. As he neared the door the face disappeared. Had he gone or was he crouching down? The officer peered through the glass. No sign. He raised his weapon and then pushed the button to let him out. The door clicked open. Cautiously he stepped outside, turned his head slowly in one direction and then the other. Nothing. The corridor was clear.

He shouted for Connie Burns. 'That bloody copper, Paul, is nowhere to be seen and Iveson's just tried to get in. You'd better let your boss know, I'll radio mine. Our man's somewhere in the hospital.'

Amina Ali held tightly on to her husband's hand. The consultant sat behind his desk reading through her notes. Why did they do that? Why couldn't they read them before they asked the patient to come in? Ali put his free hand over his wife's. Hers was cold, icy even; he was sweating. This was awful, worse than anything he'd ever gone through.

The doctor looked up and smiled. 'Good news,' he said. 'The biopsy shows the lump is benign.'

Amina sagged and Ali let his breath hiss out as if from a pressure cooker. 'You're sure?' he said.

'Absolutely sure. You can go away and forget this ever happened. Although it would be a good idea to let us take out the lump; it's doing no good in there, and it will probably still be growing.'

Amina nodded. She seemed beyond the power of speech.

'You'll only be in hospital for a day and a bit sore for another day or two. We'll send you a letter with an appointment date.'

The consultant stood up and held out his hand which first Ali and then Amina took. He held on to Amina's a little while longer. 'I know what you've gone through, but you can go home now and put it behind you. You've got your life back.'

She smiled at him. 'Thank you,' she said.

Once outside she collapsed on to a chair and allowed the tears to flow. Ali put his arm round her shoulders and she held on to him. Relief surged through him; followed by elation. Eventually for no other reason than he wanted to say something normal, he suggested they went to the café for a cup of tea. He could do with one, if she couldn't. And if she didn't mind he wanted to ring John Handford; tell him.

She agreed. 'Do that; he's bound to be wondering.'

As Ali moved into the entrance of the hospital he turned to see a man coming towards him. At first he thought he recognised him and then he was sure. 'Mr Iveson?' he said, a question mark in his voice.

Michael Iveson spun round, saw him and began to walk in the direction from which he'd come.

Ali made a grab for his arm. 'It is Mr Iveson isn't it?'

The minister pulled away and then quickened his pace.

Ali made to catch him up, but Iveson speeded up even more. As they passed Amina, Ali called to her, 'Ring John, tell him Michael Iveson is in the hospital. I'm following him but I may need back-up.' He threw the car keys at her. 'Then go home, Amina; I don't want you staying here.'

chapter nineteen

Iveson fled along the corridor, Ali following, both avoiding people as they skipped round them. Some moved aside to let them through, assuming no doubt there was an emergency. For a while Ali closed up, but Iveson knew his way and several times he turned at the last minute to follow an unexpected route. He was amazingly agile for a man of his age and sped up the stairs two or three at a time. Out of breath, Ali followed him. He was not fit and when this was over he was going to the gym. At the top Iveson ran along the corridor and then down another set of steps. Where the hell was he going? Ali's mobile rang. He put it to his ear.

'What's happening?' There was urgency in John Handford's question.

Ali continued to run. 'I'm still chasing him.' His breath came in gasps.

'There's back-up on its way. Be careful, Ali, he may be armed. Don't do anything stupid. And stay on your mobile.'

They were back on the ground floor now, dodging, side-stepping, skirting round men, women and children. Ali wanted to shout to them to stop the man in front of him, but if John was right he couldn't take the risk of him having a gun. He'd seen no sign of one, but that didn't mean it wasn't there, and if he'd killed twice already the likelihood was he wouldn't hesitate to do it again.

Iveson ploughed on until he reached a short flight of steps. He almost jumped them and at the top pushed at a door to disappear through, letting it swing back. Ali flung it open. He was in a tunnel. It was long and sloped upwards. Florescent strip lights illuminated the way; pipes and cables ran along the cream flaking walls and condensation dripped from the ceiling. In places the slated floor was wet and he had to swerve to prevent himself from slipping. He had no idea where it led or where he was going. He shouted into his mobile. 'John?' No answer. He tried again; still no reply. He'd lost the signal; he was on his own.

Iveson was several yards ahead of him, still running, but not as quickly and Ali began to gain on him, until without warning the man stopped and turned. For a moment he stood motionless, his hands in his pocket.

Ali slowed down. 'Mr Iveson, I'm Detective Sergeant Khalid Ali and I need to talk to you. Please stay where you are,' He wished he could steady his voice, but he was winded and the words came out in gasps.

Iveson made no reply. Ali took a step forward.

Iveson maintained his position and then suddenly, but calmly pulled his hand from his pocket, lifted his arm and stretched it out towards him. The gun he was holding glinted under the lights.

The sweat swathing Ali's body turned cold. He was going to die and there was nothing he could do about it. There was no escape. If he moved forward he would be shot in the chest like Dianne Ingleby, if he turned to run he would be shot in the back like Jason Lake. In front of him he saw the shadow of Amina. He'd brought her here to learn she was well and now he was going to die instead of her. He stared at Iveson, and as he did so all movement slowed. Amina's voice penetrated his brain. 'Khalid, do something.' Her voice showed no fear; she was angry with him, angry that he was making no attempt to save himself. Suddenly, as if kick-started, his training took over and he moved into automatic pilot. Nothing mattered except the situation. His voice was firm as he spoke. 'Put it down, Mr Iveson,' he said, his voice level. 'All I want is to talk.' He took a step forward.

As he did so, the blast from the gun exploded in Ali's ears and the bullet threw him sideways. At first he felt nothing but the throbbing in his head, then the pain in his shoulder intensified and his arm hung limply by his side. He clutched the wound hard with his hand, and watched fascinated as the blood seeped through his fingers and dripped on to the floor. Michael Iveson had shot him. Surprise overtook fear and irrationally his only thought was that if it had to happen, then a hospital was the best place to be.

As the reverberation from the gun-fire faded, Ali looked up. Iveson had disappeared. For what seemed an age, but could only have been seconds, he stared at the emptiness. The minister had to have gone further on up the tunnel; there was nowhere else. He needed to let John know so that the back-up could begin their search. His mobile was no longer in his hand; he must have dropped it when Iveson shot at him. He couldn't remember. If only he could think straight, but his brain was urging him to sink to the floor and sleep. Amina was there again, shadowy, but there. 'Focus and find it.' His eyes searched the ground; he saw it, only a metre away, lying in the flakes of concrete and paint that had gathered over the years. Cautiously, he sank to the floor and slid his bloodied hand along the slates. He touched it, but as he made to pick it up it slithered away from him. He stretched further until he felt it again and curled his fingers around it. Lifting it towards him, he fingered in the number to reach John and put it to his ear. There was nothing; there was no signal here; he'd forgotten. Before he could regain contact he had to negotiate the rest of the tunnel and hope that when he opened the door at the far end Iveson wasn't waiting for him. His arm hurt like hell; blood dripped on to the ground and he wasn't sure how much he was losing. He vaguely remembered a nurse once saying to him, 'There always seems to be more than there is when it's pooling.' Now for the first time he hoped she was right. But right or not, it didn't stop his head spinning as he dragged himself upwards and leaned against the wall. He felt sick and took a moment to recover, then with the wall as his prop he shuffled along it like an old man until he came to the door. Painfully, he pulled at it. In front of him, bright lights illuminated a wide hall which stretched into the distance. The ceilings were high and doors dotted the walls. Where was he? Not in the main hospital but a separate building. The tunnel they had run down obviously linked the two. Iveson certainly knew his way round. There was no sign of him now, he hadn't waited for the policeman, probably thought he was dead. In fact there was no sign of anyone. Everyone safe behind their doors except him.

Ali sank to the floor hoping that soon someone would come along to help him.

*

273

When Handford arrived at the hospital, as much of it as was practicable had been evacuated and the roads leading into and away from the city had been cordoned off. Armed officers were searching all floors. It was a mammoth task looking for a man who knew the building like the back of his hand. He was met by the sergeant on duty.

'Have you found him yet?'

'No sir, not a sign. The armed response team are on all floors and we have just about every available officer combing this building and the other one, Field House. To be honest, I doubt he's here now. He'll be long gone. We've got the girl out. She's in the safe house with Connie Burns and a couple of officers from the protection unit. Poor woman, she's in quite a state, keeps saying she wants to die and asking why we didn't let him kill her.'

'I know. I hope now, they might consider sectioning her. Mother, father and brother gone, and her desire for revenge thwarted; what has she to live for?'

The sergeant nodded, but remained silent. How could you answer a question like that? Handford couldn't. It seemed the only way Kathie could survive was to die at the hand of the man who forced her father to take his own life. Michael Iveson's only way to survive on the other hand was through killing those he thought could destroy him. Two families devastated by one man. He wished he could understand – really understand. All he could do was solve the puzzle and try to pick up the pieces. It seemed so inadequate. Thank God Ali hadn't died at Iveson's hand. 'I understand Khalid's injury isn't as bad as it could have been.'

'No, he's fine. They've taken him to the surgery up the road where as far as I know he's still being treated, but according to the doctor, the bullet nicked him rather than penetrated. A few stitches and he'll be as good as new.'

'And the officers who let Iveson go?'

'Ah well, they're not in such brilliant shape and I have a feeling things will go downhill for them when this is over.'

His hostility towards the two men simmered. 'Good,' he said with feeling.

'Look, John, there's nothing you can do here until we've completed the search. Once we've ensured it's safe we'll bring in the

274

SOCOs to hunt for the bullet because wherever it is, it's not in Khalid Ali.'

Ali was sitting on a bed in one of the cubicles, Amina at his side, his arm in a sling. 'It's not too bad,' he said. 'It nicked me rather than penetrated.'

Amina wasn't so relaxed about it. 'It could have been much worse, Khalid. What on earth possessed you to go running after him?' She turned to Handford. 'It's a good job I didn't take any notice of him and go home. I'd be opening the door to your officers now come to tell me he'd been shot.' She let her gaze fall on her husband. 'There are times when you take duty a step too far, do you know that?'

Handford understood her anger. He tried not to tell Gill if he had been in a dangerous situation, but he knew that although she pushed her concerns to the back of her mind most of the time, it only needed one incident to bring them into pole position. 'I know,' he said.

'We came here today for me, John, and he's the one on a bed.'

Handford attempted to diffuse her fears. He planted a kiss on her cheek. 'I shouldn't worry too much about him, he seems fine to me. I'm much more concerned about you. Dare I ask the outcome?'

In an instant the question stripped her of her fury and a smile lit her face. 'I'm clear, John, the lump is benign. I have to have it removed sometime, but that's all.'

He hugged her. 'I'm so pleased,' he said. 'It must be a weight off your mind. Now I'm sorry – and I know you're going to hate me for this – but I need to know from Khalid exactly what happened.'

Amina sighed. 'Of course you do. I've been a policeman's wife long enough to know that his work comes first. I'll go and get myself a cup of tea from the practice nurse who with luck will be a bit more understanding than you two.'

They waited until she had gone. 'She's taken it hard, Khalid.'

'I know.'

Handford sat on the edge of the bed. 'Right, tell me.' Amina had been right – the job came first.

Ali explained as fully as he could and finally said, 'I don't know where he went from Field House. He must have had a vehicle in the car park across the road. I'm sorry; I would have caught him if I could.'

'There's nothing to be sorry about. The chances are he could still be in the hospital. He's a dangerous man, more dangerous than we thought. We've got to find him,' Elizabeth Dutton had said he usually went back to where he felt safe and in this city it was the manse. He thumbed in her number and when she answered he described the events of the afternoon.

'He's not here, Inspector. At least not yet. He'll come back sooner or later, of that I'm sure, and when he does I *will* contact you.'

He thanked her and told her to take care.

'Don't worry about me; I'm not the one he wants to hurt.' She was a brave woman, though he doubted she realised it.

As he ended the call Amina came up to the bed. She stared at Handford. 'The doctor says we can go,' she said, her tone brooking no argument. 'He'll need to have the wound redressed tomorrow but our own GP can do it.' She searched in her bag. 'I'll bring the car round.'

Ali slipped gingerly off the bed. 'I'm going to the station, Amina.'

Angrily she protested.

Handford agreed 'Go home, Khalid, you need to rest.'

'I need to be at work where I can do some good. What can I do at home?'

Again his wife remonstrated with him. 'You can sit and watch television; you can sleep; you can do anything or nothing.' She raised her eyebrows. 'You can even work out what you are going to tell your father.'

'No Amina, I'll do all that tomorrow but today I've got to do this. I was the one who lost him.'

'It wasn't your fault, Khalid.' She appealed to Handford who lifted his hands in submission and shook his head. He knew how his sergeant felt. He had to do something to assuage the guilt, even though he had nothing to be guilty about. If he was at home he would be restless and hell to live with. 'I'll look after him, Amina, and I promise you I won't let him within a mile of Michael Iveson.'

Defeated, she gave Ali a kiss and squeezed Handford's arm.

'Make sure he doesn't do anything stupid,' she said.

The door to the manse opened quietly. Mrs Dutton appeared at the kitchen door. 'Michael, where've you been; we've been worried about you.'

He made no answer, but stood looking at her. Finally he said, 'There were things I had to do.'

'Like what?'

Again he made no reply but instead said, 'What are you doing here?'

'I was waiting for you to come home.'

'Why?'

'You missed the Ladies' Friendly Society meeting.'

'I told you I had things to do. I still have things to do. I'm going into my study.'

'I'll bring you some tea.'

'No, no tea. I want to be alone; I want to pray. I want to talk to God.'

He passed her as though she was invisible and as the study door closed Elizabeth heard the click of the lock. She turned to the phone and picked up the receiver, then on impulse returned it to its cradle and hurried through the kitchen into the back garden. By the french windows, she stopped and carefully leaned sideways to peep through the glass. Michael was sitting in a chair facing her, but obviously not seeing her for there was no reaction from him. He was staring straight forward, tears rolling down his cheeks, and in his hands he was nursing a gun.

As it turned out, Handford's promise to Amina was easier made than kept. Had they been at Central when the message came through he could have insisted Ali stayed in the office. As it was, it was passed through to Handford while they were driving back. Iveson was at the manse. He had gone to where he felt safe and was currently shut in his study holding a gun. Mrs Dutton had no idea whether he intended to use it, but she had never seen him quite like this before.

Handford pulled into a lay-by and rang Russell. He explained the situation, told him he was going to the manse, and asked if the DCI could arrange for a negotiator. 'If what Mrs Dutton says is anything like accurate, we're going to need one.'

'I'll do it straight away, John. While you're waiting I want you to keep well clear. This man is dangerous; he's killed twice and injured Ali. He has no reason not to do it again, and every reason to do so. You understand me, Inspector? You leave it to the negotiator.'

Handford agreed, but he'd been in this kind of situation before, except the last time the suspect had a knife not a gun and was holding his own sister and her child hostage. By now Iveson might be doing the same to Elizabeth Dutton. Keeping clear wasn't always an option.

The road had been sealed off at both ends and as always a crowd had gathered by the tape. Telling them there was nothing to see did no good. There might be something to see eventually, and they weren't prepared to miss it. Jane Charles was the inspector on duty. 'Can't you keep your suspects under better control, John, do you have to let them run loose with guns?' She nodded towards Ali. 'And your officers as well, by the look of your sergeant. Should he be here?'

'No he shouldn't, but he feels bad about losing Iveson in the first place.'

She sighed. 'Young and foolish.'

The small talk had gone on long enough. 'Tell me what's happening in the house.'

'Nothing much. Mrs Dutton is still in there and refusing to come out. Iveson is sitting at his desk in the study and hasn't moved since I arrived.'

'And the gun?'

'He's clasping it like a toy. Currently he's not doing any harm, but I don't know how volatile he could become if we attempt to go in. DCI Russell rang and said he has asked for a negotiator, but he doesn't know how long he's going to be and we're still waiting for a phone line to be rigged up.'

'Can we get in to talk to him?' Handford asked.

'Not through the front of the house, but the french windows aren't locked. We've tried a couple of times, but as soon as we move close he levels the gun at us. You do what you want, John, but I'm not risking my officers.'

'Somebody's got to do something.' He called Ali. 'I want you to go in and talk to Mrs Dutton. Find out when he came home and his state of mind. I'm going round the back. Let me know

278

when you've got something. And lose that sling; it makes your injury look worse than it is.'

Ali winced as he pulled it off and handed it to the uniformed inspector, then he walked slowly and carefully up to the door and pushed on it. It opened. So far so good. When Ali disappeared Handford set off round the back. At the french windows he paused. He didn't want to give Iveson a reason for shooting him. He glanced round for a suitable vantage point. If he could get to the opposite end of the garden, he would probably be able to see into the study and then make a decision as to how to proceed. He held himself against the fence and slid round the border until he came to the bushes where he settled himself between two of the larger ones, and crouched low to the ground. He could just about see Iveson, still sitting behind his desk, still, he thought, holding the gun although he couldn't be sure about that. At one point the minister turned his head sharply towards the door that lead into the hallway. Handford hoped Ali wasn't attempting to go in. He rang Jane Charles. 'Any sign of the negotiator?'

'No not yet. What's he doing?'

'Nothing. I think Ali has tried to talk to him, because he keeps looking towards the study door, but so far he hasn't moved. Keep an eye on that will you, I don't want him to give Iveson a reason to use that gun again, and let me know when the negotiator arrives.'

It was going on ten minutes later when he was beginning to feel the need to move to rub his legs into life that his phone vibrated. It was Ali.

'What's happening?'

'Nothing, although Mrs Dutton is obviously worried about him. She says she's never seen him like this before. He won't talk to her, but she says someone must make the attempt and I agree with her. I've tried though the door, but it's not me he wants. He's done a lot of crying. He has to confess, he says, and he needs someone higher up to confess to. Mrs Dutton has tried to get in touch with the circuit superintendent, but he's currently conducting a funeral service. I wondered if we could persuade him into a chapel where he can feel closer to God. We're not going to get higher than Him.'

Handford didn't think so. Even if Iveson agreed to move there was no saying what he'd do. 'When he says he wants someone

It seemed like hours before his phone vibrated again, but it couldn't have been any more than three or four minutes. 'He said yes, but for God's sake be careful. I don't know how stable he is.'

Handford stood up. He could have gone back the way he came, but suddenly turning up at the french windows might startle the minister, so instead he walked slowly across the lawn. At the windows he stood for a while. Iveson hardly seemed to notice him. He lowered the handle and the door opened. Cautiously he stepped inside, but remained on the threshold.

'Mr Iveson,' he said quietly.

Michael Iveson lifted the gun. 'Don't come any closer,' Handford spread out his hands in submission. 'I won't. I'll stay right here.'

Iveson remained motionless.

Handford said, 'You like this room. I remember you told me when I came to see you.'

'It's peaceful, quiet. Somewhere I can be close to God. Are you religious, Inspector?'

Handford gave a slight smile. 'Not especially. You don't have much time in my job to go to church.'

'You should always make time for God, to get close to Him. The dying are close to Him – Mrs Baker was.'

'You sat with Mrs Baker the night she died?'

'Some of the time. I left her for a while, but I was there when she slipped away to Him.'

'And Dianne, you were there when she met Him as well?'

'No, I was with Mrs Baker.' He stared into the distance and gave a wry smile. 'I set her on her journey, but I couldn't be in two places and Dianne had her family, Mrs Baker had no one.'

'I seem to remember you told me you liked Dianne.' Iveson was silent for a moment and then slowly the tears began to roll down his cheeks and he started to sob. 'I liked her a lot and she liked me. We used to talk about things.'

'What things?'

'Her faith, my faith, her life ...'

'Your life?'

'No, not my life. She wouldn't have understood. That's why, once she was close to knowing, she had to go to Him. I couldn't risk her not understanding.' His hands slipped and he allowed them to fall on to his knees. The gun remained in front of him on the table.

Stealthily Handford took a step forward, but Iveson was quicker. He snatched at it and pointed it at Handford again. 'I told you not to come any closer.'

'I'm sorry, I'll stay here. You were telling me about Dianne. What do you think she wouldn't have understood?'

'That I sinned.'

'We all sin Mr Iveson, but we don't kill someone because of it.'

'Kathie was about to give Dianne the name of her attacker.'

'Do you know who attacked her?'

Again he began to sob, this time louder than before. 'Why do you ask? You know I was the one. I only wanted to frighten her, to stop her from talking.'

'Talking about what?'

The crying stopped and he banged on the desk. 'About me.' His voice descended to a whisper. 'About me. She knew who I was. She stalked me and talked to me and threatened me. I couldn't turn round without she was there.'

'You could have come to us, we would have stopped her.'

The comment angered Iveson and he became agitated. 'No you wouldn't. No one would. I tried again today but the policeman was there with a gun. He was protecting her; he didn't care about me. And then there was the other detective. He said he wanted to talk to me, but that wasn't true was it? He was coming towards me, through the corridors and up the tunnel. At first I was far away from him, but eventually he was getting closer. I didn't have a choice; I could tell by his voice he wouldn't have understood, so I had to stop him. The only way to do that was to shoot him. Is he dead?'

'No, the bullet nicked him in the shoulder.'

Iveson lifted the gun higher so that it was level with Handford's head. 'I was too far away from him, but I would do more than nick you if I pulled this trigger. I could stop you right now. You're a brave man Mr Handford – or are you foolish?'

Handford could hear his heart pounding in his chest and he began to sweat. Where was that bloody negotiator? Never there when they're wanted. Gill would be furious if she knew what he was doing. 'You could, but I'm sure you won't.'

Iveson let the weapon drop, but not all the way.

It was important to take his mind off the gun, to keep him talking, give him what he had asked for. 'You need someone to confess to, Michael; you told my sergeant that. You've already confessed to me that you attacked Kathie Lake and that you killed Dianne. Do you want to confess to killing Kathie's brother?'

Iveson nodded, tears rolling down his cheeks again. 'He had come to take over where Dianne had left off. The girl would have told him tomorrow or the next day or even next week, but she would have told him. I couldn't let that happen. The only way to stop people is to shoot them. I learnt that in the army. It's you or them. People can be wicked; the only way to stop them is to shoot them. I have to stop wicked people – Kathie, Dianne, the young man and the detective, and now ...' He lifted the gun again and steadied it with his other hand. 'You've to be careful about the recoil, you know. I wasn't careful enough in the car park.'

It was pointing again directly at Handford. He knew exactly what the man intended. People who got in his way had to be disposed of. Simon Lake was the first, Kathie would be the last, with Dianne, Jason and John Handford in between.

Gill, Nicola, Clare, visions of his family flashed into his mind. No way Mr Iveson, not if I can help it. He threw himself to the ground as the gun exploded and lay for what seemed an age, wondering if he was dead or alive. His ears pounded with the blast, and the air reeked with the stench of the shot and then came silence, a harsh, unsympathetic, insensitive silence and he knew what had happened.

Handford lifted his head and slowly turned to look at Michael Iveson. He was leaning over the arm of the leather chair, a small bullet hole to one side of his head. The other side had disappeared, exploded, scattering brain tissue and blood over the walls. A crucifix seemed to have caught most of it and it was currently dripping on to the floor. He had been wrong; James Michael Gould-Iveson was to be the last.

'John? For God's sake, get this bloody door open. John, are

you all right?' Unsteadily he pulled himself from the floor, holding on to the furniture as he walked over to turn the key.

'I'm all right,' he said, 'but I think it would be better if Mrs Dutton didn't come in.'

Four days later DCI Russell called a meeting of the murder team. It had been a long four days. Kathie Lake had been returned from the safe house to the psychiatric ward. She couldn't understand why she was being moved and challenged the decision. It was a difficult moment and John Handford was loath to tell her of Michael Iveson's suicide, but once in the care of the hospital the psychiatrist insisted. Until she knew he was dead, he told Handford, she couldn't even begin to move on. If she thought there was any chance of her still being able to take her revenge on him, even by her own death, her mind would remain locked to that objective. It had to be unlocked. She hadn't progressed through the normal course of grieving when her father had been imprisoned, or when he and then her mother had died, so that when it came to her brother's death she couldn't cope. She was too filled with the desire to settle her own scores with Michael Iveson that there was no room for anything else. What had Rebecca said? 'My mother used to tell us that victims of crime go through a number of emotions – numbness, impotence, grief, anger, guilt. But all I feel is hollowness deep inside me and I can't imagine ever having the energy for any of the others to take over.' Kathie had replaced the hollowness with revenge; she had neither the room nor the energy for the other emotions. But she did have Emma who had promised to visit her every day. Eventually she would be grateful to her, but it would take time.

Chanda had given Aisha the statement she wanted, and Aisha for her part had agreed to put in a good word for her with the court. A day or two after Salma's birth, Chanda had asked if she could visit Aisha. At first she'd said no, but then had capitulated, providing Parvez was with her. It was a difficult meeting. Her sister-in-law came through the door carrying the baby.

'Oh no,' Aisha turned to her husband. 'No way. This isn't fair. She's hoping to win my sympathy by bringing in the child.'

Chanda stepped forward. 'I'm not, honestly I'm not. I wouldn't use her like that. I thought you might like to see her that's all.' She held out her hand. 'And I've brought you this.' It was her passport. 'I had it with me when I ran away; I thought if they sent people to find me, I might need it.' She dropped it on Aisha's bed.

Aisha picked it up. 'Thank you,' she said. 'You do realise, don't you, that giving this up is as much for your benefit as for mine? Without it Iqbal can't send you to Pakistan. But apart from that it means nothing, because I have no intention of changing my mind about the complaint. It stands.'

Parvez stood up 'Come and sit down, Chanda.'

When she was settled, he crouched in front of her. 'The forensic results are back from the lab,' he said, looking into the young girl's eyes. 'They've found Aisha's blood on your shoes as well as traces of hair and skin. The DNA tests proved what you did. You know there's no doubt, don't you?'

Chanda nodded and lowered her head.

'And you know you won't get away with what you've done?'

Chanda raised her head, her eyes filled with fear. 'What will happen to me?'

'When you leave hospital, you'll be charged with inflicting grievous bodily harm on Aisha. It's a serious charge. I've promised I will take you to the police station and Mr Handford has agreed I can stay with you.'

He turned to Aisha who nodded.

'I've also spoken to the inspector in charge and he has agreed to give you police bail providing you agree to live in a Social Services secure unit – there's a place available and at least you'll be with your baby. After that, Chanda, it's up to the magistrates. Plead guilty and they might let you stay in the unit rather than remand you to a young offenders institution. Either way you'll be passed on to Crown Court for sentencing. Parvez stood up and looked down on her. 'It's difficult to know what the outcome will be, but this time it's in the court's hands, not in my father's.'

Ray Braddock's future was also in the hands of the courts. He had appeared at the magistrates' court, and was remanded in custody until the plea and direction hearing at the Crown Court in three weeks' time. Darren Armitage was bailed for reports, but it was unlikely he would get a custodial sentence. Gary Marshall had been told he would go to trial. He had blustered that his brief would get him off, and PC Foxton had smiled and said, 'Not this time Gary.'

The inquest into Dianne Ingleby's death had been opened and adjourned so the family could make funeral arrangements. Handford wasn't sure what, if anything Maurice or Rebecca Ingleby would do. He had visited them after Iveson's suicide and they had thanked him for everything. Perhaps if they went through the true emotions of grief they would come out the other end. He couldn't be sure; there were more issues than the murder to be dealt with.

So for the moment it was over but for the paperwork.

The CID detectives listened as Russell addressed them. 'This is the last time I shall be talking to you in my capacity as your crime manager. So I want to thank you for all your hard work over the past few years and particularly during this investigation. It's a pity it ended as it did, but I want to assure you that no one is to blame. There will be an enquiry of course, but the general feeling is that the Reverend Iveson intended to take his own life when he locked himself in his study with the gun, and that DI Handford did him a service in listening to his "confession". Police officers take their lives in their hands each time they go out. What John did may be described as foolhardy by some ...'

'My wife for one,' Handford said wryly.

Russell smiled. 'I wouldn't argue with his wife, but even so I don't think we can deny it was a brave act or that he carried it out because he cared. It's a good trait in any one, but particularly in a detective.'

He allowed the cheers and the applause to die down, and then said, 'Finally I want to introduce you to two people. First, if you could come forward Sergeant Ali. I heard today that Khalid had been accepted into HMET and promoted to inspector.'

There were whistles and boos all of which were taken in good part.

'Do I have to call you guv now?' Warrender asked.

Ali smiled. 'No Warrender, sir will do.'

Russell held up his hands and waited for silence. 'I said there were two people to introduce you to. You all know by now – in fact I think some of you knew before I did – that I am to take over Mr Slater's position when he retires next month. I need a good DCI and I'm sure you'll all agree that I couldn't have a better one than John here. Unfortunately, as hard as I tried, he's not joining me. HMET – damn them – insisted he was theirs. So let me introduce you as well to Detective Chief Inspector John Handford of the Homicide and Major Enquiry Team.'

All Orion/Phoenix titles are available at your local bookshop or from the following address:

Mail Order Department
Littlehampton Book Services
FREEPOST BR535
Worthing, West Sussex, BN13 3BR
telephone 01903 828503, *facsimile* 01903 828802
e-mail MailOrders@lbsltd.co.uk
(Please ensure that you include full postal address details)

Payment can be made either by credit/debit card (Visa, Mastercard, Access and Switch accepted) or by sending a £ Sterling cheque or postal order made payable to *Littlehampton Book Services*.
DO NOT SEND CASH OR CURRENCY

Please add the following to cover postage and packing

UK and BFPO:
£1.50 for the first book, and 50p for each additional book to a maximum of £3.50

Overseas and Eire:
£2.50 for the first book plus £1.00 for the second book and 50p for each additional book ordered

BLOCK CAPITALS PLEASE

name of cardholder _____

address of cardholder _____

_____ _____

_____ _____

_____ _____

postcode _____

delivery address
(if different from cardholder)

postcode _____

☐ I enclose my remittance for £_____

☐ please debit my Mastercard/Visa/Access/Switch (delete as appropriate)

card number ☐☐☐☐ ☐☐☐☐ ☐☐☐☐ ☐☐☐☐

expiry date ☐☐☐☐ Switch issue no. ☐☐

signature _____

prices and availability are subject to change without notice